Historical fiction

CW00689120

BLOSSOMS ON
A POISONED SEA

Maiko Tatsumoto

BLOSSOMS ON
A POISONED SEA

A Novel of Love and Betrayal in Minamata, Japan

by

Mariko Tatsumoto

NORTHAMPTON HOUSE PRESS

Front cover image by Niadra LLC. Title page image NHP LLC.
ISBN 978-1-950668-24-3 (print edition)
Library of Congress Control Number: 2023919090.
Published by Northampton House Press, www.northampton-house.com.
Franktown Virginia USA.
Printed in the United States of America. 2

ONE

Island of Kyushu, Japan

Fall, 1976

T he young journalist stood holding a leather briefcase in one hand and a small, well-worn valise in the other. His raincoat was wrinkled, as if he'd slept in it. Which he had during the overnight train ride from Tokyo to Minamata, a small city on the southern Japanese island of Kyushu. He stepped through a bamboo gate to a well-kept garden. Large bushes of yellow and crimson chrysanthemums lined the flat-rocked walkway to a large cedarwood house. Tall pine trees shaded its front yard.

At the front entrance he knocked briskly on one of the double sliding-glass doors.

Someone inside called out, "Come in."

He entered, bowing deeply to the comely woman in the foyer, an entrance large enough for several people to stand in at once. He removed his shoes and thrust his black umbrella into a wooden stand intricately carved with gently lapping waves rolling up to stands of tall broadleaf trees. The Amakusa Islands, which sheltered Minamata Bay from the rougher open sea. Terraced tea-fields rose from its shoreline.

"Hajimemashite." How do you do, he said, offering a business card with both hands to his hostess. "I'm Sawada Tanzan from *Nihon Bunka Magazine.* Thank you for seeing me."

He surreptitiously attempted to smooth down his thick black hair, noticing in a nearby mirror that it stuck out at the top and sides like an open fan. The day was calm, and the temperature mild for fall.

"I'm Kuge Yuki. Come in, please."

The tall, slender woman wore a purple and white plaid dress. Her curled, shoulder-length black hair framed a beautiful face; her warm brown eyes sparkled with determination. "For so many years we wanted the world to see the suffering of Minamata, but no one would listen. We're so pleased you'll be telling it now."

Yuki ushered the guest down a long, gleaming wood hallway into a tatami-floored room. A long scroll depicting blossoming trees near a waterfall cascading from a craggy cliff hung in an alcove. A small light-green ceramic vase held one vibrant red spider lily. The shoji doors opened onto a covered veranda overlooking a garden where maple leaves were just turning red, promising a spectacular display in the coming weeks. Western-style armchairs and a sofa were clustered on one side of the large space. A man sat on a thick floor-cushion at a low table with rich reddish woodgrain. He removed and folded tortoise-shell glasses, tucking them in the pocket of a crisply-ironed white shirt.

This, the journalist knew, must be his other interviewee. The thirty-five-year-old doctor rose nimbly and bowed. "I'm Kuge Kiyoshi. We appreciate your coming all this way."

"Kuge Sensei, I'm honored you both consented to see me." Sawada bowed reverently. "Sorry to take time away from your patients."

"Please, call me Kiyo. And don't worry, I'll tend to them once we're done. This is far too important to miss. Please, sit."

They all took floor cushions; the men cross-legged, Yuki's legs tucked beneath her. A stout middle-aged woman in white blouse and coral skirt quietly entered. She set a lacquered tray inlaid with mother-of-pearl lotus onto the table. After serving tea and plates of rice crackers, she left.

Sawada took a grateful sip and smiled, happy to have reached his destination. "Smith-san did the world a big favor with his photo-journal article in America's *Life Magazine*. It brought the Disease to the world's attention. I'll do the same with my article. Books have been written about it, of course, but most people feel too busy to read a whole volume. But a magazine ... people read those while on the train, or relaxing at home. I'll tell the story from your viewpoint: two who fought against and lived through the tragedy."

He heard the eagerness in his own voice and thought, *If I were a dog, my big ears would be perked up right now.*

Kiyo nodded. "Smith-san's photo of the young victim being bathed by her mother certainly got the world's attention."

Yuki nodded. "No wonder it became known as Minamata Pietà, after Michelangelo."

"Yes. And I'm moved by your beautiful paintings." The writer gazed around at dozen oils of Minamata Bay, and portraits of people affected by the Disease.

"People and nature are what's beautiful. I'm in awe of them every day." Yuki smiled at him.

"Smith-san was brave to take on the project. He took a severe beating from those nasty Chisso guards," Sawada said.

"The poor man suffered so much pain. He never saw well afterward," Yuki said.

"Luckily, I'm at no such risk," The reporter's smile faded. "Those union workers should've been tried and incarcerated."

"Yes." Kiyo cracked a round rice cracker in two and ate half. "Control by big money was absolute here, back then."

"You must've been overjoyed when the court finally punished the guilty parties," the journalist said.

"Yes, but it took years, and the efforts of so many. Especially Dr. Hosokawa, who bravely testified about the cat experiment as he was dying of lung cancer." Kiyo looked sad as if again mourning his former mentor.

"A courageous, hard-fought court battle." Yuki sighed. "Yet Chisso still claimed innocence for so long. Those rotten executives." Bitterness crept into her voice. "Oh." She laid a hand over her husband's shoulder. "I'm sorry ... I didn't mean – "

"Don't worry about it." Kiyo shook his head. "Dad's long gone now." He chewed thoughtfully. "You can't imagine how hard Yuki worked and struggled, putting herself in peril." He gazed at his wife with deep admiration. "We both lost people we loved. They too suffered and died, along with the victims of the Disease."

"The Bay's animals and birds did, too." Yuki was watching a sparrow slip into a birdhouse nailed to a tall pine tree. Sunlight through the green needles made bright slashing designs on flower beds of fluffy red Kochia and white and pink cosmos.

"I want to hear every minute of those years." Sawada was eager to hear this story of a lifetime. All the fatigue from the long journey had vaporized like the steam rising from his tea.

But just then excited cries rose in a nearby hallway. Two small children ran into the room. The girl's pigtails were tied with yellow ribbons that matched her sweater. She flew into her father's lap, yelling, "Papa! Papa!"

Kiyo wheezed a laugh, knocked almost breathless by the hard landing. He gently tugged one pigtail and smiled.

The boy's face was plump, with rosy cheeks; a smaller, chubby version of his mother. His blue jeans were stained with dirt. Mimicking his little sister, he shrieked, "Mama! Mama!" and hugged her neck.

Yuki cupped his chin in her hand, laughing.

"Oh, you have company. Sorry to interrupt." A slim older woman in a chic beige skirt and brown blouse paused in the door to the hallway. She bowed slightly to Sawada.

"This is my mother," Kiyo said. Then, to her, "Remember I mentioned Sawada-san was coming to interview us about the Disease?"

"Oh yes, of course. Nice to meet you."

The journalist rose and bowed. "How do you do, Mrs. Kuge?"

"I hope your trip was not too tiring."

"Not at all. Would you like to participate in the interview?"

Kuge Etsuko shut her eyes for a moment, face pale above red-tinted lips. At last she opened them again. "No. It was . . . for me . . . for everyone, a difficult time. Still is for some." Then she smiled and glanced down at the children. "They're still excited from playing at the park."

"I swung so high, almost to the sky." The girl lifted her arms to the ceiling.

"I went on the slide all by myself." The boy grinned proudly.

"What a big fellow." Kiyo glanced at the visitor. "Toyohiro's four." He pointed to his daughter. "Koh's six."

"Cute kids," Sawada said.

"I'll take them to the kitchen for a snack," their grandmother said. "Children, want some cookies?"

"Yes!" Koh leapt from her father's lap and ran back down the hallway.

"Me too!" Toyohiro dashed after her.

"Stop running," Yuki scolded. But they were already gone.

"I'll take my leave," Etsuko said.

"I'm honored to have met Kuge-san's esteemed mother." Sawada bowed from his seat again.

"Oh, please." She waved her hand dismissively. "No need to talk like that. It's 1976, after all." But she was smiling as she went off after the children. Soon, soothing strains of a piano jazz piece – "Scenery" by Fukui Ryo – issued from a radio somewhere back in the other wing.

"Our children don't really understand how lucky they are," Yuki said.

"No, probably not," the writer agreed. "The years right after the war ... everything decimated, nowhere to live, not enough food. And then, Minamata Disease. I grew up in Tokyo, though, and didn't hear about that until I was older." He tugged a notebook and a pen from his briefcase.

Kiyo and Yuki glanced at each other. "Where should we start?" Kiyo asked.

Yuki thought for a moment. "From the beginning, I suppose. When it all started."

"Yes." Kiyo's eyes took on a faraway look. "We were only fourteen then, and had no idea of what was to come, back in 1956 . . . ."

TWO

Uncle Acts Strangely
Tsukinoura, 1956

Akaji Yuki got off the transit bus at Tsukinoura, her home village, after attending eighth grade classes. Still an hour left to wait for her uncle Higano at the bus stop, so she lay on the grass near the road. Enjoying the warmth of the spring sun, and the sweet scents of blooming azalea and wisteria. Barely noticing all the cars rumbling by, heading to or from the City of Minamata.

A stray yellow tabby suddenly brushed past her shoulder. As she looked, it convulsed, jumped and twisted, front paws scrabbling at empty air. The cat barely touched the ground before springing up again, contorting its body until its head touched one hip. All the while it yowled horribly, as if in terrible pain.

She'd seen another cat acting strangely, two days ago. Before that she'd never seen any cat behave like this, nor had ever heard one cry so piteously. A bad feeling slithered over her skin as the suffering animal staggered away, disappearing under the foundation of a nearby house.

Finally the bus rolled up. Her uncle got off in an oddly-tattered work-shirt and stained pants, stumbling once as he descended the steps.

She sprang up. "Uncle Higano, what happened?"

"Just a couple burns. I'm lucky – the acid mostly ate my clothes." He rolled up one sleeve. "See?" On his forearm was a burn shaped like a one-yen coin. Another, about the same size, had already blistered.

"*Iya!*" Yuck. Yuki winced. "That must hurt."

"Mixing chemicals is a dangerous job."

"Can't the factory make it safer?"

"Causing a ruckus would cost me my job. Chisso's a good company. Their hospital helped your Aunt Haruko when she was sick, remember?"

Yuki sighed. "I miss her."

"Me, too. Not a day goes by I don't long to see her. Though I'm grateful her terrible suffering's over."

They headed down the narrow road, toward home.

"I hope Dad and Mom caught lots of fish today. I'm so hungry I could eat a whole mullet."

Uncle stumbled suddenly but caught himself before he fell. "Hey. What tripped me?"

Yuki glanced back at the dirt road. "I don't see anything there."

"Huh. Feet must've fallen asleep on the ride home." He scratched at his hands. "Hm. They're kinda numb, too."

For some reason, the sick cat flashed through Yuki's mind again, and she shivered.

The next morning, she and her parents dug into a breakfast of grilled octopus and sea bream. "Where's Uncle?" Yuki nodded at his empty place at the table. "He'll miss the bus."

"Higano-kun!" Her mother called out. When he didn't respond, she turned to Yuki. "He's overslept. Go knock on his door."

Yuki padded the few steps to the only other room in the tiny house. Uncle Higano and Aunt Haruko had moved in when her aunt fell ill with tuberculosis. Uncle had stayed on after she died.

She knocked lightly on the frame of the flimsy *shoji* door. "Uncle? Time to get up."

No answer. She glanced back at her mother, who nodded, so she slid the door open.

Higano lay splayed on the floor, under his futon. "Uncle, what's wrong?" She dropped to her knees next to him.

He blinked up, looking confused. "Is it late?" He sat up, but swayed as he tried to stand.

She grabbed his arm to steady him. Before she could call out, her mother was by his side. "What's wrong, Higano-kun?" She grasped his other arm.

"Nothing. I'll get dressed now."

Kazuko frowned, but she nodded at Yuki, who followed her out, closing the door. They returned to breakfast, but after several minutes Uncle still hadn't appeared.

Nobuyuki got up and opened the door. His brother was fumbling with his shirt buttons, fingers stiff and awkward.

"Let me." Her father did them up and led Higano to the table. "Eat. I'll put the futons away."

Her uncle shuffled to the table, lowering himself awkwardly to the floor. He picked up chopsticks and a bowl of rice, but both slipped from his fingers, the bowl crashing to the tatami floor.

Yuki gasped, "Uncle!"

Mom hurried over and draped a jacket over his shoulders. "We're taking you to the hospital."

"No!" He banged a fist on the table. "I slept poorly last night because of the burns, is all. I must go to work now."

He rose unsteadily; Nobuyuki held his hands out as if to catch him. "I heard some girls from Modo Village were struggling like you are. They went to the hospital. You should go, too."

"Nothing's wrong with me!" Higano staggered the three steps to the entry, then tried to slip on his shoes. The right heel jutted out crookedly. He leaned over and tried to straighten that foot with his hand, but instead jabbed his fingers into the dirt floor.

Her parents exchanged worried looks.

After two more attempts, Higano finally got both feet shod and stumbled out, untied shoelaces dragging behind.

"He forgot his lunch." Yuki held up a cloth-wrapped tin lunchbox.

Mom blinked back tears. "Go give it to him."

Yuki ran out after him. Some thirty small houses scattered the forested rolling hills between the main road and Minamata Bay. Most residents were fishers. Yuki's home stood in the middle; a good baseball player could throw the whole distance in either direction.

Uncle Higano was normally a fast walker. He should've been at the bus stop on the main road by now, a mere six houses up. But so far he'd only lurched past two. The back of his neck already glistened with perspiration.

"Uncle! Here's your lunch."

He turned toward her, lost his balance, and toppled to the dirt lane. He pushed upright and took hold of her outstretched hand.

She heaved backward until he was up again, then pointed to his untied shoes. "Your laces aren't done. You must've tripped on them."

"You're right." He didn't meet her gaze. "I was in a big hurry."

She handed over the tin lunchbox, then stooped to tie the laces before he could argue. "It's a nice day. I'll walk with you." She took his hand, shocked at how cold and lifeless it felt.

The red and white public bus rolled up to the stop, belching exhaust as it idled. Several people boarded. Uncle tried to go next, but the toe of his shoe caught on the edge of one step. Yuki grabbed his waist and boosted him up. At last Higano slumped into the front seat, lips pressed tightly together. He didn't look down at her or say goodbye.

THREE

Dual Birthdays
Minamata City, 1956

Kiyo smiled when he caught sight of the first birth-day cake he'd ever had: white icing with piped green decorations, and tiny white candles aflame. His mother's obsession with emulating all the ways Americans lived definitely had its good points. The cook set the cake, which smelled sweetly of sugar and butter, in front of him, as the fourteen candles flickered.

"Wow. Thanks!" he said.

Tonight his mother wore a red and blue plaid dress; one she'd spotted on the cover of an American fashion magazine. She beamed at his enthusiasm. As usual, when-ever her husband wasn't home, she had the radio tuned to the jazz station. Watanabe Sadao's wailing saxophone filled the air.

"You're supposed to make a silent wish, then blow out the candles," she instructed. "If you blow all the flames out at once, your wish comes true."

I wish Dad wouldn't work so much and could come home for dinner. Kiyo inhaled deeply, the candles' heat warming his face, then blew out every single one.

Yanagiya, the family's cook and maid, chuckled. Unlike her fashionable employer, she wore a plain blue cotton ki-mono, and kept her long hair knotted in a bun at her nape. She sliced a large piece of the cake for Kiyo, handed it to him, and smiled. "Happy day."

He eagerly stuffed in a big bite. "So *good,*" he moaned.

Fukuzawa stood by, clapping. His father's tall, company-employed chauffeur was dressed impeccably in a black suit, as always. Kiyo assumed he was just waiting to be summoned to pick up his boss at the office. Until he disappeared, returning moments later rolling a shiny black bicycle down the long hallway to the dining room.

Mom gestured at the bike. "Americans give birthday presents. Here's yours."

"Really?" Kiyo sprang from his chair to check it out. Fukuzawa held it steady while he ran a hand over the black-enameled metal fenders, the sturdy chrome handlebars. This was nothing less than freedom!

"Thank you, thank you. I really wanted one." He bowed to his mother. "I like how Americans celebrate birthdays."

"Their ways are the wave of the future. They're all so wealthy and so stylish."

She clasped her hands and turned to face east, as if she could actually see America from across the Pacific Ocean.

"Mrs. Takahashi and her friends get the same magazines I do, but thanks to your father's position at the company I can acquire luxury items first. Our tailor sews our clothes before theirs. Nishikawa Furniture orders our furniture first. So I ordered the best bicycle for you a month ago and waited until now to present it." She giggled, laying a hand lovingly on his arm. "We shouldn't spoil you too much, after all."

He ran a finger across the smooth steel spokes, squeezed the brake handles and prodded its plump black rubber tires, which sprang back. "Dad's assistant taught me how to ride."

"So he told me," Fukuzawa said.

"So I'm going cycling!"

In his room Kiyo shed the blue suit Mom had ordered from the tailor, and slipped on a casual shirt and shorts. He rolled the new bike outside and sped west down the streets of Minamata, toward the shimmering, crescent-shaped Bay. Then, south on the narrow unpaved road that hugged the sea. Cool evening air rushed at his face. Houses and trees flew by. Some boys his age were fishing with bamboo poles off a concrete jetty. He heard a plunk as one baited hook hit the water.

I could ride on forever, he thought.

Near Tsukinoura, the little fishing village closest to his city on Minamata Bay, he wondered what it must feel like to live in a place called The Back of the Moon. Was it just as dark, cold, and airless? At last he stopped to check his watch; Dad's old one. The trip had consumed a mere seven minutes instead of the usual twenty it took to jog here.

Leaning his elbows on the handlebars, he inhaled the salty breeze, peering down at the crystalline blue waves slapping a short seawall encrusted with barnacles.

That was when he saw the cat. The poor animal was convulsing; blood glistening on its white fur. He froze, shocked, as the large white feline savagely rubbed its face against the dirt next to the pier until its nose bled.

The writhing animal then hopped up on the concrete barrier, and jerked around in a circle on its hind legs in a horrible sort of dance. Suddenly it bent backward in a sharp arc, landed hard on its side, and tumbled off the seawall. Its front paws clawed frantically to hold on, nails scratching at the ledge. But the weight of its body dragged it down, out of sight.

"No!" Kiyo dropped his bike and sprinted to the concrete barrier. The Bay had swallowed up the cat, so he leaped into the waist-high shallows. Even there, the icy water made him gasp. The sun, sinking toward the horizon, blinded him. One deep breath, and he ducked under the surface. But his dive stirred up the sandy bottom, making the water murky. He couldn't see. At the surface he took another breath, then submerged again.

Nothing. He swam out farther into the Bay. The ocean floor dropped quickly; soon he could no longer touch the bottom. He treaded water, then dove to look again. He swam in a slow circle, searching for any sign of the cat, face underwater. No luck.

Failing to save the poor animal made him feel sick. How strangely it'd been acting – as if driven insane by some horrible pain. He pulled himself up onto the seawall and stared blankly out at the Bay, to wait until his clothes stopped dripping.

Another cat appeared and brushed against him, this one smaller with gray fur. Kiyo jumped off the seawall and scooped it up.

"I'm not letting you near the water." He stroked its head and scratched under its chin. The cat closed its eyes and purred. He was glad it was acting normally. He couldn't bear to watch another animal suffer.

"Jiro, Jiro!" a girl's voice called out.

"Are you Jiro?" he asked the cat, which purred louder.

The voice belonged to a girl just rounding a bend of the shore. Pretty, about his age, hands cupped around her mouth, she was still calling.

"Hey! Are you looking for this little guy?"

"Jiro!" The girl rushed up and held out her arms. He handed over the cat.

She carried her pet away; Kiyo followed. She headed to a small wood-planked hut that smelled of dried squid. The door hung open at a crazy angle, its top hinge missing. She sat on a straw mat laid over bare ground, next to an open schoolbook. Kiyo stood in the open doorway. Gaps between the wall-boards were so wide he could see the Bay through them. The roof had lost most of its tiles; columns of sunlight streaked in through the gaps above.

Jiro writhed ecstatically as she scratched his chin, and nuzzled his head playfully with her nose. "Bad boy. You're supposed to stick around here."

"He was following the seawall," Kiyo explained. He almost told her about the strangely-dancing white cat but decided it would spoil the happy reunion. The sight had been terrible; no point in horrifying this girl, too. The white cat had obviously been sick. But Jiro looked very healthy.

When the girl finally looked up, he noticed a glittering brooch shaped like an oval tea-leaf pinned to her faded, wrinkled blouse. Her eyes shone as brightly as the faceted ruby red, sapphire blue, and crystal-clear glass on the ornament.

"Thanks for bringing my cat back," she said. "I should've kept a better watch on him, but I was drawing."

"You're an artist?"

She looked a bit sheepish. "I do sketches."

"May I see some?"

She set the cat down, slid a piece of paper from between the pages of her math book, and held it out. "That's what I saw from my father's boat today."

He sat on the edge of the mat, scrutinizing the drawing. Light filtered through the thin paper; the math problems filling the other side were visible through it.

He traced the horizon in the pencil sketch with one finger. "Yeah, there's the Amakusa Islands across the Bay. Hey, you're really good." Those islands, a barrier between the rough open ocean and Minamata Bay, created the inland Shiranui Sea.

She'd sketched the sun high above it, as well as a small flat-bottomed boat brimming with a fisherman's catch. The water between boat and islands seemed to actually glitter. Two men, a woman, and a girl, sat inside the boat.

"I can't help it, I just have to draw. My parents, my uncle, and I went fishing because today's my birthday." Kiyo started to tell her it was his birthday, too, but she rushed on, adding, "I go almost every day, even when it's not my birthday. That is, when I'm not in school. The picture's how I want to spend every birthday."

When she smiled, her whole face lit up with an inquisitive eagerness. "Everything's perfect out there." Then she slapped her forehead. "Eh. I'm talking too much."

He chuckled. "No, it's okay." He liked her ready smile, and didn't mind listening. She was lifting the gloom he'd felt after watching the other cat die.

She looked down and fingered the silver brooch. "I found this on the beach early this morning. Someone must've dropped it in the ocean, and the current brought it to me for my birthday."

"It's pretty."

"Thanks. I'm never taking it off." She sighed happily.

He looked around the shack. "What's this place?"

"Used to be some kind of tool shed. Now, just a local kids' hangout."

"Hey, it's my birthday, too."

She beamed. "Really? How old are you?"

"Fourteen."

"Like me. But your voice is already so deep." She grinned again, showing pearly teeth. "I thought you were older."

He laughed loudly. He'd never known any girl bold enough to say such things. She wasn't like the ones he knew at school. It was refreshing.

She prattled on, not seeming self-conscious about her comment. "So, what's your name?"

"Kiyoshi, but friends call me Kiyo."

"I'm Yuki. Hey, come home for dinner with me."

He raised his eyebrows. "But won't your parents mind a stranger just showing up?"

"Not when I tell them it's your birthday, too."

"Really? Well ... OK, thanks."

"Come on." She took her drawing from him, stuck it back inside the textbook and pointed at her cat. "Jiro, follow me."

"I have to get my bike. It's around the bend."

After Kiyo wheeled it up, she gasped. "*Subarashii!*" Incredible. "Is it new?"

He nodded. "A gift for my birthday."

"We both got something, then." She patted her pin before pointing southward. "I live that way."

Four big islands make up Japan, but Okinawa, the
fifth island, is actually a chain of 160 small islands far
south of the main four. Minamata Bay is on the southern-
most island of Kyushu.

It was only May first but already the trees and bushes
they walked between were lush and green. Farmers were
planting wheat and beans in fields near small, tidy farmhouses. Large vegetable plots grew thick and tall next to
each family home. Chickens strutted about, clucking and
pecking, tugging up fat worms.

They strolled to the edge of a five-story cliff, the bottom
dotted with moss-covered stones washed by perpetual
waves.

"Over there's my village." She pointed past the cliff to
where the beach again met the Bay. A spot clustered with
dozens of unpainted, mostly one-story wooden buildings
with faded tile roofs. To get there they had to keep walking
until they reached a short, graveled main street, then
turned into a narrow sandy lane. Kiyo's bicycle left tire
ruts in the soft dirt.

Houses here were set farther apart. Storage shacks
and fishing gaffs and nets filled the areas in between.
Chickens, perched atop henhouses, half-opened their eyes
as the two of them passed. Laundry was drying on bamboo
poles hung from roof eaves. Women cooked vegetables and
various kinds of seafood outside, squatting over small
portable grills that sent wood smoke wafting along, carrying mouthwatering scents.

Jiro darted away into the bushes on some secret feline
errand.

"Here we are." Yuki stopped in front of a small cottage with bleached, weathered siding which Kiyo realized was nothing more than old, salvaged boards nailed to a frame.

Suddenly Yuki yelled, "Watch out!"

Kiyo stopped abruptly. A rasping sound: one clay tile slid off the roof, landing at his feet with a dull thump.

"Are you all right?" she asked. "Dad's going to fix the old roof if we have a good fishing season."

"Yes, fine." Glancing up he saw several more crooked tiles that looked loose enough to fall. Should he ever return, he'd keep an eye out. Roof tiles were heavy and sharp; they could do a lot of damage.

He parked his bike in front and followed her past narrow sliding front doors crafted from old boards stuck onto flimsy wood frames. Kiyo had been taught to take off his shoes before stepping up and inside. Here the entry floor was unpaved dirt, the space barely large enough for the two of them to stand. Three pairs of battered black rubber boots were shoved into one corner.

From here he could see inside the whole house: a tiny kitchen to the left, a broom and duster hanging on the kitchen wall, and a slightly larger space in front of him divided in two by open shoji doors.

The wood lattices, set in frames covered by translucent paper, let light filter through. When paper in shoji doors at his own house was torn, if located where guests couldn't see the damage, Mom just had it patched. In public areas the whole door got re-covered.

But the two shoji doors in this cottage were covered with old, yellowed newsprint. A single bare ceiling bulb hung from a frayed electric cord; the sole source of light, except for two small windows. A low table was the only piece of furniture in the front room. A scratched-up dresser and homemade shelves of rough wood furnished the back room. When Kiyo glimpsed his face in a tall, cracked mirror propped against one wall, he realized he was gaping, and quickly wiped away his look of surprise.

Two men, in white undershirts and tan pants with rolled hems, were smoking cigarettes, sitting on mats in an open doorway off to one side. Beyond it lay a thriving vegetable garden where four chickens clucked and pecked and squabbled. One man was puffing out perfect smoke-rings. Outside, next to the garden, a lean woman crouched next to a small charcoal brazier. She wore a long-sleeved cotton blouse and dark pants, the usual attire for fishers, to keep the sun off. A thin towel was wrapped and tied at the nape to cover her hair.

Kiyo guessed she was probably no older than his mother, but she wore no makeup on her sun-weathered, lined face. Strong-looking hands fanned flames as she grilled what looked like fish, octopus, and colorful assorted vegetables.

"Meet my new friend, Kiyo," Yuki told them. "Kiyo, my family."

"Welcome, Kiyo," said the woman. "I'm Kazuko, Yuki's mother." She smiled; her gaze was kind.

He bowed. "*Hajimemashite yoroshiku onegaishimasu.*" Nice to meet you.

"Oh, my." Yuki's mother looked him over with even more interest. "So well mannered. Is your name written as 'clear water'?"

"Well, sort of. Meaning clear . . . or pure."

"Yuki-chan's name is written as 'having hope.' How we inscribe our names shows our true soul."

His parents had often talked about how they'd chosen kanji characters for their three sons' names, constantly reminding them to become the kind of person those names represented. Apparently Yuki's did the same.

Kazuko flipped a fish over on the grate. "You're just in time for Yuki-chan's birthday dinner."

The two men raised their hands in greeting. "Hi, I'm Nobuyuki, her father," said the darkly tanned, stocky one.

"I'm Higano, his brother." The finer-featured man jerked a thumb at Nobuyuki.

"Uncle Higano lives with us," Yuki said. "Oh, and Dad? A roof tile almost hit Kiyo-kun's head just now."

Her father winced. "Glad you're not injured. I'll fix that roof soon. So, what do your parents do?"

"Mom stays at home. Dad works for Chisso."

"I work there, too." Higano's hair was cut severely short, his skin not as sun-darkened as was Yuki's parents'. When he swiveled to face Kiyo, though, he swayed and almost toppled off the threshold.

Nobuyuki took his arm. "Careful, Higano-kun."

A shadow crossed Higano's face for a second, then he smiled. "What does he do, your father? I might know him."

"He, ah, works in the office." That's not lying, Kiyo told himself. The executive head of wastewater discharge *did* work in the office there.

"Ah." Higano shook his head. "Wouldn't know him, then. I'm out in the factory."

"Guess what?" Yuki said. "Kiyo and I were born on the exact same day. He got a bicycle for his birthday." She pointed through the open front door to the polished black bike.

Kazuko craned her neck to see. "Oh, very nice."

The two men hopped down from the doorway to go examine it. Kiyo slipped on his shoes again and joined them.

"What did she mean, *for* your birthday?" Higano asked.

"In America, you get a present on each birthday."

"I've never heard of such a thing." He looked doubtful.

"Mom's read about it in her fashion magazines."

"Hmm." Nobuyuki stroked the bike's leather seat. "What a beaut." He looked just like Yuki when he smiled: the same cherry-blossom cheeks, the same wide dark eyes.

"A bicycle's so handy," Higano said.

"True. We could get around that way so much faster." Nobuyuki nodded.

Yuki's mom laughed. "Couldn't afford one, even if the fish all jumped into our boat."

"Say." The uncle looked at Yuki. "I gave you two colored pencils a few weeks ago. Did you realize they were your birthday present?"

"Were they? Thank you, Uncle." She grinned. "The best ones I've ever gotten for a birthday."

Everyone burst out laughing. Jiro stalked up and rubbed his head against Yuki's shin. She went into the kitchen for fish scraps, and set them on a flat rock outside the side door. The cat leapt to the meal. "We had a good fishing haul so you have lots to eat today," she told him.

"Dinner!" Kazuko called.

The family kicked off their wooden clogs, Kiyo slipped out of his damp leather shoes, and they all went inside.

Nobuyuki opened a bottle of shochu – liquor made from fermented rice or sweet potatoes – and poured three cups. "We should toast to the birthdays." He sat on the floor in front of the low, nicked square table, which was just large enough for four.

Kazuko carried in a platter heaped with grilled fish, octopus, snow peas, spinach, and green onions. She went back toward the tiny kitchen alcove. All kitchens in Japan were lower than the rest of the house. But Kiyo noticed, as she stepped down into it, that this one had a dirt floor. She rushed back with soy sauce, chopsticks, and rice in chipped blue-and-white bowls.

Yuki scooted over to make room for her mother. Then her parents and Higano each picked up a cup of shochu. "To both kids," Nobuyuki said. And the adults tossed down the liquor.

"This is your birthday dinner, too, Kiyo-kun." Kazuko smiled at him.

His steak dinner suddenly seemed like a long time ago. "Thank you." He dug in, savoring the salty soy sauce coating the vegetables and seafood: crunchy on the outside, tender on the inside.

"I shouldn't do this, but it's your special day." Nobuyuki gave Kiyo a conspiratorial smile. "Want a sip of shochu?"

"How about me?" Yuki complained.

"Girls shouldn't drink," her father said sternly.

She frowned. "That's not fair. We're the same age."

He sighed. "All right. As your father, I'll allow it, just this once."

He tipped the bottle into each of their empty rice bowls, barely wetting the bottoms.

Kiyo was surprised at how the mere sip of harsh liquor burned his throat. But he liked the warmth that rose a moment later. He gazed into his empty bowl. "May I have some more?"

Nobuyuki shook his head. "Told you. Just a taste. Don't be telling anyone I did this."

Kiyo grinned. "I won't, if I can have a little more."

Everyone roared with laughter. Yuki and Kiyo joined in, as her father lifted the bottle again.

FOUR

The Strange Disease

A month later, as his math tutor checked math homework in the living room, Kiyo tried to glimpse the side-table clock without moving his head. Ten more minutes until the tutor would leave. Neither one enjoyed their twice-a-week after-school sessions, but the pimply high school senior, only a couple years older than Kiyo, was at least getting paid. Kiyo's parents expected him to get into the country's best university and study medicine. His father had used his influence to set up a meeting for Kiyo today with Dr. Hosokawa Hajime, the director of Chisso Hospital.

At four o'clock sharp his mother appeared, dressed in a brand-new plum-colored suit. A design she'd had made by her seamstress, based on a picture in a recent American fashion magazine.

"Tanaka-san." She handed the tutor a white envelope. "Your pay for the week. Thank you."

The young man accepted his fee, bowed, and left.

"Kiyoshi-kun." His mother gave him a wry smile, as if she'd noticed the relief on his face. "I know you don't like the extra lessons, but you're lucky we can afford it. Otherwise, how will you keep up with students in Tokyo?"

She turned her face north, as if she could actually see the capital. "I loved the city, it's a marvelous place. But I made the sacrifice to leave it and marry your father, to live here for his work. Maybe we'll return to Tokyo after he retires." Her face glowed at the possibility. "Anyway, you know all this work is for your future."

"Yes, Mom. Can I go to the meeting with the doctor now?"

"Yes. But remember to be extra respectful. Your father's gone out on a limb for you, setting it up."

"I will. It's great of him to do this for me."

"How could he not? You pestered him enough." She laughed and patted his shoulder.

He pedaled away quickly, but had only gotten two blocks when his friend Masa darted out onto the narrow road between well-kept houses, waving him down. Tall and beanstalk-skinny, Masa peered down at Kiyo, eyes narrowed under his mop of coarse, straight hair. He wore his usual after-school outfit: well-washed, soft-looking indigo pants and an old white shirt. He might've been mistaken for a gardener in the upper-class neighborhood, instead of a resident.

Kiyo envied Masa's height; he wanted to be tall, too. "Can't stop long. I'm headed to the hospital to meet Hosokawa Sensei."

"Oh, that's right. How long will you be there?"

"I hope quite a while."

"You were more fun before you got on this I-Want-To-Be-a-Doctor kick."

"It's not a kick. And I'm still fun. See you tomorrow. No tutoring then."

Chisso Factory had built and staffed the large, modern, two-story medical facility, and Kiyo was there to meet its chief of staff. He parked his bike, grabbed the anatomy textbook from the basket, and ran up the steps. He tried to calm down and maintain a serious, mature look, but it was hard.

The sharp scents of antiseptic and disinfectants assailed him as soon as he opened the large entry door. He rushed down the gleaming main hallway, carefully dodging a man walking slowly on crutches. Each step the gowned patient took made a squeak as the brown rubber crutch-tips hit the floor. He then passed a young woman cooing at the crying baby in her arms, and another mother dragging a screaming toddler.

At last Kiyo spotted Dr. Hosokawa's metal nameplate mounted on a well-varnished office door. He tapped on the door's frosted glass panel. After a moment he knocked again, calling out, "Hosokawa Sensei, it's Kuge Kiyoshi."

No response.

He trekked back to the main entrance slowly. Had the doctor forgotten? Or perhaps he now regretted promising Kiyo's father this favor, and had already left.

At the front reception desk he asked a young nurse with a jaunty white cap if Hosokawa Sensei was in.

"Yes. Could be in one of the treatment rooms. We've had many tourists check in after overdoing things. Just the past hour, an old man with stomach cramps, a teenager with a broken leg who jumped off a cliff into the Bay – good thing it was a low one – and a girl scraped up from falling off a bike."

"Wow," said Kiyo. "Busy day."

"Yeah. Maybe try Room 125?" she suggested.

He thanked her and hustled back down the hall. Voices were audible through a closed door marked 125. Hoping one of them was the doctor's, he knocked.

"Yes?" a man called.

Kiyo opened the door a crack. A gray-haired man in a white lab coat stood next to a bald middle-aged one sitting on an exam table. The patient was just buttoning up his shirt. The doctor held up an index finger, nodded at Kiyo and turned back to hand a brown paper packet to the pa-tient.

"Make a paste from the medication with some water. Apply it to the hives twice a day. They should clear up soon."

The man rose, bowed to the doctor, and left, clutching his prescription.

"Excuse me. Hosokawa Sensei?" Kiyo asked.

"Yes. You must be Kuge Kiyoshi."

"I am." Kiyo bowed deeply. "Thanks for letting me study here with you."

"Sorry if you had a hard time finding me, Kiyoshi-kun." The doctor sighed. "I just called your father to postpone our appointment a bit. We've been inundated."

His new mentor was medium height and thin. Probably a bit younger than Dad, Kiyo thought. That would make him fifty-five or so. But Sensei also had deep lines around his mouth, like his father. And the thick lenses of his black-framed glasses made his eyes look small.

"No problem." Kiyo assured him. "Patients should come first."

The doctor smiled for the first time. "Let's go back to my office."

When they got there Kiyo's father was standing by the doctor's gray metal desk.

"Ah, there you are," Kuge Kichiro said. "Sensei, my son, Kiyoshi. Or have you already met?"

"Indeed we did, Kuge-san."

"I must hurry back to the office. I'm indebted to you for showing my son around." He turned to Kiyo. "Kiyo, listen to the sensei."

Trying not to roll his eyes, Kiyo said, "I will, Dad."

The two men bowed. After Kichiro left, Hosokawa Sensei turned back to Kiyo. "So, you want to be a doctor?" He winced and rolled his shoulders as if they felt tight.

"More than anything."

"What's that you're holding?"

Kiyo held up the anatomy book. "I bought it with my allowance."

Sensei thumbed through. "Already looking much used."

"I read it all the time. Right now I'm learning the bones in the body."

"Good start." The doctor gave a pleased chuckle.

Kiyo glanced at a tall bookcase stuffed with medical books, the only other furniture in the small room besides a desk and two green leather chairs. "Neurology. Internal medicine. Surgery. Childbirth ... one day I want to know all of this."

The physician handed the book back. "You sound just like me. I knew from the age of seven I would be a doctor."

"Really? That's when I knew, too."

Sensei looked Kiyo over as if seeing him for the first time. "And you're how old now?"

"Fourteen."

"So you've wanted to practice medicine half your life already. I think we'll get along." He slid an index finger over the spines of a shelf of books. "Always more to learn. Fortunately, my family could afford to give me a good edu-cation. You're lucky to have supportive parents, too."

"Yeah, I guess so." Kiyo felt a momentary stab of guilt over complaining about tutoring. Especially after seeing how Yuki's family lived – in a place smaller than his living room. "I'm excited to learn more."

"You can follow me on rounds now," said Hosokawa Sensei.

He trailed the doctor from room to room as he visited patients, introducing Kiyo as "my assistant." And Kiyo bowed to them as he tried to appear serious, biting his cheeks to keep from smiling too much. And enjoying him-self immensely.

At least, until they climbed the stairs to the second floor, and entered a wing where three girls a little older than himself lay on narrow cots moaning and convulsing.

The room stank of stale sweat, feces, and vomit. He stood frozen in the doorway, staring at their splayed, misshapen fingers, their flailing arms and legs. It was like the ill-fated dancing white cat all over again.

Several sticky strips hung from the ceiling, black with trapped, dying flies. Yet, when one of the girls gave a long mournful wail, a fat black fly flew straight into her gaping mouth.

Kiyo closed his eyes. Then remembered he was supposed to be watching and learning, and snapped them open again. A white-uniformed nurse was holding down one girl, trying to keep her from falling or injuring herself.

"Can you . . . strap them down?" Kiyo asked.

"We tried that," Sensei said. "But they twist and jerk so violently, it could dislocate a joint or cause deep strap burns that could then get infected."

He picked up a long rubber tube and spoke soothingly to the patient in the farthest bed. "I'm going to carefully insert this through your nose into your stomach, my dear, so we can feed you."

But when he raised the tube and bent over her, she tossed her head violently back and forth.

"Can you lie still for me?" he added.

Instead, she bucked like a spooked horse.

Sensei turned to the nurse. "Usuda-san, we'll have use sedation. Hold each one as I administer the shots."

Once they were done with the nerve-wracking job of sedating and feeding the afflicted girls, the doctor led Kiyo from the room. "This is a terrible epidemic. So many cases recently. I've never seen anything like it before. Time to notify the public health office."

"May I go along?"

Sensei nodded, and they set off at a brisk pace. "Don't say anything, though, while we're there."

"I won't." Kiyo hurried to match the doctor's long strides as they reached the front walkway. "What're the symptoms of this new disease?"

"First, the hands and feet become numb so they have trouble walking and gripping things. After a while, they can't control limbs or muscles at all. Their mouths seize up so tightly they can't open them to eat. Vision narrows until they finally go blind. Deaf as well. And all the while they're in terrible pain. Seems to be some sort of neurological problem."

Kiyo frowned. "I saw a cat the other day. And, well... this reminded me of it. The animal looked like it was dancing," he said. "And yet so tormented by some agony, it jumped into the Bay. The poor thing drowned." He grimaced, remembering how he'd failed to save it. "But after seeing those girls in the beds, I think the cat was having convulsions. Can they get this disease too?"

"Hmm. Cats?" The doctor looked thoughtful. "That's interesting. I'll think about it."

Kiyo had also been visiting Yuki once a week since they'd met. He'd observed that her uncle Higano now had great difficulty walking, often stumbling as if his feet were numb. He could no longer hold chopsticks, so Yuki's mother made rice balls, which he could scoop up and eat with his hands. But he only nibbled at food, as if he couldn't open his mouth very wide.

Kiyo shuddered. Her uncle must have the same disease. It seemed so unfair. Didn't her family have enough trouble just getting by?

The public health office was located next door to the hospital. Kiyo followed Hosokawa Sensei up a short set of steps and into a smaller, older, one-story wooden building. The doctor passed the receptionist without any acknowledgement, gaze riveted on the door at the end of the main corridor. They passed a shiny red fire extinguisher, one of many such new devices now seen in commercial and public buildings, hung in the hallway near the men's restroom.

Dr. Hosokawa finally halted at a door near the end of the hallway, and knocked.

"Hai?" Yes? A voice called.

The doctor went in. Kiyo trailed behind him and went to stand quietly off to one side.

"Hosokawa Sensei." The man at the desk laid his pen on the notebook he'd been writing in, then stood and bowed. Tall and gaunt, a bit older than Kiyo's father, though still with a full head of slicked-back black hair.

Without even a nod, the doctor said urgently, "Miyagi-san, I have an epidemic to report."

"Epidemic?" Miyagi frowned. "Of what?"

"It's ... well, so new I don't even have a name for it yet."

"What do you know about this new disease?" As the official waited for an answer, he grabbed a swatter and swung at a buzzing fly, narrowly missing. Making a sour face, he hung the wire-handled swatter on a nail and turned back to Sensei.

Dr. Hosokawa said, "Last month I examined a five-year-old at our factory hospital. The symptoms were difficulty in walking and speaking. She was also having convulsions, so I hospitalized her. Two days later, her younger sister presented with the same symptoms. I admitted her, too. Their neighbor's daughter had similar issues. Then we discovered eight more afflicted people after a house-to-house survey of the neighborhood. They're all in the hospital now, deteriorating quickly. So far, nothing has significantly eased their suffering or controlled the symptoms. Because of its localized nature, I suspect the disease may be contagious. I'd like to isolate these patients."

"Umm." Miyagi frowned. "That does sound alarming. They should be quarantined, in case it's contagious. At least until you know more. I'll alert other doctors to watch out for the same symptoms."

"Thank you." Hosokawa Sensei bowed, then turned and hurried out of the office. Kiyo bowed as well, closed the door behind them, and rushed again to catch up. As he followed the doctor back to the hospital, he wondered, How many people will be afflicted by this hideous new disease? I never realized before what a mystery diagnosis can be.

As sickened as he'd been to see the terrible suffering of Hosokawa Sensei's patients, the part of his mind that had always been eager to become a doctor wanted very badly to learn more.

FIVE

DDT

By June, a mere two months after he'd been burned at the factory, Uncle Higano could just barely struggle along on stiff limbs. On July 1st, a neighbor found him sitting on the road two houses from the bus stop, unable to rise and go on. The neighbor, half-carrying Higano, helped him get home. The next day, Yuki's father stopped by the main office of Chisso Factory to let them know his brother must quit his job.

Now, six months later, the terrible year was almost over, and Uncle Higano could hardly do anything at all.

On a cold January morning Yuki tapped softly on his door. Hearing a muffled grunt, she entered the stale-smelling room and knelt next to his futon. He'd grown so thin she could now lift and prop him up by herself.

He couldn't hear well, so she shouted near his ear, "Good morning, Uncle!" Then wrapped a padded jacket over his shoulders. "It might snow this afternoon. Good thing it's Sunday, and I don't have school. Let's move over to the *kotatsu*. You'll be warmer there."

As did the families in every Japanese household, Yuki helped her mother set up a charcoal heater in the fall. They removed a section of flooring in the living room and fed charcoal to the kotatsu set down in a square pit, then positioned the low table over it. Then four people could sit around the table, legs dangling inside the hole in the floor. They draped a thick futon large enough to cover the table and everyone's laps over it all to trap the warmth created by charcoal embers smoldering down in the middle of the pit.

With Yuki on one side of Uncle Higano and her father on the other, they half-dragged, half-carried him into the front room and lowered him to sit at the kotatsu. While Yuki held him upright, Dad lifted Uncle's legs and settled them down in the warm pit, then covered him to the waist with the futon. He'd also nailed two boards into an L shape, which he now slid under Uncle and against his back to keep him upright. A sack of rice weighted the back of the board and kept it in place.

"Here's your breakfast." Kazuko set a bowl of rice porridge on the kotatsu table and laid a hand on her brother-in-law's thin shoulder. "I bet you're hungry." She raised half a spoonful to his lips. But the stiffened jaw barely allowed his mouth to open. She pressed his lower lip down with the spoon, but when she tipped the porridge in, it dribbled down his chin. She mopped up with a towel and tried twice more, but Uncle couldn't take in any food.

He muttered something in his changed voice, low and rasping, slurring the words.

"Did you say toilet?" Kazuko asked.

"I'll take him." Nobuyuki got up and lifted his brother from the kotatsu. While Mom held him up, Dad turned away, squatted, and slid his brother onto his back. Leaning forward so Uncle would not slide off, Dad wrapped his arms around his brother's legs, and began walking them toward the outhouse.

Higano was the only family Yuki knew besides her parents – her mother was an orphan, her father's parents lived on Amakusa Islands across Minamata Bay – and she couldn't bear to see him so incapacitated. Before his mouth had clamped shut, he'd told her his vision was getting smaller. As if he were looking through a length of bamboo, the edges of his world squeezing into a smaller and smaller perspective.

"Higano!" she heard her dad scream. She and her mother dashed outside.

Dad stood bent over Uncle Higano, who lay moaning on the ground, bleeding from a jagged gash on his forehead.

"I'm sorry! I'm so sorry." Dad wrapped his arms around his brother and sat him up.

"What happened?" Mom asked, crouching and studying the cut.

Nobuyuki glanced up, face twisted in misery. "I thought he was secure on my back, but he's too weak to hold on any longer. He slid off and hit his head on a rock. I'm sorry, Higano-kun."

Yuki got a clean rag from the kitchen and wiped the blood off Uncle's forehead. "Mom, it looks deep."

Kazuko shook her head. "We should take him to the hospital. I'll help get him up."

She and Yuki loaded Uncle back onto Nobuyuki's back, then walked alongside, bracing him with both hands to make sure he stayed in place during the trek to the bus stop.

Yuki hated the hospital. Two years ago Aunt Haruko had withered away here and finally died. The floors were still too shiny, and the fumes of some strong antiseptic stung her nose. The place was all white, like a bandage. Or a shroud. The walls, the uniforms, the beds, the sheets. Even the furniture.

In the examination room, a doctor in a white lab coat greeted the family as they laid Higano gently on a white-sheeted bed. "I'm Dr. Hosokawa."

Dad bowed to him. "My brother slid off my back as I was carrying him back from the outhouse. He hit his head."

"I see." The physician turned to Uncle. "Good morning Akaji-san. I'm Dr. Hosokawa." After closely examining the wound, he looked up and said, "Head wounds bleed a lot, and often look worse than they are. Now that the flow's stopped, I can put in a couple stitches."

He sutured the cut, then patted Uncle's shoulder. "That should do it. Now, I understand you're unable to walk. How have you been feeling lately? What's your health like?"

Uncle's jaw trembled as he strained to move his mouth. Lips quivering with exertion, he could only make incomprehensible noises.

The doctor nodded sympathetically. "I see your jaw has locked." He peered up at Dad. "What are his other symptoms, and when did they start?"

Dad listed them all, adding, "It began last April, eight months ago."

"We've seen over forty patients who present with the same signs. There's truly an epidemic of the Strange Disease."

"An epidemic?" Yuki gasped, just as her mother frowned and said, "What's The Strange Disease?"

"That's what we're calling it, for now. All we know for sure is that the victims are from fishing villages along Minamata Bay. But we've no idea what this new ailment is, yet, or what's causing it. The city government and some of my colleagues formed The Strange Disease Countermeasure Committee to confer about it. I've invited researchers from Kumamoto University to study it with me."

Nobuyuki looked hopeful. "Ah. Then they should be able to figure this out soon."

The doctor didn't respond to that, only added, "We have a special ward for Strange Disease patients. I think we should admit him."

Nobuyuki blinked back tears. "Higano's been getting worse for eight months, but he's always refused to see a doctor. We try to care for him, but he needs more help than we can give. We can't even get food into his mouth any-more."

Mom wrung her hands. "We'll do whatever might help, but he can't go on without eating."

Uncle thrashed and moaned, "No, no."

"I'm sorry." Kazuko's voice cracked. "But here is the best place for now. You'd starve at home."

"The disease appears to be localized," said Dr. Ho-sokawa. "We don't know yet if it's contagious, so the ward is isolated. You should stay away for now, just in case." Turning back to Higano, he added, "We'll transfer you there, and look after you."

Uncle grunted and shook his head. Seeing the terror and desperation in his eyes, Yuki grabbed one stiff hand. "You'll fix him up, right?" she asked.

The doctor didn't meet her gaze. "We'll do everything we can."

"*Ganbatte.*" Hang in there, her mother told Higano, gripping his shoulder in encouragement. She seemed to be trying to smile, but her lips trembled.

Nobuyuki nodded to his brother and then quickly looked away, as if ashamed.

Yuki choked back a sob and laid her head on Uncle Hi-gano's chest, so he wouldn't see her tears.

"Come on, Yuki-chan," her mother said gently. "They'll take better care of him than we can."

Out in the hallway, Nobuyuki thanked the doctor.

"But how long will he have to stay?" Yuki asked.

Hosokawa Sensei gave a long sigh. "I'm sorry to have to say this, but . . . so far, no one has recovered. Fourteen Strange Disease patients have died."

Kazuko gasped, and her father bellowed, "What!"

"No, no!" Yuki cried.

The doctor shook his head. "Wish I had better news. But it's a puzzling disease. Researchers believe it's caused by heavy metal poisoning. Victims are often from the same family."

"Same family . . . ." Kazuko covered her mouth with one hand. They all stared around at one another, eyes wide with alarm.

After school the next day, just as Yuki was nearly home, she noticed three men in all-white uniforms climbing out of a panel van parked in front of her house. The white vehicle had black lettering on the side: MINAMATA CITY GOVERNMENT. It barely fit on the narrow dirt road.

"Sumimasen!" Excuse us, one shouted as he opened the van's rear doors.

Yuki ran the rest of the way and rushed inside the house. Curious neighbors, unused to seeing motor vehicles on their unpaved back lane, peered out from open doors and windows. Yuki's friend Kumiko poked her head out, too, watching with interest.

When her mother answered the door, her face paled. "Yes?"

"Akaji Higano lived here?" one man asked.

"Yes." Kazuko nodded tentatively. "What's going on?"

"He has a contagious disease."

"Higano-kun is contagious?" called an older neighbor from across the way, a fisherman with gray stubble covering his gaunt jaw.

"Oh, no," his wife shouted from inside their house. "Honey, come back inside. What if you catch it?"

The husband crossed his arms. "Higano-kun was always at the bathhouse every night, when I went. What if he's been spreading some filthy disease?"

"He's not dirty," Yuki said furiously. "And no one can help being sick."

"We go out and disinfect homes of all victims with the Strange Disease," another white-uniformed man told Mom. "Please back up and give us space."

Higano had only been hospitalized one day, and government men were already here. What next, Yuki wondered.

The same neighbor man crossed the lane and tapped the worker's shoulder. "Higano-kun has that Strange Disease I've been hearing about? The one where you go mad?" He turned toward the street and waved his arms at the other neighbors. "Stay away from the Akajis," he yelled. "They'll infect you with that killer disease." Up and down the street, all people suddenly looked not curious but fearful. Some went inside, banging the front doors behind them.

"What're you going to do to the house?" Yuki asked the uniformed men.

"We'll spray everything in here with DDT to disinfect the whole place. Now please, everyone, step out of our way," said the one who'd spoken first.

When Kazuko still stood in the doorway, looking confused, he grabbed one of her wrists and gently pulled her outside, into the yard. The three sanitation men readied long cylindrical spray cans with nozzles.

Yuki remembered Jiro then. "Wait!" she shouted. "My cat." Ignoring shouted orders to stay put, she sprinted from room to room, calling "Jiro! Jiro!" He was not in any of the usual places: sleeping on the folded futons or atop the small wooden dresser. Reassured then that he must be outside, she grabbed a stack of pencil drawings of the seaside, family, and Jiro – worried the DDT spray might ruin them – and went back out into the yard.

She stood next to her mother and saw through the open front door the sanitizer-men pumping cans, spraying the walls, floors, ceilings, doors, table, dresser, mirror, kitchen counter, shelves, pots, pans, bowls, utensils, futons, pillows, buckets. Even their few clothes, which they tossed on the floor to treat. Soon tendrils of white fog were drifting from the open windows, and Yuki could not just smell but taste the foul chemical. Her eyes watered as it burned her lungs and made her cough. A few neighbors who'd ventured out and gathered to watch were coughing, too.

About a half hour later the DDT-spray enforcers stowed their gear inside the panel truck and sped away.

"Where's Dad?" Yuki asked.

Her mother didn't answer. She and Yuki, stunned and nauseated, stood staring at their reeking house, wondering when it would be safe to go back inside. Not a single neighbor came over to sympathize or comfort them. The two of them stood alone. Almost, Yuki thought, as isolated as Uncle Higano must feel in his hospital bed on the Strange Disease ward.

SIX

Isolation Ward

Five days without seeing Uncle Higano felt like five years. He'd always been there, all of her life. Yuki's parents now slept in his bedroom, while Yuki lay alone on her futon in the main room. Before, it had barely provided enough room for their three futon laid out side by side, but it now felt too large. No longer did she need to push the table into the kitchen every night before bedtime. She even missed hearing Uncle Higano's snoring, a muffled drone that to her was as calming as susurrating ocean waves.

"I want to go see Uncle," she told her parents at breakfast, on the sixth day.

Her mother shook her head slowly. "We're not supposed to go there."

"We lived in here with him for three years and we aren't sick," Yuki protested.

"That's true." Her father was smoking a cigarette; he'd laid out his fishing net in the living room, and was repairing sections which had ripped. "We should've caught it by now."

"Right. And we can't just let him lie in that place all alone," Yuki said. "He must be scared."

"You're right." Dad ground his cigarette out in a nearby ashtray and stood. "Let's go."

They were wandering the hospital's hallways looking for Higano's room when Yuki heard a familiar voice call her name. She turned, surprised, to see Kiyo walking toward them. He wore his high-collared, brass-buttoned, black school uniform, and had a small, thick notebook tucked under one arm. His thick, wavy hair was neatly combed and parted. Watching him approach, she wondered again, as she had often done: *Why does a smart boy of his social stature, from a well-off family, want to be my friend?* He was still visiting the family almost every week. Still, on this worrisome day, Yuki decided to stop wondering and put away her insecurity. Just seeing him made her smile; it lightened some of the heaviness in her heart.

"What're you all doing here?" Kiyo said, as he bowed to her parents. "Hello, Akaji-san."

"Good morning," said her mother, managing a small smile. Her father muttered a terse, unintelligible greeting.

"Uncle Higano's been hospitalized in the Strange Disease ward," Yuki told Kiyo. "We've come to visit him."

He sighed. "I'm sorry. He did seem worse every time I visited, but I'd hoped . . . ."

Everyone fell silent then. Yuki felt sick, recalling once again how her uncle had steadily withered from a jovial, robust man into a scrawny, inert lump on a bed.

"The ward is upstairs. I can show you where it is." Kiyo pointed at the front stairs. "This way."

"But how do you know that?" Yuki asked.

"I come here all the time to study. I want to be a doctor."

She blinked. "Really? That's so noble." All the boys in her village mostly just wanted to be fishermen, like their fathers. "But aren't you afraid of catching, well ... something bad?"

He shook his head. "Doctors are always around sick people. That's just how it is."

"So above all else, they must be brave." Yuki stared at him in awe. Before he'd seemed like a nice boy, a good friend. She hadn't realized he had such great ambitions, assuming until now that when grown he'd probably work at Chisso, as his father did.

As they climbed the stairs, Kiyo kept up a running commentary. "Hosokawa Sensei set up the quarantine a while ago, before the researchers had figured out the Disease might be caused by heavy metals. So it may not actually be contagious. But nothing's certain yet, and you can never be too careful about possible contagion. Especially in a hospital. That's why Hosokawa Sensei kept this ward separate."

When they reached the second-floor landing, Yuki thought she heard someone screaming.

Kiyo didn't react. He walked over, opened a nearby door, and peeked in. "Higano-san must be in one of the other rooms."

At the next open doorway Yuki froze and inhaled sharply. Three emaciated men were inside, their skin hanging loosely as washing on a clothesline. One was Higano. A second man's eyes were closed as he moaned and rocked on his narrow cot. The third only stared at them and whimpered like a wounded animal.

She could tell they were all fishermen from their dark, wind-burned skin, which even now still carried a faint scent of fish. But that was where the normal resemblance ended. Now their hair was unkempt, tangled and matted. Strands of long, wispy whiskers grew from their unshaven chins. The room stank horribly of soiled diapers.

Uncle Higano had a tube stuck up his nose. As she was about to cross the room to get to him, he toppled out of bed, bucking and writhing on the tile floor, arms and legs flailing as if possessed by a demon. His cotton sleeping kimono hiked up to reveal legs like thin, weathered twigs. His back arched so acutely Yuki feared it would break as she watched. He spread his fingers and toes wide, then curled them in sharply.

"Uncle!" She rushed over and crouched on the floor beside him, gripping his arms in an attempt to hold him still. But the convulsions were too violent. One arm swung out abruptly and hit her face. She fell back, head slamming against the opposite wall so hard she saw sparkling lights.

Kiyo dashed over and pulled her upright. "Yuki-chan, are you hurt?"

Her parents rushed over too as Yuki rubbed the back of her head. "No. Not really. Nothing compared to how he's suffering."

"Maybe you should go sit down over in – " Kiyo began.

"No! I'll be fine."

"He didn't mean to hit you," her father murmured sadly.

"I know," Yuki said. "Just an accident."

"Kiyo-kun, help me get Higano-kun back on the bed," Nobuyuki said.

Kiyo gripped Uncle's legs while her father grabbed him under the arms. They were just lifting him off the floor when Uncle Higano jerked again. Nobuyuki almost dropped him, and Yuki and her mother both uttered frightened cries. But the two men finally managed to slide Higano back onto his bed. Kazuko came over and covered him with a light cotton blanket. Yuki stood off to one side, panting, as if she'd been the one who'd moved him.

"Higano-kun?" she said tentatively.

His head lolled. His eyes blasted open wide, and from his stiff, constricted mouth rose a terrible howl.

"Higano-kun, we're here," soothed Yuki's mother. "Please, remain calm, if you can."

"But he's in pain," Yuki cried. "He's trying to tell us he's hurting."

Nobuyuki stood by the bed, holding down his writhing brother, tears streaming down his face. "I'm so sorry. So sorry."

"What're you all doing here?" A nurse in white uniform and starched cap stepped into the room, her thick rubber shoes barely making a sound. "This is an isolation area. Doctors and nurses only."

"It was good thing we came." Nobuyuki pointed to Higano. "My brother fell out of bed, onto the floor. No one else was around or came in to help. Why aren't you taking better care of him? And what's that tube jammed up his nose?"

Her face softened. "I'm sorry. We're so busy on the ward, and – well, the tube is there because he can't chew or swallow. So we feed him liquid nourishment through the tube, and give him vitamins and medications. We've also been injecting him with phenobarbital, an anti-seizure medication for epilepsy. We're trying antibiotics, too, and adrenocortical hormones. We try to stay with these patients all night. But during the day, we have other patients to care for as well."

Dad dragged a hand down his face. "Other patients aren't in pain like them! Are any of these men ever washed? Or shaved?"

"We try to bathe them as often as we can. But shaving is impossible. They move so suddenly, it's too risky to hold a razor, or any sharp blade, to their faces."

Kazuko wiped her tear-streaked face on one sleeve. "Isn't there anything we can do?"

"Pray, I suppose," the nurse said, shaking her head sadly.

As Yuki stood there, watching and listening, her fingers felt as if feathers were brushing against them. It was by now a familiar sensation; one that would persist until she drew something. She beckoned to Kiyo to follow her, and stepped out into the hallway. "Can you possibly get me a piece of paper and a pencil?"

He looked puzzled, but ripped a page from his note-book, then handed it to her along with a sharpened pencil from his shirt pocket.

"Thanks." She knelt in front of a wooden chair, slapping the paper onto the seat. Then quickly drew a picture of Uncle Higano relaxing on a bed. His eyes were closed, his mouth held a hint of a smile. Both hands rested on his stomach. That was what she wished he looked like right now, instead of convulsing and screaming in agony.

Kiyo said in a tight voice, "Eh! How'd you do that? He looks so ... alive. So real. Incredible."

"Uncle's the one who's incredible. I could never bear so much pain."

The feathers were gone now. She could stop drawing.

As she laid down the pencil her parents came out of Uncle Higano's room. Both of them peered down at the sketch.

"Oh, Yuki-chan, that's how I want him to be, too." Her mother's face crumpled again.

Her father gulped down his sorrow. "Let's tack that up on the wall at home. To give us hope that he'll somehow get better."

Yuki nodded. If only some image she could draw would help drive out the nightmarish sight of her uncle's suffering. If only such a picture could help ease his pain, even a little. She would draw and draw, until her arms ached and burned. Until her hands turned into cramped claws.

On the bus ride home, she kept seeing Higano's suffering. The writhing and convulsing, the impossibly-bowed back, the stiff, thrashing limbs. A block of ice seemed to

form around her heart. Even when her aunt had been dying of tuberculosis, there hadn't been such terrible agony.

The bus hissed to a stop at Tsukinoura Village. A tiny
café, a small grocery store and a general store with a post-
office counter were the only businesses there.

As the three of them walked home, Yuki looked for Jiro. The cat roamed a wide territory but usually came running when she called his name. But, no sign of him. She
kept detouring from the lane, bending to check underneath
house foundations or peering up into trees. Her parents
went inside when they reached home, but Yuki kept walking around the village until she reached a cliff. The place
where the world dropped off, all the way down to the Bay.

It was there she found Jiro. Like Uncle, her cat seemed
to be in terrible agony, hopping on his hind legs in a dance
of pain like some other cats she'd seen around the Bay. The
poor thing twisted backward until his spine was like a
crooked, upside-down U. Then he flipped over to all but
stand on his head, screeching loudly, and finally jumped
high in the air, smashing down again on the grass.

"Jiro! Jiro!" she cried, trying to catch him.

Ignoring her, he crouched low and scraped his nose
across the dirt until the skin ripped and blood oozed.

"Oh please, stop!" Yuki picked him up, trying to comfort him, but the cat fought her, dragging his claws across
her hand, leaving four deep, bloody slashes.

"Ow!" she cried, stunned. Jiro had always been sweet-
natured; he'd never wounded her before.

He leapt from her arms and stumbled toward the end
of the path and the cliff's edge.

"Wait! Come back," she cried, chasing him down the
rutted dirt path. Before she could reach him, the suffering
cat hurled himself off the precipice. "Jiro, no!" she
screamed.

Yuki held onto the gnarled branch of an old camellia
tree growing at the cliff's edge, leaning out as far as she

dared, staring down at dark blue waves slapping the rocky wall below.

"Jiro!" Her scream echoed across the Bay. "Jiro!" she screamed again, though surely he must've died from the long fall onto those sharp rocks. "Jiro, don't leave me ..."

She fell to her knees on the path, sobbing.

It'd been snowing, six years ago almost to the day, when she'd found him. Just a little gray lump on the side of the road. At first she'd thought it was a piece of rock until the gray lump moved slightly. She'd crouched to take a closer look.

"Why ... you're a kitten," she'd whispered, and picked him up. He fit in the palm of her hand. One golden eye had flicked open for a second, then closed. "You must be freezing," she'd whispered, and tucked him inside her jacket, next to her warm belly.

"*Ganbatte.*" Hang on, she'd told him, and then she'd run down the lane, all the way home.

She'd burst through the front door, yelling, "I found a kitten!" Unbuttoning her jacket to show her parents. The gray ball of puff opened its eyes again, but still didn't move. "He was lying on the side of the road."

"In the snow?" Mom tsked. "He'll be freezing. Put him on your lap in the kotatsu."

She'd held her baby cat until it was time for bed, then tucked him in next to her under the futon. No one thought he would survive the night, but he did. And once recovered, he'd followed her everywhere, sleeping in her lap whenever she sat down, curling up next to her head at night.

Now he was gone, after suffering the same devastating agony as Uncle Higano. Dying horribly right before her eyes.

A cool breeze tickled her fingers.

Wiping tears away, she found a twig and, there in the dirt, etched her beloved Jiro purring and rubbing against her legs.

"That's how I'll always remember you," she said. "A happy, loving cat who was once left for dead, but got a second chance at life."

But this time, even after the familiar prickling feeling that was the urge to draw had left her, she felt no better. It was too much in one day. To first have her heart ripped apart by Uncle Higano's hopeless misery. And then, shredded into jagged pieces by the death of her precious Jiro.

SEVEN

Uncle Is Set Free

Four months after Jiro's death, Yuki arrived home from school one day to see her mother looking pale and panicked.

"There you are," Kazuko said, grabbing Yuki's arm. "Come on. Kashiwa-san just left. We must go to the hospital, right now."

Kashiwa, the owner of the local general store, had the only phone in the village. A kind man, he often acted as the emergency contact for residents.

"Oh." Yuki pressed her quivering lips together. "Is . . . I mean, is Uncle – "

Her father closed his eyes as if the light hurt them. His lips were pressed tight, as if to hold in something he'd find unbearable to say out loud.

Her mother shook her head. "No time to explain. We must go now." She hurried them both out of the house.

Once on the bus, Yuki wanted to ask what Kashiwa had said. After looking at their faces, though, she pressed her own lips tight to keep from bawling. Each time they'd visited her uncle over the last four months, he'd been thinner. He'd also screamed more, flinging his arms around.

She shivered and glanced out the window of the bus. Houses and trees, the latter now emitting the sweet scents of blooming cherry blossoms ... somehow the bus seemed to move past it all more slowly than usual. The driver waited at the stops too long. Too many tourists boarded and then departed.

At their destination, they rushed off the bus and ran inside the hospital, then up the stairs to the isolated Strange Disease ward. There, in a dark room reeking of stale sweat and feces, Hosokawa Sensei was stooped over Uncle Higano. Kiyo stood next to him, observing.

"Oh, Higano-kun," Dad moaned when he saw his brother.

Yuki darted to the foot of the bed. Instead of jerking, twisting, and screaming, Uncle now lay still. His back painfully arched, face contorted in a silent shriek. Eyes wide open, unblinking. A small tube ran up one nostril. His hands were clenched tightly. His skin appeared as thin as a translucent cloth glued over a skeletal frame.

Hosokawa Sensei straightened, tucking the end of his stethoscope into his lab-coat pocket. With two fingers he gently closed Uncle's eyes, then pulled the blanket up to the dead man's neck and covered his face with a clean white cloth.

"Higano!" Dad's knees buckled. Mom stood beside him, quietly weeping.

"Uncle, no." Yuki sobbed. Her mother reached out and enfolded her in her arms.

"I'm very sorry. We just don't understand the Strange Disease well enough, yet." The doctor sighed, looking sad and frustrated. "Well, then..." He quietly left the room.

Kiyo hung his head. "I'll miss him."

Higano had been there when Yuki was born. He'd picked her up when she fell. His shoulders were wide and sturdy when she'd ridden on them. Unlike her father's thick-skinned hands, Uncle's had felt soft and uncallused, holding hers they'd walked.

First Aunt Haruko, then Jiro, now Uncle Higano. How could the family go on?

Kiyo escorted them out to the hall. "A nurse told me Higano-san fell into a coma after the doctor went home last night," he whispered.

Mom uttered a small cry. "Did she call the doctor back?"

"No." Kiyo looked down at his hands. "Only because ... people with the Strange Disease ... well, near the end they all go into a coma and then die. So quickly ... it's almost a good thing, by then."

"He suffered for a whole year. At least he's no longer in pain." Dad sighed and wiped his eyes.

"Why are you here today?" Yuki asked Kiyo.

Kiyo fished a notebook from his jacket pocket. "For this. I accompany Hosokawa Sensei on rounds, taking notes for him. Then he can study the progression of the symptoms."

"You already sound like a doctor." Yuki closed her eyes hard, to squeeze back the tears stinging them. "What did you write about my uncle?"

Kiyo cleared his throat. "Higano-san's deterioration was similar to the other Strange Disease patients. Hosokawa Sensei is working hard, but doesn't know enough about the Disease yet to know how to save them. He and the nurses work all day. Sometimes all night. He never takes time off. Sometimes falls asleep at his desk. I help as much I can but wish there was a way I could become a doctor faster."

Yuki roused from grief for a moment to wonder: How could someone only fourteen years old already be so far along the path to becoming a doctor? "I'm sure Hosokawa Sensei appreciates your help."

Her parents went to the front office to make arrangements for Uncle's cremation. Then the family headed to the Buddhist temple to talk to the priest about Higano's funeral.

Yuki didn't own any funeral clothes. Neither did her parents. So they bathed at the public bathhouse, put on a clean set of their least-shabby clothes, and carefully combed their hair. As they stepped outside to head to the temple for Uncle's funeral, Kiyo rode up on his bicycle.

He got off and bowed deeply. "My condolences to the family." He held out a white envelope.

"*Koden?*" Condolence money, her father asked. He reached for the envelope, then hesitated. "But you're not indebted to Higano-kun." Nobuyuki lowered his hands. "We don't need charity."

Kiyo shook his head. "It's not that. He was always so nice to me. I just want to honor him."

"Is this from your parents?" Kazuko asked.

He blushed. "No. Only my allowance, so it's not much. Please, for Higano-san. I wish I could've helped him, somehow." He thrust the envelope into Dad's hands and reached for his bicycle again.

"Wait." Yuki touched his arm. "Aren't you coming too? You have on a suit."

"Oh. I'm only here to pay my respects. But I'll come along, if that's all right."

"Yes. It is." Nobuyuki tucked the envelope into his jacket pocket. "You're a good kid, Kiyo-kun."

Unlike the fancy temple in Minamata that city people and wealthy families attended, the fishermen's village had one small wooden building built close to the Bay. As they arrived waves lapped the beach, seagulls wheeled and screeched, and the salt scent of seawater wafted around them. A Buddha statue on the far end of the main room faced the entrance, carved of unpainted pine. Sunlight couldn't reach far inside, so the temple felt cold.

Yuki, her parents, and Kiyo were the only ones there. They took off their shoes and padded over the cold, slick wood floor to the altar.

A photo of a smiling Uncle and Aunt Haruko on their wedding day had been set on a small table near the statue, next to a bronze bell and two bowls of incense. Seeing this made it indeed feel like the final farewell. Yuki wanted to curl up and cry, but she owed it to Uncle Higano to act mature and dignified.

"Why did we use their wedding picture?" she asked.

"It's the only one we have of him," Mom replied. "And we didn't want to cut Haruko-san out."

How slim and pretty her aunt looked, even in a plain cotton kimono. She posed formally next to her husband, who wore a dark kimono, and according to proper wedding protocol had kept her expression neutral. Still, her eyes flashed with happiness.

"They were certainly in love," said Yuki. "He would've liked us to remember them together."

Everyone bowed as a man in a simple dark robe stepped in. "Hello." Like all priests, his black hair was cropped short. He was very tall and broad-shouldered, with thick, callused hands. No doubt priests at the poorer temples had to do all the upkeep, too.

But he spoke with the gentleness of an obviously spiritual man. "Would you like me to wait for others?"

"No," Nobuyuki answered. "There will be no one else."

The priest nodded and went to stand behind the table. Everyone else sat on the hardwood floor, facing him. The cold quickly seeped into Yuki's legs; she wanted to hug them to her to keep warm. But her parents and Kiyo were sitting with back erect, hands folded on their laps. She straightened her shoulders, and did the same.

The priest pressed his hands together, chanting a Buddhist sutra. When he rang the bell its low notes reverberated in the large empty room. He lit incense, and then invited the family to pray.

Nobuyuki stood and moved slowly over to the table. He pressed his hands together and bowed to his brother's photograph. After a few moments, he raised his head, pinched fresh incense grains from one bowl, lifted and held them up to his forehead, then sprinkled them on the incense already smoldering in the other urn. He backed up and settled onto the floor again.

Kazuko did the same, though she prayed only half as long. She'd instructed Yuki on how to transfer the incense between vessels before praying. So after her mother sat again, she padded up to the picture and bowed. Then she talked to Higano, silently.

"Thanks for being my uncle. We always had fun together. I hope you find nirvana soon, and I'm sorry you were in so much pain."

Reaching under the sash belted around her waist, she slipped out a small piece of paper: a pencil drawing of Uncle as he used to look, healthy and cheerful. She laid it carefully on the smoldering incense. "Now you can be happy again."

A thread of smoke rose from the urn; her picture, she hoped, had helped set him free.

Kiyo prayed for a long time, in a low voice, but Yuki heard him say, "Sorry we couldn't alleviate your pain. When I become a doctor, I'll do all I can to stop suffering."

Tears trickled down Yuki's face, so she bowed her head. She never wanted to feel such a deep sorrow as this one, ever again.

EIGHT

Stick To Your Own Kind

On Kiyo's fifteenth birthday, his mother gave him exactly what he'd asked for: an envelope full of money. That afternoon, an unusually-warm first of May, he pedaled toward an art supply store downtown. The sky was bright blue save for a plume of smoke chugging out of the tall gray smokestacks of Chisso, darkening the sky above.

At the art store he looked over the colored pencils and chose a pack with ten different colors. Liking the woody aroma of charcoal pencils, he also bought a small box of those. Then picked out a sketchpad with a fresh pulpy scent, the sheets a little larger than a textbook. He paid and carried these first-ever birthday gifts for Yuki out to his bike's basket, and headed to Tsukinoura.

It'd been four weeks since her uncle died, and she still looked downhearted. He'd been busy learning the parts of the brain with Hosokawa Sensei and hadn't seen her for over a week, longer than was usual between visits. Typically he stopped by every few days.

A grin tugged at his lips. *Well, I'll be with her soon.*

He spotted her slim silhouette alone on the beach. She was turning over driftwood, the birthday brooch catching a gleam of sunshine now and then from her wrinkled blouse. The scents of seaweed and brine wafted from the Bay. Village children screamed and shouted in delight as they hopped between empty, abandoned boats. Most of the small fishing vessels now only bobbed empty at anchor or lay pulled on the beach.

Only a few years ago, fisher families would have loaded up their boats before dawn with their youngest children, tin bottles of water, and portable braziers. Then set
their single sails to pull them out into the calm Bay, cruising on a good breeze. Once in deeper waters, they'd throw
nets out for fish and retrieve pots tossed into the Bay the
night before. These they'd tow up full of octopuses, crabs,
squid, and lobsters. At lunchtime, mothers would grill the
best of the catch on the brazier, and the family would savor
fresh seafood just pulled from the pristine waters.

But now . . . .

Just then Yuki looked up and smiled, though she
looked drawn. "Hello! I've been searching the beach to see
if there's something as pretty as my pin washed up here."

"It'd be tough to find anything else that made you look
so much like a princess." His heart lifted when the compliment made her smile. "I've never seen so much kelp on
the beach," he added.

The fine sand was strewn with long streamers of green
seaweed, and the ocean scent was stronger near them.

"More and more washes up every day."

"I brought a gift for your birthday." Kiyo held out the
pencils and sketchbook.

"Oh, Kiyo-kun," she gasped, and flipped open the box.
"So many colors! Real sketch paper. And charcoal drawing
pencils. Thank you." She suddenly looked distressed. "But
I have nothing for you."

He waved a hand dismissively. "Repay me by becoming
the greatest artist ever born."

"What chance does a fisherman's daughter have to be
any kind of artist? I can't learn it all on my own."

"Then someone must teach you."

She scoffed. "Oh, yes. And that costs money."

"You're really good, Yuki-chan. Don't give up. Keep
drawing no matter what."

She sighed. "I'd never give up art, but . . . not every-one's as lucky as you. Your parents have money. They can afford a tutor, and to send you to medical school." She turned away. "Why do you even bother with me?"

He gaped. "Why? But – you're the most fascinating person I know. You don't do all that fussy girly stuff. You love the ocean, notice everything around you . . . ."

She scoffed. "I can't *afford* all that girly stuff."

"Well, maybe so . . . ." He hadn't meant to make her feel poorer than she already did. "I know your life's not the same as mine, but I'll always be your friend. You'll become an incredible artist! And sure, my parents have money, but not everyone gets into medical school. That's why I study so hard, to make sure of it."

"Sorry. I didn't mean everything's just handed to you." She touched his sleeve, then waved an arm as if tossing away the whole awkward conversation. "Thanks for the gift. I can't wait to start drawing in color!"

Kiyo paused, gazing at Yuki under the cloudless blue sky, his breath coming faster. A faint scent of soap rose from her skin. The slender fingers resting lightly on his forearm seemed to sizzle, heating his skin through the shirt. He was about to raise a hand to trace those full lips with one finger, when a girl of twelve or thirteen with a long braid down her back, stopped leaping between the boats and shouted, "Don't come any closer! My dad says you'll make me sick and I'll die like your uncle."

Yuki's hand slipped from Kiyo's arm. "I lived with Un-cle Higaro, and I'm not sick. So how can I be contagious?"

"Keep that nasty disease to yourself." The girl leapt off the boat and splashed away through the shallows.

Kiyo sneered at her retreating back. "Ignorant fool. Who cares what she thinks?"

Yuki didn't answer.

"By the way, why aren't you guys fishing today?"

"The catches aren't good anymore. My parents don't go out very often now."

But if the family didn't fish, how would they support themselves? "Those kids are catching fish with their bare hands, right next to the beach." He pointed to a boy who was showing off his catch to friends. "Let's get some, too."

Yuki nodded. "All right." She tucked her gifts back in Kiyo's basket and waded out into the shallows. "We only want fresh fish, so don't take any floating upside down."

Kiyo waded in too, but then stopped, staring at the water. Many dead fish floated at the surface. Those still alive swam slowly, as if half asleep. He could grab them easily. They were slick, though, so he clutched one in each hand, and went up to lay them on the beach. Yuki did the same. When they had twenty, Kiyo slipped the box of pencils into the waistband of his shorts, while Yuki did the same with the sketchbook. Then they piled the fish in the bike basket.

"Mom will make the best lunch!" she exulted.

The sun was at its peak. By the time they reached her home, a few houses above the shoreline, they were sweaty and tired, dried, itchy sea-salt frosting their skin.

"Look!" Yuki cried from the front step. "We caught a lot of live fish."

Her mother rushed out, looking delighted. "Wonderful! I'll cook them for lunch."

"And look what Kiyo-kun gave me for my birthday." Yuki waved the sketchbook. Kiyo handed her the pencils, and she opened the box to show off.

"Aren't you a lucky girl?" Kazuko said. "Thank you, Kiyo-kun."

"She promised to draw me a picture."

"I'm sure she will. That's all she does in her spare time."

At the neighborhood spigot, Kiyo and Yuki filled a bucket with water and poured it over themselves.

"Ahhh. Feels so good." Kiyo scrubbed his scalp with his fingers then sluiced his arms and legs with another bucketful.

Yuki washed her face and poured cool fresh water over her hair, twisting the long black rope of it to ring water out. "I feel so much cooler."

"You're cute wet or dry," Kiyo said, noticing how smooth and brown her legs had become from the sun.

A neighbor girl of about six hopped over their way, skipping rope, sending up puffs of dust every time the jump-rope slapped the ground.

"Akiko-chan!" A young woman, hair wound up in a thin towel, hands and knees smeared with dirt as if she'd been working in the garden, dashed out. She yanked at the girl's arm, spinning her around. "I told you not to get near her."

"But – " The girl's lower lip quivered.

Her mother pulled her away, behind their small house.

"What idiots," muttered Kiyo.

"Yuki-chan, Kiyo-kun!" It was Kazuko, calling them to lunch. They hurried back to the house.

She'd grilled some of the fish, while others had been filleted and sliced raw. One whole uncooked fish still lay on a cutting board. Kiyo grabbed a long knife and slit open its belly. Pointing to the various organs, he said, "Here's the heart. That's the stomach. The intestine, liver, bladder, and kidney."

Kazuko stared down, looking thoughtful. "You know, I've been gutting fish for years and never thought about any of that."

"Come on, let's eat," Yuki's father said. "I'm starving."

Sitting on the floor with the family around the low, square table, Kiyo dunked slices of fish in soy sauce and ate it with scoops of rice. The salty sauce made the rich mullet taste even more delicious. "Akaji-san," he asked Nobuyuki, "since today is my and Yuki's birthday, may we have some shochu?" He'd noticed the bottle sitting on the short kitchen counter.

"Sure. When you're ten years older." Nobuyuki burst into laughter. "To tell you the truth, it hasn't been much fun drinking without my brother."

The mention of Yuki's uncle lowered a net of sadness over the room. For a few minutes, everyone ate silently, without looking up.

"All right," her father said at last. "Just a little bit."

"Me too, this time," Yuki reminded him.

Nobuyuki got up and poured four small cups of shochu. He returned to the table and handed them around. Still standing, he said, "To celebrate life," and then tossed back his portion.

After the mountain of fish he'd eaten Kiyo cycled slowly through the village, listening to the loud, sawing song of hidden cicadas. At home, he parked his bicycle at the side of the house and stepped into a kitchen still hot from the cook stove.

"Hi, Yanagiya-san." Still ecstatic from his day spent with Yuki, he grinned at the family's cook. "I won't need any dinner tonight."

Perspiration trickled from her bound hair and streaked her broad face; she wiped it off with the hem of a long white apron. She was only about forty, but deep lines etched her face. "But I'm making your favorite. Pork cutlet," she protested.

He detected the smell of fryer grease heating up.

"Oh. I appreciate the thought, but I already ate."

"Well, all right." She sighed, still looking disappointed. "Your father's in his office."

"He's home?" Kiyo glanced at the wall clock. "It's only seven-thirty."

"Fukuzawa-san brought him home a few minutes ago." So the chauffeur had also gone home early. Kiyo headed for the office.

Kichiro was seated at his desk lighting a pipe. Many papers were spread out on the desktop before him. The warm cherry and molasses smell of his favorite tobacco filled the room. "Where've you been?" he asked, when he looked up and saw Kiyo.

"At Yuki-chan's."

His father raised an eyebrow. "That fisher's girl?"

He nodded.

His father clamped the pipestem in his mouth, shucked suit-jacket and tie, then undid the top button of his shirt. "You should spend more time with classmates."

"I do. I see Mori Masa-kun."

"Kusumoto-san's son lives just down the street."

"I don't like him."

His father looked surprised. "Why not?"

"Thinks he's the smartest guy in the world. And he makes fun of other kids."

"He'll be a lawyer, like his father. An honorable profession."

"Well, I'm going to be a doctor. That's an honorable profession, too."

"Indeed it is." His father nodded. "But – "

"And Yuki-chan's going to be a famous artist. She's really good!"

"I see."

Kiyo knew he didn't, though. He saw only a poor fisherman's family. Not good enough for *his* son.

"Sir, dinner's ready." Yanagiya called softly from the doorway.

Dad only grunted a reply to the cook. Then, to Kiyo, "Call your mother for dinner."

"I will, but I already ate at Yuki-chan's."

His father leapt up from the chair, nearly toppling it. "What? What did you eat?"

What did that matter? Kiyo wondered. "Um, fresh fish and rice. Yuki-chan and I caught them in the Bay with our bare hands."

The tips of Kichiro's ears turned red. "You *caught* them?"

"They swim so slowly, it's easy. You can snatch them right out of the Bay."

"I don't want you catching any more fish! Or eating fish at all. Especially at that family's home. They're poor. They eat the worst food because they can't afford anything else. They sell the best of the catch and eat the rotten ones."

"That's not true." Kiyo said quickly, before his father could cut him off. "I know, because I've eaten there a lot."

Kichiro bit down on the pipe-stem so hard his teeth squeaked against the briarwood. "You've eaten there before? – Yanagiya-san! Yanagiya-san!"

The cook rushed back looking alarmed. "Yessir, is there a problem?"

"You're never to serve fish, shellfish, kelp . . . or anything else from the Bay."

"Sir?" She looked astonished. "But . . . why?"

"Just do as I say!"

"*Hai.*" Yes sir, she said and nodded. "But meat, well, it's very expensive."

"That's my concern, not yours."

"Hai." She bowed and retreated to the kitchen.

"Kiyo, no seafood. Here, or anywhere else. Do you understand?"

It made no sense. "I don't see why – "

"Don't talk back! Do as I say. And quit mooning around after that girl. Fishers are low-class and crass."

Kiyo spun away and stomped outside, into the garden. "Class, class, who cares about class," he muttered. "You can stay at the factory and never come home for all I care!" he shouted back at the house. Then got back on his bike, to ride as far away from his father as possible.

A businessman in a factory could never understand the freer life fishers lived – no need to dress formally, chasing endlessly after a career, or worry about stupid social standing. Yuki's family was poor, yes. Yet in some ways, Kiyo envied them. Fishers took pleasure in being out on the sea, leading a simple life, and revering the natural world.

"Stupid, stupid," he muttered, thinking about the things his father had said.

Human beings had never been meant to live shut up inside all the time, encased in layers of cloth, breathing stale air. What about nature, and the sea? Fishers might be poor, but he still envied them that freedom.

NINE

The Lab Assistant

At the hospital the following week, Kiyo found Ho-sokawa Sensei in the isolation ward, giving shots to a new patient. Kiyo hovered by the open doorway, waiting.

Once the patient had lain back down, the doctor pulled up his blanket and patted his shoulder. Then he stepped out into the hallway and looked at Kiyo. "What's going on? You seem distressed."

"I watched my friend's uncle die six months ago, yet we've still found nothing useful to help us figure out the cause of his disease."

His mentor nodded sympathetically. "Though you've been of great assistance taking notes for me while I make rounds."

"That's not enough! May I go to Kumamoto and help the researchers at the university?"

Dr. Hosokawa looked doubtful. "I'm not sure there's anything there a fifteen-year-old can do."

"I can't just sit around and wait. Please, there must be something."

"Would your parents approve of you going there?"

Kiyo clenched his fists at his sides. "I'll make sure they will."

"Hmm." Sensei massaged the back of his neck. "Very well, let me make a call."

In his office the doctor picked up the handset of the heavy black telephone and dialed. After a brief wait, he said, "Hello, Inagawa Sensei? Hosokawa Hajime ... Yes, fine, thanks. You must be very busy studying the Strange Disease." The doctor sighed and shook his head. "I know what you mean. Too much to do, never enough assistance. I may be able to help with that, though. A young man I've been mentoring here is very capable, and wants to help with your research. If he came down for the weekend, say, is there something he can do for you? . . . Yes, absolutely. Yes, yes . . . No . . . Thank you."

Dr. Hosokawa smiled up at Kiyo briefly, then added, "Agreed. Kuge Kiyoshi will see you Saturday, then." He hung up and peered over his glasses at Kiyo. "Seems they're eager for any help they can get. You can stay with Inagawa Sensei. But you won't be paid."

"Fine. I don't need the money. I just want to help."

"No one knows that better than I do. We're two of a kind. Still it's rare nowadays to find a young person willing to work so hard." He patted Kiyo's shoulder. "You'll be preparing slides. Let's go down to the lab, and I'll teach you the process." Another faint smile. "Since I told them you already knew how to do it."

"Thank you, thank you." Kiyo grinned.

The doctor chuckled. "It's only basic slide prep. Anybody your age can do it, as long as they're careful."

In the basement lab, Kiyo scrutinized long tables full of test tubes and slides, and the many glass petri dishes stacked inside cabinets. The room had two sinks and, like the rest of the hospital, smelled strongly of antiseptic and disinfectants.

A sparkling black microscope caught his eye. "May I look through that?"

"Sure, but there's no slide in there right now."

Kiyo stroked the smooth, cool metal, then leaned forward and pressed his face to the eyepiece, peering down. Only blackness there now, but excitement rushed through him. He wished he were already in Kumamoto.

Reaching up into one cabinet, Hosokawa Sensei pulled out and gently lowered a box of thin glass slides. Then another box of even thinner, shorter pieces. Kiyo had used these before, but only in science class.

"They're going to want you to prepare slides of seawater. First, wash the droppers."

The doctor picked up a long glass eyedropper and cleaned it thoroughly in one sink, then filled a small jar with tap water. "Pretend this came from the sea. Shake the jar so you get the sediments that drift to bottom. Then take out a slide and place a drop on it. Like this."

He demonstrated. "Be careful not to get air bubbles in the dropper because we don't want them on the slide. Put the slipcover carefully on top. Touch slide and slipcover only by their edges, or you'll leave fingerprints. Then label it. Let's say it's . . . ." He leaned over the table to write.

Kiyo leaned closer too, and read *Minamata Bay 100M south from discharge pipe.*

"Now you try it," said Dr. Hosokawa, stepping back from the table.

Kiyo stopped at Masa's house on his way home.

"Hey." His friend was already out of his school uniform, as usual wearing old khaki pants and his favorite faded blue shirt – though his family could afford to buy him new clothes every day. He waved to Kiyo. "Come on in!"

As soon as he stepped into the entry and closed the door behind him, he heard music. "Is that 'Hound Dog?'" Kiyo tapped his shoe to the fast, infectious beat. He'd heard Elvis Presley a few times on the radio, but rock and roll music had been banned from TV. Conservative adults considered the swivel-hipped musician's songs and performance style too sexual and vulgar.

"My sister keeps the record hidden," Masa confided. "Only plays it when our parents are out."

"I love Elvis."

"Me too. All the songs are great."

Kiyo lowered his voice. "Hey, I have a favor to ask."

Masa grinned. "Oh yeah? What?"

Kiyo noticed his friend's upper lip was showing a faint shadow. Was he already shaving? "I need to go to Kumamoto University for the weekend. They're trying to help figure out the cause of the Strange Disease there."

"Hey, you're really taking this thing seriously."

"And I need you to cover for me."

"Cover for you?" Masa's eyes widened. "Sure. Like a secret mission. What d'you need me to do?"

"I'm going to tell my parents we're going hiking in Kumamoto. To climb Mount Aso and stuff. And that we'll be staying with your parents' friends."

"What if your mom and dad see me while you're gone?"

Kiyo frowned. "How often do you run into them?"

"Eh. Almost never."

"All right then. We'll take that chance. I'm leaving first thing in the morning."

"But ... will the university scientists be there on a Saturday?"

"Oh yes." Kiyo nodded. "Hosokawa Sensei works every weekend. So does my dad. The researchers do, too."

Masa nodded, raising his eyebrows. "It is kind of like being a spy. Oh," he added, as if he'd just remembered something. "I've got a book for you." Turning away, he disappeared deeper into the house while the rock music blared on. He returned in a few minutes carrying a hardcover volume. "Here."

Kiyo studied the title. "*The Accountant Detective?*" He looked up questioningly.

"Remember how we used to read all those detective novels?"

"Sure. I loved them."

"Well, I still do." Masa tapped his long index finger on the book. "This one's really great. So, read something a little different from that big fat medical book you carry around all the time."

"Anatomy is fascinating, too," Kiyo protested.

"Yeah. I'm sure." Masa twisted his round face in a cockeyed grin.

"Well . . . thanks." Kiyo opened the front door. "And maybe stay home for a couple days so you don't run into my parents."

He could still hear Masa's amused laughter as he peddled away.

The next morning, with a blue baseball cap pulled low over his forehead, Kiyo passed his fare money under the black bars of the station clerk's window. The first movement of Beethoven's "Pathétique Sonata" was playing from a radio on a shelf behind the man. Train schedules were chalked on a large slate next to the window, along with fare prices and railroad maps. As he stepped away with his ticket, a pendulum wall clock chimed. Five minutes until the train arrived. He stood waiting in the shadows cast by a pillar on the platform, hoping not to see anyone he knew, in case they reported back to his parents.

It was early winter still, but snow had blanketed the higher mountains on the main island of Honshu. He shivered and buttoned up his jacket. Soon he was surrounded by other travelers.

A dozen skiers in thick wool sweaters and bright knitted hats carried long wooden skis with cable bindings over their shoulders, along with rucksacks. They all looked ea-ger for adventure. Young mothers rocked infants or cooed at babies tied in slings on their backs, the long cloths criss-crossed over their chests. Men in business suits juggled briefcases and suitcases. Groups of grade-school boys in navy-blue wool jackets, matching brimmed hats and short pants – the required uniform in the country – lined up to board trains either south to Kumamoto City or north to Honshu. Each student carried a small furoshiki – a square piece of wrapping cloth used to transport goods – with cor-ners tied diagonally across. Probably their lunches.

Finally Kiyo's train pulled in, puffing smoke and dis-gorging riders. He waited until everyone else was aboard, then scurried on, glancing around the train car. Not spot-ting anyone familiar, he hoisted his backpack onto the baggage shelf and took a seat. As more passengers filed in he kept his face turned away toward the window, as if en-thralled by its view of the station. At last he relaxed a bit and bent to loosen the laces of his heavy hiking boots, since it would be a three-hour journey. Then he flipped open his anatomy book to study muscles.

But only a few pages in, he couldn't concentrate. Then he remembered the novel Masa had loaned him. He dragged his backpack off the luggage rack and dug it out. By the end of chapter one, he was immersed in a world of murder and intrigue. He fished a rice ball out of the lunch bag the cook had packed and ate it as he read, avidly turn-ing pages. Raising his head occasionally to see the coast-line's dense pine and deciduous forest flying past, and slic-es of the Bay as the land rose sharply from the water.

The express train stopped at a couple towns but zoomed past fishing villages without even a small station. A couple got on and sat across the aisle. Untying a furo-shiki, the woman drew out a bottle of sake and two small cups. The more they drank, the bigger grew their smiles.

The train rumbled into Kumamoto Station at noon. Pulling out the crude map Hosokawa Sensei had drawn, Kiyo headed to the bus stop and studied its schedule. He'd have a thirty-minute wait, so he ducked into the restroom and changed into dark slacks and a white shirt. Not as crisp as when Yanagiya pressed them, but still presentable. He pulled his cotton sweater and jacket back on, and returned to the stop to wait.

His bus looked newer than those in Minamata but was far more crowded. Kiyo helped a woman hoist a heavy suitcase onto the overhead luggage rack. She inclined her head and thanked him.

Feeling nervous, he glanced at his directions repeatedly even though the map on the bus clearly showed his stop. A block before it, a large, white two-story building behind a tall, stucco fence came into view. Men on ladders were cleaning its windows. Surely that had to be the hospital. He stilled his legs, which had been bouncing in excitement.

The hospital was easily three times the size of the one back home, but it exuded the same strong antiseptic smell. At the entrance, he changed into visitor's slippers, then at the front desk asked the receptionist. "Where might I find Inagawa Sensei?"

Up a staircase and down a long, sparkling-tiled corridor, he passed hurrying nurses and visitors with worried expressions. He read the engraved plates next to each office door until he found one with the doctor's name on it.

Inside, in an office not much larger than Hosokawa Sensei's back home, a balding man in a lab coat was shuffling through stacks of paper on his desk. A cigarette smoldered in a glass ashtray, making the room appear hazy.

"*Sumimasen.*" Excuse me, Kiyo said.

The man looked up slowly, his face so pale it might've never seen the sun. Intense dark eyes seemed to read Kiyo's mind.

He took a step back and licked dry lips before he spoke. "I'm Kuge Kiyoshi from Minamata. Dr. Hosokawa sent me here to help you."

Inagawa's tense face softened into a smile. "Ah, the assistant Hosokawa Sensei called about. How old are you?"

"Almost sixteen." Fifteen-and-a-half, close enough, Kiyo thought.

"Old enough." The man chuckled. "Sensei said you're trustworthy. A hard worker. I'll go with that. We need to stop the Strange Disease. It's a nasty one. We need all the help we can get." He frowned again, then added, "Come on, I'll show you what we've been doing." Pointing to Kiyo's pack, he said, "You can leave that here."

As Kiyo tucked his bag in a corner, the doctor's nicotine-yellowed fingers crushed out the cigarette in the ashtray. "Maybe by the time I get back, the report I'm looking for will reveal itself. Papers hide from me all the time." He barked out a laugh, and Kiyo smiled.

They ambled down the hall and turned into the patient wing. The university's hospital was even larger than he'd thought. After passing at least twenty rooms on each side, they went through a set of heavy double doors.

Screams shattered the quiet on this side of the doors. Kiyo recognized the shrill, agonized cries and winced.

The doctor glanced at him. "Yes, we transported twenty of the victims from Minamata Hospital here. Like Dr. Hosokawa, we're trying different treatments to see what might work. There are seventeen patients left now. Observing them has been helpful to our progress in understanding the Disease, but..." He sighed and trailed off.

Kiyo thought he understood the rest: *But it's still hard to watch, when you have no answers yet.*

They stepped into the first room. Two men, as skeletal as the Strange Disease patients in Minamata, thrashed on narrow beds, their haunted, sunken eyes begging for release. The familiar stink of feces and sweat hung on the air. The next room was worse. Three boys no older than seven huddled there, contorted in agony.

Kiyo shuddered. So young.

"Three brothers," the doctor said. "All contracted the Disease within a week of each other. Their parents show some symptoms, but aren't ill enough to be hospitalized." The smile he gave the children looked more like a grimace. "The nurses will come soon to feed you, boys."

"They can still eat, then?" Kiyo asked.

Instead of answering the doctor took his arm and led him outside, into the hall. "You've seen the same at your hospital?"

"Yes. Their suffering is terrible there, too."

Inagawa nodded sadly. "But it's important we tend to and study them." He glanced at his watch. "Almost three. No wonder I'm hungry. Had lunch?" Without waiting for an answer, he led Kiyo across the street to a large restaurant.

A stiff breeze had risen on this brisk November day. The delicious scent of noodles and teriyaki sauce drifted out as they opened the door. A few people were sipping tea; most would've finish lunch hours ago. So the thirty or so small tables and the counter stools were empty. Inagawa headed straight for a table pushed against one wall, as if he sat there often.

Keeping his jacket on, Kiyo sat across and read the offerings posted on the wall menu.

"Everything here is good," the doctor said.

The waitress wore a casual blue kimono with a white half-apron. She didn't write their order, merely shuffled back to the counter yelling, "One curry, one shabu shabu," to a chef in the open kitchen. Another cook was sharpening knives. The damp whetstone made sharp slapping sounds.

The doctor lit a cigarette and inhaled deeply. "Why's a boy your age so interested in a disease as heinous as this one?"

"I'm going to be a doctor."

Inagawa picked a shred of loose tobacco from the tip of his tongue. "Then go to medical school when you're older. Why subject yourself to such horror now, so young?"

"I have a friend whose uncle died of the Strange Disease." Kiyo took a deep breath. "It was . . . horrible." The mention of Higano made him miss Yuki. Her adorable face. The way she could sketch anything in the wide world and made it all jump from the paper, almost alive.

"No doubt it was horrible indeed." The doctor nodded.

"Now people just shun her family. Government men came and sprayed their house with DDT."

Remembering the white cat he failed to save from drowning, he added, "I've also seen cats show the same symptoms."

"Really?" Inagawa said, just as their food arrived. Kiyo felt ravenous; he shoveled in spicy curry-covered rice. The sensei picked out thinly-sliced beef, tofu, mushrooms, Chinese cabbage, and bean sprouts from the hotpot of boiling broth, dipped them into savory soy and lemon juice, and tucked them in, along with steaming, fluffy rice.

After two cups of hot green tea, they returned to the hospital. Its large, well-lit laboratory held a great deal of equipment. Three long islands ran the length of the room, stools shoved under them. Wheeled carts stood ranked against one wall. Glass-fronted cabinets held hundreds of small boxes. Rubber tubes connected bottles filled with liquid to beakers. Metal frames held test tubes large and small.

Two researchers gazed into a couple of the dozen microscopes lining a long counters, as a third wrote in a notebook.

Inagawa introduced Kiyo. "This is Ito Sensei, Miura Sensei, and Watanabe Sensei." Everyone lifted their heads and blinked at Kiyo. They all looked tired. "This is Kiyoshi-kun, the student Dr. Hosokawa called about. He's here to help, so put him to work."

"Sure," said Miura, the one who'd been writing. Like the rest, he appeared tired. His wiry gray hair stood up like hairbrush bristles; one long black hair sprouted from a mole on his chin. He smiled, though, as if suddenly feeling hopeful. "Then we might actually get to have dinner with our families."

"Everyone's been working late," Inagawa said.

"You can start here." Ito was the youngest, with coal black hair, wide shoulders, and short, stocky legs. He pointed to dozens of small jars filled with murky water. "I collected those from Minamata Bay. Samples must be put on slides."

Kiyo nodded. "Yes, Sensei."

"Do you know how?" Watanabe asked. The third researcher was slender and diminutive, his enormous head nearly bald save for a few gray lonely hairs on top.

They all looked so different. Yuki would've love drawing their portraits. "Yes," said Kiyo, thankful Hosokawa Sensei had already taught him this.

"Good," Ito said. "After finishing a slide, put it here." He gestured to a box with open slots on one side. "Five slides from each jar. We don't know how many particles are in each so we want to study a large sample. Understand?"

Kiyo nodded. "Yes."

"Each time you use the dropper, wash it out so there's no cross contamination. Thanks." The researcher turned back to the microscope's eyepiece.

Kiyo sat on a stool and got to work. Before he knew it, Inagawa was calling out, "Enough for tonight. We'll continue in the morning."

Startled, Kiyo glanced at the wall clock: six-thirty.

"Tomorrow, I'll show you what I need done," Miura said before bolting out the door.

"May I work a little longer?" Kiyo asked.

"Tonight, my wife is expecting you for dinner," Inagawa said. "So you must come home with me now. She's eager to meet the person who's enabling me to get home before ten, for a change."

After a fifteen-minute bus ride, Kiyo was in the entry to their house, bowing to Mrs. Inagawa. She was short and plump; her left cheek dimpled when she smiled.

"He's the boy I told you about," Inagawa explained.

"How nice to have dinner together for once. Come in, come in!"

Kiyo was surprised when she served grilled mullet with a bowl of fragrant rice.

"Don't worry," the researcher said. "The fish was caught north of here in open waters, nowhere near Minamata Bay."

"I always ask where fish is from, now, before I buy," she said. "But I don't hear of anything coming to us from Minamata Bay these days, anyhow."

"Because they're mostly dead," Kiyo said. The tender grilled fish all but melted in his mouth. "Delicious. I haven't had fish in a long time." He wondered why his family couldn't have seafood from another place besides Minamata Bay. But his father now seemed rigidly against eating anything from the sea, at all.

Mrs. Inagawa laid out a futon on the living room floor for Kiyo. In the morning she cooked more fish for breakfast. When he and Inagawa entered the lab, the other men were already working.

Ito looked up at Kiyo. "You're doing a good job. I appreciate it."

"I'll finish the rest, now," Kiyo said.

He labeled the last slide at four o'clock. The researchers had been studying the ones he'd made all day.

"Look," Ito said suddenly, motioning the others over to his microscope.

Kiyo lowered his head to gaze through the eyepiece. Gray and black blobs filled the slide.

Ito laughed. "Have any idea what you're looking at?"

Kiyo felt his face grow hot. "Ah ... well, no."

"Try this." The researcher grabbed a slide with a sample from another part of the Bay. "Notice anything similar?"

Kiyo looked again. "I think so." Eh, more blobs, he thought.

"How about sharp crystal-like things?"

Kiyo peered hard. "Oh. Really small ones? Yes! I do see them."

"All right. Look at the other sample again."

Kiyo switched slides. "Same sharp-looking things." He lifted his head. "What are they?"

"Heavy metal. Metallic elements with a relatively high density compared to water. If ingested, or inhaled, they're extremely harmful to living things. These samples prove Minamata Bay is full of them."

The other men crowded in and took turns looking too.

"And so . . . the fish are eating them?" Kiyo asked.

"Anything that lives in that water is. These samples tell us any fish or shellfish there will be loaded with heavy metal. When people eat that sea-life, they're ingesting it too."

So once-beautiful Minamata Bay was polluted. Poisoned. Ruined. It is dying too, Kiyo thought.

Inagawa said, "For three months doctors and researchers have been studying the forty people afflicted so far. We still need to isolate *which* heavy metal is causing the Strange Disease, and where it's coming from. Then stop the inflow."

Inflow.

Six months ago, Kiyo's father had ordered the cook not to buy any seafood. As the manager in charge of waste disposal, he'd be one of the first to know what was going into the Bay from Chisso's pipes. Even before the researchers, he must've suspected the Strange Disease could be linked to seafood. Protecting his family would be his foremost goal. But now that the researchers had discovered the presence of heavy metal in the Bay's waters, he could warn the general public – and protect everybody.

For the first time in over a year Kiyo felt an upwelling of hope. Surely now the Strange Disease was close to being figured out. Maybe soon there'd even be a cure. And he would be one of those helping doctors make sure Yuki, and everyone else in Minamata, would never get the Disease again.

TEN

How Can Heavy Metal Hurt You?

In the week Kiyo had been home from Kumamoto, he'd biked over to see Yuki three times, then ridden home feeling calmer and happier. Today, he was hurrying from school to get to the hospital for a meeting with Hosokawa Sensei and the researchers at the University of Kumamoto.

The scientists he'd worked with were all crammed in Dr. Hosokawa's small office, each holding copies of an official-looking report. Instead of lab coats, everyone – including Dr. Hosokawa – had on a dark suit and tie.

The men from Kumamoto turned to smile as Kiyo hovered in the doorway. The air seemed to crackle, as if a storm of important news was about to break.

"Let's go," said Dr. Hosokawa. They all rose. Kiyo followed them outside, and over to the public health office next door. Three officials of that agency met them in the lobby and ushered the group into a small meeting room that reeked of stale cigarette smoke. There Hosokawa Sensei introduced the university researchers, and everyone bowed, exchanging crisp white business cards.

The public health officers sat on one side of a long cedar conference table, the university men on the other. When Kiyo took a chair in a far corner, an agency man asked, "Who's he?"

Dr. Hosokawa barely glanced up. "My assistant."

"He stays," Inagawa added.

The official cocked his head, looking puzzled, but finally turned back to the group. Dr. Hosokawa moved a chair from the government side of the table and pushed it in among the researchers. Several men lit cigarettes.

After handing a copy of the thick report to the head official, Inagawa spoke about their research and findings, concluding, "So an immediate public warning not to eat any seafood pulled from the Bay will minimize the number of people contracting the Strange Disease."

"You've found some heavy metal in its water," said the headman, "but you haven't directly linked it to the Disease. We can't cause a panic here without more proof."

"Are you saying you won't warn people of the risk?" Inagawa half-rose from his seat. "Even though heavy metal poisoning is not just harmful but also often fatal. Not just to sea life, but to people, animals, and birds."

"I see," said the stone-faced official blandly.

"You don't see at all," Kiyo blurted.

Hosokawa Sensei turned abruptly. "*Kiyo.*"

"*Sumimasen.*" Forgive me, Kiyo said, forcing down rage. Were these pompous men even listening?

The head health official glowered at him, then turned back to the researchers. "I thank you all for coming. But until you know more, it would be irresponsible to publicly broadcast mere conjecture."

"We've been studying the Strange Disease for almost two years. It would be even more irresponsible to not tell the people of the risk." Inagawa sat back down, red-faced.

"Of course I understand your concerns," the official noted. "And will most certainly discuss your findings with the head of city council. Please, keep up the good work." He bowed shallowly. "We're indebted to you and look forward to more certainty about the cause of this terrible disease. Please, keep me informed of more specific results."

The researchers left, faces tight with anger. Kiyo was fuming along with them. If the health agency won't warn the public, he decided, I can at least tell Yuki.

The late November day was cold; most people seemed to be staying inside. As he pedaled through his neighborhood, Masa waved from his front yard. Kiyo waved back but didn't stop. He'd already taken his friend to a movie and bought him some rather expensive American cookies as thanks for being his cover story.

The wind pricked at his face like frozen needles; he pedaled faster to get warm. Red and orange leaves littered the ground; they made the road slippery. Pine trees were the only green left in the landscape. His knitted gloves let in the cold and soon his hands felt numb. He'd ask for leather ones, next birthday.

At Yuki's house, he knocked on the battered door, swinging his arms to restore some circulation. As soon as she opened the door he darted in, removed his shoes, and all but dove under the warm kotatsu. Kazuko was huddled on one side, Nobuyuki on the other. Their tatami-mat flooring was so worn, a sharp bit of rush straw poked through Kiyo's slacks.

"Mom, Dad, it's Kiyo-kun," Yuki said, laughing as she closed the front door. She took the last empty place around the heater, pushing aside a sketch of Jiro she'd been working on.

"I sure liked that cat." He tilted his head to better view the drawing.

"Me too." Yuki bit her lip, blinking rapidly.

As he was kneading his numb hands underneath the table, his leg accidentally bumped hers. "Oh, sorry," he mumbled, and quickly moved it away.

"It's all right." She smiled.

His mouth went dry; his cheeks flamed. Maybe he should bump into her more often.

Kazuko was darning a hole in a brown sweater. "Did you ride your bicycle all this way in the cold?"

He nodded. "I've got some important news."

"I have something to tell you, too," said Yuki.

"Really? You first, then."

"I saw an announcement about an art show in Mina-mata, happening right before New Year's Eve. Have you ever gone?"

Kiyo quickly thought back to various advertisements he'd seen in the newspaper and posters around in the city. He couldn't recall anything about an art show. He felt cha-grined. Art was Yuki's passion. Shouldn't he pay more at-tention to such things? "I, uh – no, I've never been. We should go together."

Her face lit up. "You wouldn't be bored?"

"Of course not. I love art. Let's do it!"

"*Subarashii.*" Wonderful. Yuki's face glowed with ex-citement. "I can't wait."

His spirits lifted. How easy it had been to make her happy, simply by going to an art show. "My news is less pleasant. I've been at the University of Kumamoto helping researchers figure out the cause of the Strange Disease."

"You did the research?" Yuki stared as if awestruck.

He shook his head. "No, I just prepared slides in the lab."

"Still, I wouldn't know the first thing about how to do that. You're amazing."

"But I can't even draw a straight line, so we're even. Anyway, I learned some very interesting things in Kuma-moto." He told them about heavy metal's connection to the Disease. "So you see, you must quit eating seafood."

"You must be joking." Yuki's father snorted as if he'd told a ridiculous joke.

"No, really. Consuming catches from Minamata Bay is causing the Strange Disease. It's not safe anymore."

"But we can't stop eating it," her mother protested. "We get most of our food from the Bay, though we catch so little these days. It's impossible to grow enough seasonal vegetables in our garden, or just live on eggs."

Kiyo hadn't considered that. Unlike his family, they couldn't afford to buy chicken or meat.

"And I love fish," Yuki added sadly. "Especially octopus."

"The Bay has always fed us." Kazuko nodded, as if that settled it.

Nobuyuki poured himself a cup of shochu. "When I was a kid, we never had enough to eat on Amakusa Island. I fled poverty there to come make a living here, off the ocean. It was the right choice. We may not have much, but we always eat." He tipped back his cup and closed his eyes. "Are those scientists absolutely sure fish is the cause?"

"Yes. They're just trying to figure out which heavy metal is the culprit, and where it's coming from."

"Ah. See there?" Her mother's face relaxed. "Then they're not really certain of anything yet."

"Well, not precisely . . . still, it's best not to take any chances," Kiyo insisted.

But everyone seemed to be ignoring his warning.

"It's a cold ride back. Why not stay for dinner?" Nobuyuki capped the bottle. "A good meal will warm you up."

"Please, consider what I said about heavy metal contaminating the Bay. There's a clear connection. If you eat fish, you're eating that too. It's causing the Disease."

"But I don't even know what 'heavy metal' is. How can plain metal hurt you?" Yuki's father plunked his cup hard on the table, as if to show he was done with the subject.

"I'm only telling you this because I don't want any of you to get the Disease."

"I know you care about us," Yuki said. "And we thank you."

"But you'll keep eating fish." Kiyo hung his head, frustrated. Now he had to study and work even harder, help Hosokawa Sensei more, and also somehow convince Yuki and her parents not to poison themselves with the dangerous food they so loved so much.

ELEVEN

The Big Show

When Yuki stepped off the bus, Kiyo was waiting at the stop. Her breath skipped a beat. He looked so tall and confident. That handsome face drew glances from other girls passing by, also headed to the art show. Yet his entire attention seemed focused on her.

She never stopped being amazed at her luck. "I'm so excited. My first show!"

"And we'll see what kind of art you'll be doing later on, as a successful adult artist."

She smiled. "Thanks, Kiyo-kun."

They headed to the Community Building. A sandwich-board sign in front of the two-story brick structure announced: *Prefectural Art Show.* Inside the large entryway a dozen people stood in line, waiting to pick up programs listing the work displayed and artists' names.

Finally Kiyo and Yuki reached the head of the line. Two people sitting behind a table greeted them warmly.

"Hello. Welcome to the most prestigious art show in our prefecture," said the man, who wore a nattily-tailored navy-blue suit.

"Many of the artists whose work is displayed here today are actually present," added the middle-aged woman, who wore a fancy persimmon-hued silk kimono.

"Thank you." Yuki bowed deeply. "Do a lot of people come to see this show every year?"

"Oh, yes," the woman gushed. "We'd be busy with just the city people and others who live elsewhere around the

Bay. But with New Year's celebration starting in two days a lot of tourists are here in town already."

The man nodded. "They love the hot spring pools, especially in winter. The ones overlooking the Bay and those up in the mountain."

Yuki had never even seen a commercial hot spring, though she'd soaked in the many of the small natural pools around the area with family and friends. At those, of course, no one waited on you with woven-bamboo baskets full of fresh towels or to hold neatly-folded clothing. But lounging in nature's mineral baths for free was still a luxurious way to spend a day.

Her family had gone the previous winter with Uncle Higano, and no one had suspected it would be his last time there. There'd been an hour-long bus ride on a narrow, curving mountain road through a valley next to a river. Then they'd trekked up a little-used path thick with bare-limbed trees. The strong smell of sulfur had assailed her nostrils as they approached the shallow hot-springs pond. Stripping as modestly as possible, they'd carefully lowered themselves into the steaming water. And Uncle had sighed a long, *"Ahhh,"* as if every worry had just melted away.

Again she sent a thought to him: *We will never forget you.* "Hot springs are really wonderful," she agreed, smiling at the woman behind the check-in table.

They moved on, approaching the large main hall. Yuki paused at the doorway and gasped, "I've never seen so much art in one place."

The walls were covered with paintings and drawings composed of everything from charcoal and muted tints to bright splashy oil-painted colors. Sculpture and pottery were displayed in the open center area. Visitors wandered around slowly and dreamily, studying the pieces.

Yuki began with an oil painting of an ocean scene to her immediate left. The waves looked as if – should you reach out and touch them – your fingers might come away

damp with real seawater. She stared at each picture in-
tensely, in turn, slowly circling the room. Kiyo walked
along next to her, and she wondered if he was only pretending to be interested, for her sake. "Isn't this the most
spectacular sight ever?"

"Absolutely." He bobbed his head, eyeing a watercolor
depicting a luscious basket of ripe persimmons. Maybe he
was just hungry?

Halfway through the exhibits, she said, "I'd love to
learn how to paint with oils and watercolor."

He nodded. "I'm sure you'd be great at those."

She felt doubtful. "I've taught myself about proportion,
shading, compositions, and other things from books at
school. But paints ... they're very different from handling a
pencil."

Kiyo looked thoughtful a moment, then said, "Come
with me." She followed him back out to the two people
posted at the table in the entryway. "Excuse me," he said.
"My friend is looking for someone who teaches painting
and watercolor. Someone local."

The woman brightened and spoke up immediately.
"Why, Goto Sensei does both, and she lives in Minamata.
She's here today. Why don't I go find her?"

"Thanks you."

Yuki tugged at Kiyo's sleeve. "You know I can't afford
to pay for lessons," she whispered, feeling mortified.

"I'll cover it out of my allowance," he whispered back.

"Oh no. I can't let you do that," she protested.

"You have to make your dreams come true as an artist,
just as I must in order to become a doctor." He smiled.
"Anyhow, I usually don't even spend all my allowance, and
what I do buy, well, it's just frivolous stuff."

"But it's *your* money."

"I insist. I have Hosokawa Sensei and the researchers
to mentor me. You need Goto Sensei to teach you. I want
you to succeed, because you're truly an artist." His look

grew mischievous. "Anyhow, good paintings sell for a lot of money. So you can pay it all back when you're rich and fa‑mous."

Yuki flushed hotly. Her heart felt full, ready to ex‑plode.

. . . good paintings sell for a lot of money.

Then one day soon perhaps she could afford to buy plenty of healthy food, have those broken, falling roof tiles replaced . . . and in many other ways make her parents' lives easier.

And if Kiyo believed so strongly in her art, well then, she would work hard to fulfill his prediction for her future. "All right," she told him. "But I *will* pay you back some‑day."

The receptionist reappeared, trailed by a very tall woman who smelled of scented face powder. Her purple kimono had large white peony blossoms woven into the hem.

"Goto Sensei," the greeter said. "These are the two young people who asked about you." Then she took her seat behind the table again.

The artist named Goto nodded to Yuki and Kiyo. "Nice to meet you."

Yuki and Kiyo bowed deeply. "I'm Akaji Yuki, and this is my friend Kuge Kiyoshi‑kun," Yuki said. "I've seen your watercolor landscapes and oil portraits. They're wonder‑ful."

"Thank you." The painter looked very pleased.

"Yuki‑chan is a talented artist too," Kiyo boasted, and Yuki felt herself blush. He added, "She wants to learn how to paint with oils and watercolors. Can you teach her?"

"Perhaps. What kind of art is it you do, Yuki‑san?"

She stammered, "Oh, well, I doubt I'm all that good ... but I like to draw with pencil."

"Did you bring any work along with you?"

"Ah, no. Not with me."

"But she's so talented," Kiyo put in eagerly, "she could just draw something for you right now." He rushed over to the volunteers' table and asked for paper and a pencil.

"Here." He held them out to Yuki.

She glanced nervously at Goto. When the artist nodded, she went over to an empty table, sat, and carefully sketched a portrait of her.

Goto leaned over the table and inhaled sharply. She took the drawing from Yuki's hand. "And you've never had any instructions?"

Yuki shook her head. "No, none."

"Well, you have much promise, indeed."

As Kiyo opened his mouth to speak again, Yuki said quickly, "Are you saying you'll teach me, then?"

The artist smiled. "Yes, indeed I will."

"Thank you." Yuki and Kiyo both bowed deeply.

"Oil paint is more expensive than watercolor," Goto added. "It takes more time to paint, and requires canvas and turpentine. I suggest we start with watercolor."

"How much is each lesson?" Kiyo asked. When she named the price, Yuki saw his eyes widen.

"She'll also need to buy boards, paint, and brushes," Goto added, ticking off each item on her fingers. "I have extra easels."

Yuki shook her head. "Thanks, but I don't really have to have lessons. This will be too expensive."

"Will you get everything for her?" Kiyo asked. "We won't know exactly what to buy."

"Yes," the teacher said.

Yuki tugged at his arm. "Kiyo-kun, I really need to talk to you for a moment."

He ignored her. "And you'll give her a lesson once a month, starting tomorrow?"

"Certainly."

As Kiyo bowed, Yuki understood it was already too late. The deal had been made. "Thank you. I'll do my best to please you."

The next afternoon she met Kiyo in front of the hospital, after he'd done rounds with Dr. Hosokawa. They walked to Goto's place, a well-kept, modest-sized house in a good neighborhood.

Yuki matched her pace to Kiyo's even though every few steps she felt like skipping. But that would be childish. *You're fifteen*, she told herself sternly. *Act calm, more mature.* But at last the excitement simply burst out. "My first art lesson!"

He grinned. "I love how passionate you are about art."

She nearly stumbled. He loves that about me?

But she'd been born to make art, and could not imagine living without it. Kiyo never seemed to mind her family's poverty or their rundown house Only what he called her talent and the love her family felt for each other, and for him. Did all couples overlook faults and flaws, determined to see only the good in each other? Walking next to him right now, she could believe it. Her heart seemed to tumbled over itself like a litter of frolicking kittens.

Goto answered the door wearing a white artist's smock streaked with paint in a rainbow of colors. She led them down a hallway to a light-filled studio with a large north-facing window. Yuki took a deep breath, inhaling the sharp scents of turpentine, gesso, and oils. She'd dreamed of having such a studio, one day; now she was standing in one. It seemed a good sign.

Instead of following, Kiyo lingered out in the hall. "I'll wait out here."

"Good idea," the instructor said. "I'll get you a chair."

Two easels were already set up, each with watercolor paper tacked to a square wooden backing.

"I've already wet and stretched the papers, so they're ready," Goto said. "I'll teach you how to do that next time. Now, I'll be over here at this easel. You take the other one."

My own easel! And a private lesson from a real artist. Yuki felt suffused with joy as she moved over to her spot.

"Today, you'll work with watercolor and brush. But first, I'll explain some basics. Watercolor paints are transparent. The tinted powder's mixed with water; the more water used, the lighter and more transparent the tone. Less water creates deeper shades. And this use of lightness and darkness gives a picture more sense of light, depth, and three-dimensional space."

Yuki realized she'd done something similar with her pencil by stumbling onto size, perspective, blurring, position and other techniques. But never before by using depth of color.

The hour flew by as they painted and Goto critiqued her composition and brush strokes. She felt disappointed when the lesson ended.

As she was cleaning her brushes, she said, "I have no money to pay you with."

The artist raised an eyebrow. "Yes, but the young man is doing that."

"I know, but I'd like to at least pay for part of the fee. Is there something you might accept in trade? I can do many things: clean, laundry, run errands, shop."

She held her breath as the artist looked thoughtful. Kiyo was kind and generous, but she couldn't let him take responsibility for everything.

"I wouldn't mind having you doing all of those things," Goto said at last. "But are you any good?"

"Oh, yes. I've been doing those tasks for my family since I was very young. I'm prompt and hard working."

"I can believe that." Goto smiled warmly. "How about two hours of chores, three times a week after school? I'll give you an hour-long lesson once a month, and your supplies."

"Oh, thank you!" Yuki bowed, elated. She set the damp brushes in a jar to dry, and then opened the door to the hallway.

"How was it?" Kiyo asked, rising from his chair.

"I worked on still life and learned so much in just an hour!"

He frowned. "What is 'still life'?"

"Oh, portraying objects like fruits, flowers, rocks. I painted a composition with an onion, some garlic bulbs, and a knife on a cutting board."

"Huh. Can I see it?"

Yuki untied her furoshiki and showed him the small painting.

He leaned over it and sniffed. "So real I can practically smell the garlic."

She laughed, feeling for once as if she didn't have a care in the world. "I want to pile up some dried leaves and paint that when I get home."

When he'd paid for the lesson, Yuki said, "Thank you, Kiyo-kun. And guess what? You won't have to pay again, after today. I'm going to work for Goto Sensei part-time in return for my lessons and supplies."

"Really?" Kiyo's eyes widened. "Wow. I'm impressed."

She faced the artist and gave a final bow. "Thank you, Goto Sensei. I'll work hard on everything you taught me, until next month."

The artist handed Yuki her colored watercolor powder and some painting boards, all wrapped in furoshiki. "You are talented, my dear, and also a fast learner. I believe your future as an artist is bright."

A few months later Yuki hummed as she swept a feather duster over Goto Sensei's low-slung living room table. The top had been hewn from one long plank of a single enormous tree. A cluster of wooden turtle sculptures was arranged on it; her teacher had told her she'd traded paintings with other artists for both table and turtles. The table was made of katsura wood, and its distinctive caramel scent lingered.

The house was also full of watercolors and oils, as well as ceramic vases and wooden figurines made by various other artists. Yuki admired each piece as she carefully cleaned it. How lucky she was to receive such valuable lessons in exchange for spending time with such beautiful art. During her lessons over the past three months, she'd soaked up everything the teacher taught her. And working like this, preparing for her own future career meant she was making her own way. That made her feel more adult. After all, she'd be sixteen in two months.

In the midst of her work, there came a knock on the front door. Goto was out, at a meeting. It might be a delivery, or something else important, though, so Yuki went to the door and answered it.

She was surprised but happy to see Kiyo on the front step, still in his school uniform.

"Hi, Yuki-chan. How's it going? I saw Goto Sensei at Masa-kun's family's hotel and thought I'd stop by."

"So nice to see you." She let him in and shut the door. "I'm almost done for the day."

"Wow, look at all this stuff. It's like an art gallery."

"I know. I'd like to have a house like this, someday. I love all the beautiful pictures and objects. Want to know who did them?"

He nodded. "Sure."

She gave him a tour, showing off each piece in the various rooms – except the bedroom, which she felt was too private to enter. Explaining who each artist was, the technique used, the title, and anything else she knew.

Kiyo listened patiently. Then, back in the living room, he pulled her close.

"It's hard to keep my hands off you," he murmured, nuzzling her neck. He smelled of road dust from the bike ride, and more faintly of clean cotton and sweat.

Yuki giggled nervously to hide the desire she also felt. She did want to be closer . . . to touch him. To be touched.

She forced down her shyness. "I like being near you, too."

"Good." He ran his hands down her back, still kissing her. His lips were firm yet soft, and tasted sweet. The heat coming off him made her pulse race. She closed her eyes and moaned.

At that moment the front door suddenly flew open. Goto stepped inside.

The artist stopped in the foyer, gaping. The grocery bag she'd been cradling slipped, then crashed to the entry's stone floor. Yellow egg-yolks oozed from the mouth of the cloth sack. A ripe yuzu fruit split, filling the foyer with its zesty citrus scent. "What're you *doing?*" she rasped, her voice a harsh whisper, as if disbelief crushed her ability to speak. "And what're *you* doing here?"

Yuki and Kiyo quickly stepped apart. He put on a contrite expression and turned to face the artist, bowing deeply. "Hello. I was . . . in the neighborhood. Just stopped in to see Yuki-chan. In case she needed any help."

Yuki bowed, too. "I – I'm sorry. Kiyo-kun just wanted to . . . I was showing him some of your marvelous art works, that's all."

"You took a stranger around my house without my permission?" Goto shouted. Her voice had recovered, its tone now more that of a great lord to an unworthy samurai.

"N-no!" Unnerved, Yuki feared she was saying all the wrong things. "Not into the bedroom." She gasped, shaking her head. "I mean . . . that's not what I meant!"

"She only showed me the exquisite art in your living area. I've been here only a few minutes. I wasn't going to stay."

"So is this what you do when I'm away? Entertain your boyfriend."

"No, no! Please believe me," Yuki cried out. "This has never happened before."

"Which part? That you're not really doing chores, or that you're instead cavorting with him?"

"I've never been here before when you were not home," Kiyo protested.

"It won't happen again." Yuki bowed again.

"I trust you alone in my home, and you two sneak around, making love like dogs in the street."

Yuki gasped at the crude accusation. "We did nothing of the kind."

Kiyo sounded angry now. Yuki prayed he'd remain calm for her sake. She didn't want to lose her job and her art lessons.

"And I'll never come over again," he added.

"Indeed you won't." Goto stepped back, away from the open front door. "Get out!"

"Yes, of course." Kiyo went over to get his jacket from the hallway.

As he was pulling on his shoes, Goto added, "And both of you, never come back."

"I apologize deeply," Yuki said. "Please, Sensei, forgive us. This won't ever happen again. I have the utmost respect for you and your home."

"If that were true you would not be found caressing a boy in my living room."

"Please," Kiyo tried again. "This was all my fault alone. Please don't punish Yuki-chan for my mistake. I'll do whatever you ask, to make amends." He dropped to his knees and bowed his head to the ground. "I beg you."

"No! The disrespect. I never want to see either of you again. Leave!" When Kiyo remained on the floor she waved her arms at him, raging, "Get out of my house, now!"

Yuki rushed out barefoot, clutching her shoes, Kiyo following. A loud bang chased after them as Goto slammed the door. The lock clicked loudly behind them. The sound of Yuki's hope of being an artist crashing down, too.

They walked quickly for a block, panting, saying nothing. A few blocks away, Yuki paused to put on her shoes.

"I'm so sorry," Kiyo raking his hands through his hair. "I never meant for that to happen."

"I know. And it's my fault too. I really shouldn't have let you inside. She's right, that was disrespectful."

"I'll find another teacher, and pay for the lessons and the supplies. Bus fare too if you need it."

She sighed. Kiyo always meant well. But at the moment she couldn't stand the shame of that scene in the house. "You can't fix everything with money," she whispered. "I feel so humiliated. What she must think of me! Loose. And a liar!"

"But you're not either one. You're wonderful, smart, beautiful."

"Please, Kiyo-kun. Enough. I'm going home now."

Shoulders slumped, she turned from his hurt gaze and trudged toward home. Her great chance, lost. Who would teach her now?

In just the three lessons, though, Yuki had already learned the joys of watercolor painting, and was still determined to master it. She experimented, learning how to let the paper itself represent the color white. Planning out the picture ahead of time in order to be able to paint quick-ly and prevent streaky strokes and hard lines and the paints swiftly drying. Blending colors without muddying them. So I was kicked out before learning about oil paint-ing, she thought. That won't stop me.

At an art store in Minamata she strolled around inhal-ing the various scents of her craft. Testing the softness of sable versus the firmness of bristle brushes. Perusing books on oil painting. She picked up several hardbacks, flipping through to see which might teach her the most.

"You going to buy anything?" the owner barked. "Stop pawing my merchandise with your grubby hands."

Other shoppers turned to stare. A woman in an expen-sive silk kimono glanced at Yuki and frowned. "What is that she's *wearing?*" She tapped the woman next to her, who was setting three large canvas frames on the counter.

"Something a farmer wouldn't be seen in to till a field," the other woman said loudly. "Hmph! Not even ironed. Probably from a fisher family."

"She might have the Disease!" kimono-woman gasped.

A man in a dark brown suit and silk tie crammed some paint-tubes back into their slots and hurried out of the store, giving Yuki a wide berth.

She looked down at her old white blouse and navy skirt, the best outfit she owned. They were clean, as she was. Nothing she was doing at the moment required nice clothes, even if she had any. And why would fishers bother to iron their everyday wear? To impress the shellfish?

She slid the book back into its slot on the shelf and left, ignoring the whispers of the remaining shoppers.

"I don't need fancy clothes to be an artist," she mut-tered as she stepped out onto the sidewalk. And now at least she knew how much the instruction book cost. She'd figure out a way to earn the money.

TWELVE

New Year's Surprise

Kiyo always looked forward to New Year's celebrations. Who didn't love the most important holiday of the year? His second eldest brother, Tadahisa, finishing up his last year at the University of Tokyo, was home for a week. His oldest brother Ichita and his wife had arrived two days earlier with their four-year-old son and baby girl. Traveling to Minamata from Sapporo, on the northern island, was a two-day trip. Now the house felt lively and full, the way it used to when his brothers were still at home.

Kiyo even enjoyed the pitter-patter of toddler feet and the baby's frequent crying. In deference to their father's love of *enka* music – sentimental ballad songs – everyone even gamely endured Murata Hideo's hit song *Jinsei Geki-jou* playing repeatedly on the phonograph.

The brothers hadn't changed a bit since Kiyo last saw them a year ago. Tadahisa took after their mother: short and slender, oval face, thin nose, high forehead. Ichita, on the other hand, was a carbon copy of their father: tall, square-shouldered, wide nose, broad cheekbones. Kiyo had looked up to them both when he was little, following them around all day if they let him.

Yanagiya had laid out futons for Tadahisa next to Kiyo's in his bedroom. Ichita and his family occupied his old room. On New Year's Eve, too excited to sleep, Kiyo turned over in bed to look at his brother. Tadahisa's head was propped on one hand as he read a book.

"Will you miss Tokyo when you graduate?" Kiyo asked. "Mom always says how modern it's getting. All the shows, and fancy stores. We actually have three coffee shops here now, but I haven't had any!" The drink had become popular in Tokyo once the coffee ban had been lifted after The War. Now it was even a popular choice in Minamata.

"So what does it taste like?" Kiyo added.

"Eh. Hard to describe. Sort of . . . chocolatey. Only not."

"I'm going to try some this week."

Tadahisa set aside his book and sat up too, mirroring Kiyo. The scar he still had from long ago, after once playing carelessly with a knife, was still visible on the back of his left hand.

"Sure, Tokyo's great. But I'm looking forward to coming home in a few months to work for Chisso."

"I'll probably go to Tokyo University, too."

"Of course you will. Dad did, like Ichita-kun and I. You have to go to the best school in Japan."

"Did you know I'm going to be a doctor? I'm studying already." He rolled over and reached for the anatomy book on his desk chair. "I'm learning a lot on my own. See?" He thrust the thick volume at his brother.

Tadahisa laughed and held out both hands, fending it off. "No thanks! You always had the inquisitive mind. Not me."

"I work at the hospital all the time. Dr. Hosokawa lets me hang out with him."

"What! But you're only fifteen. How'd Dad bribe him to let you do that?"

"It was Dad's idea at first. But now I go because I can help. I'm just like Hosokawa Sensei."

Tadahisa frowned. "How so?"

"We both knew when we were little that we had to become doctors. Medicine's the most important thing to us."

"Well, what do you know? My brother, the doctor."

Kiyo tried to stay serious, but a smile overtook his expression. Tadahisa threw back his head and laughed, crooked front teeth shining in the moonlight. How good it felt to have laughter in the house again!

"You like a girl now, I bet." Kiyo's brother slapped the floor. "So who is it?"

"Promise you won't tell Ichita-kun."

"I swear. Just tell me."

"Her name's Yuki-chan. Cutest girl you've ever seen — and an incredible artist. We also have the same birthday."

"Same birthday? Must be fate, then."

"For sure." Kiyo laid his head back on his pillow, smiling. Imagining Yuki's face. "That's exactly what it is."

By the time Kiyo had shrugged into his suit on New Year's Day, everyone was already seated around the Western-style dining table, dressed in formalwear. His mother's elaborate kimono had a scene of a creek flowing through a forest woven into dark blue silk. His father wore a navy-blue silk kimono. Ichita was in a light gray suit; Tadahisa, a trendy brown tweed jacket and brown wool pants.

"*Okaasan.*" Namiko, like all Japanese, called her mother-in-law "Mother." Ichita's wife was thin, with delicate wrists and ankles, enormous dark eyes, and a rosebud mouth. "Your kimono is so beautiful." She sighed. "We didn't have enough room in the luggage for kimonos. Anyhow, Ichita-kun prefers suits, so he didn't care." She smiled sadly, gazing down at the lapels of the fitted tan wool suit she'd worn on their trip.

Kiyo took his seat at the far end of the table, and wished everyone a happy New Year. "*Akemashite omedetougozaimasu.*"

Even Dad bowed back and recited the greeting.

"About time you got here!" Tadahisa shouted. "Now we can finally eat. I'm starving. Sit down already!"

Yanagiya and a young assistant she'd hired to help prepare holiday delicacies carried in trays of food, setting one in front of each person. A low arrangement of blush-pink peonies was centered on the table. Even with the delicious aroma rising from the traditional *ozouni* soup, Kiyo could still smell the flowers' sweet scent.

He dug into his ozouni. "Mmm. Nice." The pounded rice cake in clear broth was deliciously chewy. Instead of the usual red and white fishcake, shredded bits of chicken floated on top.

Now that his two brothers were sitting next to each other, even as different as they looked, Kiyo realized how alike they really were. Both wore black glasses. Both were whip smart and ambitious.

"Hey. Where are the kelp rolls? And the herring, shrimp, and sardines?" Ichita craned around the table, then looked toward the kitchen door.

Kichiro lowered his chopsticks, still holding a bit of sweet rolled omelet. "Eh. We must move forward. All the more advanced Japanese will eat meat from now on."

Ichita frowned. "Sure, meat's all right, but seafood's traditional. I was looking forward to those dishes. You mean to tell me there won't be any?"

"Your father wants us to be modern now." Etsuko smiled at her husband. "And I agree with him. We're going to set all the trends in Minamata."

"But what about our traditions?" Ichita argued.

"Yeah, that's just crazy." Tadahisa nodded. "For Japan to be modern, we can't eat fish?"

Kiyo leaned forward. "See, there's this epidemic – "

"Quiet!" his father barked.

He flinched back in shock. "But Dad, I was just explaining – "

"Epidemic?" Namiko stopped eating and wrapped an arm protectively around her small son. "Is it even safe to be here? What about the children?" Her eyes grew even larger as she looked around the table.

"There's absolutely nothing to worry about," Kichiro said, voice calm again, as if he hadn't just shouted at his youngest son. Then he looked down at his plate, picked up his chopsticks, and took a bite of omelet.

All day Chisso employees, neighbors, and acquaintances dropped by with holiday greetings. Proud of her latest purchase, Etsuko kept the gold and amber, dome-shaded stained glass lamp on the corner table lit even when bright sunlight beamed through the living room windows.

By the end of the day, Kiyo was sick of small talk, and only wanted to go see Yuki. They certainly couldn't have enjoyed the sort of New Year's feast his family had, but he hoped they'd enjoyed it somehow. By dinner time, his parents and brothers were eagerly drinking sake and beer. Kichiro puffed away on his pipe, filling the room with his tobacco blend scented with cardamom and coriander.

"May I have some sake?" Kiyo asked. When his father hesitated, he cajoled, "It's New Year's Day, Dad."

"All right." Kichiro poured a small cup. "That's all you get."

"Thanks." Kiyo sipped. Sweet yet bitter, the alcohol went down much smoother than the eye-watering shochu he'd had at Yuki's house. It warmed his chest just as well, though.

Mom clapped to get everyone's attention. "I had a special dinner prepared for us. Yanagiya-san!" she called out.

The cook and her helper carried in plates, each holding a small piece of meat. Kiyo's mouth watered at the delicious pan-fried scent.

"Beefsteak?" Namiko clapped too. "Thank you, Okaa-san!"

Dad eyed Ichita. "Not eating seafood isn't so bad, after all, eh?" He put away his pipe and picked up a knife.

Ichita grinned as if he'd forgotten about the morning's squabble. The table grew quiet as, unaccustomed to using knives and forks, everyone carefully cut their meat into small portions, slowly chewing each piece. The ribeye – it seemed enormous to Kiyo – was so tender. Everyone nodded and smiled over their plates, savoring the holiday treat.

"Just think. I'll be eating like this every day after April." Tadahisa goaded Ichita, holding up the piece of steak on his fork. He poured more hot sake into everyone's cups, including Kiyo's.

"Oh, you won't be coming back here," Dad said, and gulped down his refill.

"What do you mean?" His middle son dropped his utensils with a clatter. The whole table stopped eating. "I'm working for Chisso after graduation."

"No. You should join a company in Tokyo." Kichiro held out his empty cup, and his wife automatically filled it again. "That's where the opportunities are now."

Ichita looked puzzled. "But Dad, you always said Tadahisa would join Chisso and work with you."

"Once you join a company, you join forever. Give your life to it. You can't leave."

Why's he even saying that, Kiyo wondered. Everyone knows this already.

"Of course not." Tadahisa said, a bit too loudly.

"You'll be far better off in Tokyo, which will soon be the center of modern Japan."

"Why're you doing this?" Ichita knocked back his drink and slammed the empty cup onto the table. "Chisso's been your family as much as we have. You've given your life to it, been loyal, and it protects you. Chisso's been good to all of us. You promised Tadahisa-kun he'd join them."

Dad downed another cupful. "Better start interviewing in Tokyo soon as you return." Then he rose abruptly and left the room.

The three brothers stared around at each other in disbelief. At last Kiyo said, "What the hell is going on?"

THIRTEEN

The Navy Versus Chisso

Cold, misty rain fell on Kiyo as he cycled to the hospital two days after the New Year's. He climbed to the Strange Disease ward, where new patients still came in every week. They grew thinner and thinner, and screamed more and more.

In the afternoon he watched a nurse slip a feeding tube up a teenager's nose while another nurse held the thrashing boy down.

Kiyo went out to the corridor and pressed his forehead to the wall, lunch curdling in his belly. Doctors and hospitals were supposed to help people, yet these patients suffered and begged without end until they died.

"I will become the best doctor in Japan, and figure out how to help anyone who comes to me in pain," he muttered to the blank white plaster.

He missed seeing Yuki. But Hosokawa Sensei and the university researchers were working through the holiday to determine which specific heavy metal was causing the Strange Disease. He had to assist them again.

Kiyo entered the lab where Dr. Hosokawa was studying slides under the microscope. The Sensei lifted his head. "Hello."

"Did you take any time off for the holiday?"

"Two days. But our Strange Disease patients get no days off."

Kiyo looked down, ashamed to have spent three days feasting and relaxing with his family while men like Dr. Hosokawa remained hard at work. "I've a few vacation days left until school starts. I could go to Kumamoto again."

"They said you were a great help, so they'll probably be happy for you to return. I'll make the call."

Masa agreed to be the cover-story for Kiyo again, this time pretending they were visiting Masa's relatives in Kumamoto for the rest of New Year's. Kiyo's train ticket was for the next day, but he couldn't let the holiday pass without wishing Yuki a Happy New Year.

His cap was coated with frost by the time he arrived at Tsukinoura Village. He'd discovered that, by wearing two jackets, he didn't feel totally frozen by the time he got to her house. Well, except for the numb hands.

Again, he crawled quickly under the kotatsu and wished everyone a Happy New Year. He slid in beside Yuki so he could secretly hold her hand. Her small warm ones fit perfectly in his larger cold ones, and she didn't seem to mind. He was glad he'd made time to come.

Yuki's father insisted on toasting with shochu. Kiyo was happy to; he'd grown fond of the harsh alcohol, and it made him feel warmer on the ride home.

"I'm going to Kumamoto again tomorrow," he explained, "so I won't come by for several days."

"More faraway science," Yuki said, as if he were headed to the moon.

"I've got to help as much as possible. I want to make sure no one else – no one in your family – gets the Disease ever again."

"We're lucky to have you looking after us." Nobuyuki said. "Another?" And he poured more shochu into Kiyo's empty cup.

Kiyo reached Kumamoto after a long nap on the gently rocking train.

"Happy New Year." Inagawa greeted him.

All the researchers now talked to Kiyo as if he were one of them. He felt like he belonged. They seemed to understand his drive to be a doctor. Here he didn't have to justify the time he spent at the hospital, or try to explain why his anatomy book was so fascinating. If not for Yuki, he'd try to stay here until he went off to college.

"We took more samples from the Bay," Inagawa said. "Seawater and dead sea creatures for slides!"

"You can set them up," Ito said.

"Sure." Kiyo nodded.

"We've been studying samples from the victims who've died," Miura said.

Kiyo swallowed hard. "Um, samples?"

"From the brain and other organs."

He nodded again, trying to appear as if he'd always known they would be cutting up the dead patients.

Besides preparing slides of the new water samples, he was to make more of thinly sliced pieces of fish and octopus preserved in sickly-sweet-smelling formaldehyde. Miura, who was in charge of sea life, cut those. He also made the slides of human samples, a job considered too delicate for Kiyo to handle yet. Staring at the thin pale slices, Kiyo could hardly believe they'd once been part of a person.

Those people had suffered just like Uncle Higano. Animals suffered, too, like the stray white cat and Yuki's pet Jiro. He'd eaten fish all his life, but the dissection reminded him that they, like people, were individual living things. He handled each sample gently with forceps, carefully labeling them, making sure they lay perfectly flat on the glass.

At seven that evening, Inagawa said, "It's still the holidays. Why don't we knock off a little early and go home?" Everyone smiled and put away their work.

Kiyo stayed the night at Inagawa's house again. They returned to the lab at eight the next morning, and Ito was already at work.

"I wanted to take a look at the new seawater samples," he said. "Half are done. I'd like you to finish the rest now."

"You already did half?" Kiyo asked. "So fast."

"I've been here three hours."

"Oh." Kiyo's cheeks heated up. "Sure. I'll do them right away."

As he prepared each slide, Ito studied it. Kiyo was finished by noon. Ito finally raised his head from the microscope and glanced around at his colleagues.

"What is it? Did you find something?" Miura asked.

The room went quiet. Everyone stared at Ito.

"There's a high concentration of manganese in both the fish and in the organs of deceased humans. Along with thallium, selenium, and organic mercury. I feel sure one of these is what's causing the Strange Disease. Also, the concentration of heavy metals is denser near where Chisso discharges its wastewater than anywhere else in the Bay."

Kiyo froze. "So . . . so the contamination must be coming from the factory," he blurted out.

"It appears so," Miura agreed.

But this is good news, in a way, Kiyo told himself. Once the company knew what their wastewater was doing, it would stop leaking contamination. He had to tell his father as soon as possible. Once he made Chisso quit discharging the toxic chemicals, Yuki's family could safely fish and eat food from the Bay again. This knowledge had come too late for Uncle Higano, but at least the most precious person in the world to Kiyo would be safe.

The next day Kiyo entered Chisso grounds through a plain wrought-iron gate and parked his bike in one of the long racks along with dozens of others — most not as nice as his, he noticed — in a courtyard only large enough to park a few trucks. The huge plant was a plain blocky building yet it dominated the city. Train tracks ran on one side of Chisso, facilitating the loading and shipping of manufactured products as well as supplies and materials received. The Bay bordered the other side.

Long two- and three-story buildings and a number of three- and four-story concrete and wooden structures were surrounded by dozens of high smokestacks of brick or steel. Snaking metal pipes connected the stacks to their buildings. White and gray smoke puffed continually up toward cumulus clouds hanging over the Bay. Twenty cylindrical storage tanks of various sizes were scattered around the perimeter of the square-mile property.

Inside the main office three rows of four desks stood side by side, crammed into one large open room. Each table held a jar of sharpened pencils. Most of the employees, wearing cheap coats and shiny ties, had their heads down, reading and writing. Cigarettes smoldered in desktop ashtrays. The hazy air reeked of stale smoke. Abacuses click-click-clicked as bookkeepers flicked the beads up and down the wires, speedy fingers flying in a blur. Some used mechanical adding machines, but the men on the abacuses seemed just as fast.

Kiyo crossed the room, climbed a flight of stairs, then rushed down a long corridor. He passed rows of wavy glass doors until he reached the one whose metal plate was engraved KUGE KICHIRO.

He knocked softly. His father's voice called, "Yes?"

When Kiyo entered, Dad swiveled his chair to face him, looking surprised. "Kiyo. What're you doing here?"

"Are you busy?"

"Always. But come in. Sit down."

Kiyo closed the door behind him. Though his father held a high position in the company, his office was only large enough for a desk, two leather guest chairs, and a bookcase full of black notebooks.

"What is it? Is something wrong at home?"

"No. But researchers from Kumamoto University are coming today to tell public health officials that more heavy metals have been found near the factory's wastewater than anywhere else in the Bay."

His father went rigid. He clenched his jaw for a moment, then said, "And?"

"Is Chisso's discharge contaminating the Bay?"

"How dare you insinuate such a thing." His father voice was low but it vibrated with anger. "How could anyone impugn an honorable business with such flimsy evidence? The company provides me with a job that funds your good life. Chisso's why I can afford to send your brothers to Tokyo University – and you, too, in a few years. Where's your loyalty? Chisso's your company, too."

"But you told Tadahisa-kun to go work for a different company."

Kichiro huffed, "I'm only looking after him. Tokyo will be a powerful city, full of opportunity. Instead of hurling accusations at Chisso, you should be grateful for all it's done for you."

"I am. But if Chisso is discharging toxic chemicals into the Bay, even accidentally, it's making people sick. It's killing them."

"No it's not! We're as concerned as anyone else. There's nothing conclusive yet, but we're working on finding the cause, too. Until we know for sure, go home, keep your mouth shut, and don't spread unproven allegations!"

Honoring his father's order to not talk about the Strange Disease findings was what an obedient son would do. But Kiyo could not follow that order; he would be ignoring everything else he knew to be true. So after leaving Chisso he headed to the hospital. Hosokawa Sensei was in his office, fingers raking his thinning hair as he read some report.

"Pardon me, Sensei," Kiyo murmured softly from the doorway, to avoid startling him.

The doctor looked up at Kiyo and removed his glasses, rubbing the dents they'd left on the bridge of his nose. "Come in."

Kiyo took a seat in front of the desk. "Have you talked to the university researchers? Did they tell you heavy metals in the seawater are probably coming from Chisso's pipes?"

"They said they'd found the heaviest concentration at the point where the factory dumps its wastewater."

Kiyo bit his lip. "Right. But ... could the current or waves be pushing the poisons into that area?"

"No. They took multiple samples in many areas to rule out that possibility."

Many areas, Kiyo thought, remembering the hundreds of slides he'd prepared.

"The waste coming out of the pipes flowing into the Bay is even visible," Sensei said. "And it contains heavy metals. Sea life eats or absorbs the contamination. People then eat the seafood."

"So you agree with their theory?"

"Yes, I do. Chisso is making people sick. Making them die."

That night, Kiyo waited up until he heard a familiar
muffled *thump*: his father's briefcase hitting the floor of his
study. As he headed to the dining room, he encountered
Yanagiya in the hallway, carrying a pot of rice.

"Are you hungry again?" she asked. "I just set Kuge-
san's dinner out."

"No, but thanks."

Kiyo found his father alone in the dining room, drinking beer and eating miso chicken at the long American-
style table. He feared his dad's reaction, but he had to
know. Taking a deep breath, he sat down across from him.

"Dad?"

Kichiro, still chewing, set his chopsticks down and
grunted.

"I just saw Hosokawa Sensei. He agrees with the researchers. There's no doubt that the heavy metals came
from Chisso's wastewater."

His father gulped some beer, and ate another bite of
chicken. He didn't look upset. Perhaps the alcohol had relaxed him, or maybe he was simply too tired to show anger.
He leaned back in his plush, upholstered chair said in an
even, patient tone, "The researchers are wrong. At the end
of World War II, the Imperial Navy dumped a lot of explosives in a bay south of here. Kumikoma Takeji, the managing director of Japan Chemical Industry Association, has
already published an article proving that those explosives
contain toxic substances. Over the last thirteen years, the
casings have obviously corroded, and toxic contents leaked
into the water. So, yes, the researchers found heavy metal
there, but we didn't dump it. You see?"

Kiyo mulled that over. "But if the navy dumped the
explosives south of Minamata, how did the heavy metal
end up farther north, near Chisso's wastewater pipes?"

"Oh, they're everywhere in the Bay now." His father
waved a hand dismissively. "So around our pipes as well.
The researchers just happened to take samples on a day

the toxins gravitated there. The tides move around all the time; that's why things wash up on the beach. And you know Chisso wouldn't intentionally harm the community. We built a hospital, giving free medical care for the city."

He picked up his chopsticks again. Clearly the conversation was over.

Kiyo wasn't convinced that sea-currents were somehow moving toxins from the explosives to the discharge pipe. But he had also no proof they were not. And since there were conflicting theories, there was only one way to solve the twin mysteries of what, and who, was causing the Strange Disease. The university's researchers had to pinpoint the definitive cause. And soon.

FOURTEEN

Runaway Neighbor

School over for the day, Yuki was on the bus and headed home. Sitting alone in the back, she could already envision what she intended to draw as soon as she got home: a luminous forest hugging the beach.

After she got off at her stop, walking down the road she ran into Nishio Hachiko, a neighbor who'd grown up a few houses away. It was already mid-January, but Yuki said hello, and wished her a happy New Year.

Hachiko, slender and tall, had clipped her short, glossy black hair behind her ears with bobby pins. Her worn-out coat looked frayed at the cuffs and the collar; a yellow stain marred the bodice of its faded lavender wool. She'd worn it for nearly a decade now. The sides of her shoes bulged as if her little toes might burst through the worn leather at any moment. Her skin always looked tanned, even in the middle of the winter.

But it was her eyes that struck Yuki as different: they seemed filled with sadness, or deep regret. At twenty, she had married a fisherman widower fifteen years older, with two sons. Perhaps she was unhappy now?

Eyeing the half-full furoshiki the young woman carried, Yuki asked, "Hello, Hachiko-san. Are you going on a trip?"

The neighbor gave her a startled look, then tightened her mouth as if resolved about something. "We'd only been married a year when my husband got the Strange Disease. The next year, both boys also got it. I've been taking care of all of them the past three years. And we have so little money."

Having lost her uncle, Yuki felt great sympathy for her childhood neighbor, whose circumstances were even more dire than her own family's. "I'm so sorry."

Hachiko looked defensive. "And that's why I'm running away."

Yuki's mouth fell open. "You're what?"

"Please, don't look at me that way! I know it's terrible, but I just can't stay." She bit her quivering lip as if to still it. "Kinoshi-kun can't walk. He's fifteen now; the Disease doesn't stop kids from growing. He's too big for me to carry to the outhouse, so he has to wear diapers. Daisuke-kun is smaller, but he also needs diapers. I have to change two boys bigger than me, and they're not even my kids."

Her face crumpled. She wiped tears away with a wrinkled, yellowed handkerchief. "I can't buy enough to feed the family with the tiny subsidy we get. I can't stand this life anymore! I have to leave."

As she stood listening, Yuki caught a whiff of soiled-diaper smell, and the malodorous unwashed scent of extreme poverty.

"My uncle died of the Disease two years ago. And with most sea life dead, there's nothing to fish for, but . . . you can't just leave. Who's going to take care of them?"

Hachiko shook her head slowly. "I've worked so hard, I feel old already. Look at my wrinkles." She pointed to lines etching her forehead. "I'm leaving with one set of extra clothes and a packed lunch. My other things are so tattered they're not worth taking." She lifted her furoshiki, its opposite corners tied together, to show Yuki. "I'll change my name and my past. Say I'm from somewhere else and get a job."

"What's going to happen to your family?"

"They're not my family!" She looked away. "I feel awful, but I'm still young. I can't give up my whole life taking care of them." She squeezed her eyes shut and swallowed hard. "I'm sorry, I really am." She turned away and rushed off, toward the bus stop.

"No, wait! Don't go."

But the weary young wife ran faster, as if fearful Yuki might chase and drag her back to the life she hated. She climbed on the bus, the doors shut, and it pulled away. Yuki went on her way, feeling crushing sadness for the family left behind.

At home she told her parents about Hachiko. "I want to make sure someone's taking care of the Nishios. I'll visit to make sure they're all right."

"You're a kind soul." Her mother gave a sad sigh. "I suppose we can't leave them all alone."

"Ask Nishio-san if another relative can take them in," her father suggested.

The Nishios lived on the other side of the village, three streets away. Their small house with warped siding, no larger than Yuki's, was dark and quiet. Old fishing nets hung from the walls of a tiny open shed next to the house, its floor choked with dried leaves and tall weeds.

Yuki knocked on the unpainted front door. "Hello! It's Akaji Yuki. May I come in?" She heard a faint sound, perhaps a yes, so she opened the door and stepped into the entryway.

Shoji tracks on the floor divided the house's only room, but the warped divider-frames leaned against the back wall. All the paper covering the sliding doors had long since ripped into shreds. Three figures in tattered coats were around the family's kotatsu. Two lay on the floor, legs in the pit. One slumped half-upright against the table. An overpowering stench of feces filled the cold room.

"Hello. I'm going to turn on the light." Yuki slipped off her clogs and stepped up from the entryway into the living room. Then pulled a cord dangling from the sole ceiling-light fixture in the middle of the room.

She sucked in a sharp breath at what its glow revealed.

The father sat up, braced by his long bony fingers. Despite sad eyes and hollow cheeks, he was still handsome. The two teenage sons stretched their mouths, attempting to smile at her. The plank floor they lay on surely had not been cleaned in months. Diapers bulged under their patched pants. Yuki sat on the floor next to the kotatsu. She nodded around at each one, and smiled, trying to act as if she didn't notice the grimy walls, or how the moon shone through a hole in the tiled roof.

"Nishio-san, I saw your wife today. Did she tell you she's leaving?"

The unshaven husband peered at her through long straggly hair. "No, but we watched her pack." His mouth moved well enough for her to understand him, at least. "She said sorry. And left some food." He blinked back tears.

"So at least you had dinner." Yuki glanced at the tiny kitchen. An unwashed pot and a few small cloth bags of food were scattered across a rough-hewn counter. A mouse was nibbling grains of rice spilled on the floor. "Your kotatsu must be cold by now."

"There's no charcoal. We just sit under the quilt," Mr. Nishio said.

"Oh no! Well, I can set up your beds. You might feel warmer under the futon."

"That would be good," the father said. "But first, could you help me to the toilet? It's behind the house."

Yuki helped him up. When he wrapped one thin arm over her shoulder, she had to hold her breath; he badly needed a bath.

He staggered more than walked, but together they tee-tered to the outhouse, where he struggled inside on his own.

Back at the house, she breathed shallowly through her mouth. Choking down the urge to vomit as she changed the boys' diapers and eased them down onto thin futons. Then went back to the outhouse to help the father return.

"Is there some relative I can call on to help you?" she said as she laid out his bed.

"I hate to ask, but . . . no choice. A sister in Yudo. They have a farm." He looked down at his motheaten socks and gulped in a sob. "This damned disease."

"Tell me her name. I'll go speak to her tomorrow."

In the morning Yuki again took care of the Nishios, then set out for Yudo, a village south of Tsukinoura. Walk-ing at a brisk pace, she could be there in less than an hour. She entertained herself on the way by thinking about Kiyo. How he didn't just laugh but guffawed with his whole be-ing. And how strong his thighs were from all the cycling. When they held hands, hers resting on top of his thighs under the kotatsu, the muscles felt rock hard. Even the sole pimple on his nose looked cute. She giggled, then spun in a circle, raising her arms to the cold sky.

"Kiyo-kun is wonderful!" she shouted. Fortunately, the road was deserted except for her.

Nishio's directions led her to a trim farmhouse a few minutes from the main road. Curious chickens clucked and pecked around her ankles as she knocked on its glass slid-ing door.

A woman with muscular-looking arms, clad in a plain white blouse and dusty blue work pants, opened it. "Yes?" She gazed at Yuki curiously.

"Are you Hideko-san? I'm Akaji Yuki from Tsukinoura." Yuki bowed politely. "Afraid I have bad news." She explained about the Nishios' situation.

Hideko howled, doubling over as if she'd been speared
in the belly.

Alarmed, Yuki reached out a hand. "I-I'm so sorry."

Hideko waved a hand to indicate she was all right,
then sat on the rough plank floor in front of the entryway.
"I knew this moment would come." Head in hands, she
took a few slow, deep breaths.

Yuki looked away, gazing out at tangerine trees loaded
with fruit, giving her a moment to recover.

At last Hideko sighed and pushed tear-damp hair away
from her face. "I saw them on Autumnal Equinox Day.
They were having a hard time, even then. We took food,
but . . . I didn't know things had gotten this bad. He never
should've married that girl."

She shook her head. "Ran away, did she? Traitor. Cow-
ard." She covered her face and keened again. "What am I
supposed to do? It's so busy here. We have three kids, and
barely get by ourselves. Look!"

She pointed through the open doorway.

The patched shoji screens were open, revealing three
rooms. Though easily twice the size of her home, this one
would now have to accommodate eight people. Yuki's
stomach growled at the scent of freshly cooked rice and
vinegary pickled plums. The large kitchen held many
crates filled with tangerines; it was harvest season.

"We don't have room for three more. Ohh ..." Hideko
moaned again. "Even if we take them in, who'll care for
them?" She shook her head. "No. I can't do it." She peered
up at Yuki hopefully. "You live in Tsukinoura. How old are
you?"

"Fifteen."

"Really? You seem so mature."

Yuki barked a laugh. She knew what the woman was about to ask.

"Can *you* take care of them? I'll help with food."

"We're fishers, but there's hardly anything left to catch. We have no money. I may have to quit school and go to work."

"So you can't help my brother?"

Yuki was fed up with the woman's whining. "It's your family! There's no choice. You must take care of them. How do you think your brother and his sons feel?"

"What about my family? How will they feel?"

"Shamed, if you don't show them you're someone who believes in duty. Who's loyal to family."

Hideko's shoulders sagged. She stared glumly out over the fields. At last she stood and stretched her back. "I guess you're right. I'll talk to my husband when he returns from the fields. We'll go get them today."

Yuki nodded. "That's the honorable thing to do."

Ever since the Strange Disease had struck, both victims and families suffered – physically, financially, emotionally. She felt sorry for the Nishios and wished them well. Grateful no one else in her own family had fallen ill.

FIFTEEN

Post-New Year's Surprise

Kiyo was cycling slowly home after visiting Yuki when he heard someone calling his name. He looked left and braked to a stop. "Hey, Masa-kun! Didn't notice I was passing your hotel."

His friend stood before a wide bamboo gate, where a large, carved-oak sign announced: THE MINAMATA HOTEL. "I hardly see you anymore," Masa complained.

"I'm at the hospital a lot," Kiyo said.

"I figured." Masa wore black-framed glasses; he'd learned a few months ago that he was nearsighted. His ironed white shirt looked crisp, as did a pair of new-looking blue jeans.

Kiyo was envious. "Your mom bought you jeans? Mine thinks they're too ugly."

"I bugged her for a month. A little stiff at first, but the more they're washed, the softer they get."

"Yeah? Maybe I'll get a pair, too."

"You should." Masa grinned and mimicked a high-fashion model, turning to show off his outfit.

Kiyo nodded. "Good looking."

"The hotel's full. You know ... April, cherry blossom viewing season."

Three months since my brothers were home for New Years, Kiyo thought. Seems like yesterday.

"My parents are too busy to even get home for dinner," Masa added. "I've been coming here to eat. Imagine how packed with tourists the city's going to be this summer."

"Good for business, though. Your parents must be happy."

"Yeah, the money's good, but they're always exhausted. Hey, had dinner? Come eat with me. I'm tired of just sitting with my sister."

"Sounds good."

After Kiyo called his mother to say he wouldn't be home for dinner, the friends sauntered down the traditional inn's long, gleaming sugi hallway. Enka music played softly from a radio at the front desk. Passing guests dressed in fine kimonos or tailored suits headed to the stairs, hotel staff trailing with luggage. Some, still a bit damp from hot baths, lounged in the lobby, wrapped in cotton kimonos the hotel provided. Maids in matching silk kimonos carried trays of steaming, covered food orders to individual rooms, delicious scents trailing in their wakes.

As they passed the banquet room, Kiyo heard his father's voice. He glanced at Masa. "My dad's here?"

"I guess. The mayor and councilmen came in, probably for dinner. Chisso hosts people like that here a lot. Sometimes your father, the Chisso president, or the vice-president too. You know we have the biggest banquet hall in the city, right? Come on, I'm starved!"

They entered a large guestroom through a shoji doorway and sat on a tatami floor so new the woven rush-grass was still green. The reeds so smooth Kiyo wanted to stroke them. A famous woodblock print, *The Great Wave off Kanagawa*, and drawings of classical kabuki theater actors hung from the walls.

How luxurious, even compared to his own home – much less Yuki's hovel, its rough old tatami-mat floor, the newspaper-covered shoji doors. He admired the way they just carried on, and still remained a happy family. More so than many with lots of money. He figured wealthy people could learn a lot from them.

A maid brought trays, setting them next to a vase of red and yellow roses on a low polished table. It faced a window overlooking a grove of bamboo trees around a pond stocked with orange and white koi. Lifting the lids Kiyo discovered steaming miso soup, tofu in mushroom sauce, a plate of pickled eggplants, and chicken tempura. The youkan – a sweet bean-paste dessert – exuded a mixed vinegary, sugary scent.

As they ate he joked with Masa, still wondering what his father was doing at the hotel. He often came home late, but Kiyo had always assumed he was working at the office.

"I'm going to run to the restroom," Kiyo said.

He found his way back to the banquet room. No one else was in the corridor, so he paused to listen. The large room was full of conversations. Along with his father's voice, once he thought he recognized a local politician's voice through the paper-covered doors.

"Those researchers expect us to shut down our city over a little heavy metal in the bay, Kuge-san," the man grumbled.

His father said, "Unconfirmed accusations against Chisso could still force us to close this plant and move. I'd hate to see that happen."

"Chisso is the reason Minamata's a thriving city," another man added. "Along with a few other corporations, also the reason Japan's climbing out from the deep hole we fell into after the War."

A pause, as others murmured agreement.

"We can't let a few sick fisher families, and speculation by a few academics, ruin all we've built," said a third voice. "This council must protect the people."

"That's right," said the politician. "By keeping businesses strong and jobs secure. That's what matters to the city's residents."

"I promise, Kuge-san, I'll make sure Chisso doesn't take the blame for this mess," said yet another voice.

"Thank you," Kichiro said. "But rest assured we're not the cause. The researchers have no proof we are discharging the heavy metal they believe causes the Strange Disease. We all know the navy dumped explosives after the War. Surely by now those must be releasing toxic chemicals."

Kiyo heard footsteps rounding the hallway corner and quickly walked on.

So local councilmen and Chisso were colluding to keep the company from taking the blame—"to protect the city" – even when proof of their culpability had been found. They were willing to sacrifice the victims because they were poor and lived outside the city. These men cared only about profits and jobs. Money for the urban people, money for themselves. Betraying everyone's trust.

His delicious dinner felt like a stone in his belly, now.

Until researchers produced conclusive proof Chisso was causing the Disease, there was nothing anyone – especially a teenager – could do to force the company to take responsibility. The specific metal must be officially identified, as well as the source. Then Kiyo knew his father, as head of wastewater management, would do the right thing. Unlike the other men at the banquet, he was not corrupt.

A recollection of Uncle Higano clawing helplessly at the air rose in Kiyo's mind. Along with agonized, ghostly shrieks from the victims of the Strange Disease. No, he wouldn't stop fighting for them. And the best way to do that was to help prove the cause of the Strange Disease.

SIXTEEN

Unhappy Birthday

Four months had passed since Kiyo had been in Kumamoto during the New Years holiday, making slides for the scientists. Yet he'd had no further word from them on new discoveries. He tried not to dwell on his disappointment by celebrating another birthday – two years from the first time he'd met Yuki. The luckiest day of his life.

In the dining room at home he made a wish and blew out all sixteen candles on his cake. His mother, Yanagiya the cook, and the chauffeur, Fukuzawa, all clapped. Akiyoshi Toshiko's jazz composition, "Toshiko's Piano," with guitarist Herb Ellis, bassist Ray Brown, and drummer J.D. Heard played in the living room.

"Omedetou!" Happy birthday, said Etsuko, and slid a slim box across the table toward him.

"Oh! Thanks, Mom."

As she'd taught, he carefully unwrapped it, neatly folding the fancy, patterned paper. Inside the thin rectangular gift box was a pair of thick leather gloves. "Wow, I can really use these." He slipped them on; inside they were lined with soft, warm wool.

"You're welcome. Your hands will stay warm now when you ride." She smiled, her carefully made-up lips an even deeper shade of red than usual. "And now, let's have some cake. Yanagiya-san?"

The cook sliced the thickly-frosted white cake and set the pieces on small plates.

"*Oishii!*" Delicious. Kiyo took another big bite. "Dad's probably hungry, and won't get home for hours. I'll take him a big slice."

"How thoughtful of you." Etsuko smiled.

"Yanagiya-san, can you wrap up some to go?" he asked.

"Of course." She went back into the kitchen.

"I'll drive you. It'll be faster." Fukuzawa jingled the keys in his pocket.

Even at seven in the evening, Chisso's front office was full of men still working at clacking adding machines and abacuses. His father's office door stood ajar. Kiyo saw him inside, at the desk, sleeves rolled up. His suit jacket was neatly placed on a hanger dangling from a brass hook. The peculiar, acrid odor of chemicals from the factory wafted in through the open window.

These days Kiyo rarely saw his father at all. He left home before Kiyo was up and came back after he was in bed. Now he noticed Dad's hair was thinning, as if to match the weight he'd been losing. The bags under his eyes drooped even more darkly; his face almost matched the color of the poisoned, dull-gray bay.

Kiyo silently nudged the door open and slipped in.

His father was clutching his head with both hands, reading a letter lying on his desk. His shoulders sagged. As the door creaked shut, he started, twisting abruptly to see who'd entered the room.

"Kiyo," he said, and quickly turned the paper face down. But not before Kiyo had already recognized the letterhead of the note's sender: The Ministry of Health and Welfare.

"What're you doing here?" his father snapped, flushing.

"I figured you hadn't had any dinner, so I brought you some birthday cake. You get home so late."

"Oh, that's right. Today's your birthday." He took a deep breath, and tried to smile. "But . . . well, you should always knock."

"Sorry. You seemed so busy reading." Kiyo set the wrapped slice of cake on the desk. "What does the Ministry of Health and Welfare want with Chisso?"

His father closed his eyes and rubbed his temples. "It's the Strange Disease. We correspond with the Ministry and keep them updated. We've been working with Professor Kiyoura of Tokyo Institute of Technology. He believes the level of mercury, one of the heavy metals the researchers identified, isn't significantly higher in Minamata Bay than in other waterways. Fish contaminated with organic mercury have been found elsewhere, yet no one in those areas has the Strange Disease. So obviously that's not the cause."

Kiyo nodded. "If organic mercury was the sole cause, people in other places would certainly have it, too."

"That's right. And Professor Tokita of Toho University reported that toxic amine concentration is the highest in fish that's begun to spoil. Fishers can only afford to eat leftovers, so they're ingesting more toxic amines than the rest of us."

"What's an amine?"

Kichiro cocked his head. "Um, some kind of chemical. Anyhow, that's why they get sick and we don't. So you see, Chisso may discharge chemicals into the Bay, but it isn't causing the Disease." But he sagged in his chair, looking suddenly as if he'd aged ten years. "People shouldn't panic when nothing's certain, so don't speculate until we know for sure."

"I suppose." Then Kiyo added, "Why does Chisso take government officials and journalists out to dinner?"

His father's head snapped back up. "What do you know about that?"

"I was with Masa at The Minamata Hotel last month and saw you there with some city councilmen."

Kichiro huffed, "Well, we need a good relationship with the city. Chisso simply thanks those in charge. As an important part of Minamata, we've always worked with officials and the press, doing what we can to help." He picked up the letter on his desk again. "Now, I'm very busy. You should go home."

Kiyo went to the door, then turned back to face Kichiro. "Thanks for the gift," he said, though he felt sure his father probably had no idea what Mom had given him.

He was about to let the door close when a young man in a white shirt and dark blue tie hustled into Dad's office.

"There's someone out front asking for you," the employee said.

His father groaned and dropped the letter again.

"Should I send him away?"

"No, no." Kichiro heaved up from his chair, tugging up the waist of trousers that now hung loosely from his hips. He shrugged on his suit jacket, and followed the employee.

Kiyo trailed behind them.

The man waiting at the entrance wore casual khaki slacks and a blue shirt rolled up to the elbows, no tie or coat.

"Yes?" Kichiro frowned.

The visitor bowed. "Sorry to bother you. I'm Noguchi Tetsu, a researcher at Kyushu University in Kagoshima City. I've been studying Minamata Disease." Noguchi offered his business card with both hands and bowed again.

Kichiro accepted the card with only one hand, barely glancing at it. Kiyo winced at his father's rudeness. His face burned with embarrassment for the researcher, whose dignity and expertise had been not just ignored, but scorned.

"Sorry you came all this way, but I know nothing about that." Dad turned away.

Noguchi lightly touched Kichiro's arm. "Please, Kuge-san. It's important."

His father pulled his arm away, and glared at the man, who rushed on. "We must ascertain what's causing the Disease. Can you tell me all the products this factory produces, and the methods?"

"How would I know? That's not my department."

"But you're the head of waste disposal."

"Yes, but I'm not a chemist. Can't help you." Kichiro turned and hurried off. When the researcher started after him, the young employee who'd fetched Kiyo's father stepped in his way, frowning.

Kiyo caught up with his father as he reentered the office. "But you know all the things Chisso makes. Why didn't you tell him?"

Kichiro pivoted, face tight with impatience. "We make plastic products. Plastic is the future. And we compete with other chemical factories around the world, so it's crucial to keep our formulas secret. I'm not about to tell that idiot, or anyone else, our methods!"

"I see," said Kiyo. And it kind of made sense. But what if knowing those details could speed up the discovery of the cause, and a cure? That would save lives. He wanted to make sure the researchers had all the information they needed in order to succeed.

By the time Fukuzawa dropped Kiyo at home, the cook had gone for the day. His father's dinner plate sat on the dining table, protected from flies under a small mesh tent. Kiyo first changed into a pair of new blue jeans, still stiff after only two washings. Then he went to the kitchen, wrapped the rest of his birthday cake and put it in the basket of his bicycle, along with a birthday gift for Yuki.

By the time he reached her village, pink and orange stripes coloring the sky had faded. Darkness was setting in. He turned the corner to her house and braked.

"Hello!" he called, seeing Nobuyuki outside gripping a broom. But as her father tried to swing it to sweep a pile of leaves away from the front of their house, he swayed, stumbled, and missed them entirely.

No. Kiyo thought. *Not him, too.*

Her father was sick, just like her uncle. Did she know?

A man walking by glanced at Nobuyuki and made a disgusted face. "Deadbeat. Why don't you sober up?"

Nobuyuki hung his head.

Kiyo wanted to throttle the jerk. "He's not drunk," he shouted. Though wouldn't that have been preferable? Instead he had contracted what many villagers still called the Strange Disease, though people in the city now called it 'Minamata Disease.'

Stomach in knots, Kiyo rolled his bike up to the house.

Nobuyuki smiled. "Come in, come in. Yuki-chan, Kiyo-kun is here!" Turning back, he said, "Busy drawing, as usual."

Just then she bounded out. "Hi! So you did come for our birthdays." The glittering brooch reflected the last rays of sunset, and seemed to light up her beautiful face.

He smiled at her as he parked the bike. She patted its leather seat and sighed. "I'd sure love to learn how to ride this someday."

"I'll teach you." He lifted his parcels from the basket. "But first, some birthday cake and watercolor paint."

She clapped. "How wonderful! I've never tasted cake. I hear it's very good." She lowered her voice. "And, thank you for the paint."

"How can an artist work without the proper tools?"

She gave an embarrassed laugh. "With pencil, but I really want to use watercolors again." She turned toward her mother. "Mom, Kiyo-kun brought *cake!*"

Nobuyuki leaned the broom against the house and followed Yuki and Kiyo in. He walked unsteadily, but Kiyo noticed neither his daughter nor his wife offered assistance. So Kiyo didn't either.

Kazuko got out plates and cut four equal pieces. The winter kotatsu had been put away, its hole covered. The low table was back, and she served everyone there. The only uncracked plate, Kiyo noticed, was his.

"Wait," he said. Everyone watched as he drew out a small candle from his shirt pocket and stuck it into Yuki's slice. "Do you have a match?"

Kazuko pulled a box of kitchen matches from her apron pocket. Kiyo lit the candle, which left behind a pungent whiff of sulfur. "Yuki-chan," he said, "make a wish. Don't tell anyone what it is. Then blow out the candle."

She gazed at the dancing flame, expression serious, almost solemn. Closed her eyes a few moments. Then opened them and blew out the flame in one forceful gust.

"Yes!" Kiyo clapped. "You'll get your wish."

"I hope so." A small furrow remained between her eyebrows.

He guessed she'd wished for Nobuyuki to recover and be healthy again. To once more be the same strong, hearty fisherman.

Still, her face lit up with a grin after she took her first bite of the white-frosted cake. "Umm. *Oishii!*" Delicious.

Kiyo smiled back. But he'd noticed how thin everyone looked. "You know, I already had a big slice at home." He pushed his plate toward the middle of the table. "I'm too full to eat another."

Nubuyuki had yet to take a bite. At last he picked up both chopsticks and, holding them like a knife, stabbed at his cake. A small piece flew off the plate onto the table. He scowled deeply; a battle-weary warrior already sick of losing. Without a word Kazuko scooped the stray bite up and put it back on the plate.

Kiyo looked away, pretending he hadn't witnessed the struggle, to avoid embarrassing a proud man any further.

"Hey! Let's eat this with our hands." Yuki picked up the rest of her slice and nibbled at one edge. "It's too crumbly to eat with chopsticks anyhow."

"I bet Americans eat it like that, anyhow," Kiyo agreed.

She wedged her father's piece into his right palm. He successfully ferried it to his mouth and took a bite from the edge. "Mmm. Good!" He chewed slowly, but soon ate more.

Seeing his familiar symptoms reminded Kiyo to warn the family again. "Remember after I went to Kumamoto last month, I told you they still believe heavy metals in the Bay water causes Minamata Disease?"

"Whatever 'heavy metal' is," Nobuyuki muttered.

Kiyo forged on. "Well, there's a theory that it's leaking from old explosives the navy dumped after the War."

"The day we lost was a sad one," Kazuko said. "Everyone had already sacrificed so much. Not only did we not have enough to eat – "

"One potato, if you were lucky." Nobuyuki clenched a fist on the tabletop.

"We ate dandelions and grass, more often." Kazuko stared at the tabletop, wiping tears away with the back of one hand. "We all felt so ashamed we'd lost. I hope I live to see the day we're leading the world again."

Nobuyuki slapped the table weakly. "I want Japan to be a great nation."

"Yes." Yuki nodded.

No one had survived the war unwounded – physically, emotionally, mentally, or spiritually. Kiyo was nodding at all they'd said, when he noticed a new, pronounced curve beneath Kazuko's loose shirt. Leaning toward Yuki, he whispered, "Are you going to be an *oneichan*?"

"Yes, in a few months I'll be an older sister. And also a babysitter!"

Her mother smiled and blushed.

But Kiyo felt torn. A new baby was also considered to be good news, and yet . . . how would a family already struggling to put food on the table feed another child as well?

As the others were eating, Kiyo noticed a drawing lying on the floor in one corner. The room was small enough that he could lean back and study it. One of Yuki's pictures, of course. But his smile faltered when he saw what it represented: a smiling family sitting around a table piled high with seafood and vegetables, with peaches for dessert. He thought of his own bountiful, extravagant household, and felt ashamed.

"Thank you, Kiyo-kun. Yes, the cake is delicious." Kazuko was chewing and talking simultaneously, not covering her mouth with one hand. His own parents would've been appalled, but he didn't care. He pushed back from the table and stretched out his legs, feeling more comfortable here than he had at home.

"Want a bike-riding lesson now, Yuki-chan?"

"Yes!"

Outside in the small front yard, he taught her the basics. "Grip the handlebars on each side here, like this. To slow down or stop, squeeze this brake lever. Point the wheel straight and hold it steady as you pedal. Don't let it wobble. I'll hold the back of the seat until you get going."

She straddled the bike, hopped on, and put her feet on the pedals and started off. Kiyo let go a few moments later. She rolled about ten feet before the front wheel swung wildly. The bike toppled sideways.

He hooted with laughter. "Sorry, but . . . that was so funny." He added, "You're not hurt, are you?"

She scowled up from the grass. "No."

"All right then." He pulled the bicycle upright. "I got the hang of it fast, but of course I'm a boy." Actually, that was not true. Just an exaggeration calculated to make her determined to master cycling.

"A boy," she muttered. "So what." She jerked the bike from his hands and without even dusting off her clothes, remounted and took off. The bicycle swerved crazily, but this time she made it much farther before crashing into a sumac bush.

Before he could ask again if she was okay, Yuki picked the bike up and rode farther down the lane. At first still weaving wildly, correcting three times until it finally rolled forward in a straight path.

Then he noticed something alarming. She was riding right toward the cliff. "Wait!" He ran and finally caught up, panting.

"This is so much fun!" Her cheeks were red, her eyes wide with excitement. She flung her arms wide to encompass the panoramic view of the Bay. "See? I'm as good as any boy on his first ride."

"I was worried you might not stop in time, and go over the cliff."

"Like Jiro." Her jubilance suddenly faded. "I wish Dad didn't have the Strange Disease. His hands and feet are numb. He can't walk properly. He can't do much anymore, at all. Just stays home." Her voice cracked and she looked away. "Mom got a job as a maid so I can help him eat and dress. He hates it."

"I'm so sorry." He wondered whether Kazuko's job paid enough to support the family. But he couldn't bring himself to ask such a frightening question.

A surge of overwhelming tenderness gripped him. He took her hands in his. Every time they touched he could swear an electric charge zapped him. He pushed down a great desire to kiss her, not wanting to embarrass her in public. But this constant longing couldn't be satisfied by holding her hand or with a kiss or two. Instead his desire only increased; his groin ached almost painfully.

Breathe, breathe, breathe, he told himself.

It was going to take discipline to keep himself in check. He didn't really want to go, but night was setting in. And the longer they stood so close, holding hands, the more likely he might end up embarrassing himself.

"I'd better head home." He reluctantly let go of her hand and took hold of the bike again. "Tell your parents I said good-bye!"

And he was off down the road, pedaling like mad to forget the ache he still felt, from his growing desire for Yuki.

SEVENTEEN

New Places to Pollute

That summer was the hottest Kiyo could remember. When he and Yuki had turned sixteen two months earlier, the weather had still been cool. But it quickly turned warmer until, by mid-July it was sweltering. Riding a bike anywhere in the heat and humidity meant sweating buckets. Still it was his only mode of transportation, so now he was slowly pedaling to the hospital.

He'd read a puzzling article in the newspaper the evening before, and wanted to ask Hosokawa Sensei's opinion about it. He reached the hospital, parked his bike in the rack out front, and was trotting up the steps when he heard a meow. He stopped to listen. Yes, definitely the mewing of several cats. Certainly strays roamed the city, but this sounded like many cats together. That was odd.

He started to follow the sound out of curiosity, then recalled his original mission and hurried up the front steps instead.

The rotating fan atop Hosokawa Sensei's filing cabinet spun and whirled, sending out streams of humid air. Perspiration beaded on his forehead and glittered on his nose. Flies buzzed, too, and the doctor swatted at them fruitlessly, now and then.

"Hi, Sensei." Kiyo dipped his head.

"Hello, Kiyo-kun. It's so hot today." Dr. Hosokawa mopped his face with a handkerchief.

Kiyo pulled his own out to dry the sweat running down his temples. "Hotter every day." Just then a faint meow drifted in through the open window. "And I keep hearing cats."

"You're not imagining it. I'm conducting a new experiment." The doctor rose. "Come with me and see. I gathered thirty stray cats for a sample population."

In back, three sides of the hospital building surrounded a small courtyard. An eight-foot tall wire fence on the open side now enclosed it. And inside that, orange, black, white, tiger-striped, calico, tuxedo patterned, long- and short-haired cats padded around. Some hissing or batting at each other, others meowing or grooming themselves. A few were drinking from of a large shallow water bowl. A bobtailed gray cat suddenly sprang up as if to scale the fence, but fell short a few inches from the top and fell back, landing nimbly on its feet.

Yuki would love to hold and pet them, Kiyo thought. She'd missed Jiro so badly, ever since he'd plunged into the Bay. She drew pictures of him, documenting his life from the time he was a kitten up to his last agony-filled day. Maybe he could take her one of these cats for a pet.

But no ... her family couldn't afford to feed it.

"That one keeps trying to get out," Sensei said.

"Why are they in there?" Kiyo knelt next to the fence for a closer look.

"You've heard people talk about 'the dancing cats'?"

"Yes. I've also seen them." His belly felt like it was filled with ice whenever he recalled the first time: the white cat he hadn't managed to save from drowning.

"Those symptoms present much like the ones patients with Minamata Disease have," Hosokawa Sensei said. "I believe cats contract the same disease. So I'm going to divide this cage into three sections and put a third of the cats in each. I'm giving wastewater from Chisso's factory to the first group, fish and shellfish from the Bay to the second, and blue mussels from the Bay to the third, to see what happens."

"If they show Strange Disease symptoms, will that prove the cause?"

"We'll see which symptoms the various groups exhibit. More importantly, if they do grow ill, it will prove sea life is being poisoned by something in the Bay. The poison then remains in the fish and shell fish, and causes the Disease in anyone who consumes it."

Kiyo shook his head admiringly. "So logical. Stray cats survive on leftover fish and octopus. Then they get sick like people, especially the fishers and their families. The poison is affecting both animals and human beings."

He slapped a mosquito biting his arm. A red smear replaced the annoying bug. "So, how can I help?"

"Well, you can feed the cats."

"I'll come every day," Kiyo promised.

When a lanky young cat with tan fur rubbed against the fence next to him, Kiyo stuck three fingers through the wire and scratched its side. Its fur was soft and silky. He smiled when the cat purred.

"Let's go inside." The doctor wiped his face with his now-limp kerchief. "I need some water."

Even with ceiling fans whirling at top speed, the air grew hotter as they climbed the steps and went back inside. In the waiting room, patients slumped on benches waving paddle fans before their sweating faces.

Inside his office, Hosokawa Sensei handed Kiyo a glass and they shared a pitcher of water. The doctor turned the fan back on and stood in front of it. "That's better." After a few moments, he sat at the desk and gave Kiyo a turn at the fan. "I do have news. More has happened to make me wonder."

Kiyo waited, but the sensei merely drank more water.

"Like what?" he finally asked.

Dr. Hosokawa picked up a pencil and tapped it on the desktop. "Ten months ago, the company switched from discharging its water into Hyakken Harbor, which they'd been doing for over forty years, to releasing it into the Minamata River."

Kiyo lowered the glass slowly. Hosokawa Sensei was about to say something important.

"This worried me. I asked the company president to stop discharging there, but he refused. Soon fish began dying at the mouth of the river. And now new victims are appearing in fishing villages from the coast of Shiranui Sea."

Kiyo nodded. "Where the Minamata River meets the Shiranui Sea."

"Have you been around there lately?" He didn't wait for Kiyo to answer. "The stink of rotting fish and shellfish mixed with fumes from the factory waste is so noxious, it makes one ill simply to breathe there." He shook his head.

"That means the wastewater *must* be causing the Disease."

"Sure looks like it." The doctor looked wistful. "Hachiman Beach at the mouth of the River used to be a lovely vacation spot. We dug up clams and shellfish, filling our bamboo baskets. I remember soft, white sand beaches next to the blue-green pine groves. Families on holiday thronged there. But now . . . . " He shook his head.

"Is the wastewater still being dumped into the river?"

"I'm afraid so."

Kiyo scowled. "Why do they keep doing it?"

"Perhaps the executives truly believe the Disease isn't their fault. The company keeps proposing other possible causes."

Kiyo recalled his father's theory. "Like the explosives the navy dumped in the Bay after the War."

"Yes."

Then he remembered the question he'd come to ask. "I read in the newspaper that the Ministry of Health and

Welfare reported the cause of the Disease as still unknown. But the researchers from Kumamoto University did determine organic methylmercury is the cause."

The doctor refilled his glass. "The researchers feel
sure of their findings, yes. The puzzling thing is,
they've only found *inorganic* mercury in the Bay. The
inorganic mercury can't convert to organic mercury.
That's why the Ministry isn't convinced the cause is
organic methylmercury. Assuming the university people are correct, and it is the culprit, that begs the question: where is it coming from if not the factory? And
why hasn't organic mercury been found in the Bay's
waters?"

"Dad said Chisso, like all chemical plants, only re-
leases inorganic mercury, along with some other heavy
metals. But there're no other incidents of the Strange
Disease where other chemical factories are located."

Sensei gulped down another glass of water. "Yes,
and that confuses the issue even more."

Kiyo recalled the letter from the Ministry of Health
and Welfare he'd seen on his father's desk. He wanted
to think Dad was an honest man. But he was only one
man. Could someone else at Chisso be using their power, as a higher-up in one of Japan's biggest companies,
to influence local government and media? Making
them believe the company had nothing to do with the
Disease?

Clearly at this point his father alone couldn't solve
the problem. Not without proof so conclusive even the
president of Chisso couldn't deny it. And then, of
course, Dad would do what was right.

EIGHTEEN

The Cost of Anger

The temperature kept rising as summer advanced into August. Even with the cottage's front and side doors open, sweat coated Yuki's body. The humid heat on this morning made her feel as if she was strangling. And it was only eight in the morning.

As she spooned rice and miso porridge into her father's mouth, he suddenly slapped the floor with one palm. The spoonful of breakfast missed the mark and dribbled down his chin. She wiped his face clean with a towel.

Kazuko lowered her spoon. "What's wrong?" She listened attentively to her husband's slurred, labored reply. "You want to . . . go somewhere?"

Suddenly, Yuki knew. "The fisher's march!"

Dad nodded and slapped the floor again.

The Minamata Fishermen's Cooperative, made up of fishers around the Bay, was now convinced the Chisso factory's toxic waste was killing the sea life they depended on.

Since opening in 1908 as a fertilizer producer, Chisso had paid the fishery cooperative small amounts of "sympathy money" – once in 1926 and once in 1943 – for polluting the Bay with wastewater and damaging the fishing. And now, over the last few years, catches had declined again, by a whopping ninety percent. But when the Cooperative asked for compensation, this time Chisso had refused to take responsibility, or to pay the fishers, claiming it was not their fault. So the area fishers were marching today to protest.

Kazuko looked worried. "Do you think that's wise?"

Yuki wasn't sure whether her mother didn't want him to go because of the difficulty walking, or because of what could happen when a bunch of angry men banded together to protest.

Dad snarled and slammed his hand on the table. Their bowls jumped. Yuki caught one teetering near the edge.

"What?" Kazuko asked her husband.

"Oh." Yuki looked at her father. "Are you saying we won't have enough to eat?"

"For the winter. He's right." Her mother nodded. "My job pays so little. We're barely scraping by with vegetables from the garden and eggs from the hens right now. But once cold weather comes . . . ."

A worry-worm slithered up Yuki's back. "I'll take you, Dad. I'm mad, too." School was out now for summer, so she could do it. But how could she even return to school in the fall if their food ran out?

Nobuyuki struggled to rise. Kazuko shook her head at Yuki, but said nothing else to dissuade them.

"I'll pack us a lunch," Yuki said. Her father nodded and sat back down.

The first bus into the city had already left, so that gave her enough time to get ready and get her father to the stop before the second one arrived. When they got on, the next bus was only half full.

"Most marchers must've taken the first bus," she told Nobuyuki, who nodded.

All the windows were down, and a welcome breeze ruffled her hair, which she'd recently cut short. They passed tourists in bathing suits basking on the white sand or sitting under beach umbrellas eating snow cones and popsicles. Others in town were strolling past the shops, laughing and chatting, as if unaware of the dying Bay.

Close to the city she spotted a familiar bicycle headed toward their village. She stuck her head out the window and yelled, "Kiyo-kun! Kiyo-kun!"

He stopped and looked up as she waved at him. "Where are you going?"

"To the fisher's march."

"I'll meet you there," he shouted back, and turned around.

She ducked back inside, smiling. Thinking about him always made her pulse beat faster. Now, unexpectedly, she'd be seeing him again today.

By the time she was helping her dad descend the bus steps, Kiyo had caught up. In Minamata's city center, where the march would set off from, several hundred demonstrators milled around, holding up white placards and banners, or sitting on benches and curbs, waving paddle fans to cool themselves. The bold black lettering on the many protest-signs demanded Chisso pay for killing fish in the Bay.

"Hi, Yuki-chan. Good morning, Akaji-san." Kiyo crammed his bike into one of the streetside racks, along with perhaps a hundred other bicycles. "I was coming to see you." He smiled and swiped his face with a handkerchief. "Boy, it's already hot."

Dad grunted in agreement.

"I heard the Cooperative asked Chisso for 100 million yen," Kiyo said.

"Yes, but that amount will be divided between three-hundred fisher families," Yuki said.

She understood her father's next words, and interpreted for Kiyo: "Won't feed us very long."

He nodded. "No, I guess not. So you're marching, Akaji-san?"

Nobuyuki nodded.

"The route's half a mile long." Kiyo glanced at Yuki.

"You can make it, can't you, Dad?" she asked.

He grunted, and seemed to nod.

A few minutes later the demonstrators started marching toward the factory, holding signs high and chanting, "Chisso destroyed our fishing!"

Pedestrians stopped to gawk. Some shook their heads, or made revolted faces and shouted, "Go home! You're a nuisance!" or "Stop making trouble."

"Tourists will quit coming," called a diminutive woman from a bakery take-out window.

A man stepped out of a pickle-making shop right to the edge of the street as the protesters passed. A long white apron covered his white undershirt and shorts. He smelled strongly of vinegar and sesame oil, shaking a fist at them as he yelled, "You're nothing but troublemakers!"

Yuki and Kiyo walked on either side of Nobuyuki, to support him in case he stumbled. The trio moved slowly, out of necessity. Still, every dozen steps or so, one of them had to grab an arm to stabilize him. The late-morning sun baked the road under their feet, sending heat up in waves.

A woman wearing a faded housedress was sprinkling water from a bucket with a ladle onto one residential side street to keep the dust down. Yuki paused and drew the water bottle from her bag. They all stopped to drink, falling further behind the main group of protesters, which was already blocks ahead.

At last they approached the factory, its tall chimneys belching steely-gray smoke. Her nostrils flared at the vile chemical stench. Marchers crowded in front of the main office entrance, waving signs and shouting at a small group of company suits in the courtyard there.

"What's going on?" Kiyo asked a tall young man in a white undershirt, who jabbed a sign in the air as he chanted.

"Chisso tycoons refuse to admit they're at fault. They claim they're not responsible for the fish-kill. They only offered a sympathy payment of three million yen. Bastards! Our leaders are going to talk to them now."

One demonstrator screamed, "Destroy the Bay, you pay!"

Other men joined in. "That's right! You pay!"

Dad mumbled, "Company bastards."

Just then, a dark object plummeted down, striking the head of a man who was in front of Yuki. The black thing dropped to the pavement: a dead crow. The man screamed and brushed at his hair. People stepped back, creating a large circle around him.

"Another dead crow." Kiyo said. "Birds are dying, like the cats."

A man next to him sneered, "Chisso's not satisfied killing us and the Bay. It murders animals who eat from the sea, too. Soon we'll have no more birds."

The man who'd been clobbered by the bird brushed a few black feathers off his shirt and gasped, "Am I bleeding?" He ducked his head so those around him could check.

"Oh yeah," said another man, slapping the fellow's head lightly. "Just as ugly as before the bird hit you."

Everyone around him guffawed.

Yuki and Kiyo took advantage of the opening created by the dead bird kerfluffle, helping Nobuyuki stumble up closer to the front. More marchers quickly filled in the space behind them. And as the sun beat down on the demonstrators, a reek of sour sweat rose to join the factory's chemical stench.

A woman on the front line yelled back, "Hey! They're gonna raise the payment."

A man flapped a hand at her. "Shh!"

"Someone just came out," said the tall young man waiting next to them.

A man returning to the crowd from the front entrance shouted, "Thirteen million yen!"

"That's all?" The young man with the placard spat, as if he'd tasted rotten fish. "They can't treat us this way!"

"That's right!" another fisherman shouted.

Soon more people were cursing and shouting in rage. A whole mob of angry faces. Yuki decided she'd draw their twisted, anguished features when she got home, to re- member the day.

Just then, without warning, the crowd surged forward. Yuki, her father, and Kiyo were swept along with the wave of sweating bodies.

"Dad!" Yuki tried to grab him, but he was pushed from behind by the crowd, and fell. Kiyo stood over him, flinging out both arms out to prevent anyone from stepping on No- buyuki. Then he was knocked down too. Yuki bent to help them both up and her bare knee touched the scorching as- phalt.

"Ah, hot!" she screamed. And with a superhuman effort she yanked her father to his feet, hoping he wasn't badly burned.

Kiyo scrambled up too. "Are you both all right?"

"I'm okay. Are you hurt anywhere, Dad?" She checked him over. "Your elbows are scraped and bleeding, but the asphalt didn't burn your hands, at least."

Around them, men were now throwing rocks and pro- test signs at the factory's windows. A sharp shattering of glass echoed from the concrete buildings. Fishers shouted more demands. Angry marchers waved fists at the few Chisso employees in the courtyard as they scurried back inside to cower against the far wall of the front office. Some ran down an alley, away from the uprising.

The sea of men frantic for money to feed hungry wives and children pushed against the front doors, trying to force their way in.

The wailing of sirens drew closer. Yuki turned and saw at least a half-dozen black-and-white police cars turning into the parking lot.

"Oh, no," she said. "We have enough trouble without being arrested."

Kiyo chewed on his lower lip. "Dad would kill me if I get caught by the police."

The cruisers screeched to a stop, surrounding some of the fishermen. Police officers in black uniforms and hats, shiny badges flashing, climbed out. One spoke to the crowd through a cone-shaped loudspeaker. "*Everyone leave, now! Or we'll arrest you!*"

Glaring at the protesters, the other officers lined up, smacking their palms with thick black billy-clubs.

"Let's get out of here," Kiyo whispered.

They shouldered their way between rioters, sometimes leading, sometimes dragging or lifting Nobuyuki, trying to cut away.

As they passed, other fishermen lowered their signs, grumbling, "Damn police," and "I don't want to get beat up," and "Chisso has everyone on their side." The crowd was slowly, grudgingly shifting away from the Chisso office building.

Someone trod hard on Yuki's toes; she grimaced and kept walking. A dipping sign struck her head. The demonstrator carrying it didn't seem to notice; he was too intent on escaping the police. Nobuyuki stumbled repeatedly, but they kept going. Police officers jabbed nightsticks into the backs of any protesters moving too slowly.

"Come on, we have to move a little faster," Yuki urged. How could she explain to her mother if Dad got hurt?

After what seemed a nightmarishly-long trek they reached the bus stop and collapsed on its bench.

"Thirteen million!" Yuki's father kept mumbling, venom in his tone as he pounded one thigh. "Chisso the criminals!"

"It should be a lot more," Kiyo agreed.

Yuki leaned close to Kiyo's ear and whispered, "I'm sorry. He doesn't mean it's your father's fault."

Kiyo shook his head. "It's all right. Who could blame him for being mad? Practically everything in the Bay is dead. And Chisso, well . . . ." He trailed off, but she understood the unsaid words.

Chisso doesn't care.

Three weeks later, Nakamura Todomu, Minamata City's mayor, announced an agreement he'd mediated between Chisso and the Fishing Cooperative: a 15 million yen fund to aid the recovery of fishing, plus 325 yen for each of the 300 affected fisher families.

"At least we can buy food for a while." Kazuko hung her head; they'd all been hoping for more. "The monthly aid from the prefecture helps, and I'll keep growing the garden as late in the season as possible."

Dad mumbled angrily, "Damned company!"

"You're right, Nobuyuki-kun," Kazuko said. "They destroyed our way of life, our income, and our food source. Yet that's all we get. The crooked mayor must be in bed with Chisso. The Cooperative only accepted this measly amount because a pittance was at least better than nothing. Three-hundred twenty-five yen . . . unbelievable. It should've been a hundred times that."

"They're getting off way too easy," Yuki agreed.

How would they survive after the payment was spent and a new baby arrived? Anxiety swirled in her gut more and more these days; she felt almost too sick to eat anything, anymore.

NINETEEN

Snubbed

Six months after the fishers' demonstration, Kiyo rose early on a November Sunday feeling restless. The clanging of pots from the kitchen meant breakfast was an hour away. He wanted to visit Yuki, but no one welcomed a drop-in visit at dawn.

So, he pedaled to the Bay through morning fog, the brisk, icy air stinging his cheeks. The city was quiet; only a few lights burned here and there in windows. To ignore the biting cold he tried to think of the discomfort as simply feeling alive. Minamata Disease victims would be thrilled to be outside, alive again, riding a bike. A little slap on the face from Old Man Winter was nothing. But he did mind the lingering stench of dead sea creatures, where there'd once been the briny scent of a living ocean.

The sky was lightening to the east. Sun like a large orange plate was rising above the houses, casting rosy light over the Bay's lifting mist. He noticed movement on the water and looked again.

One rarely saw any vessels out in the harbor now, at Chisso's wastewater dumping site. Yet there it was: a small boat gently bobbing on the ripples between several long piers. Dozens of fishing boats used to launch daily from that place. Now only a few remained, tethered to the docks. A couple years back, fishermen would be out calling greetings and good-natured insults at one another as they set out for the day. Those boats were all dry-docked now, or had been sold.

So he was surprised when a man on the skiff threw a bucket into the water, paying out the attached line until it went slack – the pail hitting bottom. Then he hauled it up and dumped what looked like sludge into a large recepta-cle. As he bent over the container, the end of the blue scarf around his neck loosened and slithered into the pail. The guy jerked it out, shook it off, and wound the rest of the scarf more tightly around his neck.

Still puzzled, Kiyo watched him gather more mud. At least until the sun began to warm his back, and his stom-ach growled ferociously to be fed. Yanagiya would have breakfast ready by now, so he headed home.

The scents of freshly-steamed rice and grilled vegeta-bles made him glad he'd returned. He stretched out his back and shook his arms and wrists to loosen up. They were stiff after being locked so long over the handlebars.

Dad, dressed in a thickly-padded robe, was already eating. Kiyo took a seat. His father hadn't shaved yet. The gray stubble on his face and wrinkled neck made him look much older. Mom wasn't around.

Probably still making herself beautiful, Kiyo thought. She always comes to the table all dressed and made up.

When the cook brought his plate he exclaimed, "Smells great!"

Yanagiya gave a pleased smile before retreating to the kitchen.

Still chilled from the cold ride, he cupped his hands around the miso soup bowl. Ah, the heat felt good.

"I was out on the Bay this morning," he said, then slurped some broth.

"Already?" His father raised an eyebrow. "Pretty cold out there."

"Yeah. And someone was taking mud from the bottom of the harbor, next to Chisso's pipes."

"What?" Kichiro dropped his chopsticks, which clat-tered on the tabletop. "But how?"

Kiyo described what he'd seen.

His father sprang up. "I've got to get to the office."

"But it's Sunday."

Without replying, Kichiro telephoned Fukuzawa to come pick him up in the company car, then dashed up to his room. A few minutes later he returned dressed in dark slacks and a white shirt under a blue sweater. Still unshaven, he threw on a coat and rushed out.

Kiyo ate his breakfast, bemused. What had the man on the boat been doing to make Dad so upset? Clearly both must have to do with heavy metal in the discharge water.

After breakfast, Kiyo settled in with his anatomy textbook, but was thinking about riding out to see Yuki later in the afternoon. Maybe it would warm up a little by then.

Someone knocked at the front door. He left the book open on his desk and went to answer it.

A young man, thick blue muffler wound around his neck, stood waiting on the front steps, carrying a briefcase. He nodded to Kiyo. Not tall, but he had wide shoulders and a patch of dark beard on his chin.

"Good morning," the visitor said. "I'm Takeda Jun, a researcher from Kyushu University studying Minamata Disease in conjunction with University of Kumamoto. I'm collecting hair samples from victims and other people around the area who've shown no symptoms yet. May I take a sample from you?"

"Um, yes. Sure. Come in." Kiyo let him in and hung up his coat in the hallway. "What can you learn from hair samples?"

"We hope to determine the level of certain heavy metals in the body," he said.

"*Sugoi.*" Incredible, Kiyo said. "I didn't know you could measure such things just from hair. And what'll that tell you?"

"Research is often about trying to prove existing theories. Mine is that people with no symptoms won't have much of certain heavy metals in the hairs. Or at least only small amounts. While those with symptoms will have more. Our goal is to discover which heavy metals are caus-ing the Disease."

"That's so clever." Kiyo smiled, wishing he'd thought of something like it.

Takeda set his briefcase on the tatami floor in the liv-ing room, next to the kotatsu. He sat and opened the case. Not much inside: a pair of scissors, pencils, paper, enve-lopes, and a thin notebook. He set everything on the ko-tatsu table, then picked up a pencil and opened the note-book. "May I have your name, please?"

"Kuge Kiyoshi."

The man licked the tip of his pencil-lead and scribbled at the top of a page in the notebook. "Any numbness in hands or feet?"

"No."

"Lack of coordination?"

Kiyo shook his head.

"All right. I'll name more symptoms of Minamata Dis-ease. Just speak up if you think you have any. Trouble hearing? Vision narrowing? Hard time talking and eating . . . ."

Kiyo shook his head as the researcher listed all the symptoms he'd seen firsthand in victims.

"Good," the man said. "Now – age?"

"Sixteen and a half."

"So, non-symptomatic." He scribbled that down, then stood and studied Kiyo's head. "Excellent. You have thick hair. I can cut a sample from the back without it showing."

He shuffled through his notebook, drew out a clean sheet of paper, and wrote Kiyo's name and age on it. Then picked up his scissors and stood behind Kiyo. A snip of the scissors blades. Then the researcher set the sample on the paper, folded it into a neat square, and tucked the packet in an envelope.

"Are you taking samples from the local fishers?" Kiyo asked. "They tend to be the most afflicted. It'd be interest-ing to see the comparison between their hair and that of city people." He wondered what level of heavy metal Yuki had. High enough to be diagnosed with the Disease? He wished he could do more to protect her.

"Yes, I'm planning on doing that. You have an interest in these things?"

"For the past year I've helped the Disease researchers at the University of Kumamoto. May I go to Kagoshima and help you analyze hair samples?"

The man stared at Kiyo curiously. "They let you work with them?"

"I know how to prepare slides, and use a microscope."

"It's an admirable offer, but my boss would never allow a child in our labs."

A *child*?

"Yes, I'm not quite seventeen, but I've been working with Hosokawa Sensei. I'm studying medicine. See?" He tapped his textbook, its edges worn from use.

"That's nice." Takeda's condescending little smile irri-tated Kiyo. He acted nothing like the researchers in Ku-mamoto.

"Thanks for the sample," Takeda added.

Kiyo took a deep breath to calm his annoyance.

Just then his mother came into the room, hair freshly curled, makeup perfectly applied. "We have a guest? Someone should've told me. Did you offer him tea?"

That would be all Kiyo needed, for his mother to learn what he'd just done. He stepped in front of the scientist. "Um, he was just leaving."

Etsuko frowned at Kiyo and stepped past him. "Hello," she said brightly.

Takeda bowed. "How do you do, Mrs. Kuge?" He ex-plained the reason for his visit. "Your son gave me a sam-ple. May I take yours as well?"

"What?" She took a step back, holding out both palms as if to ward off an attack. "No."

"I promise not to mess up your beautiful do."

Etsuko's lower lip quivered for a second, then she pressed her lips into a tight line. "Please leave."

The man nodded. "Of course. My apologies."

Kiyo tried to slink back to his room, but she called after him. "Kiyoshi, you shouldn't have done that. Your father won't be pleased."

He felt quite sure she was right.

When Kichiro came home very late in the afternoon, he looked just as unhappy as when he'd bolted off that morning.

His wife greeted him with a smile. "Kiyoshi-kun, tell Yanagiya-san to make tea for your father."

She waited until her husband had handed his coat to the chauffeur and dropped onto a cushion on the living room floor. Fukuzawa left with the coat draped over one arm. Kiyo set the tray of green tea and rice crackers the cook had handed him on the table.

Kichiro picked up the cup and took a sip.

"*Anata.*" Honey, his wife said calmly. "A researcher from one of the universities came by today."

He started, spilling tea on his sweater. "Why? What did he want?"

As she carefully blotted the wet spot with a handkerchief, he set the empty cup back on the tray. She refilled it and he lifted it again.

"To take hair samples," she told him.

Kichiro's eyes narrowed. "What! You didn't let him, did you?"

"Of course not. But, well . . . Kiyoshi-kun did. You know how he – "

"You *let* that man take some of your hair?"

Kiyo tensed. "If it can help cure Minamata Disease – "

"Don't you know those so-called researchers only want to blame Chisso for everything? And I hate the name 'Minamata Disease.' It's bad for our city."

"But only people who live around here have it. That's why the doctors and researchers call it that. And if Chisso doesn't want to be blamed, it should do more to help them find the cause," Kiyo shot back. "I'm doing my part by giving a sample of my hair so they –"

Kichiro smacked the teacup down so hard on the tray, it cracked in half. "You bullheaded idiot!"

Kiyo grabbed his anatomy textbook and left the room, shaking his head, disgusted. Clearly he and Dad would never agree about how to deal with the Disease – at least not until some new discovery forced Kichiro to look deeper, beyond the company's official line.

TWENTY

Make Japan Great Again

The dark November sky threatened a coming storm. Kiyo hurried to the hospital, wondering, Will I even be able to get to Yuki's house if it snows or sleets? Enduring a long, cold ride was nothing compared to the joy of being with her. Seeing the loving way she looked at him, her eyes full of warmth. He'd ride to Tsukinoura in any temperature for that. But snow was one obstacle his bike tires couldn't deal with. Luckily, snowfalls were infrequent in the area. Maybe the storm would hold off until tomorrow.

He stopped to feed the cats, as he'd been doing for the past four months. Their cage stank of urine and feces; there were too many of them confined in a small space. With Hosokawa Sensei's permission, though, he'd nailed some boards together and roofed the top of the cage to shelter them from bad weather. He'd spread rags begged from the cook on the ground inside the cage to serve as makeshift beds.

Some of the cats were huddled together on those scraps of cloth now. A black one looked up at him and meowed. Two younger cats chased each other, tumbling across the ground like acrobats. He knelt to spot his favorite tan-colored cat – whom he called Chibi, "Little Cutie." The perfect name for such a small, sweet animal.

"Chibi, Chibi," he called. A flat-faced gray cat padded over and sat by the fence, washing its face with a forepaw. Kiyo called again. When he couldn't find the cat, a wretched thought stopped his breath. *The Minamata Disease.*

No. Surely, Chibi was all right.

Kiyo took the back stairs to the doctor's office two at a time. No one there.

He turned around and headed for the second-floor ward for those afflicted with Minamata Disease. As soon as someone in there died, another victim was admitted to the empty bed. He rushed into the ward, and all the patients looked up at him with the same frantic eyes, begging for relief. Some screaming in pain.

"I'm sorry," he said, as he passed each beds. "I'm so sorry."

He didn't find Hosokawa Sensei there. So he went back out into the hallway and asked a passing nurse where the doctor might be.

"Try the lab," she suggested, then walked on with her stack of patient charts.

Kiyo found him there, perched on a stool in the basement room, face pressed to a microscope eyepiece. Not wanting to interrupt, he waited until his mentor lifted his head.

"Ah, Kiyo-kun. I'm studying some brain tissue from Cat Number 400. I sent the same samples to Kyushu University for analysis, and just received their report."

"Brain tissue?" So that meant Chibi was probably – The world spun for a moment, and Kiyo grabbed the doorframe.

"Oh, no." Dr. Hosokawa groaned. "Surely you knew that when one of the cats exhibited symptoms, I had to autopsy it. That means it must be euthanized. Did you forget?"

"No." Kiyo took a few breaths. "I mean, yes...of course." But knowing, as opposed to having it actually happen ... he wanted to run outside to the cage and set all the cats

free. But he was supposed to be an objective medical researcher, not a child mourning a dead pet.

He dug his fingers into his thighs. *Don't embarrass
yourself in front of Hosokawa Sensei.*

The doctor rose from his stool and came over to rest a
hand on Kiyo's shoulder. "You're a kind soul. But you
know, once a cat contracts the Disease it would ultimately
die anyhow. Not letting it suffer at length is kinder."

"But *we* gave it the Disease."

"Yes, we did." Sensei sighed. "That's how we learn how
to cure illnesses. But also remember that those stray cats
would've lived on fish from the Bay even if we hadn't kept
them caged here. I gave Cat 400 a shot, and it just went to
sleep."

Everything the doctor said was right. But that didn't
ease the pain he felt for all the confined cats, for the first
poor white dancing cat and for little Jiro. All innocent animals who had no idea what was happening. Yuki could
lessen the sting of her losses by drawing a picture, but he
had no such talent. Her gift eased her family's pain, too.

Kiyo feared the answer, but had to ask. "What did Cat
400 look like?"

Hosokawa Sensei frowned, thinking. "A tan-colored
male with small delicate paws."

Kiyo moaned. "Chibi."

The doctor looked surprised. "Don't tell me you named
the cats."

"Just that one."

"Ah." Sensei patted his shoulder. "I'm sorry."

Kiyo nodded, throat constricted.

"And do you still want to be a doctor?"

"I – yes," Kiyo said, straightening and wiping his eyes.
So he needed to act more like one, starting now.

Dr. Hosokawa returned to the microscope, beckoning
Kiyo over, too. "It took Cat 400 – I mean Chibi – four
months to show symptoms. The pathology lab at Kyushu

University reports the cat had begun to lose cerebellum cells. Also, there was an abnormally high amount of mer- cury in the internal organs. These same results appear in human victims. My instruments are crude compared to the university's. But here, take a look."

Kiyo compared Chibi's slides with one of a human brain. The cells did look similar.

"This is important." Sensei slid off his stool. "I must report this to Chisso right away."

"Can I go along?"

Sensei hesitated, then nodded. "But I'm going to see your father. He may not be happy to see either of us there."

Kichiro's voice called "Come in!" when the doctor and Kiyo knocked on his office door. He looked surprised to see them standing in the hallway, but waved them inside. Kiyo hung back while Hosokawa Sensei told his father about the cat experiment, and showed him the university pathol- ogy report.

"So this shows a direct link between the contaminated fish in the Bay and the Minamata Disease." The doctor's eyes were shining with excitement.

Kichiro's were not. He frowned and looked up over the report, at Kiyo.

Dr. Hosokawa shook his head. "He has nothing to do with this discovery. Just tagging along to learn more."

His father sat down behind the desk, silent for a mo- ment. At last he said, "You may be right. But there's no proof there that it's *our* wastewater affecting the fish."

"What?" Dr. Hosokawa huffed. "But look at all the peo- ple getting the Disease along the Shiranui Sea, after Chisso changed the dumping location to the river there."

Dad's mouth tightened. "The president will need more evidence than that before authorizing changes to how we discharge wastewater here."

The doctor leaned forward, hands propped on the desk, bringing his face closer to Kichiro's. "Please. If this company is the cause of so much illness and death, you must clean up the wastewater now. People are – "

His father looked away. "I'll let the president know of your cat experiment, Hosokawa Sensei."

"Thanks, Dad," Kiyo blurted out. But his father didn't meet his gaze. After a few moments, he turned away and followed Dr. Hosokawa out of the office

Between visits to Yuki and studying for midterm exams, Kiyo had just enough time to go feed the cats every day. He hadn't talked to Hosokawa Sensei for at least a week. But on this day, when he found him in the office, the doctor's expression was hard.

"What's wrong?" Kiyo had seen him sad or distressed over patients he was unable to help, but he'd never seen him actually angry before.

"I've been ordered to stop the cat experiment."

"What? But why?"

"The president of Chisso didn't give me a specific reason. Just an order."

Kiyo gaped at the doctor. "But he can't do that! You're the best hope for a cure."

"He can do it, and he did. Chisso funds this hospital facility, remember? And I work for Chisso."

"No!" Kiyo ran from the office and pedaled furiously over to the factory offices. Hurrying past his father's closed office door, he rushed past the executive secretaries at their desks in the administrative assistants' office. He'd all but grown up in this place. So he knew the righthand door led to the president's office. Without pausing, he lifted a hand and pounded on it.

"Yes?" called a gruff voice.

Kiyo pulled the heavy cream-colored door open just wide enough to slip past. He entered the office and bowed, forehead almost touching his knees. When he straightened, the confusion and annoyance on the president's long face was plain.

Yoshioka Kiichi sat behind a wide desk of gleaming mahogany. He wore an expensive-looking dark blue wool suit, crisp shirt, and a dark, figured silk tie. He was nearly bald, and the overhead light reflected off his slick-looking skull. A good bit of gray hair still sprouted from his ears and nostrils, though. Behind him, on the back wall hung a large oil painting of Minamata Bay. The painted version still looked clear, blue, and beautiful.

"You look familiar but I don't know why," snapped the man. "Who are you?"

"Sorry to disturb you." Kiyo removed his school hat. "I'm Kuge Kiyoshi."

"Ah, yes. Kuge-san's son?"

"Yes sir. I'm working at the hospital with Hosokawa Sensei. I heard you wanted him to stop the cat experiment. But, Yoshioka-san, it's very important. The first cat to develop the Minamata Disease had brain cells that had changed the same way as the human victims'. We can learn a lot from those cats. Maybe even find the cure, at last."

The president's face seemed to swell before Kiyo's eyes. His cheeks mottled with red. "Leave. Now!"

"Please, I'm begging you to allow Dr. Hosokawa to continue the experiment."

"Does your father know you're here?" Yoshioka snarled.

"No, he doesn't know."

"If he did, he'd tell you the same thing I just did. Now go on, get the hell out."

"Sir, have you ever seen anyone afflicted with the Disease? It's painful. Horrible," Kiyo said quickly. "They can't walk or use their hands. Some can't hear or see. Their mouths quit working, and then they can't eat. And after that – "

"I'll call a guard to throw you out!" the president shouted, rising from his seat.

Kiyo opened the door and stepped out. But instead of closing it behind him, he turned back and bowed again. "Please reconsider, sir." Then before the president could rage at him again, he quickly shut the door. Muffled shouts and curses trailed him as he walked stiffly between the desks of the two startled looking secretaries, who stared at him as if viewing a dangerous lunatic.

As he hurried down the hall he spotted a brass plaque for the vice president's office. Kiyo knocked softly on the door. No reply. He knocked again.

"Hey. What do you want?" A short chubby man was headed up the corridor, glaring at him. The man's ears gave him an odd look; they lay so flat against his head it appeared they'd been pinned back and stapled in place.

"Are you Murata-san, the vice president?"

The scowl deepened. "Who're you?" A gold-capped front tooth glinted under the ceiling lights.

"Kuge Kiyoshi." He bowed deeply. "I'm working with Dr. Hosokawa to find a cure for Minamata Disease."

The vice president looked Kiyo up and down, curled his lip, and shoved him aside. He entered his office and slammed the door.

"Please!" Kiyo shouted to be heard through the door. "People in Minamata are suffering. May I explain our research to you?"

"Get away from there!" Someone shouted from down the hallway.

Kiyo turned to look. His father was hustling toward him. "Murata-san called. Told me, 'Get your son out of here or I'll call the police.' " Kichiro's ears burned red with rage.

"I'm sorry I caused you problems. I'll go now." He followed his father toward the stairway. But as they neared it, he said, "Dad, did you know the president ordered Dr. Hosokawa to stop the cat experiment? He's close to finding answers."

Kichiro grabbed Kiyo's shoulders hard, and turned him around roughly. "Shut up. Go to my office."

"But I – "

His father shoved him hard. "I said go!" His voice was a deep growl of anger.

He marched behind Kiyo all the way to his office and closed the door behind them. "Are you insane, harassing Murata-san? My own son – "

"I just wanted him to consider letting the cat experiment continue. Yoshioka-san said no, so then – "

"You actually said that to the president?" His father gaped at him.

"Don't worry. I made clear you didn't send me."

"How could you do something so rash?" Dad clasped his head between his fists. "Shaming me in my place of business."

"The Ministry of Health and Welfare's Minamata Food Poisoning Subcommittee published findings that the Disease is caused by eating large quantities of fish and shellfish from the Bay," Kiyo said. "And then the cats – "

"Now you listen to me." Dad leaned down, his face inches from Kiyo's. The dark circles, the wrinkles around his eyes and mouth were carved deeper than just a few months ago. "You will not say another word about the Disease or what's been published or what some university people claim. They're wrong!"

"But – "

"Neither seafood nor mercury compound are causing the Disease. The Ministry of International Trade and Industry and the Japan chemical industry are studying the real reason. Their answer is to be published soon."

"But the hospital cats got the Disease from eating fish from the Bay too."

"That's wrong! Don't you understand? We're trying to save Minamata! Chisso pulled it from the dust and made it prosper. It's the reason an express train stops here. Going around saying our bay is polluted, that Chisso's causing the pollution . . . the city will collapse. We might have to move the factory somewhere else."

"But Dr. Hosokawa believes – "

Dad slammed a fist on the desk, and Kiyo fell silent.

His father stepped over to the window. "Let me explain something." He looked out at rows of brick buildings, tall, smoke-belching chimneys, and a dozen flat-topped, cylindrical storage tanks.

"You were too young during the War to recall how degrading it felt to surrender. We'd fought hard, sacrificing most of Japan's young men. We ate grass and weeds because there was no food. Many homes burned to ash in air raids. The world now regards us as broken, stupid. Only capable of producing trinkets for export. So Japan must rebuild. Why do you think I work so hard, missing time with the family? For you. For Chisso. For our country!"

His father was right. Kiyo could never truly understand what his parents had been through. "You do work long, hard hours, and I appreciate it. I know your generation suffered a great deal just to live through the war."

His father grunted. "And now, around the world, the label 'Made in Japan' means the product is cheap. Inferior. I feel humiliated by that. You should, too. Industry leaders like Chisso will reestablish our place in world trade, alongside other leading nations. This factory's the most advanced in all of Japan. That only happened because Chisso employees work hard and sacrifice to better the country. So quit thinking only of your own interests! The victims of Minamata Disease are few. Their pain incidental compared to what Chisso's done for our city and the country."

Kiyo frowned. "I know Japan needs to regain status, and that the city depends on Chisso to prosper. But working-class people, farmers, fishermen ... they should matter too."

His father nodded. "Well, Chisso will be installing a wastewater purifier soon."

"Really? That's great!" Sunlight seemed to suddenly brighten the room. "Why don't you announce that in the newspaper?"

"We will, soon. Now, go home. You've caused enough trouble for one day."

Kiyo pedaled to Tsukinoura feeling ecstatic. The snowstorm was smaller than forecasted. The inch of accumulation had melted; the roads were barely wet. And now he knew his father was doing all he could to help stop new cases of the Disease. The new purifier proved that.

He dismounted at Yuki's house and ran inside without knocking, shouting, "Guess what? Chisso is putting in a wastewater purifier!"

The family, which was sitting under the kotatsu, all turned to look at him.

"They admit they killed our fish? And caused this Disease?" Nobuyuki mumbled. When Kiyo listened closely, he could still understand most of what he said.

"Not exactly. But it'll stop heavy metals flowing into the Bay. Isn't that what we wanted?"

"I suppose." Kazuko, a hand resting on the mound of her belly, looked doubtful.

"They should grovel," Nobuyuki muttered.

"It's very good news, Kiyo-kun." Yuki smiled at him. "Come over and warm up."

He settled next to her, picking up her warm hands in his chilled ones. "Even after the purifier is installed, you should avoid eating anything from the Bay. It'll take a long time for the water to be clean again."

"A clean bay. Can you imagine?" Yuki looked wistful.

"Yes, yes." Her mother brushed away a tear.

Nobuyuki said nothing.

After warming up with a cup of hot green tea Yuki prepared for him, Kiyo rose to leave. "Wish I could stay longer, but I should get back to the hospital with this news. See you soon," he promised Yuki.

"I hope so." She waved goodbye as he backed out the door.

As Kiyo pedaled the long road to the hospital, an idea formed. A way to perhaps continue the cat experiment. Once there, he threw down his bicycle and rushed inside, up to Dr. Hosokawa's office.

He knocked. But then, unable to wait, he threw open the door before being invited in. "Sensei, why don't we find some place away from here to keep the cats. Then we can still continue the experiment!"

The doctor looked up at him from his desk, and slowly shook his head. "Too late," he said grimly. "Chisso guards came this morning. They already took them away."

A newspaper article announcing the Cyclator, Chisso's new wastewater purification system, appeared the following week. A few days later it was to be unveiled in a public ceremony.

That morning his father came down to breakfast looking pale. His dress shirt seemed to billow from his shoulders and around his thinning frame as if it was instead drooping from a wire hanger.

His wife looked up from her plate and frowned. "*Anata.*" Honey, she chided. "You look exhausted. You've been working far too hard. Why not take a day off?"

"Don't be ridiculous." Kichiro hitched up his suit trousers and tightened the belt a notch. "I'm just annoyed. Those fishermen, creating too many problems. The government instructed us to switch dumping from the Bay to the river. Now, they want us to discharge into the Bay again. Industry creates waste. It can't be helped. Our products are vital to the nation, but government people keep hamstringing us."

His wife reached up and gently patted his arm. "Yes, and I know Japan will be strong again. With the help of Chisso and other corporations."

As his father rolled his head, wincing, his neck made audible cracks and pops. "There's no proof our wastewater killed fish. No proof we caused the Disease. But still, we have to give sympathy money so they don't starve. And now, an expensive purification system. That wastewater is my responsibility; I can't fail. But at this rate, we might have to close the factory."

"Have some tea," urged his wife.

He rubbed his temples. "I have to go."

Kiyo laid down his anatomy book. "May I come? I won't cause any trouble. "

"Hmm." His father regarded him with narrowed eyes. "You'd better not."

At the public unveiling, a black bird flew low over the head of Yoshioka Kiichi, president of Chisso. A very unusual sight, most birds having disappeared since the Bay became polluted.

Despite the brisk, cold December wind that morning – and the fact that it was a Saturday – many important city officials, Chisso's department heads and other employees stood around the water purification machine. The dark metal hulk was large enough Kiyo could've rolled inside with his bike. Clear water drained into the river from a protruding pipe.

The president and department heads wore their expensive wool suits and coats. Cashmere scarves protected their necks. Above them, well-fed, unweathered faces reflected great pride. Only a few dozen spectators could crowd in around the water's edge, though.

As the president rose from his folding chair on the wooden platform and headed to the podium to speak, a lone crow swooped low over his head, cawing as if in protest, or derision.

Kiyo had been thinking how privileged he was to attend. But the bird . . . could it be a bad omen? Surely not. Anyhow, that was superstition. He was supposed to be a man of science.

Nothing else will go amiss, he decided.

Just then, a large rat crawled out from under the machine.

"What's that thing doing here?" the president whispered to the younger man standing near the podium.

His aide's eyes widened. "Sorry, sir. There're lots more mice and rats since all the cats disappeared."

With some help from Chisso's guards, thought Kiyo bitterly, thinking of the scuttled cat experiment. But the aide was right. Cats were simply no longer seen on Minamata's streets or the piers of the Bay.

"I don't care. Get rid of it!" The executive growled.

The employee kicked at the rat, and it scrambled away, under a nearby foundation.

The president bared his teeth in a tight smile and launched into a speech. "Chisso, one of Japan's most respected companies, will lift our country back to greatness again. But it's also a company that cares about Minamata, its beautiful bay, and its people."

Beautiful? Kiyo peered out at the Bay. He used to love the clear blue water, the silver fish flashing, skimming over and under it. Now the water was sickly gray and white, studded with the upturned bellies of floating, stinking dead fish. Did Chisso's president think the people here couldn't see that? Couldn't smell it?

"In order to do everything possible to keep our river and bay clean, we've installed the Cyclator." Yoshioka swept a hand out to indicate the hulking purification machine. "This wonderful device cost the company sixty million yen, but it was money well spent. For the wastewater is now crystal-clean. Let me show you."

The same aide slipped a drinking-glass from a black bag embroidered with Chisso's name. He leaned out and held it under the outflow pipe where water was still gushing. Then wiped the sides dry with a small white towel and handed it reverently to the president.

Yoshioka tipped his head back and drank the contents down in one extended gulp. When he held up the empty glass, the crowd applauded.

Kiyo clapped, too. At first a bit grudgingly. But as the applause rose in volume he, too, felt swept up in the excitement of the day. Perhaps the president, though slow to act decisively, wasn't such a bad man. This expensive advancement surely meant there'd be no new cases of Minamata Disease. And that, in the end, showed Chisso was still a good company, after all.

It seemed his father had been right.

TWENTY-ONE

Sister, Won't You Turn Over

Tomoko-chan, the family's new addition, was born on December 18th. On this May morning, Kazuko sat at the table nursing her four-and-a-half-month-old daughter as Yuki chopped onions in the kitchen.

Yuki set down the knife. "Mom, Dad went to the outhouse half an hour ago."

Nobuyuki could still walk, if slowly, but he couldn't use a cane; his nearly-numb hands couldn't grasp the handle. So he sometimes stumbled or bumped into walls or trees, but still insisted on going to the outhouse alone.

"Should I check on him?"

Kazuko shook her head. "A man must retain some pride."

As Yuki went back to chopping onions she thought unwillingly of the Nishio family again. The staggering father she'd had to half-carry to the outhouse. The two nearly-grown boys in soiled diapers. All of them deserted by an overworked second wife, and thrown on the mercy of overburdened family in the country. Were they even still alive?

Just then she heard a wail. Tomoko had slipped out of their mother's arms and dropped into her lap. "I'm sorry, Tomoko-chan." Kazuko was trying awkwardly to scoop her up again and comfort her. "So sorry."

"Here, Mom." Yuki put a long towel on the table, laid her baby sister on it, and then strung one end of the towel under Kazuko's arm, the other around her neck, and tied them together. "That'll make nursing easier. I'll help you over to the wall. You can lean against that for support."

Tears spilled from Kazuko's eyes. "You know I have it, too."

"No! We don't know that."

"But my hands and feet are almost numb. I'm so clumsy now, so slow. My body has betrayed me."

Yuki had felt a crushing blow the first time she'd noticed her mother's faltering gait. First her uncle, then her father. Now with Mom also developing the Strange Disease, she'd soon be unable to work. How would the family survive?

No. She couldn't think about that, or the sorrow would make her curl up in a ball and cry. She shrugged her shoulders hard, as if that might dispel the worry. *Keep moving forward, stay a step ahead of the gloom.* She was all the family had left. Good spirits were now even more important.

"You can still do most everything," she lied, patting her mother's hand. "You're just having trouble with ... little things. Kiyo-kun told me some people get bad quickly, even die. But some get the Disease just a little. You're probably one of those."

Mom shook her head and wiped her eyes on one sleeve. Leaning back against the wall, she stroked the baby's head.

"Dad hasn't gotten so bad," Yuki added.

"But it's your birthday. And I can't do anything for you."

"Don't worry, I'll make dinner." Yuki turned back toward the kitchen, squeezing her eyes shut. *Hide the pain. Don't let them see the terror.*

"When's Kiyo-kun coming?" Kazuko asked.

"He can't this year. He's got to go to a Chisso family banquet with his parents."

"Those companies have such silly, expensive events."

Yuki was relieved when her father finally teetered back inside but said nothing. He needed to retain some sense of dignity, as her mother had noted.

While sweet potatoes boiled, she went to the garden and picked tender early snow peas, then pulled radishes – the cold-loving plants. Mom had been well enough to till and seed them before her hands grew too stiff. No school on Sunday, so Yuki would plant more of the seeds they'd saved from last year's harvest. She'd have to grow many more vegetables over the summer, by herself, and pick and dry or pickle them, for winter. A couple older hens had quit laying, so they'd eaten them, leaving only two to produce eggs. Mom had sold some of their vegetables and bought barley. She also had applied for more government assistance, but who knew when or if help would come.

Before leaving for school the next morning, she prepared barley porridge and boiled potatoes. The monthly rice subsidy from the city, which they'd applied for and received, barely lasted two weeks. But she still considered her family luckier than many.

She ate a bowl of porridge, then fed her parents their portions.

"And here's your lunch." She set a plate of six potatoes on the table. If they tried to reach the dirt-floored kitchen, one step lower than the house, they might fall.

Worry crawled up her spine and swam in her belly while she attended classes. She made secret little sketches in her notebook: the family smiling or eating. But the drawings no longer made her feel better. Real food obviously wasn't going to appear from her pencil and paper.

In the afternoon she hurried home, breathing in short shallow gasps, afraid of what she might find. Stepping past the front door, she saw her dad sleeping on the floor in the bedroom. Little Tomoko lay crying on the floor of the main room, wearing a shirt, but naked from the waist down. Kazuko sat next to the baby, blinking back tears.

Yuki picked up her sister and smelled the ammoniac stench of urine. The worn tatami was dark and wet where Tomoko had lain.

"Mom, what's the matter?"

"I t-tried to change her diaper, but I cou-couldn't get it on. She's been crying all afternoon there, hungry and wet." Kazuko turned her face to the wall and sobbed.

"Don't worry. I'll take care of it."

Yuki heated water on the brazier and bathed Tomoko in a bucket. The washed diapers, thick cloth ones Kiyo had given them, were still damp, so she pinned a cut-up shirt around the baby's bottom.

"Tomoko-chan, here you go." She tied the baby securely to her mother's chest with the long towel. Kazuko fumbled at the buttons of her blouse until Yuki undid them for her. The baby latched on, making strong sucking motions. But her arms and hands lay still. She didn't clasp the breast as she used to do.

What could it mean? Yuki shook the thought away. The baby was just tired from crying all afternoon.

Kazuko closed her eyes and sank against the wall.

Once Tomoko let go, Yuki laid her on an old quilt on the floor and knelt beside her. "Tomoko-chan, Tomoko-chan," she chanted, offering her sister a finger. Usually the little girl clutched it, kicking and gurgling. Today she only jerked her arms and legs awkwardly and cried.

"Has she turned over today?"

Mom thought a moment. "I don't think so."

"Strange. She should be turning by four months."

They both stared at Tomoko, frowning.

"She's not putting her fingers in her mouth either."
Yuki felt a stab of fear. "But she never . . . she couldn't . . .
." She shook her head. "No."

"Minamata Disease?" whispered Kazuko. Panic contorted her face.

Yuki regretted mentioning the unusual behavior. "How
could it be? She hasn't eaten any seafood, only your milk.
Maybe she's just full and sleepy." She smiled at her sister.
"Right, Tomoko-chan? I'll lay out your futon, Mom. You can
take a nap, too."

Yuki was so busy scrubbing laundry on the washboard
she forgot about gathering firewood until it was time to
make dinner. The last of the wood had heated water for
Tomoko's bath.

She picked up two large deep-sided, rectangular bamboo baskets with handles and hurried to the forest, intend-
ing to gather enough wood to cook a couple of meals. Her
arms already felt tired when she thought about having to
stockpile enough cooking fuel before winter arrived.

One basket was half full when she saw Kiyo waving
through the trees. "Hi!" He came over, smiling. "Akaji-san
said I'd find you here. What're you doing?"

Yuki's mouth trembled. She bit her lip to still it. "Just
getting firewood. We can't afford charcoal anymore."

"Oh." Kiyo's expression slowly morphed from surprise
to comprehension. "We'll have to do something about that
before winter. It's dangerous, constantly burning wood in a
kotatsu. I'll help gather some now, though. Hand me a
basket."

He began picking up branches and fallen wood from
the forest floor. When his load almost reached the top and
the basket leaned precariously, he set it down and helped
Yuki finish filling hers.

When she lifted it, preparing to head back, he touched
her arm. She set the basket down again. He took her
hands in his, and their warmth radiating a bit of hope.

"Let's pretend it's still our birthdays, and say *omedetou* to each other."

Yuki smiled. "I'm so busy, sometimes I forget about things like that. Happy Birthday, Kiyo-kun." She clutched his hands tightly.

"*Omedetou.* Seventeen!" he said. "We're almost grown up."

"Almost." She wrinkled her nose. "Did you come from the hospital?"

"Yes." He chuckled. "Why, do I smell like antiseptic?"

She nodded.

"Oh – I brought you some paint." He dug in his jacket pocket and pulled out a box of twelve watercolor dry-pan paints. "I heard you can mix them to make more colors?"

"Right." She admired the set. "Thanks, Kiyo-kun. I was all out."

"I promised I'd do anything to make you a world-famous artist."

"World-famous," she repeated, then giggled. "Think I'd better use them today."

"Let's take a walk. Forget about everything for a while."

Hand in hand, they strolled the dense forest pretending to spot foxes, deer, and badgers. Glittering droplets of water from the previous night's shower clung to broad fan-like leaves, shimmering in the columns of sunshine streaking between tall, moss-covered cedars. They crossed a small rushing brook paved with smooth gray and brown baseball-sized stones. Long slippery roots grew like long, crossed fingers under their feet. Bush warblers and long-tailed tits sang from the branches.

"It's beautiful. I'm out here every day but just don't see that anymore." She took a deep breath. "Pine and juniper resin. I seem to notice the world only when I'm with you."

"I'm sorry about your parents. Will you be all right?"

She considered telling him about Tomoko, but again pushed the thought away. "You know how some members of the Mutual Aid Association sat in front of Chisso's front gate for a month, protesting? Demanding compensation for Minamata Disease patients."

Kiyo nodded. "The company still claims they didn't cause the Disease, so the payments are small."

"They called it 'condolence gifts offered in sympathy.' We finally got our small annual payment. That'll carry us for a while. And the garden's growing well."

"How will your family eat this winter, though, after you've spent the money and the garden's done?"

"I don't know."

But she did know. Then, there'd only be one avenue left.

He pulled her close. "Let's walk out here every time I visit." His deepening voice vibrated against her ear. She wanted to stay in this embrace forever.

"No matter what happens you must keep drawing and painting." He pulled back and gazed into her eyes. "We'll never give up on our dreams. Right?"

She sighed and stepped back, crossing her arms. "It's easy for you. Your family has money. There's nothing to concentrate on except studying. I have a whole family to take care of, and no money. But don't worry, I'll keep drawing. I have to."

Art was like oxygen. Always there, keeping her going. Drawing and painting gave hope and beautified a less-than-lovely world. Lifting her from everyday despair by illustrating what life *could* be.

"I'm sorry about your parents. And the Bay. I'd trade places if I could. But I'm happy you won't forget your gift."

Back at the house they made a neat stack of wood next to the front door. Yuki forced a smile. "That'll keep us for a few days."

"I'll come back to help then, too."

"Kiyo-kun," Kazuko called. "Stay for dinner."

"We do have great garden vegetables on the menu." Yuki pointed to the table, where several small baskets of snow peas, green onions and radishes sat.

"Looks great, but Mom told me to be home by six."

"Next time then," Kazuko said.

Yuki waved as Kiyo cycled up the unpaved lane. Recalling the feel of his strong hands, she eagerly looked forward to their next embrace. "Goodbye," she whispered. And then turned back to the house. Time to feed everyone and wash the dishes.

Later, as her own way to pray her sister would grow up strong and healthy, she drew three pictures: Tomoko crawling and smiling, then as a toddler chasing a butterfly. And finally, as a grade-schooler walking to classes, laughing and talking with friends, books in hand.

TWENTY-TWO

A Bad Trade

Autumn leaves usually turned the bay area a brilliant red, orange, and gold. But this year, an early frost in September froze the leaves, leaving them black and shriveled, barely clinging to the branches. Like dead hands unwilling to let go and depart this world. Those who lived around the bay feared this winter would be far colder than usual. That meant Yuki would need to stockpile more wood than usual.

Kiyo, riding through Tsukinoura, saw her late in the afternoon. She stood back, watching a few customers at a vegetable stand pick through the last of the day's produce, and talking to someone. He braked, then turned into the road.

When Yuki looked up and saw him she quickly turned away from the woman she'd been talking to.

The shallow basket at her feet held a half-dozen fish. The woman's bamboo carrier was filled with kelp.

He blurted out, "Where'd you get those?"

Yuki raised her chin defiantly. "We went fishing today."

"Out in the ocean?"

"That's right. Now, I'm selling them."

Kiyo dismounted. "All the way through the Bay and out on rough seas, in that little boat?"

"It took all day to sail there, yes. But we caught plenty of fish."

The woman, who'd been listening, wore loose navy-blue pants and an old worn sweater, the everyday uniform of fishers. Her hair was a youthful black, but worry lines etched her thin face. "Of course, they're from deep in the ocean. I had to go out there, too, to get delicious seaweed from safe waters."

Kiyo picked up the woman's basket and lifted it to his nose. The stench was so revolting, he jerked back, gagging. "Smell that." He stuck the bamboo container in Yuki's face. "Not delicious. Not from deep waters."

The woman tugged the basket back, clutching it to her chest. "Take pity on me. My husband died of the Strange Disease. I've no money. What does it matter where it came from? We're all sick now." Her eyes shone with tears. "My family needs fish to eat. How about a trade?"

Before he could object, Yuki said, "I love kelp. How many fish do you need?"

As they were making the exchange, a girl of seventeen or eighteen came walking up the road.

"Hi, Reiko-chan," Yuki murmured. "Haven't seen you in a while."

The young woman's baggy pants and long-sleeved blouse were as worn as Yuki's clothes. When she saw who'd spoken, though, she froze and raised a fist to her chest as if warding off evil. "I heard all about your family. What did you do to get the Disease?"

A flame of anger lit Kiyo's belly. "Why, you – "

Yuki clenched her jaw and sneered. "Nothing," she said coldly. "But you might come down with it any time."

Reiko shook her head. "We're clean. We don't do bad things. We stay away from infected people."

Kiyo's anger turned to fury. Before he could speak though, Yuki pointed at him. "He works at the hospital, around people with the Disease all day long. Yet he's not sick. The victims are mostly from the villages around the Bay, and it comes on suddenly. You may feel fine now but could lose feeling in your hands and feet tomorrow."

Reiko squealed like a trapped rabbit, clasping her shaking hands. She wheeled and ran the other direction.

Yuki barked a laugh, but then dropped her arms and looked sad. "Sorry. I shouldn't have said that. It's just . . . she made me so mad."

"I'm glad you spoke up. She made me mad, too. People are so cruel. I'd like to drag every healthy person to the isolation ward and make them see what the Disease does."

She nodded. "I was afraid you'd think badly of me. I used to believe she was my friend."

She turned back to the seaweed woman and wrapped four fish in newspaper. The woman folded half of the seaweed in her basket the same way, and they traded.

Kiyo grabbed the packaged seaweed from Yuki's hands and thrust it at the woman. "Take it back."

"No." The woman coughed phlegm into a handkerchief. Then, picking up her carrier, she trudged down the road.

"You can't eat this," Kiyo told Yuki. "It's from the Bay. I think your fish are, too. You shouldn't be selling them."

Yuki squared her shoulders and scowled at him.

"Everyone's eating fish and seaweed caught in the Bay now. We have to. Summer is over. We've no money like you to buy other food."

"But the cat experiment proved the Disease is contracted from eating that fish."

"We can't survive on a few withered vegetables all winter."

"No. You're right. Come with me." He walked his bike over to a shop on the main street. Looking sullen, Yuki hesitated, then followed. But she hesitated at the door. "I don't have any money."

"I have my allowance."

The shop was barely bigger than his bedroom. It smelled richly of dried bonito and mushrooms, soy sauce and vinegar. Rice and barley filled a few wooden bins.

Canned persimmon and tangerines, and dehydrated kanpyo were stacked on shelves against the back wall.

The proprietor, missing two front teeth, smiled and nodded at them.

Kiyo nodded at the shelves. "Five kilos of rice. Miso. Dried bonito and kelp not from Minamata Bay. What other dried foods do you have?"

"Some soybeans and kanpyo."

"Kiyo-kun, no." Yuki looked stricken. "You can't."

"Doesn't dried gourd shavings and wheat gluten sound good?" he asked.

"Yes, but – "

"Do you have any eggs or tofu?" Kiyo asked. The last of Yuki's hens had quit laying, and the family had finally been forced to eat them.

"I have six eggs and one cake of tofu left."

"We'll take those, too," he told the shopkeeper.

"Kiyo-kun," she begged. "Don't."

"It's the least I can do." He set her basket on the small table next to the cash register and pulled a handful of coins from his pocket. Mom had given him his monthly allowance yesterday, but he had no idea how much groceries cost. "Is that enough?"

"Yes." The shopkeeper's hand, missing the tip of its index finger, counted out what was owed and plunked the money into the cash register.

"My parents will never accept this." Yuki whispered, looking embarrassed. "It's charity."

"Do I have enough left for shochu?" Kiyo figured Yuki's father hadn't had his favorite drink in ages.

"Perhaps a small bottle."

"I'll take that, too." The bottle was added, and Kiyo picked up the parcels.

The storeowner smiled broadly. "Come again soon." As they were walking out, he shouted, "Hey, you forgot your fish."

"Throw them away," Kiyo said. "Don't eat them."

"Thanks," Yuki said, smiling. "But it's too much."

"It's not a problem. I get allowance once a month. I'll get you as much food as it'll buy. Just promise you won't eat fish. I couldn't stand it if you got sick, too."

"All right. Thanks, Kiyo-kun."

"I'll buy food, you concentrate on art. What kind of a world would it be without pictures, music, books? You're going to bring joy to many people someday."

"Sometimes I'm not sure I know what joy is anymore."

He knew her life was hard, but couldn't help feeling like he wanted to shake sense into her. "You've taught yourself a lot! Many famous artists are self-taught."

"Really?" She frowned. "Like who?"

He couldn't come up with a name. "I don't recall right this minute, but ... I even study anatomy on my own. Sure, I'll need to go to medical school, but I'm learning lots now."

She sighed. "I know what you're saying. Don't worry, I'll keep drawing. You're going to be a wonderful doctor. And I am getting better at watercolor."

It began to rain, pouring down hard, the drops flinging up mud from the dirt road until it clotted the hems of their pants. They squeezed under a narrow eave on the side of the store to wait out the storm.

The overhang was narrow. To fit, they had to press tightly against each other, thighs and hips touching. Walled in by a curtain of water, it felt like they were alone in another world. The press of her hip, scent of that smooth skin was intoxicating. He took a few deep breaths to calm down. Her face was so close, he could smell the clean scent of the baking soda she used to brush her teeth.

He quickly leaned down to kiss her mouth. She kissed him back.

"I like it when you do that," she said.

Heat suffused his body, his face. "Me too."

He saw now how her breasts filled out her blouse. The narrowness of her waist, the gentle swell of hips. She was incredibly desirable. He squeezed his eyes tightly shut, as if that would lessen the throbbing between his legs. He thought about her throughout the day. And at night, when he couldn't stand it anymore, he had to satisfy himself. Imagining her hair spilling over him, drinking in the sweet, remembered scent of her.

About ten minutes and at least as many kisses later, the rain let up a bit. She said, "We'd better get these home."

"Eh. You're right."

They tried to jam the whole basket of food into Kiyo's carrier, but it wouldn't fit. He took all the items out and neatly stacked them in the bike-basket.

She picked up the sack of rice and the eggs, tucking them under her jacket. "I don't want the rice to get wet. And on these bumpy roads, the eggs might break."

They trudged on through the steady rain. Muck splattered their legs and filled their shoes. Rain whipped all but blinded Kiyo, but he couldn't let go of the heavy bike handles to wipe it away.

At her house, they unloaded everything. Yuki's mom burst out crying. "Oh, Kiyo-kun, thank you." She handed them each a towel. "Now dry off, both of you."

Kiyo rubbed his hair briskly with the thin, hole-pocked cotton. He felt embarrassed to be thanked so often. After all, he'd done nothing to actually earn his allowance; he was merely an executive's spoiled son.

While Yuki went into the bedroom to change, he handed the bottle of shochu to Yuki's father. "For you. A gift."

Laughter like a series of huffs erupted from Nobuyuki. "But I get some, too," Kiyo added.

Yuki's father jerked his head up and down in renewed mirth.

"Put this on, it's dry." Yuki's mom handed Kiyo one of Nobuyuki's old shirts. He changed into the too-large, soft cotton.

"What a meal we'll have tonight!" Yuki lined up the food on the kitchen counter. "And several more nights, too."

"Look." Kiyo pointed outside. "It finally stopped raining." He picked up two large baskets stacked in one corner of the kitchen. "I'll get some firewood."

Wearing Nobuyuki's jacket, he searched the woods for dead tree limbs. He'd already filled one carrier when Yuki came up and tapped his shoulder.

"I need to ask you something," she whispered, looking back over one shoulder. She sounded serious.

He lowered the baskets to the ground. "Sure."

"Tomoko-chan isn't acting like a ten-month-old should. She doesn't turn over, or grab at things. She acts . . . well, as if she has the Disease. But that's not possible! She's never eaten any fish."

Kiyo gazed at her, worried. She'd been through far too much in just seventeen years of living.

"I've heard of other babies presenting that way. Mothers have brought them to the hospital. The doctors think they have cerebral palsy."

Yuki's hand rose to cover her mouth. "What's that?"

"Similar symptoms to Minamata Disease, like poor coordination and weak muscles. Some don't see or hear well. Those babies don't roll over, sit, or crawl."

"Sounds just like Tomoko-chan." Yuki rubbed her forehead.

"I'll bring my anatomy book next time and show you parts of the brain. Easier to explain cerebral palsy, that way."

"Understanding it better won't cure her. I'd better get dinner started." She turned and shuffled back to the house, head low.

By the time he'd lugged the overflowing firewood baskets to the house, Tomoko was asleep in a towel sling, resting in Kazuko's lap.

"Shochu," Nobuyuki reminded Kiyo.

"I'll get it." He did, then sat next to him and pried the
cork from the liquor bottle.

"Here." Yuki retrieved two cups from the kitchen. He
poured them half full, then held up one. "Ready?"

Nobuyuki tipped his head back a little, with obvious effort. Kiyo slowly, carefully, poured the drink past his lips.

"Ah." Nobuyuki smacked his lips and closed his eyes,
mouth stretched in a slight smile. Kiyo gave him another
shot, then drank one himself. Understanding why he loved
the feel of the almost-burning liquor sliding down his
throat. He wanted more, too, but left the rest. His mother
would be angry if she caught the scent of liquor on him.

He spied a small painting in the corner of the room and
stretched out from where he sat at the table to grab it. A
view of the Bay, a beautiful white-sand beach in the fore-
ground. "You are getting good at watercolor."

Yuki was in the kitchen, grilling carrots, onions, daikon radishes, tofu, and eggs in a pot over the brazier. "I'm
working on it. My third try. The others weren't worth
keeping."

"No, no, it's good . . . really good."

"It's easier to paint on an easel. I made one from scrap
wood. I make frames for canvases, too. Not so hard."

"Resourceful." He'd never made a thing in his life, always buying whatever he wanted or needed.

"Everything's ready." Yuki went back and forth from
the kitchen to table, carrying four bowls of rice and four
small plates loaded with grilled vegetables.

"Thanks," Kiyo said, "but my mother expects me to eat
dinner at home tonight. I'll just take a little taste." He divided most of his food among the others' plates.

"So good." Kazuko smiled, chewing slowly, clearly savoring the meal.

Bits of unchewed food slipped from her father's mouth onto the table, repeatedly, despite Yuki quickly spooning it up. He felt a deep sorrow at the sight. His gift was really only a short-term fix. The Disease was their most dire problem, and finding its cause the only possible solution. Though that discovery might come too late, perhaps, for Nobuyuki and Kazuko.

TWENTY-THREE

A Dose of Reality

Over the next few months, it was clear that the groceries Kiyo's allowance would buy were not enough to feed Yuki's family for a month. He began sneaking small sacks of rice from the barrel in his mother's pantry, along with canned and dried food; anything he thought she wouldn't miss. But on this particular November day, his mother was a day late paying his allowance. Now he worried, Had Yuki's family gone without food for a few days?

Finally, money in his pocket, he biked quickly to a large grocer in Minamata after school, stomach clenched in anxiety. He bought a bag of rice and cans of taro. Also miso, dried gourds and mushrooms, a bag of tea leaves, and ten eggs. They didn't all fit in the bike's basket, so he shoved a few cans into his school backpack and slipped his arms through the straps.

The load was so heavy he had to stand on the pedals to set out. In the rush to get going he misjudged the size of a rock in the middle of the narrow gravel road. The front tire struck it and stopped cold. He clutched at the handlebars, but the bike swerved like a wild horse and bucked him off.

He fell hard onto one side, legs still wrapped around the bike's frame. After a stunned moment, he raised his head and groaned, "Aah, my shoulder." How it hurt! And then, "Stupid damned rock!"

He managed to untangle his limbs and slowly get up. A few food-cans were rolling down the road. The whites of the cracked eggs had oozed out, darkening the cloth bag.

The rest of the groceries lay scattered across the dirt and gravel road.

He set the bike on its kickstand and rushed around retrieving everything. Just as he was putting the last few items back into the basket, a car pulled up behind him. The driver got out.

Kiyo gaped. "Fukuzawa-san, what're you doing here?"

"I was driving past and saw you fall."

"But you never drive Dad around here."

The chauffeur's normally neatly-combed hair was falling over his forehead. He gave a strained laugh and scratched his chin. "Actually, I was following you. I've noticed you taking food from the kitchen, and wondered why."

Kiyo tensed. If he knew, who else did? "I bought these," he said hastily.

"But you often do take things from the pantry, too."

"Yeah." Kiyo's shoulders slumped. "Have you told Mom?"

"Of course not."

"Thanks." Relieved, Kiyo said all in a rush, "I've been taking food to my friend, Yuki-chan. Her parents have Minamata Disease. Her sister may have cerebral palsy. They're starving."

"You know, many people too lazy to work fake the symptoms to get sympathy money." Fukuzawa nodded slowly as he spoke, as if explaining some unpleasant truth. "They don't fish anymore, just take the government money and drink shochu."

"That's not true!" Kiyo clenched his fists. "They don't fish because all the fish are dead. Sympathy and government money isn't enough to feed anyone for long. They can't buy rice or even charcoal for cooking and heating, like we do."

The chauffeur gave a resigned sigh. "OK then. Why
don't I drive you there? That's quite a load, and it might
sleet. It is November, you know."

Kiyo took a deep breath. "Fine. Thanks."

The driver stored bike and food in the trunk. He
seemed to already know the way. As they approached Tsukinoura, Kiyo gazed at the kids' hangout hut where he and
Yuki sat the first time they'd met. The door's last hinge
had finally given way, leaving it lying crookedly on the
ground, surrounded by nails rusted to dull orange. Unable
to work the water, many of the young people from fisher
families had moved away. He rarely saw anyone playing
around the dilapidated shed anymore.

Just as well, he supposed. It could crash down any
moment.

In Tsukinoura, Fukuzawa parked in front of the
Akajis' house, and they divided the food to carry between
them.

Kiyo said, "Mind staying out here? I won't be long."

"Not at all." The driver carefully stacked his share of
the cans and parcels atop Kiyo's already precarious load
and wandered out into the small side-yard.

Since his arms were too full to knock Kiyo shouted,
"Hello? It's me!"

Yuki grinned when she opened the door. "Here, let me
help." She took the bag of rice off the top. He slipped off his
shoes and stepped inside.

"Kiyo-kun," Yuki's mom gasped. "More food? I don't
know how to thank you."

The parents and Tomoko were around the kotatsu. Kiyo and Yuki stacked the groceries on a kitchen shelf.

"Did another man arrive with you?" Kazuko asked.

Kiyo blushed. "Er, yes."

"Have him come in too. It's cold outside."

Kiyo opened the door. "Fukuzawa-san! They'd like you
to come inside, too."

He did, pausing in the doorway to remove his shoes and hat, then bowed to the family. "Hello. I'm the chauffeur."

"*Chauffeur!*" Yuki looked astonished. "You have your own driver?"

Kiyo shook his head. "No, no. He's my father's company driver. I ride a bike everywhere, remember? Fukuzawa-san just happened to be coming this way today."

Her eyes shone with awe. "A real chauffeur."

"Yuki-chan, get them tea," her mother said.

"I brought green tea and canned taro," Kiyo said.

"How nice! Thank you." Kazuko looked happy. "Real tea, then. Yuki-chan, would you mind serving?"

"I'll help you." Kiyo stepped down into the kitchen with her. Something gray was nibbling barley from a hole in a grain bag slumped on the floor. "A rat!" He raised his foot to stomp on it, but the rodent squirmed under the outside wall and disappeared.

Yuki picked up the barley bag, cupping the hemp to keep more grain from spilling out. She set it high on a shelf. "They get into everything. Jiro used to catch them. I'd like to get another cat, but . . . there aren't any."

"Rats are everywhere now." He wondered why there weren't more of them in his house. "You should probably keep your food in metal cans or ceramic containers."

"You're right, but that's the only one we have." Yuki pointed to a large stoneware jar. "I ferment vegetables in *nuka* in there."

"I'll bring you some more." Maybe Mom would advance him next month's allowance. He didn't want to wait a whole month while rodents ate Yuki's food.

Kazuko said, "Fukuzawa-san, please have a seat."

"Thank you." The driver moved to an open spot at the table and folded his long legs under the kotatsu.

After Yuki poured the tea, she took her sister from her mother to go change the wet diaper in the other room.

"Ahhh. So good." Nobuyuki managed a stiff smile. "Generous, Kiyo-kun."

"Gotta have tea." Kiyo noticed that the several new watercolor paintings leaning against the wall looked so ... real. But feeling constrained with Fukuzawa there, he didn't comment.

Kazuko took a sip, closing her eyes to savor the taste. "Delicious!"

Yuki padded back in, cradling Tomoko.

"Cute." The driver reached up and tickled the baby's belly, then picked up one small hand. The baby's gaze followed him, but her arms hung flaccid. Fukuzawa frowned and tucked his hands back under the futon. "Botchan." Young Master, he said. "I need to get back."

"Of course!" Kazuko rose slowly. "You have work to do. Kiyo-kun, thank you again."

He wanted to stay longer but reluctantly left with Fukuzawa. Back in the car, though, the chauffeur didn't start the engine. Just stared out the windshield at the rutted road, the warped unpainted buildings.

"I thought I knew what poor was." He shook his head. "You're right. These fishers need more help. I saw rats running around as if they owned the place." He turned to Kiyo, eyes full of sympathy. "They can't even buy some tea or rice?"

"The government gives a little rice every month, but it doesn't last long. They grow vegetables in the summer, but they can't in the fall and winter. They can't fish anymore. If I didn't bring some food, they'd starve. But it's not enough."

"I'll help you bring more. Yanagiya-san will be happy to donate a few things from the pantry."

"That'd be great. They use wood from the forest for cooking, but soon I'll need to start buying charcoal for their kotatsu."

"Charcoal's heavy. I'll help deliver that. How old is Yuki-san?"

"Seventeen."

"Ah . . . same age as you."

"We have the same birthdate."

Fukuzawa chuckled. "Now, isn't that something?"

The chauffeur started the engine, and Kiyo was grateful for the comfort of a car – a luxury Yuki and her family had never known, along with the bountiful amounts of food in his own kitchen. Some people had too much, others so very little.

Fukuzawa cleared his throat. "It was hard to understand the father."

"The muscles around Minamata Disease victims' mouths grow stiff," Kiyo explained. "He can't open it very well. He can still eat, though it's difficult. Many victims can only scream."

Fukuzawa looked shocked. "I thought they just swayed when they walked."

"Lack of coordination from neurological damage. That's why walking and gripping things is hard. He can't hold chopsticks now. And vision narrows until they go blind. Deaf, too. On top of that, they're always in great pain."

"I've heard some jump in front of trains to commit suicide. I thought they just didn't want to work, and took the easy way out."

"No." Kiyo closed his eyes, but that never kept the images of disfigured patients at the hospital from flashing through his mind. "They're killing themselves because they can't stand the agony anymore. They don't want to be a burden on their families. Come to the Minamata Disease ward at the hospital with me, and see for yourself."

Fukuzawa shook his head. "No, I believe you. I've seen enough."

"Chisso's tainted wastewater was causing the Disease. But Dad's new filter remedied that problem. There'll be no new cases, at least."

"Yes." Fukuzawa nodded. "He's a good man, your father."

TWENTY-FOUR

Long and Lengthwise

On a cool November morning, Yuki's father inclined his head at the clock on the kitchen shelf. "Better hurry. Be late for school."

"I'm not going," Yuki said.

"What? Why not?" Mom, nursing Tomoko, looked up in shock.

"I got a job as cook's helper at Chiyo's Café in Minamata."

"But you need only two years more to graduate," Mom said sadly.

"I'm seventeen. I know math and how to read and write – enough to get by. We need the money, so I'm going in to work at ten. I'll be home by seven."

Dad didn't say anything. Only looked away, his expression pinched.

The sky was cloudy as Yuki walked the two miles to Chiyo's, a family-owned tempura shop located in a middle-class Minamata neighborhood. The wooden houses around the cafe were mostly two stories with modest, enclosed yards. Everyone had at least a small garden, where the last of summer's drying bean-vines hung limp on their bamboo poles. Only sparse rows of carrots and daikon radishes remained.

Yuki slid open the sliding glass door to the restaurant. Five tables dotted the main room. A counter, four stools tucked under it, faced the open kitchen. An elderly man in a long-sleeved tan shirt sat slumped at one of the tables, smoking a cigarette. She'd met him when she applied for the job. Mr. Sato had started the eatery thirty years ago. His son and daughter-in-law ran the place now, but the old man still whiled away the time here.

"*Konnichiwa.*" Hello, Yuki said, and bowed.

"Good, you're here." Mrs. Sato was a stocky woman with arms bigger and more muscular than her husband's — not a difficult feat. Mr. Sato was short and wiry with an unusually high-bridged nose. Yuki wondered if that hawkish promontory obstructed the view when he glanced sideways.

The wife had mounded onions, sweet potatoes, bell peppers, green beans, eggplants, and mushrooms on a cypress-wood table in the kitchen. "Wipe the tables and sweep the entry. When you're done, wash your hands and cut up the vegetables," she instructed.

Yuki nodded. "Yes, Sato-san."

Mrs. Sato turned to her husband. "With no more seafood from the Bay, the fish vendor has been shipping it in by train. It's getting too expensive. We're not making any money on the shrimp and mackerel dishes."

"We'll have to raise prices." The husband shook his head.

"Customers will complain." Mrs. Sato started scrubbing more vegetables in the sink.

Once Yuki finished wiping down the tables and sweeping up, she washed her hands and picked up the heavy knife lying on the huge chopping board.

She started with the onions, peeling and cutting them into tidy chunks. She snapped off the ends of the beans, then peeled the potatoes and eggplants and chopped them into pieces. She was about to start on the bell peppers when someone nearby started screaming.

"What've you done?" Mrs. Sato's mouth hung open. "You chopped them into little bits."

Yuki's mouth went so dry, a towel might've been stuffed in her mouth. "But . . . you said to cut them up."

"*Baka*!" Imbecile, shouted the owner. "How're we supposed to batter and fry those tiny pieces up? We're a tempura shop."

Yuki hung her head. "I'm sorry. I've never had tempura."

"You've never – " The woman clutched her face in disbelief. "Lunch customers will start arriving in an hour.
How am I . . . *Ahhhh*!" she screamed, fists clenched.

The husband dashed in. "What's wrong?" He gasped
when he saw the piles of chopped-up vegetables on the cutting board. "No! Why?"

"She says she's never eaten tempura." The wife bowed
to her husband. "I'm sorry. I had no idea she wouldn't cut
them up properly."

Mr. Sato cursed loudly, grabbed a pot, and hurled it
across the room. It bashed the white tiled wall, and
crashed to the floor, along with one broken tile. Yuki
flinched, afraid to breathe. Would he throw something at
her next? That big knife, perhaps. She'd made a huge
blunder. And now he was so angry and violent . . . would
he kill her? She wanted to flee, but felt frozen in place. Her
knees shaking so badly she wasn't sure she *could* run.

"Now our regular customers will go to Sakura's," Mr.
Sato ranted. "They may never come back! How stupid can
one person be?" Yuki didn't know if he was swearing at her
or his wife. "Chiyo, go buy more vegetables," he snapped.

"That'll take half an hour. I haven't washed the rice or
made the sauce."

"Go!" he yelled. Mrs. Sato grabbed three large sacks
and hurried out.

"I know how to make rice," Yuki whispered.

"Ha!" He stabbed his index finger in her face. "No
chance. You're fired!"

"I'm very sorry." She bowed, then ran out to the street.

Shuffling toward home, she was wondering what work
she might find next when two teenage boys rode past, then

turned around. Kiyo stopped his bike in front of her. "Hel-lo!"

The other boy was a bit taller, round-faced, with mis-chievous eyes behind black-framed glasses. He tilted his head as if trying to recall how he might know her.

"Hi, I'm Yuki."

"Oh, sorry," Kiyo said, "Masa-kun, this is Yuki-chan."

"Hi." Glancing at Kiyo, the taller boy said, "Ah. The one you've been seeing."

Kiyo's cheeks turned red. "Well, I – "

Yuki's face grew warm, too. "I started working today at a tempura restaurant." She glanced away from Masa. "To help my family."

"What about school?" Kiyo asked.

"I stopped going."

"You quit?" Kiyo blurted out, then looked as if he'd like to take back those words. "Of course, I see. Ahhh, sorry you have to do that ... No more aid money?"

"We've been careful, but that's all gone. And just now . . . I got fired."

"Eh?" Kiyo and Masa both looked confused.

"For cutting up vegetables wrong. I made some into square bits. I guess that's not how tempura vegetables are prepared."

"They should've taught you, first," Kiyo huffed.

"Tempura vegetables are cut long and lengthwise," Masa said.

Kiyo shot him an annoyed look. "You're not helping."

"Oh. I see." Yuki looked down, picking at a fingernail.

"Hey, I'm hungry. Let's get some lunch," Masa said. "There's a great okonomiyaki cart nearby."

"Ah, but . . . the thing is," Kiyo stammered, "I'm out of money."

"Already?"

Yuki's face burned again. Kiyo had spent everything he had on her family.

"Eh. I'll buy," Masa said lightly. "I love egg pancakes."

"Well." Kiyo hesitated.

"I always have money left over every month. Let's go!"

"Yeah?" Kiyo smiled at his friend. "Yuki-chan, you can sit in my basket."

Not eager to eat the cold potato she'd brought for lunch, she agreed.

Kiyo held the bicycle steady while she squirmed her rear end into the large wire carrier, folding her legs up until her thighs were pressed to her chest, knees to her chin, feet sticking out in front of her. Almost as tall as Kiyo now, she just fit. Being skinny has its good points, she thought, leaning back on the handlebars and gripping the basket's sides.

Kiyo could barely see over her head. The front wheel wobbled under her weight, but he gripped the handlebars hard and pumped the pedals.

Yuki gave an exhilarating scream to release the morning's frustration. A brisk fall wind blew her hair back and raised goosebumps on her arms, but she didn't care. For once she felt free – Kiyo behind her, the surge of the bike every time he pumped the pedals. She loved his nearness, even the earthy smell of his sweat.

Five minutes later, the trio coasted into a bus stop marked by a solitary bench. The food bar behind it was dark, too early for it to be open for lunch.

"What about this place?" said Masa.

He was looking at a man in a wide-brimmed straw hat who stood nearby at a food cart. Its shingled roof shielded vendor and food from the sun. The heat radiating from the glowing fire beneath the cast-iron grill felt good. Yuki scooted closer, rubbing her hands together. At eleven-thirty, they were apparently his first customers.

"You're early." When the cook smiled, one crooked incisor stuck out past his other teeth. "I was just making batter. What would you like on your pancakes?"

"Everything," Kiyo blurted out.

"Me, too," Masa and Yuki chorused.

They watched as he cooked shredded cabbage, green onions, and mushrooms on the grill. While the vegetables sizzled, he mixed eggs with flour and water. Then spread three large circles of batter on the hot griddle, sprinkling generous portions of all the fillings on top. After the batter began bubbling, he flipped them. Miraculously, nothing fell off.

The delicious smells made Yuki's mouth water. Her stomach growled like a bear, and everyone laughed.

When the okonomiyaki was cooked through, the man cut each pancake into four pieces and set them on folded newspaper. Masa paid, and they sat on the bus bench to eat.

Yuki picked up a piece, and savory steam rose. She bit into it, then fanned at her mouth. "Hot! But good!" The vegetables were crunchy, yet the pancake was soft and sweet. "So happy I got to try them. Does tempura taste like this?"

"Don't you know?" Masa looked astonished, but he kept eating.

Kiyo slammed one knee against his friend's leg as if to say *keep quiet.* "Thanks, Masa-kun," he mumbled around his mouthful of pancake.

After they'd eaten, and Masa heard Yuki would have to walk all the way home, he insisted on giving her bus fare.

After she'd boarded, and was sitting on a seat up front, relaxed and belly full, she replayed that pleasant hour spent with the boys. How nice it'd been to let go and have fun again. She'd savor the outing for a long time.

"Tadaima," she announced as she reached home, bending to pull off her shoes.

Tomoko lay on a towel in the main room, gurgling to herself. No one else seemed to be in there, and the door to the bedroom was closed.

Something's wrong, thought Yuki, alarm bells clanging in her head. She kicked off her shoes, bolted inside, and banged open the shoji door to the bedroom.

"Dad!" she screamed.

He hung from the ceiling truss, a rope around his neck. The living room table lay in its side next to his kicking feet, his fingers clawing at the noose squeezing his throat.

Yuki ran to the kitchen and grabbed a knife. Back in the bedroom she heaved the table upright and climbed onto it. Left arm around her father's waist, she sawed through the noose, a length of mooring line. Luckily it was old and frayed; she hacked through the top part with seven desperate slashes.

Nobuyuki fell heavily onto his feet, and his knees collapsed. Yuki dropped the knife. She wrapped both arms around him, then gently lowered him to lie over the small table, head and back supported, legs dangling over one side. His cheeks were almost purple. He was gagging, frantically gasping in air.

Kazuko staggered in on trembling legs. "What happened?"

"Dad ... he ... he tried to hang himself," Yuki said. She carefully cut the noose from his neck, then eased him onto the floor. His breathing became more even.

"*Anata!*" Honey, Mom cried, collapsing on her knees next to him.

He looked away, neck ringed by an ugly red line, shrouded in a haze of hopelessness.

"Oh, Dad." Yuki slumped next to him, adrenaline draining away to exhaustion. How had he mustered enough strength to move the table from the living room, to toss the line up over the rafter? Thank goodness she'd come home when she did.

What agony, inside and out, he must be suffering to try to commit suicide.

Kazuko draped herself over his chest, embracing him. "You tried to kill yourself while I was away in the outhouse?"

"Pathetic," he rasped, neck mottled with beads of blood. "Can't even . . . kill myself."

"We have two daughters! We're a family, and must stay together." She stroked his shoulders; a teardrop splashed onto his undershirt.

"A burden. Yuki-chan quit school to feed us. Better off without me."

"We're all three a burden," Kazuko sobbed.

"No, no." Yuki shook her head so hard her neck hurt. "I can't live without my family. Promise you'll never try to leave us again."

Nobuyuki looked away, at the opposite wall. He said nothing. Yuki worried, Will Dad try again?

And the next time, he just might succeed.

TWENTY-FIVE

Unexpected Visitors

Yuki breathed through her mouth as she scrubbed the pit latrine's porcelain toilet with a hard-bristled brush. This chore was the hardest one she had to do for her new employer, the old woman whose family owned the largest lumber store in Minamata. Her daughter-in-law usually cleaned the house but she was visiting family in Fukuoka, to the north. The young bride was not a good housekeeper anyhow, so the mother-in-law took advantage of the girl's absence to pay for a deep cleaning.

Yuki hadn't minded the two weeks of polishing floors on hands and knees and digging dirt out of corners with a toothbrush. The easiest task had been to carefully remove and wash everything from the kitchen shelves and cabinets. And she was grateful to have temporary work, at least. Now she could buy tofu and a few cans of food.

She'd be starting a new full-time job next week, packing dried vegetables from huge sacks into smaller packages at one of the large nearby farms. For now she was lucky to have some indoor work in January.

She hurried home, wondering how badly her sister's diaper needed changing. Nerves as taut as the rope on which she hung wet laundry. She always left potatoes for lunch and her sister strapped to Mom so she could nurse. Still, if either parent fell, could they get up again? If anything happened to Tomoko, could they save her or go for help? As she neared her village, she passed a cottage where chickens clucked in the yard, pecking for insects and stray grain. Yuki sighed. These people were fortunate; they had at least a half-dozen laying hens.

When she neared her own house, she was surprised to see two people at the front door. The man was knocking; the woman turned to look at Yuki as she approached.

He wore a nice wool overcoat over suit and tie; older than her father but with smooth, untanned skin and a gentle expression. The woman in worn-looking wooden clogs held a notebook. A heavy woolen shawl draped her dark-blue cotton kimono.

"Hello," Yuki said uncertainly. People carrying notebooks and briefcases rarely came to this village.

"Hi. I'm Harada Masazumi." He dipped his head slightly. "Sorry to intrude. I'm a doctor. I understand there's a baby here?"

"Yes. What do you want with her?"

"We've seen an abnormally high frequency of infants with cerebral palsy symptoms in this area. I'm doing research to see if it's something else, instead." Nodding toward the woman, he added, "This is Ishimure Michiko-san, from Minamata. She's been keeping a record of what's happening in the Bay and with Minamata Disease. Mind if we see your baby?"

"She's my sister." Yuki understood the doctor's misapprehension. Seventeen wasn't too young to have a baby, though she only envisioned a child of her in some distant future.

"Of course. I didn't mean to imply . . . I apologize." He bowed.

The man spoke such proper Japanese, Yuki felt flustered as to how she should respond. "Um, think nothing of it. Please, come in."

Her parents sat at the kotatsu. Tomoko lay in the towel tied around her mother's neck. Yuki scooped up a stack of clean diapers from the living room floor and hid them in the bedroom.

"Here are my parents," she said.

Yuki's mother bowed from where she sat. "How do you do?" Her father only dipped his head slightly, studying the strangers with narrowed eyes.

"Please excuse me a moment," Yuki said, "I must change a diaper."

She cleaned up her sister in the bedroom then tied her back into the sling. The charcoal under the kotatsu had burned out, so she replenished and lit it.

"Please, sit. You must be cold." She gestured at the table, and their guests sank gratefully into the two empty spots.

The doctor bowed, introducing himself, explaining about his research on infants with cerebral-palsy symptoms. "Not many may actually have it, though. May I ask about your baby's health?" He smiled at Tomoko.

Ishimure Michiko opened her notebook, pencil poised to write.

Kazuko frowned. "What else could it be?"

"Perhaps Minamata Disease."

Her mother looked astonished. "That's impossible. She's only ever had my milk, porridge, and mashed vegetables. Nothing from the Bay. I didn't get the Disease until after she arrived. Tomoko-chan was just born this way."

Yuki nodded. "And now, with the Cyclator, Chisso isn't dumping toxic wastewater anymore. A friend told me, because I worried about Tomoko-chan's development."

"Who was the friend?" the doctor asked.

"Kuge Kiyo. He's studying to be a doctor and assists Dr. Hosokawa at the hospital," Yuki said. "He said babies with cerebral palsy have symptoms similar to those of people with Minamata Disease."

When the doctor nodded, she wondered if he was agreeing with her or merely being polite.

"May I examine the baby?" he asked.

Mom dipped her chin in assent. After Yuki gently laid her sister on a cloth on the floor, Harada Sensei knelt next to her.

"Hello, Tomoko-chan. May I play with you?" he asked in a kind voice. Smiling, he thrust a finger into her hand. The baby kicked, but didn't grasp it. He tried again with the other hand. Same result.

He looked up at Kazuko. "When was she born?"

"December eighteenth. In 1958."

"So she's thirteen months old. Does she hold your breast while she nurses, or reach for it when hungry?"

Mom swallowed, looking anxious. "No."

"Has she made any sounds besides crying?"

"No. None."

"Does she turn over on her own?"

Kazuko shook her head, eyes shiny with unshed tears.

"Does she react to faraway sounds?"

Yuki met her Mom's stricken gaze. "She only looks at us when we're close to her. Like Uncle did."

"Oh, no." Mom collapsed over the kotatsu, sobbing.

Ishimure made more notes. After she and Dr. Harada left, Yuki pulled out her sketch pad and quickly drew her sister waddling around their house, laughing and clutching a ball of twine.

Even if this picture never came true, it gave her a little hope. She needed more courage now, just to face each day.

TWENTY-SIX

The News Unfit to Print

No further developments came from the university researchers proving the cause of Minamata Disease. Not since Hosokawa Sensei had made the initial link between seafood and the Disease during the ill-fated cat experiment. And with the Cyclator in place for sixteen months now, Kiyo had assumed the Disease would stop spreading. But that wasn't the case. Dr. Hosokawa was still baffled on how to best treat new victims.

Kiyo encountered Masa on this spring morning as he was cycling to the hospital. They rode on, enjoying the cherry blossoms perfuming the air, when Kiyo caught sight of a former neighbor.

"Kikuko-chan? What're you doing here? Didn't you get married and move to Osaka?"

She was the older sister of Hiro, a boy in his same grade at school. Her parents had arranged for her to marry an Osaka man.

But now her wide, once-smiling mouth sagged at the corners. She shook her head, burying her nose in a handkerchief, only sniffling when they rode up to her. Kiyo glanced at him but said nothing, waiting for Kikuko to speak. Masa opened his mouth, then blinked and closed it, having gotten the message.

"It was terrible!" she blurted out at last, clapping her hands over her damp face.

Kiyo raised his eyebrows. "Know what she's talking about?" he whispered. No answer.

She lifted her head and sighed. "My parents and I met my husband-to-be and family in a private dining room at a fancy restaurant in Osaka, the day before the wedding. They asked about our trip from Kagoshima. My father said, 'Oh, we're from Minamata.' They all looked shocked. The matchmaker had told them Kagoshima. We explained he knew we were from here; we hadn't lied. And then they said, 'We can't take in a bride from there and risk our family getting the Disease.' "

"But it's not contagious," Kiyo said. "You obviously don't have it. And now with the Cyclator, the Bay isn't polluted anymore."

Masa nodded. "Yeah. That's right."

Kikuko shook her head. "We said that, too, but they still feared being ostracized by friends and relatives. The father might get demoted at work."

"My brother's an engineer in Tokyo," Kiyo said. "He told me people around the country are only now hearing about the Disease. They still believe the original rumors about it being contagious."

She re-pinned a lock of hair that'd fallen onto her forehead. "They said the marriage was off and rushed out as if we were diseased. My parents spent all that money for my wedding kimono, our travel there." She laughed bitterly. "They even stuck us with the bill for dinner."

"That go-between only wanted the fee." Kiyo spat out. "Bastard."

"Choke him until he gives you your money back," Masa suggested.

"I guess." She wiped her nose with the hankie. "I was supposed to have a beautiful spring wedding with all the cherry and plum blossoms, their sweet fragrances everywhere." She tightened her lips and clenched her trembling chin. "Oh, well."

"I'm sorry that happened," Kiyo said.

"Thanks. See you later." She gave a little sigh and continued on her way.

"The Disease is giving the city a bad name," Masa said. "Someone should do something about it."

"They already are!" Kiyo pounded the handlebars.

"What's wrong with you?"

"Many researchers are working on it. No one seems to notice."

"They'd better hurry before Chisso moves away. Without the company, the city'll shrivel up. No tourists will come, even for the hot springs. Most have already abandoned the beaches. People who work for Chisso will have to move somewhere else for jobs. Our hotel will collapse."

"Is that all you care about?" Kiyo snapped. "People are suffering and dying."

Masa's mouth popped open. "But most of them are just faking to get handouts."

Yuki's uncle screaming and thrashing on the floor. Food spilling out of her dad's mouth when he tried to eat. These images invaded Kiyo's mind. And their misery filled him with rage. "They're not faking! They become weak, and can't do anything, even eat. And they're always in terrible pain."

Masa glanced at Kiyo's face and said quickly, "All right, all right! Maybe they really are sick. But the samurai gave their lives for their lords. Soldiers died for our country. Japanese have always sacrificed for the good of our people. So a few must suffer to make Japan a global power again, right? It's too bad, but we have to think of the city, our country."

"You're such an idiot," Kiyo snapped, then pedaled off, afraid he'd say something worse.

He was still angry when he arrived at Dr. Hosokawa's office. The pile of books on the desk had grown so tall it completely obscured his left side.

Surely that leaning tower would crash soon. "Sensei, people outside of Minamata Bay still believe the Disease is contagious." He told Kikuko's story.

"I'm distressed to hear that." The doctor removed his glasses and rubbed the lenses on a handkerchief. "In the beginning, we knew nothing about the Disease. I was only trying to prevent its spread when I announced it could be contagious. I wish I could undo that now. Once people get misinformation stuck in their heads, it's hard to change their minds." He put on his glasses, looking dejected.

Kiyo thought about Yuki's parents and sister. "Sensei, do victims ever get better?"

"I'm afraid not." The doctor shook his head slowly. "Neurological damage can't be reversed. Especially the kind that causes these symptoms."

"So, those people will never walk well or see clearly or be without pain?"

"That's right. Though the Disease won't progress as far in the lucky ones."

"Lucky!" Kiyo barked a bitter laugh.

"Sorry, poor choice of words. Would you close the door, please?"

Kiyo did, then sat down. "Is something wrong?"

"A friend of mine from the prefectural government's office smuggled a copy of a joint survey between Kumamoto and Kagoshima cities to me."

"He . . . had to smuggle it? But why?"

"Government officials and Chisso are hiding crucial facts that tie the company to Minamata Disease." The doctor opened a side drawer in his desk and pulled out a sheaf of papers. "They had researchers take hair samples from people who live around the Shiranui Sea, and analyzed mercury levels."

"I gave hair samples a year and a half ago. What happened?"

"Organic mercury has been found to have spread all around the inland sea, which means people are still being poisoned by something in the Bay."

"But Chisso's installed the Cyclator, and discharged wastewater is now clean. The president even drank some." How elated he'd felt that day, at the unveiling of the Cyclator, believing Yuki was now safe from the Disease. Perhaps he's been a fool to think so.

Or was it possible everyone had been conned?

"Hundreds of those hair samples contain levels greater than 50 parts per million of mercury. The highest was 920 ppm, a very high exposure. Samples from Minamata residents without any Disease symptoms were around 190 ppm. The average outside the Bay area is 4 ppm. Even at 50 ppm, people can experience nerve damage."

"I wonder what my level is. I never heard back. The fishers' levels must be very high."

"That's the thing. The government didn't publish any results at all. The participants weren't informed of their own status even when they requested it. Our government did nothing."

"Then they've betrayed us all. We must do something if the mercury level's still so high!"

"Shh." The physician tapped his lips with a finger. "I'm not supposed to know about this."

Kiyo bent over the desk and whispered. "People should be told. The contamination has to be stopped."

"I'm just a doctor. A small pawn in a game controlled by Chisso and the government."

Kiyo felt a rage so strong it made him dizzy. "Well, if you won't say something, I will!"

"Kiyo-kun!" Sensei cried, as he dashed from the office.

The city newspaper was two blocks away. He pedaled there furiously and rushed inside. Its main office stank of stale cigarette smoke. One long room held six desks ranked down the middle, side by side. The one big window looked out on a small dormant flower garden and a large brick building beyond. Reporters occupied three desks, writing. A telephone was ringing somewhere nearby. Tendrils of smoke curled up from cigarette stubs in ashtrays or between nicotine-yellowed fingers.

Another man sat at a larger desk at the far end of the room, facing the front door. A formidable-looking young woman with a tight, red-lipsticked smile, was seated next to the front door.

He approached her. "May I speak to the editor?"

She eyed him coolly. "Why?"

"It's about Minamata Disease. There's new information the paper should print."

"Tell me, then, and I'll let him know."

"I must speak to him directly."

She shook her head, and went back to a magazine she'd been reading. Kiyo hesitated a moment, then darted past her desk, heading for the man at the back of the room.

"Hold on!" she called after him. "You can't just barge in like gangbusters."

The nameplate propped on the large desk read NOMO, EDITOR/PUBLISHER. The plump man with an oddly-long neck peered up at Kiyo. "What do you want?"

Kiyo bowed. "Nomo-san, I'm Kuge Kiyoshi. Hair samples taken from hundreds of people in the Bay area prove Minamata residents have ingested very high levels of mercury compared to those outside our area. So high it caused nerve damage. You must print the findings and warn everyone not to eat anything taken from the Bay."

The editor leaned back in his chair. "Our Bay is famous for its delicious seafood. Printing such a warning would ruin the city's reputation. Tourist visits will fall. Businesses will fail. Besides, most fishers aren't working anymore, since their catch is no longer salable."

"So you'd rather everyone in Minamata gets the Disease? Yes, most Bay sea life is dead. But the poor still are forced to eat it, to survive."

"Then why has no government official or medical person told me to publish these so-called findings? If I did so, based on some teenage boy's demand, my paper could ruin our economy."

"I understand." Kiyo took a deep breath; he must sound authoritative to convince the editor. "Check with government officials, of course. But they're in cahoots with our top city officials and the Chisso corporation, working together to hide these very facts."

"Oh, really?" The man didn't sound surprised.

"Yes. So we must act to protect the citizens. Please." Kiyo bowed again.

"I see. Thanks for stopping by." Nomo picked up a red pencil and continued writing in the margins of a stack of pages on the desk.

Kiyo felt like spitting on him. Instead, he spat out more words. "The lucky ones die quickly. The unlucky go blind, deaf, can't eat, drink, or walk. They die in agonizing pain."

Nomo looked up wide-eyed, recoiling from Kiyo. He held both hands out as if to ward off a physical attack.

"What if something like that happens to your family?" Kiyo hissed, spittle spraying the shocked man's face. "Come to the hospital, I'll show you the victims. Your own neighbors."

He reached out for Nomo's hand, to pull him to his feet. The editor shouted, "*Tasukete!*" Help.

Suddenly three reporters were grabbing at Kiyo's arms and clothing. They dragged him away between the gauntlet of desks, toward the exit.

He struggled to free himself, shouting, "I'll attend your wife's funeral when she dies of the Disease!" His shoe heels left a trail of black scuff marks on the floor.

The men shoved him out of the doorway, hard. Kiyo tumbled down the steps to the sidewalk. Salarymen in gray suits rushing off to work skirted around him without stopping. Women with babies tied to their backs stared before gingerly stepping around, making sure not to brush against him.

Kiyo sat fuming on the pavement, grinding his teeth. Angry not just at the editor, but at himself. He'd stupidly lost his temper and ended up looking like a maniac.

He'd even failed to keep Yuki's family from eating seafood from the Bay. He hadn't convinced his father and Chisso to stop dumping mercury. He couldn't get Hosokawa Sensei to go public with the secret study outcome. And now his father would surely regard his talk with the editor as a betrayal.

Am I even effective enough to become a worthwhile doctor, one who actually saves lives?

Kiyo pressed his fists into his temples. The city's people had a right to know what was going on, to protect themselves. But the men in power only cared that business go on as usual. Was Dad as callous as them, or was he just being a loyal company man?

Kiyo's head felt ready to explode. He lurched up and stumbled away, feeling for the moment utterly defeated.

TWENTY-SEVEN

Unfriendly Sea

On Yuki's eighteenth birthday, she helped her father walk out to the yard, where he stood unsteadily, eyes closed, face lifted to the sky. *I like to feel the summer wind and sun on my face,* he used to tell her, back when he was a fisherman.

She tilted her face up too, The warmth felt nice, and the air was fresh. "Good wind today," Nobuyuki muttered stiffly. "Your day. Let's sail." Most people couldn't understand him anymore, but she could. He was barely able to open his mouth. The tips of his teeth showed now, and she knew he was trying to grin.

Mom chimed in. "Shall we? We always sailed on your birthday."

"Yes, let's," Yuki said. "Maybe Kiyo-kun will get here early enough to join us. I'll leave a note."

The Minamata plumber she was currently digging holes for didn't need her until after lunch, so today was the best one for a family sail. Probably the last time, she thought sadly. Who knew how long either parent would be able to walk to the beach or maneuver the sail? Tomoko had never been out on the water. Yuki wanted her to sail at least once with the family, even if she wouldn't remember when she was older.

Yuki grilled sweet potatoes and filled a jar with water. She tied her sister to her back with a long cloth, then stuffed several diapers, the food, and jar into a large furoshiki. Together, the family walked slowly down the dirt lane that ran from the main road to the water. Small houses, though most larger than theirs, stood along the road, a few hundred feet from each other. Unable to fish anymore, men young and old sat outside on sun-bleached wooden chairs smoking cigarettes. They silently watched Yuki's family go slowly by. Women were washing laundry or hanging wet clothes on bamboo poles under the roof eaves.

"Perfect fishing day." Dad inhaled deeply. "Nice salt breeze."

"No one could tell better than you," Yuki said.

"I can remember when it smelled clean, though."

"It was a wonderful life, fishing every day." Mom closed her eyes, smiling.

"Tomoko-chan," said Yuki, "We used to do this every summer day. I found this pretty brooch on the beach on my fourteenth birthday. Uncle Higano was still alive. Everything seemed perfect, back then."

How she longed to have that life again. The brooch wasn't all she had left from that time, though. Kiyo had appeared the same day. He was a well of strength; she felt she could get through anything with him beside her. A smile tugged at her lips. This summer, he could visit almost daily after she'd finished work. He'd help with their garden, so there'd be time to stroll through the woods and by the sea on warm evenings.

With Dad tottering and Mom moving very slowly, the usual two-minute walk on the narrow road was taking ten times that, but Yuki didn't mind. She wanted to remember every minute of their last sailing outing.

They were almost to the beach when Kumiko, her best friend from childhood days, came around the side of a house they were just passing. The once-slender girl's rounded hips swung; her neat pink blouse was impressively filled out. Her mother must still sew for wealthy people, Yuki thought. Kumiko wore a new-looking sleeveless top with tiny ruffles trimming the chest pocket, and a pretty

pink-and-white striped skirt. Only the few pimples sprinkled on her cheeks made her appear less than perfect.
Since quitting school, Yuki had rarely seen her, so she
waved.

Kumiko froze, seeming panicked, and looked wildly
around. She'd obviously been heading from her house to
the main road, this route being the only way to town. But
now she darted off the path so quickly she bumped into a
shed.

"Go away," she begged. "Don't give me the Disease."

Yuki frowned. "We're not contagious. That's ignorance.
Don't be afraid."

Kumiko shook her head and collapsed to the dirt, a
hand cupped over her nose and mouth as if to avoid
breathing contaminated air. She wailed like a child.

Nobuyuki's face was red with rage or humiliation.
Kazuko looked stricken.

Yuki stomped over to Kumiko and stood over her. "Do
you think they like being ill and in pain? We've lost everything." She punched the shed wall, startling Tomoko, who
began to wail along with Kumiko.

"Hey, what're you doing?" A middle-aged man wearing
stained shorts and an old undershirt stood barefoot in the
doorway to the house beside the shed. A fisherman who'd
lived there as long as Yuki could remember. "Don't bang on
my property. Move on."

Yuki spat on the grass, close to her one-time friend,
then trudged back to her family. "Come on. Let's go."

"You told her," Dad muttered.

The family continued on. When Yuki glanced back,
Kumiko was running up the lane as if pursued by a demon.

Few people came to the seashore anymore. There was
one white-haired woman using a long bamboo stick as a
support as she limped slowly over the smooth sand. Under
a blazing sun, gray mullet, sea bream, octopi, crabs, and
squid lay rotting on the beach; lives taken for no good rea-

son. At least when fishermen caught them, they'd nour-
ished people.

Yuki stepped over lifeless fish, trying to ignore the
stench. Washed-up kelp and spindly seagrass lay in piles,
straggling dark green tendrils outstretched on the sand
like arms begging for help. Unable to lift their feet, her
parents had to shuffle around these obstacles. When Dad
accidentally stepped on a dead fish and slipped, Yuki had
to catch his arm to steady him.

Some fishers had left their boats anchored in the Bay,
but Nobuyuki had pulled theirs up and left it overturned
on the beach. A few barnacles were stuck to the hull, but it
was far cleaner than others with large patches of the tena-
cious brown crustaceans.

Financial aid from Minamata City had been based on
the applicant's assets. Boats were considered an asset, but
Dad, like other fishermen, was reluctant to sell his – even
though it meant he could get more assistance.

"Boats aren't cheap," he'd raged, back when he could
still speak more clearly. They'd scrimped and saved to buy
it. So he opted to receive only the small payments from
Chisso and welfare rations from the government.

Yuki thought she understood. Maybe fishing wasn't vi-
able now, but what was life without hope?

She eased Tomoko from her back and set her down
next to Kazuko. She'd squatted on one side of the boat,
about to turn it over, when Kiyo appeared at her side.

"Here, let me help."

They flipped it over without much trouble. A few tiny
sand crabs who'd been sheltering under it scurried away.

"Happy birthday, Yuki-chan," he said.

"Happy birthday, Kiyo-kun. You found my note. Why
not come with us?"

"Sounds like fun. But Mom wants to take me shopping
for new clothes. I've grown too much this year, she claims.
I just came by to drop off some food. I left it at the house."

"Thank you!" Kazuko said.

He looked sad, though. "I'm sorry I have so much, while you – "

Yuki huffed. "If you didn't have so much, we wouldn't have enough food."

He looked startled. "I never thought of it that way."

"Thanks, Kiyo-kun."

She often lay on her futon at night imagining his hands stroking her. Dreaming of their bodies nestled together. Of pressing her face into his solid chest and smelling sweet vinegar on his breath – a pricy condiment her family could no longer afford.

"I also left you another sketchpad," he said. "You're still drawing, right?"

"Of course. Whenever I can."

"Here, I'll help push the boat into the water. Let me pull the rope –"

"The mooring line," she corrected.

He grinned. "The *mooring line*. And you can push."

It made for light work with Kiyo's help; the boat was launched in no time. Everyone stood gazing down at the water swirling around their ankles, gray-green and murky.

"It used to be so clear." Mom shook her head. "I can't even see the bottom in the shallows. And this sick green color – the sea was once the same blue as the sky, so you couldn't tell where the bay ended and it began. The air used to smell fresh, with a hint of salt. Not like stinking garbage. Remember, Nobuyuki-kun, when seaweed grew up so tall from the sea-floor?"

He nodded.

Yuki recalled those days too. "Sea anemones bloomed like chrysanthemums underwater. Like bamboo groves stretching for the sun from the sea bottom. I loved watching schools of sardines, turning so precisely." Now there was only darkness under the dead, floating fish.

Kiyo said quickly, as if hoping to dispel the gloom, "If you all get in, I'll push the boat out."

Yuki set their lunch and water in the hull. She steadied her parents as they climbed in, then set the baby in her mother's lap.

"Have a great sail!" Kiyo shoved the boat into deeper water.

Yuki unfurled the canvas sail. The wind filled it until it bulged like a fat man's belly. She twisted in her seat to wave at Kiyo, and he waved back from the shore. They picked up speed, a freshening wind blowing her hair back.

Don't look down, she told herself. For on the surface floated so many dead things they might as well be skimming over a cemetery. She sat next to her mother, resolutely facing forward, and took the baby back onto her lap.

Tomoko squealed in delight.

"She likes sailing!" Yuki stood her up so she could take in the view. The Disease had made the little girl's body so stiff that clasping her felt like holding a piece of driftwood.

Her father sat back against the hull. Staring out at the jagged green islands on the horizon that partially enclosed the Bay, creating that inland sea.

"Want to work." He made a jerky motion as if steering or dragging in a catch with the net. "But lucky." He encircled his arms, as if embracing the whole family.

"I noticed you right away." Kazuko smiled fondly at him. "The handsomest man at the *obon* dance."

Dad pointed stiffly at her. "Prettiest." His eyes glittered. "Good house."

"The house was a barn," Mom said. "Nobuyuki put the floor and kitchen in it."

Yuki nodded. She'd heard the story many times.

Her mother stroked the baby's arm. "Not everyone gets to own a home. I had that, and everything else I'd ever wanted. Being out here every day, and plenty to eat."

Yuki wanted to say how much she had loved those glorious days on the Bay, too. But her parents' growing afflictions and the death of the sea congealed the words into a lump of sadness that clogged her throat.

The farther they sailed, the clearer the water became, the fresher the air. She managed to shed some of the darkness. "Maybe we can go around the Islands and into the open sea," she said. "There're healthy fish out there."

"Clear ocean!" Kazuko declared.

With his coaching, she took them to the end of the tranquil Bay. But as soon as she coaxed the small sailboat around the promontory of the last island and into the rough open water, she grew nervous. White-capped waves as tall as her father churned here, their crests frothing white as they tossed the boat up and banged it down again. Tomoko screamed; their mother held her close, crouched over to protect her.

Yuki tacked quickly, fighting the ocean as she tried to sail them back into the safety of the Bay. Once they rounded the point, the boat again bobbed peacefully, like a toy in a gigantic bathtub.

Nobuyuki gave a sigh of relief. "Fool." He pointed to himself. "Sell this. More aid."

Mom smiled sadly at him. "I think that's best, *Anata*. Then Yuki won't have to work so hard."

The old life, their passion for living from the sea was now in the past. For a moment, everyone silently mourned its passing.

They ate lunch then, Dad gazing west at Amakusa Islands that sheltered the Bay – his and his brother's original home. Her mother faced the opposite direction, toward the thick forest lining the beaches of Minamata Bay.

In the beginning, when Uncle had first contracted the Disease, Yuki could lift the dark net it cast over her life to let a ray of happiness or pleasure inside. Now, it felt as if the net had melded into a shroud.

She stood at the edge of the stern and held her sister; a child who'd never have any sort of a normal life. She might never walk or even crawl. Her eyesight seemed impaired, and she had trouble hearing. What would it be like to lose all your senses? Would Tomoko know the difference between living and dying?

Damn whoever was responsible for the Disease! How could the world be so unfair?

Yuki hummed to her sister, swinging her back and forth above the water. How simple would it be to let her grip slacken. To let the baby slip away into the sea. Her parents couldn't swim. If they tried to save her, they too would drown. Maybe a death by drowning was the kindest end for all of them. They weren't happy. She wasn't either.

This far out, the freshness of the air seemed to clarify things. She didn't want her family to live an extended life of agony. She could end that misery. She was responsible for every aspect of their lives, now.

Dangling the baby over the opaque water, she whispered, "I love you." She looked down, ready to let go, and glimpsed a glimmering on the surface. Her birthday brooch, reflecting light back. How excited she'd been to find it four years ago, when she'd still believed a bright future awaited. But now she knew life was not kind. Not even worth living.

A deep hopeless ache throbbed in her belly.

Lowering her head, she whispered to her sister, "You deserve so much better. I'm sorry."

Yuki slowly let Tomoko sink over the gunwales until the baby was immersed to her waist in the calm Bay water. Her tiny blouse and the thin blanket wrapped around her billowed, making a small float. As Yuki gazed down at her sister's face, Tomoko made a gurgling sound. The corners of her mouth twitched.

She was smiling. Her eyes seemed ... happy. Through them, Yuki saw that her sister's soul was as pure as new snow. Tomoko was the only one in the family free of malice, anger, or hate.

Whatever was her future, no matter how bleak it appeared, depriving her of it would be a terrible betrayal. It wasn't her place to end anyone's life. She could not kill, even out of compassion.

She swiftly straightened, sweeping Tomoko up and back into the boat. She cradled the baby until her clothes dried under the hot sun, then returned Tomoko to the sling.

Perhaps her drawings were images of a future that could never be. Still, she already envisioned the new picture she would sketch at home: her family in the boat, the Bay as clear as Kiyo's name. Schools of healthy fish skimming over the surface. Dad lugging in nets full of jumping silver fish, Mom cooking a nice lunch over the brazier. And Tomoko, slapping the hull and shrieking in delight.

TWENTY-EIGHT

Tomoko's Diagnosis

Yuki tipped back her conical straw hat and swiped a handkerchief – a scrap from an old blouse she'd outgrown – over her perspiring forehead and neck. Spring had been cool, so she hadn't burned to a crisp under a broiling sun as she tilled fields. The pleasant spring had turned into a summer of intense heat and humidity, though. The farmer she was working for grew a variety of vegetables for locals: onions, daikon radishes, potatoes, green onions, and carrots.

After six hours of whacking a hoe-blade at soil that'd hardened over the winter, to break it up, her shoulders, back and arms screamed. Blisters on her hands were still bleeding, making the hoe handle slippery.

She tried to concentrate on the sweet earthy odor of tilled soil, instead of the pain. As she hoed, the farmer planted seeds and shoots behind her. At least this week of backbreaking work would earn her enough money to buy groceries.

A few weeks later, with planting season over, the only work she could find was killing rats at a food distribution warehouse. The rectangular, wood-clad structure, undistinguishable from other boxy, boring-looking storehouses in the industrial section of Minamata, was large enough to park four delivery vans. The best part of the miserable job was the scent of dried mushrooms, persimmons, seaweed, squid, tuna broth base, and candy that permeated the place. Rodents ate through sacks and cardboard boxes, ruining stock and profits. They had to be eradicated.

One scorching August day she crawled under the shelf of the warehouse, slapping the mosquitos feasting on her face and neck. She'd sprinkled rat poison in the corners yesterday. The concrete floor felt cool under her knees, but the warm, humid air was hard to breathe through the gauze mask covering nose and mouth.

There they were: the corpses. Whole families of rats lay on their backs, bloated, thin legs sticking up in the air. She felt sorry for them. They were just trying to survive, like any human family. They didn't know they shouldn't eat the rice and dried vegetables packed in the sacks. But for her family to live, she had to do her job, and kill them.

She picked up the dead bodies one by one with gloved hands and dropped them into the large cloth bag she carried. Then carefully swept the leftover poison into the bag and crawled to the next corner. Not all the rats ate the poison. Some seemed too smart for that, and they kept breeding. New ones found their way in, too. But that was good. She could count on two days of work every week.

As she approached her home, Harada Sensei, the doctor studying disease symptoms in babies, was at the front door. The note-taker Ishimure Michiko stood next to him in a much-washed, summer cotton kimono, white-and-blue striped. It'd been eight months since his first visit.

When he saw her, he gave a little wave. "Hello, Yuki-san." He carried the same tan briefcase; Ishimure seemed to have the same notebook and pencil. "I have results about your sister," he added.

Yuki wanted to know what was wrong, but was also afraid to find out. What if it was some horrible, uncurable disease? What if she was going to die? She felt like turning and running away, back down the lane. Instead she said, "Please, come in."

All the doors were propped open to funnel in any passing breeze. Her parents sat leaning against the living room wall. They bowed from the waist, and their guests removed their shoes, lining them up as neatly as if they were entering a mansion, and bowed as well. Lying on a cloth on the floor next to her mother, Tomoko stared up at them.

"Thank you for taking the time to see us," Mom said. "Please, have a seat."

Yuki hurried to the kitchen. "I'll make some tea."

"Thank you," the doctor said, "but cool water might be better. It's so hot."

"Yes, water, please," Ishimure Michiko said.

Yuki was grateful. They'd run out of tea last week. Ever since, tea meant old leaves and boiled water. She filled two glasses from the water jar and set them on the table.

"Thank you." Sensei drank it all in one long gulp. He opened his briefcase, swatting away some flies buzzing around his head, then pulled out a sheaf of papers.

Next time I get paid, I must get some sticky fly strips, Yuki thought. The insects were relentless, and her parents could no longer swat at them.

"By the way." The doctor pointed to a half-dozen watercolors leaning against the living room wall. "Who's the painter?"

"I am," Yuki replied.

"My goodness. They're as good as any in art galleries."

Yuki's face grew even warmer. "I've a long way to go."

"Astoundingly good," murmured Ishimure.

"Well," Yuki said modestly. But inside, she was jumping up and down.

"Anyhow, as I mentioned on my previous visit, local doctors and medical officials have noticed an abnormally high frequency of cerebral palsy and other infantile disorders in the Minamata area. Deaf, blind, and mute babies and toddlers. So we reexamined those diagnosed with cerebral palsy. They present similarly or identically as adults with Minamata Disease. Yet many mothers of those afflicted had no symptoms. Children born after the initial outbreak never ate contaminated fish, so the parents didn't think the infants had the Disease."

"Like Tomoko-chan," Kazuko said.

As Ishimure opened her notebook, a welcome breeze filtered through the open doors, riffling the pages. She lifted her pencil to take notes.

"Yes," Harada Sensei continued. "At that time, we believed the placenta protected the fetus from toxins in the bloodstream, as with most chemicals. So, even if a mother ate contaminated seafood, we assumed the fetus was protected, and so doctors believed these children must have cerebral palsy. However, after several years of study and autopsies of two children – "

"Autopsies . . . of babies?" Kazuko clapped a hand over her mouth.

"I'm sorry. Perhaps I shouldn't have mentioned how we arrived at our conclusion."

Nobuyuki mumbled, "Go on."

Harada Sensei nodded. "We now know that, with methylmercury, the placenta actually removes the chemical from the mother's bloodstream and concentrates it in the fetus."

Ishimure Michiko nodded as she wrote in her notebook.

Yuki's parents looked confused.

"Methylmercury, the same chemical as organic mercury, is believed to cause Minamata Disease," the doctor added. "It travels through the blood. So the chemical is withdrawn from the mother and flows into the baby while it's in the womb."

"No!" Kazuko cried. "So, instead of me protecting Tomoko-chan, she protected me." She stroked the baby's head. "I'm so sorry."

"It wasn't your fault." The doctor wiped his forehead with a white cotton handkerchief. "No one knew. Your baby was misdiagnosed. She has Congenital Minamata Dis-

ease. Once she's certified, you'll receive government compensation to help support her."

Her parents turned away from the sensei, weeping,
clasping at each other's hands. Yuki picked up her sister
and rocked her.

"Ishimure-san here," the doctor gestured to the note-
taking woman, "has been observing and writing about the
plight of Disease victims, hoping to bring compensation
and justice. Her articles have appeared in national newspapers. She receives telephone calls and letters pressuring
her to stop writing about the Disease, but still works tirelessly."

To Yuki's surprise, the woman laid down her pencil in
her lap and finally spoke.

"Of course I do. We just can't let it go on! People suffer
with no chance to speak out. The gentle sea, our mother,
has been ruined. My husband is a middle school teacher.
The school board threatened to fire him to make me stop.
The school administrators want to stay on the good side of
Chisso executives. Some of their children attend classes
where my husband teaches. I don't care. I refuse to stop
telling the truth just because those in power fear the truth
will impact our economy."

Her voice rose, her right fist pounding the palm of her
left hand. But her gaze seemed far away, as if she saw a
future utopia where everyone was well again. "My own son
demands I stop writing. My father's ashamed of me. But
I'll keep sending the truth to newspapers and magazines
and anyone else who'll listen. Until not one more person is
afflicted with this cruel Disease."

Yuki's parents' gaped, while she sat mesmerized by
Ishimure's passionate speech all the way to the end. Then
she applauded. "Thank you, thank you!" Her fingers
twitched in the way they used to do. She grabbed her
sketchbook and started sketching Ishimure's strong, defi-

ant face. She never wanted to forget someone who was fighting so hard for justice.

"You are brave to help the victims, people like my family," Yuki said, bowing. "As Kiyo-kun does, too."

"You mentioned him before," the doctor said, looking curious.

"He's helping Hosokawa Sensei search for a cure for the Disease. He's the reason we get by."

"Lucky for you," Ishimure said.

"No one is as generous, kind and caring." Kiyo's gentle nature and fiery dedication to helping people overwhelmed her sometimes.

Harada Sensei returned his report to his briefcase. "I'm sorry to be the bearer of such upsetting news."

Then the two visitors rose and left, on to the next household with Disease victims.

"I gave my sickness to Tomoko-chan," Kazuko mourned. "She is why I have such a mild case." She began to weep. "What kind of a mother am I, letting my child protect me?"

"You didn't know." Yuki hugged her sister. "Poor Tomoko-chan . . . ."

Dad's eyes burned with rage. Yuki understood what he said, though the words were slurred: "I want to kill whoever is causing this."

"Me, too," she said.

TWENTY-NINE

Caught in the Act

While the Kuges' cook was out shopping for dinner, Kiyo and Fukuzawa quickly bagged some rice, dried mushrooms and persimmons, along with canned bamboo shoots, and pickled cucumbers. Then hauled these to the car for their monthly trek to Yuki's house – the August delivery. Kiyo feared Yanagiya would detect the pilfering, thanks to the strong scents of dehydrated fungi and fruits now permeating the kitchen.

"We can't stay long," the driver said, backing out. "I've got to pick up Chisso's reports from the printers by four."

"Sure. Thanks for helping."

"I'm not doing anything, just pressing my foot on the pedal."

In Tsukinoura, they parked in front of Yuki's house and lugged the packages up to the door.

"Kiyo-kun! Fukuzawa-san!" Yuki's mother cried when she hobbled to the door. "More food. You're too generous. How enormous your allowance must be."

Kiyo shook his head. "It's nothing." The lavish praise embarrassed him; this food had cost him nothing. Even when he bought groceries with his allowance, he hadn't earned it. He'd done no work for the money his mother simply handed him every month.

"Hi." Yuki laid her sister on a futon and came to the entrance. "Let me help." She took two bags and carried them to the kitchen.

"Come in," Kazuko beckoned.

"We can't stay." He and Fukuzawa set the rest of the sacks just inside the door.

"I'm sorry to be rude." The chauffeur bowed.

"Don't apologize." Kazuko bowed shallowly, careful not to lose her balance. "We owe you our lives."

Nobuyuki lifted a hand from his seat at the table. He was using the wooden back support he'd made years ago for his brother Higano. "Thanks," he mumbled.

"Bye." Yuki smiled at Kiyo. Even five minutes in her presence made his day brighter.

He got back in the car. The chauffeur pulled away, musing, "I never get used to seeing a whole family devastated by the Disease. Except Yuki-chan, of course. She must have a strong constitution."

"She's tough, hardworking, and nice. Nothing gets her down." At least, it seemed that way. Or else she was good at hiding sadness. This idea hadn't occurred to him before.

"Is she some kind of an artist? I saw some paintings leaning against the wall."

"Those are hers. She's really good."

"I'm no art critic, but I sure liked them. I can see why you admire her."

Kiyo glanced over and grinned. "She's the best."

"Cute, too."

"Yeah." Kiyo slid his fingers over the glossy leather seat, as if he was slipping them through her hair – which she kept short now due to the work she was doing. Someday he'd lie in a bed with her, holding her close all night long.

He took a long deep breath, trying to think of other things, before he embarrassed himself.

Fukuzawa shot him an amused look.

Ahead, a transit bus with a flat tire sat diagonally across the road. Three women stared from its windows. The driver, a middle-aged man in a dark blue uniform and matching hard-brimmed hat seemed to be arguing with two older men who were gesturing at the flat tire. The jack was beneath the fender but not cranked up. A spare tire lay on the ground nearby.

The chauffeur stopped and rolled down his window. "Need help?"

The bus driver glanced over. "My jack's not strong enough to lift this monster. I don't know why they gave us something that won't work," he grumbled.

"I have a jack. We should be able to raise it with two."

"Thanks."

Kiyo got out too. Fukuzawa removed his suit jacket and left it folded neatly on the driver's seat. Then opened the trunk and retrieved a jack from under its mat. He and the bus driver positioned the second jack in front of the flat tire as traffic rumbled past, kicking up dust.

"Could you ask the passengers to get off? Less weight," Fukuzawa said.

They must've heard, because they immediately descended. Two women in stylish dresses, carrying smart leather purses, stood off to one side. The third, wearing a faded green smock, helped a young man around Kiyo's age come down the bus steps. They sat on the tall green grass at the roadside. Kiyo realized the teenager had the Disease. He staggered when he walked and swayed even when sitting. Kiyo quickly looked away so as not to be rude. Patients had told him how they hated it when city people stared as if they were lepers.

"Let's raise them at the same time," the chauffeur said.

The driver nodded. "Good idea."

The chauffeur grasped his jack handle, while the driver gripped the rear jack's lever.

"Ready?" Fukuzawa asked.

The bus driver nodded. The two men leaned hard on the handles and pumped. The vehicle creaked as its frame rose.

"It's working!" the bus driver yelled.

"Can I do anything?" Kiyo asked.

"Thanks, *Botchan*." Fukuzawa swiped the back of one hand across his perspiring forehead. "But you'd get dirty. We'll handle this."

"I don't mind getting dirty."

The chauffeur chuckled. "I know."

Soon, the two men had spun the lug nuts off the wheel and changed the tire. When they lowered it again, the pas-sengers cheered. The bus driver bowed and thanked Fuku-zawa.

Back in the car, he wiped his hands on a rag and dried his perspiring face with a handkerchief. "Now I'm running late. You'll have to come to the printers with me."

"Sure."

After retrieving and dropping off some boxed stacks of reports to Chisso's office, the chauffeur drove them home. Kiyo kicked off his shoes in the foyer, expecting to smell dinner cooking. No scent of frying onions or cooking rice drifted from the kitchen.

"Want some cold wheat tea?" he asked, and they went to the kitchen.

There his mother sat slumped on a stool, head droop-ing.

"What's the matter, Mom?"

"It's Yanagiya-san. She's been stealing." She huffed a loud sigh. She fiddled anxiously with the strand of pearls around her neck. "How could she betray us like this?"

"Stealing?" said Kiyo. From the corner of one eye, he glimpsed the chauffeur's anxious look.

Mom nodded. "I was looking for my favorite rice crack-ers and noticed many cans and dried foods were missing. I started looking around. We're low on everything! We should have 50 kilos of rice, but I only found half that. I give her the same amount of money every week. Extra for parties. Obviously she's been pocketing the money and not buying what she was supposed to."

Kiyo dug his fingernails into his palms. He shook his head and said casually, "You know, I'm hungry all the time, and raid the kitchen after school. Sometimes even in the middle of the night."

"You couldn't possibly eat all that. No, she's been stealing. So I fired her."

"What? No!" Kiyo shouted.

His mother flinched, staring at him. "No choice. I can't employ a thief."

"But she wasn't stealing. It was me!"

She smiled and patted his shoulder. "You're too softhearted. I'll hire another cook. One who can also clean. I've ordered takeout for tonight. It'll be fine."

Kiyo shook his head. "You don't understand. She did buy all the food with the money you gave her. I've been taking some to Yuki-chan's family because … they're starving. This has nothing to do with Yanagiya-san. You've got to hire her back."

Mom dropped her outstretched hand and scowled. "You mean the fisher's daughter? You've been taking my food to them?"

"Her parents and sister have Minamata Disease. And nothing to eat."

Mom's shoulders jerked back. "They get a subsidy that people like us pay for."

"Well, it's not enough for a whole month. They can't work, so Yuki-chan takes care of her whole family. Please, it's not the cook's fault."

"She let you take the food. That's the same as stealing. I'm not hiring her back."

"She didn't know!"

"She's the cook. It's her duty to know how much food is in the pantry."

"*Okusan.*" Madam, the chauffeur said. Startled, Kiyo and his mother turned to look at him. "If you fired Yanagiya-san. You should fire me, too. Because I've – "

"You're too loyal," Kiyo interrupted. He turned to his mother. "Such a nice guy, sticking up for Yanagiya-san. Don't listen to him. This is my fault. Punish me, but bring her back."

"I can't have an employee I can't trust in the house. Don't you see, Kiyoshi-kun?" Her tone begged him to understand. "She has access to everything here. She knows everything we do. I can only keep servants who are trustworthy."

Kiyo gritted his teeth. How to fix this injustice? "Take away my allowance until I've paid for the food."

"I won't do that. I'm going to take away your bike."

Kiyo gasped. "No! Not the bike." How would he get to Yuki's and the hospital? "Take my allowance, my clothes. Make me cook. I'll clean the house, take care of the yard too. But the bike – it's my transportation."

"Fukuzawa-san, please go buy a chain and lock and padlock the bike."

"But Mom – "

"No more." She held up a warning hand, and left the kitchen.

"Damn it." Kiyo kicked the wall.

The chauffeur gripped his shoulder. "You should've let me confess."

"Neither of you should be fired. This is all my fault."

"I'll drive you to see Yuki-chan, and help buy food." As if he'd read Kiyo's mind, he added, "Your allowance just won't be enough."

"You have a family to support."

"We're healthy. We can sacrifice a little."

"My mother has everything but won't help, even when I beg. Yet you volunteer to."

"She hasn't seen the things I have. I'll help as much as I can – but I do have to take care of my wife and kids."

"Do you know where Yanagiya-san lives?"

"I gave her a ride one day when it was pouring out. Why?"

"Take me there. Please. I need to apologize."

The shiny black car wound between narrow dirt streets. On this side of the city, laundry flapped on long bamboo poles in front of tiny wooden houses. The homes were packed shoulder to shoulder, facades built right up to the street. Most were one-story, but every now and then someone had added a second story that put the house to its north in shadow. In the middle of the narrow street, a young girl swung her hips, twirling an orange hula-hoop. She stopped and moved over to let the sedan by.

The chauffeur stopped the car and nodded to a single-story dwelling with a cracked window. The dry wood siding needed oiling. Some of the slats had warped.

"Can you come in with me?" Kiyo begged. Now that they were here, he felt anxious. What could he say to the cook that could ever right this wrong?

Fukuzawa shut off the engine, pocketed the key, and got out. The street was so narrow, if another car turned in it would have to back out. Kiyo dragged himself to the sliding glass front doors, moving so slowly he might've been wading through mud. He forced himself to knock. After a few moments he heard footsteps, and the door opened.

"*Botchan!*" The cook, who'd alternated between two simple kimonos at work, one blue and one green, wore a faded pink one he'd never seen before. She usually wrapped her head with a thin towel to keep hair from dropping into food, and dust or grease from dirtying it. Now he was surprised to see her gray hair pulled into a bun at the nape. "What're you doing here? Never mind, come in before the flies do."

They stepped into the tiny foyer. Neither attempted to take off his shoes because there wasn't enough room for even one of them to bend over and untie them.

The main room's intact shoji doors, neatly patched in a few spots, were open. Kiyo saw a small kitchen in the back. The sweet aroma of cooking rice almost brought tears to his eyes. That same smell had greeted him every morning in his own house. This place had two well-maintained rooms, perhaps a bit larger than Yuki's. A couple of old jackets hung from wall hooks. A small, well-polished tansu dresser was the only furniture in the other room. A bare light bulb hung from both ceilings.

The cook said mildly, "Your mother fired me today."

Kiyo bowed deeply. "I know. I'm sorry. You did nothing wrong."

"True, I didn't steal. But I knew you were taking food."

He glanced up, startled. "That's not the same thing."

She looked upward and pursed her lips in a 'maybe' gesture.

"I'll talk to my father and get you rehired."

Fukuzawa snorted. "Your mother already said no."

Kiyo waved him off. "I'll reason with him."

"Bad idea to go behind the lady's back."

"Don't bother," Yanagiya said.

"Why not?" Kiyo frowned.

"I don't want to come back. Sorry, but I don't like your mother. Like most wealthy women, all she cares about is impressing everyone. People like me are nothing to her."

Kiyo protested, "I'm sure – "

The cook laughed. "She's in love with her new crystal glasses, inviting friends over just to use them, wanting me to wash and polish each piece for hours so everyone will admire them. I was always petrified of breaking something. She pressured me constantly to learn foreign cookery, then berated me when it didn't taste the way she'd expected. How could I know what such dishes should taste like? I wouldn't have quit, but being fired ... it feels good. So long as the Chisso factory's here, people do okay in this city. I'll find another job."

"But – "

"You're a nice boy, Kiyo-kun. Nothing like your parents." She patted his shoulder. "I'll get by. Let me know when you become a doctor. You can take care of me then."

"I will! I definitely will." He nodded enthusiastically.

"Come on," the chauffeur said. "Your father probably has work for me."

Kiyo wasn't sure Yanagiya would find a better job easily. He'd been prepared to beg his father to give her old position back. Now he was ashamed he felt relieved that wouldn't be necessary. In his single-mindedness about helping Yuki's family he'd failed to consider the risks to others. Now the damage was done.

THIRTY

Who Was That Man?

The next day the family set off to Minamata to apply for Tomoko's certification. Yuki had offered to take her alone and fill out the paperwork, to save bus fare. But her parents insisted the officials would require them to sign.

Sweat glazed Nobuyuki's face as he swayed laboriously down the road in the sweltering heat. It took enormous effort for him to remain upright. Yuki, Tomoko on her back, put her hands on his back to steady him as he heaved himself up the bus's steps. He swayed, then regained his balance and staggered to a seat.

Passengers on the opposite side of the aisle made disgusted faces. Some rose and took seats farther away. Yuki pretended not to notice, handing Dad a handkerchief to mop up his perspiring face. When the bus lurched off, gears grinding, she was thankful for the cooling breeze through its open windows.

They got off at a stop in the middle of the city, and walked slowly down the bustling main street lined with small shops. Salarymen at stationary stores checked the quality of the paper, or ordered business cards and announcements. A mechanic at a bicycle repair shop was replacing a broken chain. Mothers at curbside produce stands called to children to stay close as they chose the best tomatoes and cucumbers stacked neatly in wooden boxes.

Yuki drank in the luscious scents wafting from ripe strawberries and shiso. She noted a few tourists were dining in restaurants as madly spinning fans ruffled their short, modern hairstyles and stylish clothes.

Down an alley between two buildings across the street, Yuki was surprised to spot the main Chisso office, barricaded behind a wrought-iron fence. No wonder the clackety-clack of the train had sounded so close.

"Look." Kazuko pointed to a basket of bruised peaches with a 75% OFF sign. "We could afford that. Let's buy one and split it."

Dad nodded. Yuki chose the least damaged peach and strolled inside to pay. The shelves of the small produce market were packed with watermelons, apricots, yuzus, cherries, plums, eggplants, bell peppers, and edamame. Canned and bottled goods were stacked on shelves in back. Her mouth watered; her first peach of the year. She plucked money from her coin purse and offered it to the sour-looking shop owner with an apron tied over a faded yellow dress.

"Get out." The woman narrowed her small eyes and breathed hard. Her breath reeked of garlic.

Yuki resisted the urge to step back. "I need to pay for the peach."

"I won't touch your money. I don't want the Disease. Get out." She backed away, into the wall behind her.

A bitter taste flooded Yuki's mouth. "We're not contagious."

The owner shook her head. "Leave. Now!"

"It's not our fault my family has the Disease."

"Maybe it is and maybe it isn't, but you people give our city a bad name. No one wants to come here anymore. I work hard, but have to pay taxes to support you."

"My parents can't work. They would if they could."

"Just leave." The woman made a shooing motion with big callused hands. "Go away!"

Yuki set the peach on a shelf stacked with blocks of dried noodles. The owner picked it up with a square of newspaper and started to toss it in the trash.

Someone behind Yuki said, "I'll buy that."

She turned to look. A gentleman in a gray suit with polished black shoes and nicely-trimmed graying hair was holding out his hand. The saleswoman gently set the peach in his palm and dipped her head. He gave her a coin and handed the fruit to Yuki.

"It looks delicious," he said, and then walked out.

She stared open-mouthed after the stranger as he crossed the street and headed toward the Chisso office's tall smokestacks.

Dashing outside, she yelled, "Thank you!" And tried to smile, but a hot tear rolled down one cheek. Such cruel treatment by the shopkeeper; such compassion from an unknown man. Drying her face on her sleeve, she held out the peach for her parents to admire.

"We'll have it with lunch," she said brightly, as if nothing unpleasant had occurred.

They walked in silence the remaining five blocks to the office of the Committee to Certify Victims of Minamata Disease. Yuki was trying to calm down, but her stomach knotted up whenever she recalled the incident at the shop. Doctors and health officials constantly reiterated that the Disease was not contagious, yet city people still shunned and berated the afflicted.

Inside the small government office a fan rotated, alternately blowing a warm breeze towards two men at separate desks. The one at the newer, moss-green metal desk had a deep scar running down his left cheek. He looked middle aged and seemed like the supervisor. He glanced up at them, then continued shuffling papers.

The clerk at the scratched, dented desk had such a sharp widow's peak his hairline looked like a bat attempting to fly away from his head. But when Nobuyuki wobbled in, his eyes narrowed and his mouth tightened.

The family bowed.

"We're here to apply for certification," her father said.

"What'd you say?" Widow's Peak muttered.

"We've come to apply for certification for our baby daughter," Kazuko repeated. Yuki unstrapped her sister and held her up so the man could see her.

Widow's Peak curled his lip. "She's too young to have even eaten fish."

"She has Congenital Minamata Disease. Dr. Harada Masazumi examined and diagnosed her."

"That Harada." The official growled and yanked some forms from his desk drawer. "Fill these out. We'll need to see her birth certificate."

There were only two wooden chairs for visitors. Yuki let her parents sit in them, and presented the required certificate to the scowling clerk. Then she bent over the desk, filling out forms.

Tomoko began to cry; Yuki checked the diaper and told the clerk, "I need to change her."

The office had a tall filing cabinet and wall shelves, but no place like a table on which to do so. Yuki set Tomoko on the pitted wood floor, replaced the soiled diaper with a clean one and stuck the folded up one carefully next to the water bottle in her cloth bag, away from the peach and their lunch.

Widow's Peak wrinkled his narrow nose in distaste and slapped a mosquito on his forearm. "You should do that somewhere else."

Yuki was tired of being abused by those not affected by the Disease – the ones who acted as if they were superior because of luck, or their ability to buy and eat foods not from the Bay. But she swallowed back the angry words threatening to fly out of her mouth, and loosened her clenched fist. These ignorant men could decide her family's very survival. They enjoyed abusing the little power they held. Her family desperately needed that money. She hated to grovel, but said, "I'm so sorry. You're right. I would've if I could. Please forgive me."

He exhaled a long annoyed breath. "Let's just get this done." He reviewed the completed form, squinting as if farsighted, studying the birth certificate. He stared at Tomoko as if he thought her deformed, and insisted Nobuyuki sign the document despite his nearly-illegible signature.

When it was time to use the family's seal, though, Yuki pressed the Akaji stamp proudly and firmly on the paper.

At last, the clerk dismissed them. "We'll let you know."

She prayed they'd be approved for the small allowance. When she'd first met Kiyo, she hadn't understood what a windfall he was: fine-looking, smart and kindhearted, he also kept her family alive with food faithfully and regularly delivered. All she had to offer to him in return was her love.

But she had to stretch the seasonal vegetables from the garden, a few eggs, the rice subsidy and Kiyo's gifts to last a whole month. Some days, no matter what she did, there wasn't enough.

The family bowed to the still-glowering clerk and left. It was lunchtime; restaurants and food carts were busier. The aroma of udon noodles and grilling chicken made Yuki's belly grumble. She saw the furtive looks her parents gave to eateries, their noses twitching, stomachs longing – no doubt as much as hers – for more than just potatoes.

"I saw a school a block down that way." She pointed away from the busy avenue. "Let's eat there."

They walked slowly to the end of the block. They passed an open-air café. A woman eating at a sidewalk table there wore a bright dress with oversized buttons down the front. She looked over and shouted at them, "Quit trying to close Chisso."

A schoolboy next to her in a pink-stained white shirt and brown shorts was kicking his feet and eating a large slice of watermelon. Other diners stopped eating and drinking to gape at Yuki's family.

She savagely wished they would all fall down dead.

A man in a blue coveralls at a food-cart counter lowered his chopsticks and stared. "You lazy bums pretend to walk funny so you don't have to work, and get government dole."

His insult was the last straw. "My father's not pretending, you idiot! He has the Disease. He can't fish any more. We're the victims, not you."

A pregnant woman carrying a large shopping bag stopped on the street, fanning herself. "Chisso built us a hospital. What will happen if my child – " she cradled her belly – "gets sick, and there's no hospital because the company moved?"

Yuki felt exposed, almost naked. But she couldn't let such ignorance go unchallenged. "You respect a company that throws away the people it harms, like garbage. The hospital's for everyone in the whole Bay area, not just you. But so long as you've got what you need, to hell with anyone else. Who cares about the fishers, who provided you with seafood all these years, before the Bay was turned into a cesspool?"

The man with the pregnant woman yelled, "You're going to ruin the lives of 50,000 people. The whole city will die if Chisso leaves. My shop will close."

"Yeah!" shouted a mechanic, straightening from bending over a car engine. "Where's your loyalty to Japan? Chisso is rebuilding our country."

Nobuyuki's face turned purple with rage. "Bastard," he rumbled and lurched toward the man. His feet, unable to keep up with the sudden movement, stumbled. Yuki reached out, but he went sprawling. A few people snickered. The pregnant woman gasped.

"Dad! Are you all right?" Yuki pulled him up with one hand, the other one keeping Tomoko safely in place on her back. She brushed tiny stones from his scratched face and hands. Then pulled a clean diaper from the bag slung over her shoulder, and dabbed away beads of blood oozing from a cut on his arm.

"You're horrible!" Mom screamed, pointing at the gawking bystanders. "My brother-in-law worked for Chisso, caught the Disease, and died in agony. He couldn't eat, couldn't see, couldn't hear, couldn't talk or walk. Do you think he faked all of that – even his death?"

Some people lowered their chopsticks and looked away. Others kept staring, as if entertained.

Tears streamed down Kazuko's face. "My husband and I worked hard as fishers, but we were happy. Do we look happy now? Imagine what's it's like to be unable to feed your family, to see your child have to quit school to go to work and support you? I can stand being cold, going hungry, even being humiliated by clods like you. But I can't stand to see my baby girl never walk, talk, marry or have children." She stroked Tomoko's cheek. "You're the most heartless demons I've ever met."

"Ah, take your filthy Disease away," said a man in a light summer suit who'd stopped to listen. He flicked a hand as if shooing flies away.

Yuki wanted to claw his eyes out. "Here's some filth for you." She pulled the rolled up, stinking diaper from her bag and hurled it at him. Her arms were strong from manual labor. The dirty nappy hit him square in the chest, unfurling, dripping feces down his jacket and pants.

He screamed like a child, swiping at his clothes, only to get excrement on his hands. "You, you ... look what you did! Where's the nearest bathroom?" He ran away, still howling.

Mom clasped Yuki's arm. "Let's go."

"Nice work," her father said. Yuki knew he was laughing by the shaking of his shoulders.

She was feeling a little better by the time they arrived at the school, which was closed for summer vacation. For several minutes they sat silently on a bench under the shade of a large cedar tree.

"Good for you, too," Nobuyuki said to Kazuko, laying his hand atop hers.

"I couldn't stand it anymore," she said.

"I know." Yuki sighed.

They all knew, far too well.

"But throwing that diaper?" Her mother snorted.

Everyone burst out laughing. Tomoko joined in with a hiccupping chortle.

Yuki grinned. "Yeah, that was good. Now, let's eat."

Her mother held the baby while she pulled their lunch from the bag. She poured water and passed the cups around. Then a small metal lunchbox for each person. She fed Nobuyuki barley, pickled cucumber and eggplants from each of the tiny compartments before eating her own meal.

The peach was dessert. She studied it, cupped in her palm. A small dark spot marred the otherwise perfectly fuzzy-skinned fruit. Her life before the Disease had been much like this peach: beautiful, full of sweet promise. The dark spot, the Disease. Starting small, the rot had spread until – as this bruise would do – it rotted everything. That was what Chisso had done to her family.

She closed both hands around the peach, fighting the urge to squeeze it to a pulp.

Mom looked questioningly at her. "Are you all right?"

Yuki sighed and nodded.

She wasn't, though. Sometimes she felt so sad she could barely move. Other times, the rage inside made her want to scream until her lungs ruptured.

"Dessert." Yuki didn't have a knife, so they passed the fruit around, taking bites, enjoying its sweet perfume and luscious taste.

"Delicious." Kazuko smiled; one finger blotted a drop of nectar from the corner of her mouth. Then she fed Tomoko.

Watching them, Yuki felt that familiar sensation of feathers brushing her hands. She found a sharp stone and drew a picture of her family in the playground dirt: herself holding hands with an older, adult Kiyo. Her little sister, too, was grown. Everyone stood strong and upright, smiling . . . .

Staring at that etching in the soil, she suddenly felt repulsed. She'd done the same thing for so long, wishing their lives were like that. But they'd never be that way again. No fishing, running, talking, living normal lives. *Don't be stupid! You're not a kid anymore,* she berated herself. She must accept reality: the Disease had robbed them forever of dignity and respect. Their fate was to be shunned and mocked as subhuman by those more fortunate and ignorant.

She stood and scuffed at the image in the dirt until her toes were bruised. Until soil jammed into her shoe through a hole in the toe. Until her ridiculous fantasy world was erased, obliterated. Just like the life she'd once had.

THIRTY-ONE

Riot

The fishers and the Minamata Fishermen's Cooperative had sent numerous requests over the previous
year and a half, asking that someone from the Diet –
Japan's national legislature, in Tokyo – visit to view the
devastation Minamata Disease and the contaminated Bay
had caused. Finally, an investigative commission was coming. Hopes ran high; surely the federal government would
give basic aid so fisher families could sustain themselves.

The scheduled visit was during school hours, but Kiyo
wanted to go and see what happened. Perhaps at the end
of today, he could report good news to Yuki's family. He
rose early. Then, before the new cook arrived to start
breakfast, he took a deep breath and, shuddering, quickly
gulped down a whole glass of soy sauce. He followed up
with a large glass of water to wash away the taste. If this
trick worked, he'd be able to skip class and attend the
meeting.

He declined Fukuzawa's offer of a ride to school. Instead he'd take his bike, thankful his mother had finally
unlocked it after the two-week punishment was complete.
Scorching summer had transitioned into cool fall; it was
quite cold already on November 2nd. Scattered clouds
spotted the sky but didn't appear to threaten snow.

By the second morning class, he felt feverish enough to
raise his hand. The teacher looked over at him. "Yes?"

"I'm not feeling well, Sensei."

Kubo Sensei sauntered over and laid a hand on Kiyo's
forehead. "My, you are hot. Better go home."

Drinking the soy sauce had done exactly what he'd heard from upperclassmen who used this trick to skip classes or tests. After slowly, ostentatiously dragging himself down the hall he cycled like mad to the train station.

No one was there, save the usual few passengers waiting for trains. Was he too late?

He caught sight of a black limousine cruising slowly away down the city's main street. Limos were an uncommon sight in Minamata. This one must be ferrying the investigative committee members to City Hall to meet with local officials.

He cut through alleys and side streets, arriving at City Hall just as the limousine was parking. Thousands of fishers – men, women, and their supporters – waited in front of the building. Many held up banners and placards. *Give us our Bay Back. Return our beautiful Shiranui Sea! Stop factory wastes that murder the sea!*

A dark-suited man bowed deeply as the limousine's passengers got out. Kiyo recognized him from newspaper photos: head of the Mutual Aid Association of the Families of Minamata Disease Patients. He bowed again, offering sheets of paper with both hands. And then he introduced himself.

"If I may, sir . . . we used to support our families by fishing in Minamata Bay. But its waters are now hopelessly polluted. All sea life, including fish, octopi, squids, kelp, and shellfish have died. Now we have no means of earning a living. Our families are starving. It's not our fault the Bay is poisoned with toxins. Please, we beg you. Help us!" He bowed again.

A woman with a weather-beaten face, wearing coarse hemp pants and cracked though polished shoes, shoved her way up toward the visitors. "Please, please, listen to what we have to say!"

Onlookers and the Diet members all turned to face her.

"We're honored you've come to meet with us. Our children have died from the Disease. Our husbands have no fish to catch, no livelihood. No one will buy the few sick fish that remain. We have nothing left. Please, help us!"

A soft-looking legislator in a nice three-piece suit gazed out above the heads of the crowd. "That's a sad state of affairs. We'll see what we can do," he said firmly, nodding.

Then all the men from Tokyo climbed the steps to City Hall. "Thank you!" The fisher's representative called after them. The whole bowed again, to their retreating backs.

People made themselves comfortable for the wait. Some sat on the concrete steps smoking cigarettes, others squatted or sat on the sidewalk.

Kiyo still felt warm from the soy sauce overdose; sitting on a cold, grassy patch near the steps felt good.

To pass the time, he thought about Yuki: her artist's hands, slender and graceful despite the work-calluses on the palms. She recreated life. Scenes that depicted what it was, but also the way it could, and should be. Viewing her works, a person could understand what a human life is worth, and how best to live it.

As a doctor, he would someday know all about the physical body. But she was teaching him the essence of the soul.

An hour passed. He grew tired and cold, his trousers damp from the grass. He glanced enviously at a nearby woman who sat drinking hot tea from a thermos. The scent of matcha green made him consider slipping over to a little ramen café across the street for a cup. But just as he was rising to do so, some men and women also rose, pacing and staring at the building's entrance.

A man grumbled, "What's going on in there?"

"Yeah, how long must we wait?" said the woman beside him.

A young, well-muscled man with a fresh shaving cut on his chin had been holding up a banner the whole wait.

Now his gloved hands threw it to the ground. "Chisso polluted our bay!" he yelled toward the government building. "Chisso must pay!"

Others around him nodded. A grumbling rose: "Let's go there, and demand payment now."

"Yeah, let's do it."

"They can't hold us all back."

"We want compensation!"

The young man picked up the banner again and waved it like a battle flag. "Onward to Chisso!"

The crowd roared. They followed this new pied piper, chanting, "They killed the Bay, Chisso should pay."

Intrigued, wondering what would happen next, Kiyo trailed after the hundreds of chanting protestors.

After a couple blocks, he realized he too was shouting, "Chisso should pay!"

This time, the factory's iron double gate was locked. Smoke puffed from the tall smokestacks behind the concrete office building, as usual. A train-whistle blew from the tracks behind it.

Marchers, four and five deep, spread out in front of the chain-link fence enclosing the empty courtyard parking area. A wall made of angry men.

Gloved Hands shook the bars until they clanged. "Let us in! We're Minamata Bay fishermen. We want to talk to the president."

The main office door remained closed. He bellowed his demand again. When no one responded, other men took up the cry.

Kiyo began to think they'd try to break the lock if no one responded. But just then a thin young employee in white shirt and dark tie stepped outside, closing the door

behind him. One hand still gripping the doorknob, he
shouted, "The president isn't here today. You must leave."

Gloved Hands leaned his sign against the fence. "We
just want to talk."

The Chisso employee shook his head. "But he isn't
here. Please, go away."

A large middle-aged fisherman stepped up to the gate.
The kanji for COMPENSATION was inked in black on his
white headband. He too shook the bars. "Call him! Send
him out to us!"

The employee looked frightened; he scurried back inside.

Fishermen began screaming at the building's façade:
"We want the president!" "Open this gate!" "Let us in!"
"Tell him to get out here!" "He must listen!"

Now Kiyo worried things might turn violent. He sided
with the fishers, but didn't want to be caught in a brawl.

When no one else from the company came out, a burly
protestor said, "If he won't come out, I'm going in!"

He scaled the six-foot chain-link fence and rushed toward the office entrance.

Trespassing on Chisso property? Kiyo's heart beat
faster. The burly man grabbed the doorknob and rattled it.
"Locked!" he shouted back over one shoulder, then banged
his fist on it, shouting, "Open up!"

Another young marcher cried, "I'm going in, too." Hundreds of men, mostly younger ones, strong and lithe from
heavy work, started scaling the fence. Soon most of them
were inside the courtyard.

Kiyo moved closer to the gate, hoping no one would do
anything reckless. But the protesters sounded more and
more angry. He began to fear there'd be violence, even
bloodshed.

The large brawny demonstrator stepped back, then
kicked hard at the middle panel of the front door. With a
splintering crash it flew open, and protesters swarmed in.

Kiyo stood outside the fence, gaping. The once-peaceful assembly was now a riot. Window panes exploded outward as a few of the fishers who'd charged inside threw type-writers, adding machines, and office chairs through them.

Some brave or foolish employees – depending on which side you were on – charged out into the courtyard to scuffle with the intruders. Fists flew and men shouted curses while a hail of black telephones came through the now-open windows, crashing to the pavement along with tea cups, boxes, desk drawers, account books, metal lunchbox-es, inkbottles, lamps, framed pictures, and clocks. Even a small sofa came hurtling through, thudding like a dead body onto the pavement.

Kiyo knew the company's executives abhorred physical confrontations. Believing instead that discussion and di-plomacy was the only solution to problems. This invasion would enrage them. And, though he understood the fisher's rage, he feared it would only make them appear both crim-inal and dangerously insane.

Now passersby – men in suits, women with babies strapped to their backs and holding the hands of toddlers, clusters of schoolchildren – stopped in the road to stare, clogging the street. A black limousine cruised by slowly, and the rubberneckers parted to let it pass. The car stopped in front of the gate, and one back passenger win-dow rolled down. It was the Tokyo Diet members. They sat openmouthed, watching fishermen throw punches at office workers.

The legislator next to the open window twisted his mouth up in revulsion. His nostrils flared. And then, he cranked the window back up again.

Oh, no, Kiyo thought. They've made a terrible mistake. Now the lawmakers may not approve aid. I must warn them.

As the car drove off, he heard a familiar voice calling. He turned to see Yuki running up a side street toward him, shouting his name. She stopped before him, panting.

"What're you doing here? Aren't you normally at work now?"

"Yep. See my lovely dishpan hands? I came to pick up a box of soup bowls from the ceramic shop, for the restaurant. Then saw all these people and came to see what's going on."

"Oh no." He gently ran his fingers over her cracked, bleeding fingers.

"It's all right. At least I have an indoor job." She turned to look at the chaos in the factory courtyard. "What happened?"

He opened his mouth to tell her, but just then a desk was heaved out through a top-floor window, crashing onto the pavement below. It landed in a twisted ruin, as if a train had run over it. Around it, broken chair legs and shredded paper littered the ground. And still the punches and kicks flew; the screams and curses went on.

"They're destroying the office," he said.

"I never wanted them to become violent," Yuki said.

"I know. But . . . I'd better go in there and see if my father is all right. It's not safe here. You'd better go back to work."

He left his bike on the kickstand and climbed over the fence. Dodging descending debris, he darted around fistfights and ruined furniture, and finally reached the front door. He was about to go inside when the wailing of police sirens rose, so near it drowned out the men's shouts and screams.

He glanced back at Yuki. She stood in the same spot amidst the bystanders, hands cupped around her mouth, shouting something he could not hear.

"Go on!" he yelled, waving an arm to send her off.

A Chisso employee, blood trickling from his scalp, ran past him and up to the gate, unlocking and swinging it open. As police cruisers drove up, sirens whooping, rioters fled through the open gates and scattered. Kiyo froze, looking around for an escape route. *I can't get arrested.*

Policemen leapt from patrol cars and waded in, smacking protestors with batons. The marchers, easy to distinguish in faded pants, old shirts, and white headbands, were their targets. Those inside the factory scrambled to flee, but there was only the one narrow doorway. Some, more desperate, dove through broken-out windows and ran.

Kiyo dashed to the gate, but someone smashed into him. He stumbled, then fell, hitting the pavement hand first. No time to think about a scraped palm. He scrambled up again and kept running.

Where's my bike? he thought frantically. Will my parents have to come get me at the police station? I'd be better off dead.

Outside the gate his bike had fallen over. It looked undamaged, so he righted it to pedal away, but the street was packed both ways with cars and with thousands of men, stinking of sweat and fear, trying to shove through and escape.

Someone knocked Kiyo down from behind. His elbow smacked the pavement first. The bike crashed onto this leg. "*Itai!*" That hurts, he screamed.

People kept rushing past. One stumbled, kicking Kiyo's ribs. Another man tripped over the bike and fell onto him. The broad-faced rioter scrambled up and peered at him, looking surprised. "Just a kid. What're you doing here?"

A deep cut above the man's right eye was bleeding, and one jacket sleeve was torn away. Though skinny, he managed to pull Kiyo up, then righted his bicycle. "Better go home," he said, and dashed away into the crowd.

Kiyo hurried off, pushing the bike, but after half a block he encountered half a dozen police officers standing side by side across the road. A barricade.

Yuki stood behind them, along with other curious spec-tators.

"Kiyo-kun!" she shouted. "Come on over." She waved at him to come to her.

A man in a fedora standing next to her said, "You're siding with those rioters? Lazy fraud!"

"The fishers are entitled to restitution," she shot back.

"While they loot and break the law? I'm sick of people like you. Crawl back into a hole."

He shoved her with both hands. She staggered and fell hard on her side.

"Yuki-chan!" Kiyo called, but the barricade blocked his way. "Are you hurt?"

She got up, pressing her ribs, and grimacing. Then she gasped and stared down at her bloody hands.

"You're all under arrest!" an officer yelled at the rioters who'd come up to the barricade. "Into the paddy wagon!" He pointed his baton at the van's open doors.

"Officer." Yuki tapped one policeman's shoulder. "This man pushed me down." She pointed to her attacker and held out bloody palms.

"Eh. She's a sympathizer," her attacker shouted. "Says they're entitled to more of our hard-earned money."

"He shoved me down and injured me!"

The officer squinted dubiously. "Your kind always lie. I wouldn't believe you if you said police cars are black and white. Your kind should suffer and die."

"My – " she gasped. "We're not worthless – "

But he'd already turned back toward the rioters. The other officers began manhandling demonstrators into the paddy wagon.

"Yuki-chan," Kiyo yelled again. "Get out of here."

She stood there for a moment, looking as if she wanted to argue with the cop. At last she started fighting through the crowds, away from the barricade and the protestors.

Relieved, Kiyo tried to back up his bike but instead got pushed forward. Trapped in the seething throng, he saw an ambulance drive up. Three men in white lab coats, black doctor's bags in hand, and two women in white nurse's uniforms hopped out.

The doctors began treating the fallen wounded. The nurses talked to injured people, sometimes calling a doctor over. The driver and one physician carried a suited employee on a stretcher out the gates toward the ambulance. One of the man's arms was bent at an impossible angle, and he was moaning. The ambulance took off, siren wailing.

Behind Kiyo, back in the courtyard, men with bleeding faces, limping or cradling broken arms, righted defenestrated chairs and sat on them. Some rioters lay on the ground. Medical personnel worked their way through the wounded, cleaning cuts, applying bandages, putting arms in slings. And more protesters backed up behind him, until he couldn't retreat at all.

The ones at the barricade reluctantly climbed into the police van, until Kiyo was the next one facing the officer standing guard at its double doors. His dark-blue uniform was crisply pressed, but his flat gaze unsympathetic. He pried the bike from Kiyo's grip with white-gloved hands, and let it crash onto its side on the pavement. Then, to Kiyo's astonishment, he picked him up as well and tossed him into the paddy wagon.

"Wait! You can't arrest me," Kiyo protested. "I'm only eighteen."

The officer merely shoved more men inside, trapping him in the middle. When the van was full, everyone squashed like tinned sardines, the cop slammed and locked the doors. The motor raced, the gearshift ground, and he was thrown forward as the van peeled out.

I'm going to jail, he thought, stunned. Could a criminal even become a doctor?

THIRTY-TWO

Arrested

Outside the station everyone in the van shuffled out, prodded by glaring, sneering policemen who herded all of them through a side door and down a corridor. The air here stank of stale sweat and cooked cabbage.

Kiyo paused at the open door of the cell before him. He glanced over and read the nametag of one of the officers set to guard its inmates. His name tag read EGASHIRA.

Kiyo bowed, narrowly missing hitting his head on the bars. "Excuse me, Sir?" He tried for the most respectable tone he could muster. "There's been a mistake. I'm not part of this."

"Oh, really?" Officer Egashira snorted out a laugh. "Well, your parents'll be happy to hear that. Until we inform them about your actions today."

"Wait, no, I'm – "

The man smacked his head with an open palm, shocking Kiyo into silence. His parents had never struck him. Obedient in school, he'd never even received a rebuke, much less a slap, from his teachers.

"Get in there!" The officer raised his hand again. Kiyo rushed into the cell to avoid another blow. He found an empty corner amongst the milling protesters packed inside, and sat on the cold, hard concrete. Trying to stay out of the others' way, knees pulled up to his chest. Most of them now looked dejected, not angry or defiant. Heads hanging, shoulders slumped. Fishers were not known to be a violent bunch, anyhow, and now they looked as scared as he felt. A few men whispered to each other, but most remained glum and silent.

Before long, more arrestees arrived, filing past into more cells down the hall. Some still looked angry, lips curled, fists clenched. Kiyo wondered how long that would last.

Beginning with his cell, a guard called men up one by one to a small office at the head of the corridor, to give their names and addresses. Kiyo thought about giving a false name, a made-up phone number. But when no one answered, would he remain forever in jail? He'd heard rumors that inmates were treated harshly here. Poundings for the smallest infraction, like speaking out of turn. Pressure to confess to crimes they hadn't committed.

Officer Egashira came over to the cell again. "So, what's a Saikou School kid doing here?"

Kiyo started. How did this guy know where he went to school? Then he realized: the uniform. So now the officer could find out who he was simply by calling the headmaster and describing him. Defeated, when they hustled him down the hall to the cramped office, Kiyo gave his correct name, those of his parents, and his home phone number.

"Hello, is this the lady of the house?" drawled Officer Egashira, smirking at Kiyo. "Well, your son, Kiyoshi, is here at the police station. For participating in a riot at the Chisso factory."

"That's not true," Kiyo protested but fell silent after an ugly scowl from the officer.

"Yes ... I see. All right." The man hung up. "You've got a smart mouth for a private-school kid. Get back in the cell."

"Is my mother coming?"

"Doubt it. Who cares about a delinquent like you?"

"I'm no delinquent. I'm studying to be a doctor."

"Ah. No wonder you're in jail. Now get back to the cell before I throw you in."

"All right." Kiyo went back. Since he did side with the fishers, he'd stay in jail quietly, to show support. He leaned against one wall, ignoring the coppery smell of so many fearful, sweaty men.

The officers were up to the second cell when Kiyo's name was called. He looked up. His father stood on the other side of the bars, staring in at him.

"Dad!" He shouldered through the other inmates toward the door.

"How could a son of mine do such a thing?" Kichiro gritted out between clenched teeth. His ears flamed red. His hands squeezed the bars as if he'd like to strangle someone.

Kiyo bowed low. "I'm so sorry. I just went there to watch."

"Really. How'd you get out of school?"

"I, ah . . . pretended to be sick."

"So you lied to take part in a riot!"

"No!" All his life, Kiyo had only ever missed a day or two of school each year, and always from a real illness. Now his father was making him sound like a habitual truant, and a criminal.

"I went to City Hall to see the Diet members," he said quickly. "Waited with everyone an hour, but then some fishermen decided to go to Chisso. I followed, just watching. But when they broke into the front office, I was afraid you might get hurt. I was trying to get to your office to make sure you were all right."

"I'm fine," Dad snapped. "You shouldn't have even been there."

A policeman sauntered to the cell door, unlocked it, and pointed to Kiyo. "You. Come on out."

He followed Kichiro outside. The street was shining with a recent rain. He looked up; ragged black clouds were still rolling out. He inhaled the clean rain-washed air, glad to be out of that stinking jail.

Fukuzawa was pacing next to the black car. "Botchan! We were worried. You all right?"

Kiyo nodded. The driver held the back door open for his father, then went around and opened the trunk. "Where's your bike?"

"I don't know. They made me leave it at Chisso."

Kiyo walked around and got in from the other side. Dad fumed silently, clenching and unclenching his fists while Fukuzawa slowly drove them home. The tense silence was far worse than a lecture or shouting, but Kiyo didn't know what more to say.

At home Etsuko stood in the foyer, arms tightly crossed, her glossy red lips pinched together.

Kiyo bowed. "I'm sorry, Mom. I only went there to watch, but – "

"You were arrested!" she said. "How will we live down the shame? You've disgraced our family. Joining in a riot against Chisso! I heard on the radio over a hundred people were injured. I was so worried for your father, I called the office, but he and the president were at the City Hall meeting with Diet members and the mayor. What's going to happen when Chisso finds out what you've done? He might get fired or demoted."

"I never thought anything like that would happen. I didn't mean to involve you, or him."

His father's anger seemed to have burnt out, though. Now he just looked exhausted. "Luckily, I was able to speak to the head of the police station," he told his wife. "I got him to take our son's name off the list of those arrested. He'll keep quiet. We have to hope no one at Chisso finds out."

"Thank goodness!" Etsuko closed her eyes and sank onto a nearby chair.

How much had his father paid the police for their silence? At least his actions wouldn't shame the family now, but . . . .

The phone shrilled.

Kichiro heaved a sigh and picked up, listening for a minute. "Yes, right away." He slammed the receiver down. "I must return to the office. Seems thousands of fishermen and their sympathizers accosted the Diet members."

Kiyo opened his mouth to say, *But that isn't true.* One glimpse of his father's expression and he closed it again, quickly.

"We'll have to repair most of the front offices. Those rioters wrecked everything. All the furniture, phones, doors, and windows. Ten million yen in damages! And only a hundred arrested. They should've dragged them all in. The Diet members meant to tour the factory, but saw the riot and left in a hurry. They'll never give them money now."

But Yuki and her family needed that assistance. The fishermen had started peacefully, with good intentions, hoping for understanding and sympathy. But no one could be oppressed and starved for too long without eventually reaching their limit and lashing out.

"They wanted attention," Kichiro said bitterly. "Well, now the national papers are covering this. Those fishermen must pay for the damage!"

With what? Chisso had oceans more money than the fishers, but now *they* wanted remuneration. The government wasn't going to help. Apparently impoverished village people were expendable, possibly not even thought of as human.

But what good would it do to say so now? His impulsiveness had already stoked his father's rage. To go on would possibly make things worse. So he turned away and went silently to his room. He'd had a scare, yes. But the day couldn't have ended up worse for those already near starvation. Without food or money, what would happen to them now?

THIRTY-THREE

Doing a Man's Job

Even working six days a week, Yuki's current dish-washing job paid very little. She didn't earn enough to keep her family in groceries, much less fix the leaking roof. After two years of working the menial jobs reserved for women, she'd decided to make a change. She was eighteen now, tall and strong. So this morning she stood in front of a shipping warehouse outside Minamata, determined to enter a man's world.

Because anything considered "men's work," whether in an office or warehouse, always paid far better. Even when women did the exact same tasks, men got more pay. Yuki had worked alongside farmers, hauled rocks, and dug ditches, but still been paid less than half of the wages the men were given. If she could prove she was capable of the work and thus the same wages, life would change for the better.

At least, that was her plan.

While working at the restaurant she'd overheard the chef complaining about not getting food orders promptly enough. "The food distributor's shorthanded," he'd groused. "And I have to suffer!"

Now here she was, ready to fill the vacancy.

She closed her eyes, took a deep breath and murmured, "I can do it." Pulling her shoulders back, standing tall and confident, she walked inside.

This rectangular one-story warehouse in the industrial section of Minamata – a windowless cube, except for a small grimy one set high in one wall of the corner office – took up a quarter of the city block.

A panel truck was parked in front, before the warehouse's loading dock, its sides stenciled FUJI DISTRIBUTION COMPANY. A broad-shouldered workman, biceps straining the sleeves of his dusty jacket, was tossing huge bags of dried seaweed into the back, while another worker stacked them. A third man in brown work pants and a shirt with *Zumoto* and *Manager* stitched on the chest pocket, stood next to the truck. He scribbled on a clipboard each time an item was loaded.

Yuki walked up to him and bowed deeply. "Hello. I used to get rid of mice and rats in your warehouse."

Zumoto stopped writing and looked her up and down, a smile flickering over his lips. "Yeah. I remember."

"I want to get a job doing what these men do." She gestured at the truck. "I'm tall, and very strong. I've tilled fields, sailed boats, dug ditches. I can do this work, too."

"This is work for men, not girls."

"Back when I was killing rodents, you lost a man who got sick." She pointed to the inside of the warehouse. "There's still many bags heaped up on the floor that should be stacked on shelves. I'll do it."

She went inside, over to a mound of burlap sacks marked SUSHI RICE, and picked one up. Then hauled it over to another area of the warehouse floor. One shelf was marked by a small wooden sign also printed SUSHI RICE. She hefted the bag onto it.

"See? A hard worker. I'll show up on time and do whatever's needed. I did a good job with the mice and rats."

The muscular man, with the name *Tatsumi* stitched on his shirt, stopped tossing bags into the truck. "We could use another hand. We're behind on deliveries."

Zumoto looked thoughtful. "I am tired of helping these two out. Not really my job."

"I can start today," Yuki said. "Right now, in fact."

After she hauled more rice, then sacks of barley, her back ached. But she made sure to smile as if the work was easy. She loved the rich aromas: dried salty seaweed, powdered tuna-fish soup stock, green tea leaves, mirin, rice vinegar, sugar, yam cakes, fish cakes, and more. Foods her family couldn't afford ever since fishing died out. The winter sun now felt warm enough for her to shed her jacket and take a lunch break outside. She'd worked up an appetite, and wished she'd brought three yams instead of two.

Tatsumi was shoveling rice and grilled vegetables into his mouth from a lunchbox. He mumbled, mouth still full, "Why're you here? Doesn't your father work?"

Maybe he was just one of those ignorant city people who thought the Disease was contagious, but she took a chance. "He has the Disease. Can't fish anymore."

"Oh." He shook his head slowly as he chewed, jaw muscles stretching and tightening. "Sorry to hear that. I know a family with it, too. Father and daughter. Terrible. And everything in the Bay is dead."

"Yeah." She didn't want to get into who was responsible. Though Kiyo seemed sure it was Chisso's fault, city people still tended to be loyal to the company.

At the end of the day, she felt exhausted. Her thighs and arms were tight and sore; her shoulders ached. Yet she felt lighter on the trek home.

Once there she stoked up the kotatsu with charcoal, changed Tomoko and began cooking the last of their rice until the next subsidy. Which, luckily, would arrive tomorrow. Then she announced her big news. "I got a warehouse job at Fuji Distribution. I'll make three times more money now."

Mom frowned. "Isn't that men's work?"

"Yes. So I'll be paid a man's wage. I'm strong, I can handle it."

"It sounds too hard." Her mother shook her head.

"With men? Warehouse?" Nobuyuki mumbled.

"Two. Plus the manager." She kept her voice light, her expression unconcerned.

"No place for a girl." He shook his head.

"I'm eighteen, Dad. Not a little girl. I'm a woman."

"Not safe."

"Don't worry. They've all been nice to me."

"Where is it?" Mom covered Tomoko with the kotatsu futon.

"On Harumi-dori, a few blocks from the dock and train station. Some other warehouses are on the road, too."

"That area's full of rough working men."

Yuki hadn't thought of that. But she refused to worry. The pay was double what the family used to make fishing. Trying to stretch a couple potatoes and some pickled cucumbers and eggplants to feed a family of four each day was worse than aching muscles and working with men. She'd have enough money to take the bus, and get home earlier to take care of the family. Once she could afford oil paints, life would even be better.

"No," her father grumbled. "Different work."

"Dinner's ready," she said, ignoring his comment.

On Saturday, her third day at the Fuji food company, a shiny black Toyota Crown purred up. She paused from stacking boxes of dried squid to gape at the gleaming sedan, with silver mirrors mounted right above the headlights.

Matsuyama – the employee who did most of the driving – nudged her arm. "Beautiful, isn't it? When you first see those mirrors, you think they're hood ornaments, like wings on some mythical animal. That's the warehouse owner, Fuji-san. Comes every week to go over the books with Zumoto-san."

"Must be rich."

A short, square-faced, thin-necked man got out of the backseat. He wore an expensive-looking overcoat with a dark gray wool fedora. A white-gloved chauffeur held his door open.

"Better not let him see us dawdling," Matsuyama said, and they lifted their sacks again.

A few minutes later, while working in the front of the building, through the office's glass door she saw the owner bent over Zumoto's desk, studying a ledger. He seemed very intent on the numbers, running a thin finger down the columns on each page. When he lifted his head and glanced her way, she quickly scooped up a box and moved on.

Later, when he came out of the office with Zumoto, she heard him say, "You hired a girl?"

"Yeah. Great worker. Never misses a day."

"A woman can't possibly keep up." Fuji shook his head.

"Yet she does, sir. As good as any man we've ever had."

Was she going to lose her job? Insecurity fluttered in her belly. The possibility of starvation terrified her.

Fuji frowned, and huffed a long, hard breath. "She'd better be as good." He shot Zumoto a warning look before returning to the office.

As Yuki heaved another bag onto the shelves, a skinny woman rushed up to the warehouse. Her hair was loosely covered with a thin towel wrap, as if she'd been cleaning house. She carried a small metal lunchbox.

"Jun-kun," she called out at the open door.

Matsuyama set down the box he'd been carrying and rushed over to her.

"You forgot your lunch," she said, blinking at him from behind unattractive wire-rim glasses.

"Oh, yeah." Matsuyama took the lunchbox, shooting a quick glance at the office. "Thanks. Better go before they see you."

"I understand." She rushed off, not looking back.

"What would happen if they saw her?" Yuki asked.

"Having visitors means you're not working. One guy got fired because too many people kept popping in. I value my job; got a family to feed."

Yuki nodded. She needed to learn the rules. At other jobs, Kiyo had sometimes dropped in to see her. She felt an unpleasant drop in the pit of her stomach recalling his disastrous visit at Goto Sensei's house. Though seeing him brightened her day, she'd have to ask him not to come here. She couldn't risk losing a job this good.

Sunday was glorious, brisk but sunny. The weekend meant she could spend some time painting, and taking her sister for a walk. Without such pleasures to look forward to, life *would* be dark – a mere cycle of drudgery.

She set up her easel and paints and began an ocean scene, dabbing dark blue to show depth, streaking lighter blue near the beach. Enjoying the lapping of waves on sand. Pretending the Bay wasn't merely a dead zone, but the pristine aqua sea it used to be.

She could create any world she wanted with paint and a brush. To start with a blank canvas, and make skies, forests, people or animals come alive, gave a deep pleasure only another artist could understand. No one died or got sick if a painting didn't turn out as she'd imagined. She could merely take another white panel and create again. No pressure, no stress, only the joy of expressing what she felt at that moment. Problems briefly melted away, like watercolors in the rain. She saw only the creation before her.

A whir of spinning gears, and Kiyo's bike coasted up. "Hi," he said, dismounting. "Your mother told me you were here."

"Hey." She lowered her brush, "How'd you get your bike back?"

"Fukuzawa-san found it still lying at the riot site. Fenders are a little dented. I thought my parents might take it away again, but they only ordered me to avoid demonstrations. Still, even after four weeks, the atmosphere at home is chilly. Brrrr." He wrapped his arms around himself and mimicked shivering. "Though Mom's finally starting to warm up. Dad, who knows? He's always at work."

He glanced at the easel, eyebrows rising. "Hey, you're using oils."

"I'm making good wages now, so I bought some. Plus canvas, and a book on how to use the paints. It's very different from watercolor. Oil paints are more versatile than any other medium. I still have lots to learn, though."

"But you're already really good. The Bay in your painting looks the way it used to. Before it was ruined." As if afraid he was dampening the mood, he quickly added, "You're probably already the best artist in Minamata."

She laughed, waving him off with her brush, though it was flattering. She thought she was improving, but it was hard to judge. And Kiyo had complimented her art since the day they met; would he truly notice progress?

They'd met in the days before heavy metal pollution and the Disease: clear water, the sandy beach, trees with red and gold leaves fluttering. In that life she'd breathed clean air, played with friends, eaten the plentiful meals her mother cooked, spent time with her uncle. She'd hoped art would soften the hard lump that was always in her stomach. She wanted to open her heart to Kiyo, recall how joy had felt. But sorrow left so little room for anything else, now.

"Your parents mentioned you found a higher-paying job," Kiyo said. "That's good. Where is it?"

When she told him, he gasped. "A warehouse? But don't only men do those jobs? Are there any other women?"

Clearly he didn't think she should work there, either.

"No. Fuji distributes food. And it's going well. The best part is, I'm paid the same wage as the men, three times more than I've ever made. Isn't that terrific?"

"Yes, but . . . it's not in a safe area. I'll give you my allowance so you won't have to work there."

"You already spent all of it buying us food. Now you won't have to do that anymore."

"I don't mind."

She knew he truly meant it. But she didn't want to be told what to do. She was finally making progress. "I'll be fine," she said blithely. "They treat me like one of them. And I can handle the heavy lifting."

"It's not that. I know you're strong. So tall now, and with broad shoulders, and your, um . . . ." He looked embarrassed, and cleared his throat. "But I've heard stories about how dangerous it is for a lone woman to walk among a pack of men. You're so pretty, and, well, not a girl anymore. Men notice such things. And I doubt the police patrol there."

She tightened her jaw, annoyed. "I don't expect anyone to protect me."

"If you report a crime, they may not believe you. Or even take the man's side. You know what cops think about fishers." He paused. "I'll stop by to check on you."

"Ah, actually you'd better not." She bought time by dabbing a touch of black on the painting to create shadow. Then set her brush on the easel ledge, and slowly screwed the cap back onto the paint tube. She wanted to phrase her next words carefully.

"The manager thinks anyone stopping by is a distraction. He wants us to work diligently. So if you wouldn't mind . . . I'll see you after work. Or on weekends." She smiled to lessen any sting her words might carry. "That'll give you more time to study with Dr. Hosokawa."

"Sure, but I'll always make time to see you." He gazed at her for a moment, frowning. "I won't come by there if you don't want me to. But I've got a bad feeling."

"Bosses don't want the help chit-chatting with friends, that's all. It's a good job, really. Best I've ever had."

"Just be careful, all right?"

"Of course." She smiled, glad that was over. "Now let's just enjoy this beautiful day."

The first of many just like it, she hoped, now that life was taking a turn for the better.

THIRTY-FOUR

Honor

T he next day at work, Yuki was loading a shelf with bags of hard candies, which exuded the deliciously-blended scents of sugary watermelon and tart lemon. As she lifted the next one, she noticed something strange. The same shelf had been full of this product the previous week; why was it over half empty now?

"Matsuyama-san," she called out to her coworker, "Did you deliver a lot of candy last week?"

"No. No orders for that in at least two weeks."

Worried she might be held responsible for missing or misplaced products, she went to see the manager in the office. "I'm stacking hard candy again on shelf thirty-nine. I'm sure it was full last week, but it's half gone now. Matsuyama-san said we haven't sold any in weeks."

Zumoto glanced over at the shelf, scratching the maroon birthmark on his forehead. "Oh, yeah. I had an emergency order over the weekend and delivered them myself. Don't worry about it."

"I see. Thanks for explaining that." Yuki bowed slightly and hustled back to work.

In the following weeks, though, she noticed other products seemed suddenly low in inventory, even when there should've been plenty. She reported the shortage to her boss each time. She'd been there about a month when she walked into the small office, and saw the desk was pushed away from the wall where it usually sat. Zumoto was squatting behind it; perhaps he'd dropped a pen?

"Did you lose something?" she asked.

He flinched and turned quickly, banging his head on the side of the desk. He cursed, then straightened and turned toward her, rubbing the bruised spot. "Just dropped a pencil. Found it. What'd you need?"

"Now there's a low inventory of buckwheat flour."

"Very diligent of you to notice. Those were sold. Now go back to work," he flipped a hand to dismiss her.

Funny how Zumoto always had a ready explanation for the vanishing merchandise. Back at the shelves, she said to Matsuyama and Tatsumi, "Have you noticed products keep disappearing? Boss always says those got sold, but I never saw either of you delivering them."

They looked briefly puzzled, then both shook their heads. Matsuyama said, "Boss has it handled. Anyhow, inventory's not our concern."

Obviously they didn't think, or even care. But she still worried the missing sacks might cause problems.

After four weeks of loading, unloading, and moving heavy boxes and sacks around, hard muscles developed on Yuki's thighs, shoulders and biceps. She no longer felt sore at night. Now, gathering firewood and moving charcoal at home seemed as easy as lifting pillows.

When Zumoto handed her a white envelope containing her first month's wages, she wanted to jump around and shout ecstatically. Instead she calmly bowed and thanked him. On the way home, filled with excitement, she bought rice, tea, tofu, eggs, miso, and even splurged on a can of tangerines. Now the family could have some variety at meals, as well as full bellies.

Another six weeks passed, Yuki working alongside the men, chuckling at their silly and sometimes rude jokes. Sometimes telling one, herself. With the second month's pay, she proudly presented each family member with a set of new clothing and new shoes.

The following week, Tatsumi and Matsuyama were hauling products inland to small towns in the mountains. They wouldn't be back for four days. So Yuki worked alone in the warehouse, unpacking cases of canned peaches and tins of sardines, stacking the boxes on shelves deep in the back of the windowless warehouse. The doors of the loading bay were open, and a darkening sky was visible: a storm blowing in.

Rain suddenly pounded upon a dozen crates of karintou candy and dried squid she hadn't yet moved from the bay. Zumoto ran out of his office to close the wide loading-dock door. Then, even with all the lights on, the building was dim.

He went into the office and returned with a green metal thermos. "Just us today. Let's take a tea break."

She wouldn't say no to a short rest. "Thank you."

She dusted callused palms on her beige work pants and sat on a box of soy sauce bottles yet to be unpacked. Rain drummed loudly on the metal roof. Zumoto took a seat on a crate of rice vinegar, and filled two metal cups with green tea.

Yuki warmed her hands on the cup, then took a sip. "Delicious." Luscious warmth trickled down her throat, and she smiled.

"You're a good-looking girl," Zumoto said. "Got a boyfriend?"

Her face heated up. She didn't want to talk about Kiyo; too personal. "Not really."

"Oh, yeah? I could show you a good time."

A chill greater than cold rain could bring crept down her spine. "I'm so busy taking care of my family. I don't have time for such things."

"Here. I'll show you how much fun we could have."

Zumoto set the thermos and cup on the crate and stood. She put her cup down and began to rise too, uncertain of his intentions. He lunged at her suddenly, grabbing her hair and pulling her to him, then kissed her hard. His lips were oily, and his mouth stank of the sardines he must've eaten for breakfast.

She jerked her head back, freeing her hair and pulled away, then shoved him in the chest. "Please, leave me alone!"

"Come on, I know you want it."

Those muscular arms dragged her close again. She leaned away and tried to push, but his grip on her arms was tight. Even with all the new hard muscles, she was no match for him. Half a head taller, twice her weight, he, too, was fit and strong from hauling bags and crates.

She turned away from his foul breath. "Stop! I want to go back to work."

He tightened his hold, crushing her so tightly against him it was hard to breathe. "Told you, no work today. Only play."

He slid a cold, groping hand down the back of her workpants. She reached behind her, clawing at his arm, frantically looking around for an escape route. Glimpsing the metal teacup on the crate, she leaned over to grab it, and swung it hard into his temple.

"Shit!" he exclaimed, finally letting go. "That hurt!" Rage contorted his face. The birthmark darkened from maroon to purple. "Bitch!" he snarled.

She raked her fingernails across a cheek, leaving three red furrows.

Now he looked angry enough to kill. "I was trying to be nice, you fisher scum."

She was already sprinting to the entrance, tugging desperately on the door. Freezing rain whipped in through the few inches it had opened when he threw himself on her from behind.

"No!" Yuki cried as they tumbled onto hard concrete, he on top of her. Her head bounced off the floor so hard, for a moment she saw two of him. He jerked his arms from under her, using sheer bulk to hold her in place, then sat up and straddled her. From this angle his birthmark looked like a purple spider.

She swung a fist at his face. He caught the arm, then pinned both wrists above her head. He began unbuckling his belt as she thrashed and kicked.

"Stop that."

"No, let go of me!"

He bared his teeth and slapped her so hard her head whipped sideways. The world dissolved into black and white, stars bursting everywhere.

With the brown leather belt Zumoto tied her hands to a shelf post. His thick fingers ripped her blouse open so violently, flying buttons hit her face. He shoved his pants around one ankle.

She tried again to throw him off, and he jammed a knee into her diaphragm. Choking for air, helpless as an octopus pulled up in a pot, she wanted to fight, or get up and run. But now she could barely breathe. His penis, long and bent, was her shocking first look at male genitals.

He pressed it against her. "Shut up, or I'll hit you again, harder."

She spat at him, and some hit the mark. He slapped her with his free hand, pulled down her pants, and pressed his knee between her thighs, forcing them apart.

The pain seemed to rip her apart.

"Stop!" Cold from the concrete floor chilled her back, but otherwise it felt as if she'd been shoved into a bonfire. He pounded against her, and she still couldn't get enough air. His gross sweaty bulk crushed her lungs; tears and saliva clogged her throat.

Stay alive, just stay alive, she chanted in her mind. She squeezed eyes shut, clenched her teeth, and prayed it ended soon.

Then, she would find a way to kill him.

His body finally stilled, and he rolled off. After a few moments he stood and dressed.

"You just earned the rest of the day off." He smirked. "Now I'm good and hungry for lunch." He untied her, and left.

She lay shivering on the cold concrete, too traumatized to think. Finally she slowly levered herself up in both elbows, and groped her way over to sit on a box, panting in short painful gasps. She gathered her clothes and bent to put them on, then froze. There was blood on the floor. When she slipped a hand between her legs, her fingers came away bloody. With the hem of her blouse, she wiped herself and dressed. Her blouse hung open, no buttons left, so she buttoned up her jacket, and limped outside.

The storm had passed, leaving the road full of puddles. Walking was painful. She talked to herself as she staggered home under the harsh eye of the winter sun.

"One step at a time. One step at a time."

Eventually she would reach her home and family, where she'd be safe.

People on the street stared as if she were a tramp or an alien being. Some gave her a wide berth, others sucked in a breath and quickly looked away. Could they tell what had happened to her?

A few minutes later she caught sight of herself in a store display window: hair tangled and knotted, face dirt smudged and slick with tears. A red bruise rising on one swollen cheek. Her clothes torn, wrinkled, and soiled.

As they passed Yuki, a woman in a tweed suit whispered loudly to her companion, who wore a beautiful kimono, "Do you think she has the Disease?"

"She's not swaying, just walking. But more like she's a
– " The kimono-clad woman gasped, and they hurried on.

Yuki had felt humiliation when people mocked her
family. But this was a new form of degradation, being
viewed as a prostitute.

She rubbed her face on one sleeve, and slapped warehouse dust from her trousers. She tried to comb her hair
with her fingers, but it did little good in this biting north
wind. She didn't want to spend any money, knowing the
days of good income were over. But she felt sure she'd never make it home on foot. Keeping her gaze down, she hobbled to the bus station.

She hadn't noticed the peculiar odor until she took her
seat on the bus. A mix of salt and bleach and something
vaguely like shellfish: the smell of semen. She suppressed
a gag.

She stared down at her scuffed work boots to avoid seeing anyone's expression. Clutching her hands tightly, wishing she could somehow undo the morning, undo the whole
day. Now that the shock and pain had receded a bit, anger
rose. *That evil, demon bastard.* She hated him. Her heart
pounded, her jaw clenched. She wanted to punch him,
knock out his teeth, bite an ear off.

She wanted, as she'd fleetingly thought back at the
warehouse, to kill him.

As she staggered inside her mother cried out in alarm,
"What happened?"

"What?" Dad asked, staring. "Accident?"

Seeing the worry and fear on their faces, Yuki's anger
fled. She collapsed on the floor, sobbing. Kazuko set Tomoko on a towel and lay on the floor next to Yuki. She gently
took hold of one hand. "Yuki-chan, you can tell us anything. We'll understand."

The compassion in her voice made Yuki weep harder.
Finally she sat up and faced them.

"Were you attacked?" Nobuyuki asked.

She stared at him. "How ... How did you know?"

"You mean . . . raped?" her mother gasped. "Oh, no, no, no, no." She hugged Yuki tightly, howling like a bereaved mother wolf. "He hit you? This mark on your face?"

"Yes," Yuki replied. "He hit me. And he – "

Her father's eyes burned with fury. "Who?"

"Zumoto."

"Your boss?" Kazuko cried.

"The other men?" Nobuyuki asked.

"No. They're making deliveries in the mountains. So I was alone."

"Tied you?" He pointed to the red bruises circling both her wrists.

Yuki nodded.

"I'll kill him." Dad tried to close his hands into fists.

Tomoko looked from the anguished faces of each of them, and cried. Yuki crawled over to the towel she lay on, picked her up, and buried her face in her little sister's hair. "It's all right," she said over and over.

But how could it ever be, again?

"This is terrible, so terrible. My poor girl." Kazuko wrung her hands. "We'll go to the police?"

"No! You know what'll happen then."

"Yes, yes, all right." Her mother clapped her hands over her face for a moment. When she lowered them her fingertips had left white indentations. "You should never have to see that monster again."

"Except to kill him," Nobuyuki muttered through stiff lips.

"There must be something we can do!" her mother insisted.

"If I go to the police, they'll just say I'm a whore who asked for it. We're a fisher family, and I took a job meant for men. They'll say I'm promiscuous, or not even believe it happened. Then we'd never be able to show our faces again in public." She fell silent a moment then said softly, "I'm no longer a virgin. Will Kiyo even want me anymore?"

"Of course! He'll understand." Kazuko's face crumpled. "Not your fault. You're still the honorable person you've always been."

I am, Yuki thought. But will anyone else think so? Prostitutes and women who slept around were scorned by society. Most families would not accept a slut as a daughter-in-law. *I'm not a tramp*, Yuki thought. Surely Kiyo knew that, would recognize how hard she'd fought. She wanted to put faith in his acceptance, but what if she was wrong? She wanted the beautiful future they'd dreamed about. The thought of losing the man she'd loved for four years, and still believed she was destined to be with, was gut-wrenching. But if he regarded her as spoiled goods, her heart would become a stone that no longer beat.

After a moment, her mother straightened, mouth twisted. "That horrible Zumoto. You should tell the owner what kind of a man he employs. Get him fired."

"But that would still announce to the world that I was raped. Anyway, he won't care. The owner never wanted me working there. All he cares about is money, not how the work gets done. And Zumoto makes him money."

"I'll get even," muttered Nobuyuki.

Yuki didn't reply. She felt not just dirty, but soiled to the core. The memory of Zumoto beating and violating her kept running through her mind in an endless loop.

She rose, wincing at the renewed pain that brought, and sighed. "I'll stoke up the charcoal, then go to the bath-house."

Yuki couldn't muster energy to get up the next morning. The bruising, now a dark midnight blue, covered half her face. She hurt all over. But at last she finally rose, moving slowly, fixing meals and caring for her sister.

"Just rest," her mother said.

How could she? The very idea was strange. She'd rarely been sick, her whole life. Just lying on a futon during the day seemed shockingly lazy, so she cuddled there with Tomoko.

Dad continued to mutter threats about killing the manager. Unable to stand being in her own skin anymore, Yuki returned to the bathhouse again and scrubbed until her skin was raw and pink. Yet somehow she could still smell Zumoto's anchovy and semen stench. She soaked in hot water, got out, and washed herself four more times.

She longed to see Kiyo, who had exams this week and so could not come by. At the same time, she was afraid to talk to him.

The next day she felt well enough to go into the city to ask for her last two weeks' wages. She passed a clothing shop with a display of baby outfits for sale, and froze on the sidewalk, unable to move. *What if there's a baby inside me, now?* No, she thought in horror. She refused to have a child by that monster.

She walked on again, stomach clenching with fear as she approached the warehouse. Zumoto's rough grimy fingers on her skin, the agony –

"No," she said sharply. She never wanted to lay eyes on him again, but had half a month's pay coming and couldn't give that money up. Who knew when she'd find another job? Nothing would pay even close to what she'd been making. But what if he refused to pay her? If only she had something else to blackmail him with. Something that did not involve her own public humiliation.

She'd hoped Matsuyama and Tatsumi were back from the mountains. But the truck was not in its parking place. She'd have to confront Zumoto alone. Taking a deep breath, she turned the doorknob to the office and stepped inside.

Zumoto was writing in a ledger at his scratched-up desk. He looked up and gave a nasty little laugh.

"*Akaji*. Good. Go put together the order for Minamata Grocer."

"I don't work here anymore. I want my pay."

"Quitting?" He leaned back in his chair. "See, women just can't cut it. I can't possibly reward you for not sticking it out to the end of the month. Work till then and I'll pay you."

"You hit me, you raped me. I quit. And I want my pay," she rasped.

"What? You had your eye on me the day you started work here. With Matsuyama-san and Tatsumi-san gone? Your big chance. I just gave what you'd been begging for."

"I'll never work for an ogre like you."

"Get out of here." He flipped her as if she were a fly buzzing around his head, and went back to the ledger.

"I want my pay, now!"

His chair legs grated on the hard floor when he pushed it back. He stood and began unbuckling his belt.

"Sure. You have to earn it, then."

"Then I'm going to the police."

Zumoto roared with laughter and sat back down. "Go ahead. I'll tell them you've been offering yourself for money. They'll believe me. No decent girl would work in a place only meant for men. You'll be a big joke at the station. Go ahead. See what happens."

Yuki glared at his ugly, smirking face, hatred like acid eating at her belly. He was as bad as Chisso: malicious, lying, criminal. Unfit to live. Worse, he was right. No one would believe her, especially the authorities. She'd be scorned as a whore, deserving of her fate. Maybe never able to get another job anywhere.

She spun away and ran out, stumbling down the street. After ten blocks she still heard his laughter reverberating in her head. How weak and ineffectual she'd been! If she kept on walking she'd be letting him get away with two crimes: first rape, now theft.

She had to return and make him pay, somehow.

But when she slipped back into the warehouse, two men were scuffling next to the stacked boxes of dried persimmons. A knife glinted in the sunlight. The taller, bulkier one was Zumoto, but he blocked her view of the other one.

She ducked down the aisle dividing the rows of tall shelves and peered through a gap between boxes. The knife-holder staggered as if drunk, screaming something she couldn't make out. He lifted the knife and slashed wildly at Zumoto.

The boss danced back; the blade sliced through his shirt. A little blood spotted the white cloth.

"Shit!" he yelled, and grabbed the other man's arm. Wrenching the knife away, he stabbed him in the belly.

The wounded one toppled onto his side, clutching his stomach, blood oozing between his fingers. "Die, you bastard, die," he gasped out.

It was her father's voice.

"Dad!" She ran to him and knelt there. He was moaning in pain. Blood poured from the stab-wound, his life force spreading over the floor in a lost red tide.

Yuki lifted his head. "I'll get help!"

Nobuyuki glowered up at Zumoto. "Rapist! My daughter. Die!"

"Help him," she begged the manager.

The knife was still in Zumoto's hand, the tip dripping blood. His face was expressionless. "Too late to save him." He dropped the blade and it slid under a shelf.

"No it's not! Dad, we're taking you to the hospital."

She was about to rise when he whispered, "No. The end now . . . for your honor . . . I failed."

She sat and took his hand. "You're the best father ever, the best in Minamata. Please, let me – "

He smiled and closed his eyes, body relaxing as if the anger had bled out of him.

"Dad? Dad!" She pressed her face to his bristly, poorly shaven cheek. He gave no response. She sobbed for a few moments, then glared up at Zumoto. "Murderer!"

"He came at me with the knife. Self-defense." He looked around for the blade. "Bastard would've killed me if I hadn't gotten it away from him."

"He has the Disease. He could barely walk. All you had to do was get away – not kill him!"

"How was I supposed to know? I didn't even know who he was." Zumoto straightened. "Look, I'll take him to the mortuary. I won't go to the police or press charges."

"Press charges? You killed *him*."

"He started it. Shame will fall on your family, but I'll let you skate."

She reached out and pulled the weapon from under the shelf. The nicked and worn handle . . . Nobuyuki's fishing knife. "He came to avenge me, knowing he might be killed. He gave his life for me."

"But I'm wounded!" Zumoto cried, clutching at his slashed shirt. Only a few spots of blood marred the cloth. "See? Proof I was attacked."

"Murderer! Rapist!" Yuki sprang up and lunged at him, knife outthrust.

Zumoto caught her arm, wrenching it up behind her.

"Ah!" she cried, desperately gripping the blade. But he forced the arm upward until the pain overcame her, and she let go. When he released her in order to retrieve it, she clawed at his eyes. He dodged and swung a fist, connecting with the side of her head.

Her left ear rang. She fell hard against a shelf of ripe tangerines, hip slamming the wooden ledge. Fruit flew from the box and went rolling across the floor.

"You won't get away with it! I'm calling the police." She ran into the office, pants sodden with her father's blood. She snatched the handset from the cluttered desk, then realized she didn't know what number to call.

"Go ahead, call." Zumoto's bulk filled the narrow office doorway. "Then I can press charges against you and your old man for trying to murder the respectable manager of a trucking company. Who'll they believe – me, all cut up and bleeding – or the whorish daughter of a dead, diseased fisherman?"

She recalled being pushed to the pavement at the fishers' demonstration. The policeman snarling that people like her should suffer and die. If she went to jail there'd be no one to take care of her family. She slammed the receiver down onto the base, leaving sticky red fingerprints.

Dad was dead. She hadn't even gotten the wages she was owed, to put toward a funeral. When Uncle Higano died, the hospital took his body to the mortician for cremation. Dad must go home to Tsukinoura to be properly mourned, then to be cremated, but how could she do all of that? Her stomach burned as if plum pits were roasting inside her.

She closed her eyes, and said tiredly. "All right, you can take him to the mortuary."

Zumoto zipped up his jacket over the bloody shirt. He backed the company pickup truck over to the loading dock and dropped the tailgate. Using an old blanket, he dragged Dad's body away from the pool of blood, then lifted him onto a length of clean hemp fabric. To Yuki's surprise, he gently, almost reverently wrapped the ends and laid him in the bed of the truck.

It was a freezing, cloudy, December afternoon. She rode in back, sitting with her father's body, her hair whipping around her head. She uncovered Dad's face, then tugged his hand, so tough and callused heaving up crab pots and fish nets, and held onto it. She traced the deep creases on his bloodless, pale face with an index finger. The wrinkles seemed softer, shallower. In death, his tortured face had taken on a serene look. She smoothed the thick gray hair back from his temples, and wept.

How had he marshalled the strength to get to the bus stop, then from bus to warehouse? Rage must've fueled him. He'd wanted revenge, since legal justice would never arrive. Perhaps he hadn't cared if he died in this last act as a man, as the head of the household.

"Thank you," she whispered. "What a strong man you were, feeding and protecting us all those years. Telling stories and playing games with me. I'm so lucky you're my father. And sorry I shamed the family, so you had to avenge our honor."

She glimpsed the back of Zumoto's head through the cab window. The rage burst forth again. She leaned over and smacked the glass hard, wishing it was the murderer's ugly face.

Jerking his head around at the sound, he looked over one shoulder. "Whaddya think you're doing?"

"I'll get even!" she cried, but he'd already turned back to face the road.

Then she made a decision. She must keep her temper in check. But only until she no longer needed Zumoto's help with her father's body.

The undertaker who slid open the door of the mortuary wore round wire-rim glasses, a dark suit and tie. He greeted them at the entrance and directed them to carry the body to a table in a small windowless room that smelled strongly of incense.

Yuki and Zumoto did as instructed.

The mortician frowned down at Nobuyuki's body. "The state of this man's corpse . . . what happened?"

"Suicide," Zumoto said calmly, as if he'd thought it all out on the drive over. "He had Minamata Disease."

"Ah." The mortician nodded sadly.

The ease with which Zumoto lied infuriated Yuki. He was a monster. How repulsive his large flat nose was. How hard his piggy little eyes. One ear was even larger than the other. The memory of that gross, heavy body pinning her to the floor made her feel she was suffocating again. She longed to kill him right this moment. He'd robbed her of an experience that should've belonged only to Kiyo and to her.

"That's not true," she protested. "My father was retaliating because this bastard raped me." She pointed to Zumoto. "Call the police. It was murder."

"What?" The undertaker drew back, looking shocked and then skeptical.

Zumoto tapped his temple, implying Yuki was mad. "Eh. She used to work for me. Always hysterical. Maybe because her poor father had the Disease. You know about those fishers."

"Oh yes." The mortician nodded. "Too lazy to work. Always blaming everyone else."

"What? No!" They disparaged her, and her family, as if they were owed no decency or courtesy. She felt as if she were morphing into a fire dragon, from the inside out.

"Look." Zumoto opened his jacket. "See this wound? When I saw the man was going to kill himself, I tried to stop him. Got slashed for my trouble. I couldn't prevent him falling on his knife. But his daughter did work for me for a bit." He handed the mortician a wad of bills. "So I'll pay for the cremation."

"Thank you." The mortician bowed. "Some families can't pay, so I appreciate that."

"How can you swallow his lies?" Yuki held out her hands.

The man stepped out of reach, pocketing the money.

"My father was murdered. I was raped. And he won't even pay me the wages I earned."

"I'm sorry about your loss," the funeral director said blandly. "Your father must've been in great distress." A knowing look passed between the two men. "But young lady, selling your body is not the answer. Get a decent job."

"I'm not a prostitute!" she cried.

"These people are so pitiful," Zumoto said. "One lie after another. But I have sympathy for a daughter who's just lost her old man. So I'm gonna help her out."

He counted out more bills and held them out to Yuki. She hesitated, loath to take his money. But her mother and sister needed food. She snatched it quickly, before he changed his mind.

"You're lucky to have this good fellow looking out for you," said the undertaker. "I'll take care of your father. Come back in five days for his ashes."

Yuki shook her head. "Good man? See this bruise on my face?" She turned her head to show him. "He beat me, then raped me."

"So many ways one can get bruised," the man mused, narrowing his eyes. "Please, leave now."

"He killed him!" How could she leave her father on this cold table, falsely labeled a suicide?

When she didn't move to leave, though, the mortician grasped her shoulders and steered her toward the door.

Defeated, she took a last look back at Nobuyuki, murmuring, "I'm sorry." Then, fumbling at the door, she left.

On the long walk back to Tsukinoura, she despaired; how to break the horrifying news?

But her mother seemed to know as soon as she saw Yuki's face. "Where's Dad? He said he was going to the outhouse right after you left, but never came back inside. He's been missing for hours."

Yuki burst out crying.

"What happened? Tell me!" Kazuko grabbed Yuki's shoulders, leaning on her, almost knocking her down.

"I'm sorry, I'm sorry, Mom." Yuki wrapped her arms around her. "Dad took the bus. To the warehouse, to kill Zumoto. I saw them . . . but Zumoto got the knife away and murdered him."

"Nobuyuki was . . . killed?"

"He . . . yes."

"No. No, no," Kazuko moaned. They slumped to the floor next to a sleeping Tomoko. The toddler stirred and woke. She must've sensed something was wrong, for she began to cry.

Yuki picked up her sister and pressed her face to her belly. "I'm sorry, Tomoko-chan. So sorry. He was such a good dad."

The little girl swung her stiff arms in the air. "To, to, to," she uttered. Her word for Dad.

"How? *Tell* me," Mom pleaded, digging her nails into the thin, woven rush-grass floormat as if to anchor herself to something tangible, something that made sense in a mad world.

Yuki told her everything; at first, in a voice low and faint. But as she recounted the deadly struggle between Nobuyuki and Zumoto, then holding Dad as he was dying, what he'd said, and finally the scene at the mortuary, her voice grew stronger, more enraged.

Kazuko's lips trembled as she listened, tears pouring down her face. When Yuki finished, she said softly, wiping her eyes, "Such a good man. So proud. Proud of his family. Did I ever tell you how we met at the *obon* dance?"

She had, many times. But Yuki willingly listened for perhaps the hundredth reiteration of her parents' love-at-first-sight encounter. The story always made her smile, and love them even more. She could actually imagine them at her age – two good-looking, resilient young people looking forward to a happy, satisfying life.

"Honorable to the end." Kazuko dried her face on one sleeve, her expression faraway, sad. "He hated what the Disease did to him. I'm glad he perished in a noble fight. It's what he'd have wanted."

"Noble fight? He was murdered, Mom! He should be revenged."

"But that's how he was killed, seeking revenge for you." Her mother looked alarmed. "Don't put yourself in danger trying to avenge him. I won't lose you too!"

"But I'm young and healthy, stronger than Dad."

Kazuko shook her head slowly, decisively. "Yet that horrible man still overcame you." Another tear slipped down one cheek; she compressed her lips until they were thin as a slash from a scaling knife. "I'd kill that beast with my own hands if I could. But I know I can't," she rasped. "I've already lost Higano-kun and Nobuyuki-kun. I can't lose my daughter, too. What would happen to Tomoko-chan then? I couldn't take care of her. What would Kiyo-kun do if he found out about all of this?"

Yuki's rage suddenly evaporated. Fear gripped her. *What will Kiyo think of me now?*

"I must tell him, but . . . I don't know how. If his family finds out, they may never accept me as a daughter-in-law."

"Oh, Yuki-chan."

They sat holding each other, lost in their old memories and new regrets. Both sad, bitter, and angry.

When at last they drew apart, her mother cursed. "Men run around on wives and girlfriends, and no one cares. But women are expected to stay faithful and chaste, and blamed even if they're attacked. So unjust."

"Mom?" Yuki whispered, "What if I'm . . . pregnant?"

Kazuko shook her head. "Let's hope not. But there are ways to take care of that. I'm not totally useless."

"You're not useless at all. I couldn't live without you and Tomoko-chan."

"Kiyo-kun's a decent young man. I don't think he'd ever throw you away." She gave her a reassuring smile. "But I'm afraid he too will want revenge. No stopping a man whose sweetheart's been violated. We must let go of the rage and pain, to keep living."

But Yuki could not let go of the rage over her father's murder, the next day, or the next. Added to the continuous belittling of her family by the ignorant, the constant struggle to stave off starvation. No time to make art as she itched to paint every minute of the day.

She snatched up Nobuyuki's bottle of shochu, and tipped it to see what remained. She'd bought it with wages she'd earned working for Fuji Distribution. Only about half, but it would do. She plunked two cups on the table.

"Want some?"

Kazuko, who rarely drank, said, "Yes. I do."

And so Yuki kept pouring. They slugged back cup after cup until not a drop was left in the bottle.

THIRTY-FIVE

Is Anyone Listening?

After taking his last midterm exam Kiyo stopped by the hospital. He found Dr. Hosokawa pacing the boundaries of his small office, frowning.

"What's the matter?" Kiyo closed the door behind him.

"Organic mercury's been found in the Bay."

"Finally!" Kiyo exclaimed. "How?"

"A Kyushu University professor collected sludge samples from the bottom and found it in the sea-floor sediment where Chisso empties wastewater. Methylmercury is one of the heaviest metals; it only makes sense it'd been sinking to the bottom. That's why none was found it in the water."

"Wait, that was two years ago." Kiyo frowned. "I saw that researcher heaving up many buckets of mud. The same scientist who took my hair sample." He recalled the deep chill of that winter morning, and his parents' anger at him. "Why'd they just figured it out now?"

"Maybe they were merely prevented from announcing it, before."

"So why now?"

Sensei shook his head. "One can only hide the truth so long."

"So, researchers knew organic mercury caused Minamata Disease but previously found only *inorganic* mercury in Bay water. Chisso admitted they use inorganic mercury in production but claimed the fact that organic methylmercury was never detected in the water proved they were not at fault. Now we know they are."

"Yes. Since the contamination is right next to their dis-charge pipe."

Kiyo kicked at an imaginary rock. "So Chisso lied. They must have known all along they were discharging or-ganic mercury." He felt lightheaded and dropped onto a chair. All this time, he'd believed the factory wasn't at fault. Dad had lied to him. "Does the company know their wastewater is responsible?" Kiyo whispered, as if not speaking too loudly would alter the facts.

"Yes, but they won't make any changes."

"But, the Cyclator. It was installed *after* the scientist took the sludge samples. So even if Chisso was dumping the chemical back then, it's cleaned up now."

"You'd think so." Dr. Hosokawa tapped his chin, "And yet people over the past three years continued to contract the Disease."

"Maybe the Cyclator doesn't remove organic mercury." Kiyo squeezed his lids shut so tightly, flashes of light stabbed his eyes. "What're you going to do?"

"I can't do anything. I work for the company." The doc-tor was breathing hard, as if he'd just run a marathon.

"Stop using that as an excuse!" Kiyo shoved the filing cabinet against the wall so hard it teetered.

"Careful!" Dr. Hosokawa steadied it.

"Physicians are supposed to save lives, not cover for companies. People are dying up there." Kiyo pointed to the ceiling, to the second-floor ward above them. "But you're just afraid of losing your job?"

"The other doctors here are very busy. They don't know much about the Disease. I've been caring for the victims for five years, working closely with the researchers. If I leave my post, who will take over?"

By then he and Kiyo stood inches from each other. So close Kiyo could smell *natto* – fermented soybeans – on the doctor's breath.

"You could make sure more people don't get Minamata Disease," Kiyo insisted. "Tell government officials, the newspapers and magazines. Travel to Tokyo and demand the Diet listen to you. That they force Chisso to stop dumping mercury."

"You've forgotten one thing." Hosokawa Sensei turned and shuffled back behind his desk, shoulders slumped. "Chisso controls the officials, and the media."

Kiyo remembered the local newspaper editor who'd refused to warn people not to eat food from the Bay.

The doctor shook his head slowly. "No one will release the information. The company will make sure no one hears it. They'll fire me, then if I go public, they'll claim I'm just seeking revenge."

"But you're respected, liked. The media will believe you. Quit being a puppet. Take this public!" Kiyo pounded the desk. The tower of books that'd threatened to topple for months careened over and crashed to the floor. "Remember why you became a doctor." Once *he* began to practice, he'd always put his patients' welfare first. Why couldn't Sensei see this?

Hosokawa Sensei looked stricken. "You're right, Kiyo-kun. I haven't really helped the victims. Maybe it's time for someone else to take over."

"What? No! I didn't mean . . . you're just giving up?" Kiyo bolted from the office. So angry he barely felt the icy wind whipping through his clothing as he cycled like a demon to the factory. He sprinted up the hallway and into his father's office without knocking, slamming the door behind him.

"Dad! Organic mercury was found in the mud where your department discharges wastewater." Kiyo's face was hot, his fists clenched. "Did you know this?"

Dad stopped writing and set the pen on his desk. He slowly looked up and said calmly, "One should always knock. Now, sit down." The office's dim light carved the lines on his face deeper. His skin drooped, as if too tired to fight gravity anymore.

Kiyo didn't want to sit. His nerves were on fire, heart pumping like an open hydrant. But he saw now his father's face was nearly as gray as his suit jacket. Instead of anger, as Kiyo had expected, his eyes showed nothing. His whole affect was flat, expressionless.

Unnerved, Kiyo lowered himself into the chair facing the desk.

"I've already done everything I can." Dad spoke slowly, listlessly, as if too tired to raise his voice. His pipe had tipped over, spilling tobacco onto his desk, but he didn't seem to notice. "If you hurt someone, I'd stand by you. And you by me. It's the same thing, don't you see? Nothing is more important than loyalty to your family. And your company."

"But all you have to do," Kiyo sputtered, "is take the mercury out before you put wastewater in the Bay."

Dad looked away. "We've already given sympathy money."

"Barely enough to purchase food for a few months!"

"The payments are based on the fishers' income, a for-mula used by the government. They make very little, so they get even less. We don't control that part." Dad took a shallow breath, wincing as if it hurt him.

Kiyo stared incredulously. "And you kept telling me lies about military explosives left in the Bay, and other rubbish. There's hard proof now Chisso's to blame, so you have to fix it. Is business more important than human life? Anyhow, the word's going to get out. Then what?"

His father blew out a long, defeated breath and rubbed thin, bluish eyelids. His shoulders slumped like a tired boxer's. He'd grown so thin, when he leaned back in his chair the springs didn't protest. The seat didn't even tilt back. This was a skeleton masquerading as his father.

"I did the best I could for the company, and for you. I wanted Chisso to make a better future for Japan," he said wearily. "And yes, now they will be forced to take responsibility."

He looked beaten. "Study hard," he added. "Become a doctor. I failed, but . . . you can still help people."

Kiyo didn't have the heart to berate him anymore. Dr. Hosokawa and his father seemed to have both been pushed into a corner from which they saw no escape. Sensei said he might resign, but surely Kichiro could never quit. He'd been hired by Chisso right out of college, and committed to them for life. Yet he was talking as if his life, and Chisso's were over. His hopeless look worried Kiyo.

The government wasn't going to tell the truth, anyhow. And the local paper wouldn't jeopardize itself by revealing the origin of the pollution. Everyone was either afraid or had been bought off. But he didn't care about Chisso or the economy. He would not let Yuki suffer as so many others had. He'd failed Higano, her parents, and her sister. He would not fail her.

He rushed home and wrote an anonymous one-page article explaining the course of the Disease. Detailing how methylmercury affected the brain, the scientific evidence connecting Chisso's waste discharge to the Disease, warning everyone to not eat anything taken from the Bay. Donning a brimmed cap to shadow his face, he biked to a print shop on the other side of the city. He'd been with Fukuzawa when the chauffeur had picked up some printed work for Chisso. But he'd stayed in the car, so no employee had seen him.

The shop was one big room that smelled overpoweringly of ink. A husky man, sparse beard darkening his chin, stood next to a large printing press in the back. The machine chugged like a small locomotive. Shelves held stacks of white paper in varying sizes and weight. A petite woman, back turned to Kiyo, cranked the handle on a mimeograph machine. Samples of posters covered one wall: An announcement of a show by a Kabuki troupe from Osaka; Kiyo's favorite monster movie Gojira; a welcome sign to the city's annual art show.

The clerk stopped the press and came to the counter. "May I help you?"

Kiyo pulled the article from his brown leather brief-case, a hand-me-down from his father. He slid it across the counter. "A hundred mimeographed pages please."

The man barely glanced at it. "We'll have to reproduce this on a master page first."

"Oh?" That meant someone here would read every word he'd written. Good thing he'd worn the hat. "When will it be done?"

"Well, it's pretty short. Three o'clock now, so, by six."

"All right. I'll be back then."

As usual, his father was not home yet, so he and his mother ate an early dinner of grilled chicken and egg-plants.

"The general election's coming up in a couple weeks." Mother daintily slurped a bit of miso soup. "I want a repre-sentative who's going to quash those violent Miike coal miners."

"They only want to keep their jobs. I know oil's the fu-ture, but what're 30,000 men going to do if the mines sud-denly close?"

"Striking, picketing, and clashing with police is not the proper way to get what they want." The evening newspa-per lay next to her place setting. She shook her head and tapped the front-page picture: Men fighting, some carrying knives and clubs.

"It's hardly a fair fight when the Mitsui Corporation brings in yakuza." Mitsui was even larger than Chisso. Definitely unjust, Kiyo thought, using the Japanese mafia against your employees.

"Violence is never the way."

"But aren't the yakuza also . . . never mind." He sighed and went back to eating. His parents were so insulated from the working poor, they were never going to under‐ stand their plight.

After dinner he returned and picked up the mimeo‐ graphed copies. And then, while the city lay dark and qui‐ et, and everyone else was in bed, he rode around the city, pausing now and then to surreptitiously tack his article up onto lampposts and utility poles.

THIRTY-SIX

Who's a Murderer?

The next day Kiyo took some time off to visit Yuki. But when she came to the door, the morning sun lit up her bruised face like a spotlight. "What happened?" he gasped.

She turned her head away when he reached for her hand. "Oh, Kiyo-kun." She was blinking hard, her eyes shining with tears. Then the shell seemed to crack, and she fell against him, sobbing.

He turned to look at Kazuko, who stood a few feet behind her. "What's going on?" Clearly instead of seeing Dr. Hosokawa and writing the article yesterday, he should've come to see Yuki.

Her mother shook her head, looking anguished.

"Please, tell me," he begged. "I can't stand not knowing." He gently pulled Yuki inside, and then down to sit on the floor next to him.

"I don't know how to tell you," she whispered. "I've been . . . disgraced. I'm afraid you won't want to be with me anymore."

"That's not possible. Just tell me," he pleaded.

She looked up into his eyes, took a deep breath, and began the tale. Kiyo remained silent as the torrent of horrors inflicted on her and her father spilled out. As he listened, though, he had to clench his jaw tighter and tighter, until the muscles twitched. By the time she finished, his hands were clenched into fists. "I'm going to kill Zumoto."

"Are you disappointed I'm no longer a virgin?"

"What?" He looked astonished. "It was assault. You're not at fault!" He pounded on his chest. "But I am. I failed to protect you. It's my fault, *my* shame. I knew you were in danger working there, and did nothing. I'm sorry, so sorry. The terrible things you've endured." He stroked her hair. "Why didn't you come to me, after? If I'd helped then, maybe Nobuyuki-san would still be alive."

Yuki looked stricken. "I didn't know if you . . . ."

"Oh!" he cried. "Listen to me, blaming you. You don't know my phone number. You've never been to the place I live. None of this is your fault. Please, forgive me."

"You still want to be with me?" Hope shone in her eyes.

He clasped her hands in his. "Don't you know yet that I love you? I'd never leave you."

"But your parents!"

"Even if they objected, I'd choose you over them."

"Oh, Kiyo-kun." Her face lit up. She almost smiled.

"And I'm going to kill Zumoto," he added.

"Kiyo-kun, no!" Kazuko pleaded. "Don't destroy your life, your future, simply for revenge."

"But no one should walk away, free, after committing such heinous crimes."

"I haven't told anyone except you and Mom. The weight of it was crushing. But now I feel I can think clearly again." She shot a defiant look at her mother. "And I do want revenge."

"The law says crimes this terrible are punishable by death," Kiyo said grimly.

"But the police will believe him. Not me."

"Then we have to ensure justice is done. But it would have to look like an accident."

Yuki nodded. "Perhaps he disappears and is never found."

"Tell me about the warehouse layout. And the work schedule."

"During the day the other men are there, working," she said. "There's a lot of activity in the stocking and loading area. We'd be spotted."

"All right, then let's follow him home at night, find an opportunity then. Does he live in Minamata City?"

She shook her head. "I don't know."

"We'll find out."

"I don't want you doing this, even to avenge the family," Kazuko said. "Too dangerous. We've seen how violent and ruthless he is."

"Don't worry," Kiyo said. "We'll be careful."

At six that evening, the time Zumoto usually left for the day, he and Yuki met a couple of blocks from the warehouse. Exhaust fumes from cars passing by hazed the air. Kiyo wore dark pants and a dark jacket; Yuki her old, dark-blue work pants, faded brown jacket, and her father's old fishing cap. They meant to look like any teenagers strolling down the city's street, blending into the night.

He pointed to her head. "I can still smell the sea."

She nodded. "I like being reminded of him."

As they walked on, Kiyo pulled something from his pocket. "Look." When he unfolded the knife, its silver blade glinted in the waning light.

"Oh." Yuki sucked in a breath. "Where'd you get that?"

"From a store across the city. I wore a hat to shadow my face. Anyway, people buy knives all the time for everyday purposes."

"You're right. Good thinking."

They stopped half a block from the warehouse, and waited behind a tall hedge, watching three men who were leaving the building.

"That's Matsuyama·san and Tatsumi·san. I don't know the third. Must be my replacement. Ah – there's Zumoto."

The stocky manager locked up, lit a cigarette, and set off, arms swinging. The glowing end of the cigarette made it easy to track him as he sauntered down the street, whistling. The warehouse district was quiet, almost empty. Only a few people were out; most had the weary yet anticipatory look of those heading home from work.

They let Zumoto get a block ahead before following him. The evening was chilly; Yuki stuck her hands in the jacket pockets. Soon they were in the heart of the commercial district. Many shops were closing, proprietors closing shutters or turning keys in door·locks. But the red, white, yellow and blue neon signs and brightly lit lanterns in front of restaurants and bars were still lit. Some salary·men in dark suits, carrying briefcases – lucky enough to only work fifty hours a week – were entering these establishments, while others hurried past.

Zumoto trekked through the main business section for about ten minutes, until he reached the dimly·lit food cart area. A dozen vendors with portable·kitchen pushcarts offered various dishes in a greensward under some tall trees; good protection rain or shine. Tangy and salty, sweet and sour, opposing yet delicious scents competed for customers. Cooks tapped knives on cutting boards. Lanterns hung from roofs built on top of each portable kitchen. Some were setting up folding tables and chairs, but most merely offered a stool or two in front of a makeshift counter unfolded from the cart itself.

Yuki and Kiyo slipped into the shadows beside a cottage across from the eatery.

At the *oden* vendor, Zumoto took a seat on a rickety stool facing a narrow, hinged plank counter. The man at the brazier had a thin moustache above full lips, and a tweed beret.

"A bit pretentious for a cook," Kiyo whispered to Yuki.

The proprietor bowed slightly and, before Zumoto could even order, popped open a bottle of Nippon beer and set it before him, pouring half into a glass.

Zumoto downed the alcohol in one gulp, then refilled his glass and drank that down too. He seemed to be bantering with the cook as he ate the hot-pot set before him. After another beer, he paid for the meal, lit another cigarette and continued on his way.

"I think he's heading for the red light district," said Kiyo. He and Yuki fell into step about a block behind him.

She tried not to gape as she noticed women of various ages wearing everyday dresses or cotton kimonos, but with obi belts tied in the front, apparently to more easily disrobe. They loitered in the lantern-lit entrances to brothels, smiling at passing men who slowed to view the merchandise. Sometimes one stopped, spoke to the woman, and went inside with her.

Zumoto ignored the beckoning sex workers. He ambled on, stopping finally at a plain wooden building much like the rest, two stories tall with a sliding-glass entry door. All the windows were lit, but no one stood outside. He dropped his cigarette butt on the dirt lane, ground it out with the toe of one work boot, and entered. A few minutes later he appeared in one of the second-floor windows, talking and laughing as he closed the shutters.

"It might be a while," Kiyo remarked. "Better find a place to sit."

The buildings here closely abutted each other, so at first any hiding place was not apparent. Finally, in the recessed doorway of a carpentry shop, they sat on the cold stone threshold. Street light illuminated only the main road. The night was dark, the moon not yet risen, though brilliant stars already blazed.

Men traipsed past, seeming to take no notice of two youths gazing at the night sky.

"Cold?" Kiyo asked quietly.

A chill, risen from the icy floor, made her shiver. "I'm all right."

Of course he knew she was used to much worse discomfort than this. They leaned into each other for warmth and the pleasure of being close. She didn't mind the wait or the cold, so long as they were together. He swung an arm over her shoulder, and she rested her head on the hollow between his neck and clavicle. She smelled sweet yet fresh, a bit like roses, though he knew she didn't wear perfume.

"I love being close like this," Kiyo said. "You have no idea how you make me feel."

"I feel the same."

"No, it's different for men."

"Oh?"

Just speaking of it aroused him. He shifted to conceal his erection. The last thing he wanted to do was frighten or upset her, after the horrors Zumoto had inflicted.

"Never mind."

"All right. What's new with your work on the Disease?"

He explained what the sludge study had proved. "Yet Dad won't do anything about it. He looks ... almost sick, though. I posted an article around the city about how Chisso's causing the pollution. I hope it wakes some people up. Unless the Disease strikes someone close to them, people ignore what's going on."

Just then a tall man coming up, swinging a fancy cane, slowed and eyed them suspiciously. At last he sauntered on.

Once he was gone, she said, "I wonder if Chisso will get what they deserve, like Zumoto's going to."

"I'll do my best." He closed his eyes, enjoying the bond between them.

Yuki suddenly straightened. "We're here to kill Zumoto."

"Right." This wasn't a date. He nodded. "We'll get him."

A few moments passed. She absently slipped a hand under her jacket and rubbed her belly.

"Oh. Are you worried about, you know?" Kiyo asked.

"A baby. You've thought about that?"

"Well, I'm studying to be a doctor."

"Right, right."

"But you won't know for a few more weeks."

She nodded, and he felt her shudder.

"The idea of that despicable bastard's seed growing inside . . . I want to claw my own belly out."

He squeezed her hand. "Then we'll get help to deal with it. Whatever you decide, I'll stand by you."

"I know." She relaxed a bit, leaning against him again.

Two hours later Zumoto finally emerged, smiling, and ambled over to a residential street full of small, similar-looking houses. On the front stoop of a modest, one-story wooden cottage he fumbled a key from his pocket, unlocked the glass door, and went inside. Moments later, a faint glow of electric light flared.

"So this's his home," Yuki said.

"Yeah. I bet this is his usual routine, but we'd better follow him a couple more times, before we decide on the best plan. Can you come out tomorrow?"

"Yes. But aren't your parents going to wonder? Don't you have to study?"

"We're on break after exams. Anyway, I'll just tell Mom I'm out with a friend."

"Oh, that's right. After not going to school for a year, I'd forgotten." She looked wistful a moment, then added, "Meet at the same place, tomorrow night?"

The next night's events proved similar, except Zumoto ate at a different food cart, devouring a steaming bowl of rice, heaped with what looked like donburi: cooked eggs, chicken, onions, and greens in a thick sauce. He drank two large bottles of Nippon beer, then visited a different brothel and went home after two hours there.

The third night it rained torrents. Kiyo called the Tsukinoura General Store and asked the owner to give Yuki a message: *Meet tomorrow night.*

On that third surveillance, they whispered as the manager ate at a yakitori cart, stuffing grilled chicken and vegetables down, then guzzling beer. She'd brought a small sketchpad, and quickly penciled a portrait of Zumoto as ugly, self-satisfied villain, as if committing their mission to paper.

"I've been thinking," Kiyo said, frowning. "There're too many other people out until he's heading home. So the best place to kill him would be at the corner, just as he turns onto his street."

"I was thinking the same." Yuki put away her drawing. "In the gap between those two houses where a huge pine towers over them."

"Exactly. The street's all but deserted that late. The darker area beneath the tree will conceal us better, if anyone should pass by. We'd hit him on the head, knock him out, drag him into the empty opening and slit his carotid."

Yuki blinked. "His what?"

"The carotids are major arteries, right here." He traced each side of her neck. "If even one is cut, he'll bleed out and die quickly."

"How handy that you know all about blood."

"Well, it's actually the circulatory system. Our cells get oxygen and nutrition through blood and waste is removed, so – " He broke off and chuckled. "Sorry, didn't mean to start a medical lecture. So, we slit his throat and leave him lying there. That way, he shouldn't be found until morning."

"That's a good plan." She looked thoughtful, though, as if ruminating on something else.

"What're you thinking?"

"I knelt in a pool of my father's blood. I saw the horror of the Disease, over and over. And I'll never be able to shake those memories."

"I see your point." He would never have believed he'd be planning to take a life, even in self-defense. Doctors saved people; they didn't kill them intentionally. Yet, here he was, plotting to do just that. Both of them risking their future together, for a moment of vengeance. But he'd committed to help, and couldn't back out now.

"We'll follow him from the red light district again, I imagine," he said. "Once he's home, we'll go inspect the killing spot."

She nodded, swallowing hard. "I look forward to it." Yet her expression seemed anything but eager.

The next night, Kiyo packed a spare pair of pants and a light jacket in a small backpack, in case he was splattered with blood. He tugged the brim of a baseball cap low over his eyes to hide his face. It would also keep blood out of his hair.

He walked briskly to their meeting place, all the way wondering: *Am I doing the right thing?*

Zumoto should not get away with his crimes. But plotting to become a killer . . . didn't that make Kiyo more like the man, than not? Even if no one ever knew he'd slaughtered the manager, for the rest of his life he'd know. Kiyo and Yuki, the Murderers. Would Nobuyuki even want justice taken in this way?

But only he could choose his path in life. So he walked on to the meeting place.

They stalked Zumoto through his usual evening routine. Yuki was quiet, and seemed tense; her face looked tired and drawn. He occasionally felt for the knife through the cloth of his pocket. She kept tapping her teeth with one fingernail until he finally grabbed her hand and begged her to stop.

As they waited, Kiyo said calmly and firmly, as if stating their case to a judge. "He deserves to die."

"Yes, he does." She coughed as if trying to clear her throat, voice barely a whisper.

"He's a criminal who should pay for his actions. Yet only those who hold power seem to get such justice. Men blame women for being assaulted. That's not right. Just because men are stronger, they shouldn't be able to do whatever they want with women and children. Or with older or ailing men like your dad."

She nodded. "That's why we must kill him ourselves."

"Yes, but . . . well, I have to admit I don't feel right about it. I want to inflict pain on him – a great deal of pain. But I don't know if I can. Or if I want to stand by while you do it."

"But I – "

"Even if we don't get caught, you'll carry the burden of killing someone, for the rest of your life. Your future as a great artist could be tainted."

"I don't even know if I'm that good." She protested, laughing nervously, then abruptly fell silent when she glimpsed his face. "Your future could be tainted too. You wanted to save lives and cure people. But this," she gestured at his knife and bag of clothing. "It's the opposite of your dream. I don't want you to have regrets."

He nodded slowly. "I understand. Taking a life would haunt us both forever. And his death . . . well, it will be over quickly."

"Perhaps there's a better way to punish him," she said.

A man passing by glanced over curiously, and they fell silent. If asked why they were lingering here, Kiyo would say Yuki was unwell. That they'd sat down until she felt better. But the man kept walking.

"Do you have another plan?" Kiyo whispered.

She tilted her head, thinking. "I always wondered if Zumoto was stealing products and selling them under the table. Inventory came up short sometimes. Whenever I mentioned it, he always had an excuse. Said it'd been sold when I wasn't around. Yet I never missed a day of work."

"I remember you mentioned that."

"I feel sure he's a thief as well," she said, voice rising.

"Shhh!" Kiyo looked around.

"Sorry," she whispered. "Could we get him arrested for stealing?"

"Did you ever find any proof?"

"No." She sounded discouraged.

"Let's think about that. If he was stealing, it'd have to be concealed from the owner, right?" He tapped his temple. "Which reminds me of a detective novel I once read. *The Accountant Detective* was about some guy who was embezzling."

"A detective novel? I thought you only read medical books."

"Yeah. I used to love them. But I'm too busy with studies right now."

"I see." She laughed quietly. "Go on."

"In the novel, the embezzler kept two ledgers. One showed what should be happening: How much money came in and where it went. But an embezzler must also keep track of how much he's taking, and when, so he can concoct stories if any missing money's noticed. So he keeps a second ledger he doesn't show the owner. With me so far?"

She nodded. "Yep."

"Zumoto could be doing the same. One ledger shows stock coming into the warehouse and where they supposed-

ly went. In a second ledger, he records the real situation:
where the inventory actually went, who bought it, and how
much he's pocketing. He might record the wholesale cost of
food as more than it actually was, then pocket the difference. Or sell regular goods to legitimate buyers but charge
more than what the owner specified. Then there's still
some profit and the owner's none the wiser. Meanwhile,
Zumoto's dealing under the table and keeping the extra."

"So, there should be two sets of accounting books?"

"Yes, probably."

"If I can find them, it would prove he's a thief!"

"Right. If you can."

"He always spent a lot of time in the office writing in a
large book with a plain cover. I assumed it was the ledger
Fuji-san, the owner, saw every Saturday. Maybe Zumoto
actually has two books that look the same."

"In the novel, when the accountant finds the two books,
he figures out the identity of the murderer."

"But where would Zumoto keep the extra book?"

"The one the owner sees is kept in the office, right?"

"Yes. On a shelf in there. I've never seen Zumoto arrive
or leave carrying a ledger. So he must keep it in the warehouse. We could find and take it to the police."

"Mmm." Kiyo stared into space, mulling it over. "Right
on both counts. But we must bring the second book as evidence. Also, instead of going to the police, it might be better to just let the owner know. He'd have more credibility
for getting the police to charge Zumoto."

"Good, good." She nodded. "Fuji-san wouldn't like anyone cheating him. And the police might not credit our story, but they'd believe a respected businessman. Let's go to
the warehouse now."

"Also a good idea." Kiyo smiled. "Since we know he
won't be going back there tonight."

"Do you know how to pick a lock?"

"No, but I'll take a crack at it. Make some use of our decommissioned weapon." He pulled it out of his pocket. They both laughed nervously. Kiyo felt a wave of relief.

The block where the warehouse of the Fuji Distribution Company stood was dark and silent. Kiyo set to work forcing the knife-blade between door and jamb, not as easy as he'd imagined it would be, in the dark. Once it slipped and he gouged the wooden door-pull.

"Do you have a match?" he whispered.

She shook her head.

Feeling the edge of the door with his fingers, Kiyo finally slipped the blade into a slightly wider space, working it up and down, trying to ease up the lever. At this point he felt doubtful it would work.

He was about to withdraw the blade again when, amazed, he heard the sound he'd been waiting for: *Click*. He had to bite his tongue to hold back a triumphant shout.

Inside, Yuki turned on one of the warehouse lights. The smells of dried herbs, fruits and fish rushed at them like a breeze through an outdoor market. The cavernous interior was as cold as it had been outside.

"Fuji-san is in the office every week," she said, "so I doubt if the ledger is kept in there."

"But that would be the most logical place," Kiyo said. "Let's start there. And keep your gloves on. No fingerprints that way."

The office was only a little larger than his mother's closet. The walls were plywood, hammered directly to the studs supporting the siding. A small pine desk was shoved close to one panel. A cheap three-shelf bookcase across from it held dozens of notebooks.

Kiyo quickly read their labels, then with gloved hands awkwardly opened them to see if the contents matched the labels. The top two shelves were past years' ledgers. The middle shelf held notebooks with records designated by customer name; what they'd bought, any special requests, regular orders.

Yuki was searching the desk. She yanked out all four drawers, but none held notebooks or ledgers. She found only boxes of labels, wads of rubber bands, a stapler, pens and pencils.

She slammed each drawer shut and muttered, "Nothing!" All that was left in the cramped space was a metal trashcan full of pencil shavings, cigarette butts, and wadded-up paper.

Leaving the office, they examined the warehouse, scrutinizing boxes and crates on the aisles of shelves. The scent of curry dominated the spice section as they shifted bags of powdered wasabi, ginger, salt and pepper around. Bottles of sake, shochu, and whiskey, crammed the next whole aisle and were heavy to move. Colorful photos of mackerels, sardines, clams, and oysters decorated cans in the fish area. Despite the cold, by then they were both sweating. His stomach rumbled when he spotted a label for his favorite tins of butter biscuits and caramel candy.

They peered under and behind boxes of rice crackers, sesame seeds, furikake rice seasoning, panko, green tea, plum paste, dried seaweed powder, potato starch, and Ajinomoto.

"Hopeless!" Yuki huffed. "We're wasting our time in here. The inventory's constantly rotated so he couldn't keep hiding a ledger in with boxes of food."

"Right. And the wall is just uninsulated siding. The floor, solid concrete." He stomped on it. "Ceiling's too high. He'd have to move a ladder around all the time just to access it. And up there's only rafters." He looked around the warehouse. "Where else could it be?"

"Only the office, but we already searched it."

"It has to be there. Let's look again."

Back inside, Yuki pulled every notebook from the shelves, then scrutinized the wall behind it. "Nothing here." She shook her head, looking disgusted.

Kiyo drew all the drawers out again and set them on the floor. He carefully tapped and inspected the sides and bottoms for false compartments, then felt around inside their empty slots. At last he sighed and slid them all back into place. Slumping onto the desk chair, he propped his head on hands, muttering, "Think, *think*."

"It's just not here," Yuki cried. "Now he'll get away with everything!"

Kiyo grimaced at the unfairness of life. Then his head snapped up. "You know . . . in the same detective novel, the accountant found the other set of books hidden in a wall."

Yuki sprang up. "Once I saw him moving the desk out from the wall. When he saw me he seemed flustered. He said he was looking for something he'd dropped, but – "

Before she could finish, Kiyo was dragged the desk into the middle of the room. All he saw was the plywood partition.

"Wait. What's that?" Yuki pointed to what appeared to be a dark knot in the wood's grain. "It looks like a hole."

She came over and crouched there, poking a finger at it, then running it all the way down to the floor. "Here the wood feels a bit bulkier."

She hooked one finger into the plywood hole and pulled. A neatly-cut section popped out, leaving a gap about two feet above the floor. She slid a slender arm inside. "Oh. There's something here!"

She tugged out a notebook and flipped it open. "Columns, figures, records of transactions."

"He cut carefully around the knot and with the grain. Camouflaged, so no one would notice. Smart bastard."

They opened the ledger on the desk and bent over it. After a few moments of scanning the pages, they looked up at each other and smiled.

Kiyo pulled the latest real ledger off the shelf and opened it next to the newly-discovered notebook. He ran a finger down the date columns on the first page. "There are more smaller transactions in the second book than in the official one for Fuji-san. Zumoto's secret sales. And look at the prices for those purchases and sales. Not the same. This proves he's been embezzling. You figured it out!"

"We did it together." When she squeezed his hand, he never wanted to let go.

If only it could be as simple to get the public to understand mercury caused the Minamata Disease. Or to make Chisso stop the wastewater discharge and help the victims.

Clutching the precious evidence – the original ledger, and Zumoto's secret sales notebook – they slipped out and hurried to the bus stop, half an hour before the last bus of the night. They waited on the bench, hearts skipping erratically with exhilaration.

"I'm a burglar," Yuki blurted out, and giggled uncontrollably, shoulders shaking.

"Shhh." But Kiyo too was snickering, clapping a hand over his mouth to muffle his mirth. "Do you know where Fuji-san lives?"

Yuki looked stricken. "Oh! No, I don't. How will we deliver these? Do you know how to find an address?"

"Companies have to register. The registration must show the owner's name, so he'd be listed on the papers. I'll go to City Hall tomorrow morning and look it up. When do you want to deliver those?" He pointed to the ledgers.

"Very early. Zumoto might notice they're missing. I don't know if he'd figure out I took them, but I want them out of my hands as soon as possible."

"Yeah, that's only smart. Let's meet at Minamata Park at nine tomorrow."

When Yuki approached Kiyo the next morning, she smiled. "You found the address. I could tell from that satisfied look." She paused. "And more good news. I'm not pregnant."

"Oh, good. Very good!" He smiled with relief, then held out a piece of paper with an address scribbled on it. "Two men are listed as representing Fuji Distribution Company. Must be partners. One lives in Kobe. Fuji-san lives here, in the Second District. A pretty wealthy area."

She frowned at the address. "Know where that is?"

"I think so. Let's go."

After an eight-minute bus ride, they reached a much nicer stop with a freshly-painted bench and a shiny red post box as large as Kiyo. In this neighborhood, only the second stories of the homes and tops of mature pine and camphor trees were visible behind tall cedar fences.

It's even richer than my neighborhood, Kiyo thought.

A five-minute walk got them to the owner's address. Yuki pressed open the large, ornately-carved front gate, and they both peered in. The house was two stories, quite modern and Western-looking.

My mother would like it, thought Kiyo. Dormant wisteria bushes climbed its red-brick façade. Immaculately-trimmed maples, cherry trees, and azaleas lined the circular drive. A polished black Toyota Crown was parked in front of the house.

Yuki pointed at it. "That's his car."

"So it's the right place. Do you want me to do it?" Kiyo asked.

She hesitated. "No. I will."

"All right." He nodded. "I'll wait here."

She took a deep breath and pushed the gate wide. No guard dog rushed out or barked. The house still looked dark inside, even though the curtains on the front picture window were drawn back. She hurried past a lily-dotted koi pond reflecting clear blue sky and white clouds floating above. Then she set both ledgers on the step in front of a wooden door, and tapped the doorbell. Cocking her head as if listening for the pealing inside.

Suddenly, she turned and ran back toward Kiyo. The front door opened and the man Kiyo assumed must be Fuji stood there. He stared right at her as she hovered in the open space between gate and wall. Then looked down at the ledgers.

Yuki swung the gate shut, and she and Kiyo sprinted away.

At the bus stop, sounding winded, she gasped, "I shouldn't . . . have looked back."

"Even if he saw you, he doesn't know who you are."

"He's talked to me before. I'm sure he'll remember the warehouse's only female employee." She rubbed her palms on her pants. "Sweaty hands. My heart's still pounding. Do you think he'll report me to the police for stealing the books?"

"No, but no use worrying about it now. Zumoto is the criminal. You're doing the owner a favor."

"I suppose." Still, she looked around anxiously. On the bus ride back, she clicked her fingernails on her teeth, a bad habit.

Kiyo knocked on Yuki's door two days later. As soon as she wrenched it open, he shoved a newspaper at her. "Look! Read last night's headline." Only then did he nod to Kazuko and Tomiko. "Good morning."

The front page screamed, HUMAN REMAINS FOUND SCATTERED IN HINOKI FOREST.

"I don't . . . what does this mean?" Yuki asked.

"Read it. Out loud, so your mother can hear."

Starting at the headline, she began to read. "*At 3:23 p.m. yesterday, Umemura Takuma reported to police that his Shiba Inu dog came home with a man's forearm in his mouth.*"

Yuki frowned up at Kiyo, then went on.

"*After a search, police found a dismembered body, chopped into nine pieces by what appears to be by an ax: four limbs severed in half, a torso and a head. The discovery was made near Midori Road in Hinoki Forest. The victim has been tentatively identified as Zumoto Takeyasu, manager of Fuji Distribution Company's warehouse.*"

She dropped the paper. "Zumoto!"

"The murderer's dead?" Kazuko screamed, hugging Tomoko.

Kiyo picked up the paper and handed it back. "Read the rest."

"*An autopsy determined the limbs had been amputated while the victim was still alive. Police speculate that scattering the body parts instead of burying them indicates the perpetrator wanted them found – perhaps to send a message. An investigation is in progress.*" Yuki looked up again. "Do you suppose?"

"Yup. Fuji-san."

"Oh, my. I can barely breathe," she said. "I have to sit down."

Kazuko looked up from the kotatsu. "Yuki-chan told me of the change of plan, your delivering the two ledgers, so Fuji-san knew Zumoto had been stealing from him. He must've been very, very angry. Though I never expected him to kill to protect his profits."

"Me neither!" Yuki said. "Fuji-san seemed stern. He clearly didn't like me working there. But to chop a person up? Wow. Pretty drastic punishment for theft."

"Maybe the other partner ordered it done," Yuki's mother suggested.

Kiyo nodded. "You could be right. He lives in Kobe."

"Ah. Then we're both thinking the same thing." She smiled grimly.

"Home base of Yamaguchi-gumi, the largest yakuza gang in the country," Kiyo said.

Yuki gaped at them. "Wait. What would the mafia be doing here? Trafficking in vegetables and rice? They're loan sharks, drug dealers. Prostitution and . . . and stuff."

"Loan sharking," Kiyo said thoughtfully. "Maybe Fuji-san borrowed money to fund his business and was forced to make the yakuza a partner," he speculated.

"*They* wouldn't take kindly to anyone stealing from them," Kazuko noted.

"You must be right," Yuki said. "I bet Zumoto didn't know about that partnership. Surely even he wouldn't be crazy or stupid enough to anger the yakuza." She huffed. "I mean, I just thought he'd go to jail. Not that he'd be murdered."

"Funny how the world works," her mother said. "You wanted to kill him, and did so without wielding the knife. You've avenged your dad and yourself."

"Yeah. I suppose it was what I wanted. What I *thought* I wanted," she admitted. "But this . . . I wished him dead a million times. But, well, now that he's been killed, I'm not sure I feel good about it."

They all sat lost in thought for a few moments.

"I still want Chisso to pay," Yuki said suddenly. "To suffer for killing our pristine Bay and ruining the lives of thousands of innocent fishers and Disease victims. For killing Uncle and Father, and making us worry and starve. But how do I get revenge on a company?"

"Can a company even suffer?" her mother asked.

"Exactly." Yuki nodded. "They're staffed and run by people. Do I want revenge against all of them? Life's not so black-and-white as that. The only thing clear to me is the power of art. There's no right or wrong in it, only how the artist and the observer relate through imagery."

"And thanks, Kiyo-kun, for always being on our side," Yuki said, smiling at him. "But Zumoto's killing will weigh on me for a while, as you said. Justice and revenge? Maybe they're not always the same thing."

A week later, Kiyo and Yuki's family returned to their house after attending Nobuyuki's funeral. A huge sack of premium rice sat on their doorstep. Enough to feed them for a year. "Look," said Yuki.

A folded note was tacked to the front door, the edges fluttering in the breeze. She opened and read it aloud.

"*For Your Honesty.*"

It was not signed.

THIRTY-SEVEN

The Life of a Maid

Kiyo was studying anatomy and trying to ignore his mother and her friend Sakagami as they drank coffee and chatted and laughed in the living room. But the rich brewed aroma reached even to his room. He and Masa had been going to coffee shops occasionally over the past year. Masa, totally crazy about the drink, was always happy to treat Kiyo. Who was satisfied with just having a cup every now and then. But at the moment it just smelled so *good*.

Oscar Peterson's "Oscar's Blues" was playing on the phonograph in the living room, one of Mom's favorites. Kiyo bent his head over his desk again, trying to focus on the medical text open there. But just then Sakagami said, loudly enough for him to hear, "You wouldn't think a thirty-year-old woman could find a husband. But somehow she did, and she's moving to Kagoshima. Where does that leave me, without a maid and cook? You're lucky to have found a replacement so quickly, Etsuko-san."

He could almost hear the smile in his mother's pleased reply. "A young one. She's only worked for me for two months. But a pretty good cook so I'm sticking it out."

Kiyo perked up. Was this a good job opportunity for Yuki? She'd been unemployed for a month, since the terrible events at the warehouse, and Zumoto's strange murder. Surely she could make more money as a full-time maid and cook than doing backbreaking outdoor labor for little pay – like those she'd held before being hired at the warehouse. He closed the textbook and donned a heavy jacket, hat, and gloves. The northern wind was cold, but with no snow, so the roads would be dry.

After arriving at Yuki's, he told her, "A friend of my mother is looking for someone to clean and cook, fulltime. Her last employee got married and moved away. Probably pays pretty well."

Kazuko nodded. "And that's indoor work. Warm in the winter."

Yuki looked uncertain. "But I only know how to grill fish and vegetables, or make rice and soup. I got fired from the tempura café, remember?"

"Yeah. But I think she'll train you. I'd give a good re-ferral if you're interested."

Perhaps she was worried about pleasing some wealthy woman, or merely tired, but her smile held no joy. "All right. Can we go there now?"

Kiyo was surprised. "Sure, but I'm on my bike."

"Why don't you go tomorrow?" Kazuko said.

"She might hire someone else by then," Yuki said. "I can't pass up a chance at a full-time job."

It wasn't surprising she'd been unable to find work since leaving Fuji Distribution. The economy had slowed due to the Disease, lack of fishing, and diminishing tour-ism. Kiyo imagined the money from selling the boat must be gone by now.

"Kiyo-kun, let's just go now. I'll change."

He hadn't counted on pedaling the two of them in this severe cold. He'd offer bus fare, but the next scheduled route wasn't for another hour. And, while not eager, she clearly wanted to leave immediately.

"I, ah, suppose," Kiyo said. "Sure."

The Sakagami house turned out to be far grander than his family's home. The property was fenced all around with wood slats. A peaked, red-tile roof sheltered the large, elaborately-carved front gate. The sizeable two-story cedar-clad house was visible behind it.

"Before we go in," Kiyo said, parking the bike, "I should tell you that Mrs. Sakagami comes from a really rich family in Kyoto. Servants, a vacation home in the mountains, that kind of thing. That's how they can afford this place."

"OK," said Yuki, smoothing her hair and checking the buttons on her jacket.

"Her husband's the head of city council, so don't say anything bad about the city, the mayor, or Chisso to her. Oh, and maybe don't mention your family having the Disease. The husband has lots of power over subsidies and stuff."

Yuki brushed road-dust off her pants. "Got it."

"And, um, better not explain how we know each other. I'm going to say your mother worked for someone my dad knows."

"That's fine."

He saw her resetting her expression from annoyed to neutral; almost literally swallowing her pride. Rich people so often degraded and humiliated poorer ones. Healthy folks shunned the sick. Discrimination and intolerance seemed an ugly and ever-present fact of life.

He clasped her cold hands in his gloved ones, rubbing them to get a little warmth going again. "It'll work out, I'm sure."

Past the gate they stepped into a well-tended front garden, passing neatly clipped cypress bushes and a large pond. Multicolored koi, some orange and white, some dabbed with black, some gold or silver, lay torpid at the bottom in the cold water, as if dreaming of the spring sun and warmer waters. Lush, neatly clipped grass, the pale yellow of winter, shimmered under the weakly shining sun.

Kiyo knocked on the heavy front door. A woman answered, wearing a charcoal-wool dress with a wide patent leather belt cinched tightly around her waist. A bright topaz brooch on the left shoulder sparkled like gold ore. Her hair had been waved to perfectly frame her narrow face, and she smelled of lavender.

"Yes?" She gazed out at them thoughtfully, two fingertips resting on her chin. Then she smiled, a layer of thick powder cracking around her red-lipsticked mouth. "Oh! It's you. From my daughter's class."

"Yes." Kiyo bowed deeply.

"What're you doing here? I was just visiting your mother today. Never mind. come in. It's so cold out." She stepped aside so they could enter. "And who's this?" She blinked at Yuki. "I don't believe we've met."

Yuki bowed low.

"This is Akaji Yuki-san," Kiyo said. "I heard you needed a new cook and housekeeper. She'd be perfect for the job."

Mrs. Sakagami's penciled eyebrows rose. "Is that so? Well, come in. I'll get Sumiko-chan."

Kiyo had no desire to see the daughter, who was a terrible snob, treating any students at school not as wealthy as her as inferiors. But he forced a smile. "I'd be happy to say hi."

"Sumi-chan!" her mother called. "We have a visitor."

Kiyo and Yuki removed their shoes, and followed their host down a perfectly-polished wood hallway to a large living room. The only Japanese furnishings were an expensive-looking antique scroll hanging in one alcove, and the crane-patterned ceramic vase on a stand below it. A glass chandelier, similar to the one Kiyo's mother had imported, hung from a chain, glowing. A television set sat atop a big maple cabinet. Television shows had started broadcasting

the year before in the city. Kiyo's mother had bought the
first set to arrive in Minamata.

Mrs. Sakagami seated herself on one large sofa. Kiyo
removed hat and gloves and sat opposite, on its mate. The
low table between them held a large blue-glazed ceramic
vase filled with white Christmas roses. In this elaborate
setting, alongside the richly-dressed owner, Yuki's only set
of new-but-modest clothes looked even more plain and inexpensive. She perched next to him on the edge of the seat
cushion, shoulders squared, and folded her hands on her
lap.

A teenage girl stalked into the room. "Oh hi, Kiyo-
kun." A smile lit up her broad face as she settled next to
her mother.

"Hi, Sumiko-chan." Kiyo smiled back, trying to look delighted to see her. "How's history coming?"

"Ugh. I hate that class. So boring."

"I know what you mean," he said, though he didn't.

"So what're you doing here?" she said, then stared hard
at Yuki. "Who's — "

Her mother broke in. "Kiyoshi-kun brought this girl to
interview as a possible new servant."

"Good. My room's getting really messy." Sumiko
frowned. "We need someone right away."

"Then Yuki-chan should be perfect," Kiyo said cheerily.
"She can start immediately."

"You *could* learn to clean your own room," Sumiko's
mother said tartly.

"Oh, Mom!" Her daughter laughed and waved a hand,
as if this was a truly ridiculous idea.

Kiyo chuckled agreeably, but not too loudly, trying to
stay on the good side of both women.

"How old are you?" Mrs. Sakagami asked Yuki. "Where
are you from?"

"Eighteen. I live in Tsukinoura Village."

"Oh." Her nostrils flared. "Don't a lot of fishing families live there? Some with that Disease."

"*Iya!*" Eek. The daughter made a dismayed face. "How can you stand to live there? No telephones, no coffee shops, just a bunch of rickety hovels."

In a moment Mrs. Sakagami was going to ask Yuki about Minamata Disease. Or Sumiko would insult his sweetheart again. Kiyo said quickly, "Yuki-chan can do anything you need, really well. And she's so honest, you'd never need to worry about anything."

"I'm glad to hear that." The mother snorted. "Especially since your last cook turned out to be a thief."

Kiyo bit the inside of his cheek to stop himself from defending Yanagiya. Now being not an optimal time for that.

The woman glanced at Yuki again with a faint frown, her long face reminiscent of a horse's narrow visage. "Have you graduated from school?" she asked.

Yuki shook her head. "I'm not much for academics. I'd rather earn a living."

"Yes, so long as you can read and write, and know arithmetic, why waste time learning things you'll never be able to use?" She glanced at Kiyo. "And Kiyoshi-kun, how do you know this girl?"

"Her mother used to work for a Chisso employee, and sometimes Yuki-chan helped out."

"Please hire her." Sumiko grabbed her mother's arm. "I can't stand to live one more day without a maid." She turned to Yuki. "Can you start tomorrow?"

"Yes."

"All right," Mrs. Sakagami said. "Only because I trust Kiyoshi-kun's family, and he's giving us his assurance."

Sumiko clapped and beamed. "Yes! Great."

Yuki bowed to her new employer from her seat. "Thank you."

"Be here at six in the morning to make breakfast. Oh, and Kiyoshi-kun?" Mrs. Sakagami turned a radiant smile his way. "Come visit here anytime."

The sky was still midnight-dark the next morning as Yuki forced herself from her futon at five o'clock. She yawned. Afraid of oversleeping, she'd woken every hour or so to check the time. The house was stone cold; she shivered as she turned on the hanging bulb. Over her long underwear she quickly slipped on the white blouse she'd worn yesterday for the interview, a sunny yellow sweater, and dark blue pants.

She set several rice balls – stuffed with pickled plums and covered with dried seaweed – on a plate on the kotatsu table for her family's breakfast and lunch. The unexpected gift of first-quality rice from the warehouse owner allowed her to vary the usual potatoes or yams. Finally she lit fresh charcoal in the kotatsu. Then the embers would be nice and warm by the time Mother and Tomoko got up.

The buses didn't run until six, so she walked fast to warm up, and to reach the Sakagami house on time. A steamy plume of condensation puffed from her mouth with each breath. Pebbles poked her soles through her old, worn-out shoes. Here and there roosters crowed; lights were flickering on inside farmhouses. The moon had set and the sun not yet risen, but she knew the road well. The Milky Way sparkled, as if some artist had stretched a black canvas overhead, then loaded a giant brush with white paint and flicked it, painting the inky sky thick with dazzling stars.

Maybe I should paint some nighttime scenes, she thought. As she trekked past it she glanced at the remains of the neighborhood kids' old tumbledown shack, recalling her first encounter there with Kiyo. Its rotting boards had caved in one by one until the whole thing had collapsed. Her childhood playhouse, back when the Bay was clear and beautiful, was now only few broken slats. Most of the boards and nails had been pilfered by locals for firewood or repairs. Like the hangout, everything good from those days was gone.

Yet she was the lucky one. The only family member who hadn't succumbed to the Disease. And she had Kiyo, keeping her family alive and working hard to help all Disease victims! And she still had art. How many people were born to draw and paint?

Fishing a rice ball from her jacket pocket, she nibbled a quick breakfast as she walked. A little farther on, she noticed a thick scent of smoke, and worried a house had caught fire from a kotatsu like the one back home. A few steps more and she saw, in the dawn's weak but growing light, a farmer burning a pile of trash next to his house. The city hauled urban refuse to landfills, where some of it was buried, the rest burnt. But rural people mostly had to take care of their own rubbish.

She passed by, feeling relieved. Her new position would be a good job, even though it still didn't pay nearly as well as the warehouse. Still, maybe she could save a little money every month, and buy more paint. Even take another art lesson from an accomplished artist ... one other than Goto Sensei, of course. The book on how to paint with oils had been helpful, but not like learning from a real artist. Come summer, when the days were longer, she'd paint outside after dinner.

Of course, first of all she'd buy more varied, delicious food. She'd become adept at stretching the money she made, the subsidies from the prefecture, and extras Kiyo brought them.

She'd almost reached the Sakagami house when a small dark animal slinked across the path in front of her, wriggled under some leafless bushes, and vanished.

"A cat!" she gasped.

So some were still alive? Probably only the ones belonging to people wealthy enough to feed their pets something other than leftover fish.

Poor Jiro. How she missed him, still.

She arrived at the Sakagami house just as the six-o'clock whistle blew at Chisso Factory. Their savior, the city people believed. But maybe karma meant that somehow bad people were punished, eventually, in their own way.

She knocked on the front door with a frozen, numb hand. Mrs. Sakagami, in a Western-style pale yellow flannel nightgown trimmed with lace, opened the door.

"The hired help does not come in through the front entrance. Come around to the back."

"*Sumimasen.*" I'm sorry. Yuki bowed and hurried around the side of the house, following a stone-paved path to the back door.

Her employer let her into the kitchen. "Another chilly winter day," she said, quickly shutting the door. "Now, cook two cups of rice. Make miso soup, and eggs. Serve them with pickled vegetables and tofu. It's a pity we can't have fish from the Bay." She made a forlorn face. "But why risk getting that Disease? Even though some of those people are just pretending to have it, to get subsidies."

Yuki's hands clenched into fists; she hid them behind her. "I know some folks with the terrible Disease," she said softly. "They're not pretending."

Mrs. Sakagami drew back. "You're *around* them?"

Yuki recalled Kiyo's warning. "No, I just know of some."

"I see. Well, we eat at seven. Find your way around."

She left the kitchen. Yuki heard her footsteps ascend-
ing the stairs, presumably headed to a second-floor bedroom.

The house seemed very cold. Yuki left her jacket on as
she opened the double doors to the first of five large cabinets set against one long wall. Perfect plates, bowls, platters, saucers, glasses and cups filled all the shelves within.
Enough for her family to use for a year without washing a
dish. She was shocked when the next cupboard was also
filled with dishes, except these were thinner, lighter, more
intricately painted.

The ten tea sets on a lower shelf could serve half her
village. She held up a bowl to the light and stroked the
pale green glaze. So delicate and beautiful. She'd never
touched anything so exquisite before. She carefully put it
back in its spot among a row of nine identical bowls.

When she opened the third cabinet, the grassy scent of
green tea drifted out. She'd only had it when Kiyo brought
some for the family, but immediately recognized the magnificent scent of matcha. Below that shelf cans of soy sauce
and bamboo shoots stood in ranks along with other fruits
and vegetables she didn't recognize. Huge bags of dried
mushrooms, rice, flour, and sugar, baskets of onions and
garlic, dried bonitos and fresh persimmons, cooking oil and
vinegar filled the other two cupboards.

She stood staring in disbelief. This single family pantry stocked more food than her village grocery store. If she
ever had a kitchen half as nice, her family would never go
hungry again.

Better stop gawking and get to work, she chided herself.

At the ceramic sink across the room, when she twisted
the stainless steel faucet handle, a tsunami gushed out.
She gasped and quickly shut it off, staring down at the
dark spots on her jacket where water had splashed. Some
of the homes she'd cleaned in before had had indoor plumb-

ing and a few modern appliances. But this was the first time she'd be *using* those conveniences.

She continued exploring, carefully opening a white re-frigerator that stood almost as tall as she did. Air cold as winter rushed out to chill her face. Inside she found three slender bottles of milk, miso paste, butter, and a number of other containers she didn't open.

After finding a heavy pot in a lower cupboard, she washed a half-liter of rice and set it in water on the stove, then realized she didn't know how to light it. She went outside to see if a fire could be built from the other side, the same way one heated water for bathtubs. But there was no fireplace.

Her pulse began to race. She had to start cooking the rice soon if it was to be ready by seven. Should she go up-stairs and ask the wife? But if she admitted her lack of knowledge, as she had in the tempura place, wasn't that asking to again be fired on her first day?

Back inside, she finally noticed some black pipes run-ning underneath the grill. Knobs on the top had markings: HIGH, MEDIUM, LOW. But when she turned them there was only a faint hissing sound. She could smell gas. The restaurant where she'd washed dishes for a few weeks had this kind of stove, but how had the cooks lighted it? She rummaged in a wooden box on the counter next to it and found a matchbox. She turned a knob and held a lit match to one iron ring.

The burner burst into flames. She gave a little shriek and jumped back, then laughed at herself. What an amaz-ing place! She played with the knob until she figured out how to control the flame. Now all she had to do was watch the clock to make sure she turned the heat off at the right time.

Soon, the kitchen was steamy and warm. Yuki re-moved her jacket and hung it on a hook. A fragrant pot of rice and miso soup with tofu perfumed the kitchen.

She got the remainder of breakfast ready with two minutes to spare. Mrs. Sakagami bustled in dressed in a fuzzy white sweater under a maroon jacket with a matching skirt. A pink cut-glass brooch was pinned to one lapel. She smelled sweetly of face powder and lavender oil. Her thin lips were colored a bright red.

She looked around. "Why aren't the trays ready?"

"Sorry. Trays?"

"Don't tell me." She closed her eyes and huffed. "I have no idea how you people even manage to live." She opened a cabinet and pulled out three black and gold lacquered trays, bowls, plates, a decorative glass container of soy sauce, and three pairs of black chopsticks inlaid with mother of pearl. "Now, fill the bowls and plates with the food." She frowned, looking at the eggs. "Wait. What is that?"

"Your eggs."

"They're not omelets."

"What are omelets?"

She groaned. "How shall I ever explain this disaster to my husband?"

Yuki bowed. "Sorry, I'll get everything set up on trays."

Finally, Yuki carried them out and set them in front of Mr. Sakagami and Sumiko at the large table in the dining room. Sumiko had on her dark blue school uniform: a wool dress piped in white with sailor's collar, its ends knotted in front like a tie. A glass bowl of perfectly-arranged pink camellias in the center gave off a sweet scent. The husband was hefty but handsome in a tweed wool suit, starched white shirt, and thin blue tie. He studied Yuki for a moment, then nodded.

Mrs. Sakagami took her seat. Yuki stood nearby, holding her breath as the family began to eat.

"Eew, yuck." Sumiko pushed her plate away.

"I'm sorry." Her mother shook her head. "Our new maid doesn't know how to properly cook eggs." She glanced over at Yuki. "Don't you have cleaning to do?"

Yuki bowed and went into the kitchen, peering from the doorway, watching the family eat. Each time Mr. Sakagami opened his mouth for a bite, a gold-crowned front tooth glittered under the light. He chewed some rice and pickled vegetables and nodded. "This isn't so bad."

"Because the previous cook pickled them," the wife said. "I bought the tofu from the tofu maker so that should be fine."

Once the family had left – husband off to work, Sumiko to school, wife to somewhere more mysterious – Yuki washed the dishes and cleaned the kitchen. She then stared nervously at the electric washing machine, wondering how to use it. Laundry was one of her duties, but she normally used a scrub board and tub. Neither one was anywhere to be found, inside or out. She gave up for the moment and went out to the neighborhood shopping street, buying a list of ingredients for dinner from small local vendors. Then, cradling a basket full of vegetables like a young housewife, she strolled into an appliance store that had a washing machine in its display window very much like the one at the Sakagami house.

"Are you interested in purchasing one?" asked a neatly-dressed man in a brown suit.

"Maybe." She smiled as if she liked the looks of the machine. "Could you show me how it works?"

In just a few minutes, she learned how to use a washing machine.

Now, on to a cooking lesson. She'd just checked out the menus of some moderately-priced restaurants when she passed a mahjong parlor. She jolted to a stop and backed up. Five small square tables covered with white cloths were filled with mahjong players. At one of them sat Mrs. Sakagami with three other women, scowling at a rack of tiles in front of her. A dozen other tiles were scattered in the center, painted-side up. A red tea kettle on the pot belly stove in the middle of the room spewed steam. The walls were paneled with polished Japanese redwood, and hung with framed photographs of Mount Fuji. Yuki had never played the game but could see her employer didn't like her hand.

She chuckled. *So that's how Mrs. Sakagami spends her free time.*

On the next block she found a small café she liked the looks of, and sauntered up to the cook. He was in the open kitchen behind a low counter, chopping onions.

"Good afternoon," she said as confidently as if she was there to eat. "I see you offer omelet on the menu. I'm very particular about how they're made. Can you tell me how you do yours?"

After he'd explained his method and ingredients, she bowed shallowly like a good customer, and thanked him. "That sounds delicious. I'll come back tomorrow with my friends."

She felt like skipping on the way back. Laundry and cooking wasn't going to be so hard, after all, now that she knew so much about modern conveniences.

Since he'd been invited to do so by Mrs. Sakagami, Kiyo stopped by every day to see how Yuki was faring. Usually no one was home anyway until late in the afternoon.

She'd been at the new job for two weeks by then. Kiyo entered the kitchen with her and reached for her hands, pulled her close for a quick kiss.

"Glad this job's working out. I get to see you more often."

She smiled, enjoying the warmth of his hands. But then, remembering the humiliating episode with Goto Sensei, she pulled away. "We can't."

The back door suddenly opened, and Sumiko entered. Yuki and Kiyo quickly stepped apart.

"Kiyo-kun!" The daughter beamed at him. "I'd have come home earlier if I knew you were waiting for me. Don't hang out in the kitchen. You're a guest."

She tugged off her stylish cashmere coat that looked a bit too tight and held it out to Yuki. "Hang this up and make us some tea. Bring out the best *senbei*. Kiyo-kun, you're good at biology. I need some help."

"Sure." He nodded and followed her into the living room, glancing back at Yuki with a remorseful grimace.

She came out and served them tea and rice crackers. Then, back in the kitchen, she listened to Kiyo explaining anatomy to Sumiko. A few minutes later Mrs. Sakagami came in through the front door. "Oh, Kiyoshi-kun! I'm so pleased to see you."

Yuki, hearing the pleasure in the woman's voice, opened the door between kitchen and living room just a crack, so she could watch.

The mother tossed her coat on a small side table. "How nice of you to drop by. My husband says he and your father always work together well to make this city prosperous. And your mother, such a graceful socialite. I admire her excellent taste. I could never hope to keep up."

She covered her mouth with one hand. Her high-pitched laugh was reminiscent of glasses clinking against each other during an earthquake. "You two look so cute together. Need more tea? Yuki, Yuki!"

"No, please." Kiyo smiled. "I've had plenty. I'm so impressed with Yuki-chan's skills as your new maid. She's doing a great job."

"Well." Mrs. Sakagami forced a slight smile. "Adequate, I'd say."

There was a knock at the front door.

"Who could that be?" Mrs. Sakagami rose to go answer it. When she opened the door, a skinny man dressed in a tan, too-thin raincoat stepped into the foyer. He held out a small box. "Madam, I have rubber bands, toothbrushes, cleaning brushes, and pencils for sale."

Yuki's employer glowered at him and stepped back. "I have no need for those. Please, get out. Hurry, you're letting in cold air."

"Very good quality." He began to open the container.

"I don't need to see it!" Mrs. Sakagami's voice rose. "Please, leave." She made a shooing gesture, closed the door firmly after the departing, and muttered, "Annoying peddlers." Then she rejoined Kiyo and her daughter. "Sorry for the interruption. Last week a hawker wanted to sell me a toaster."

Sumiko sat gazing adoringly at Kiyo. "Kiyo-kun was helping with my homework. He's so smart. Knows all about biology. He's going to be a doctor, Mother."

"Oh really?" Mrs. Sakagami's smile broadened.

"I've wanted to be one since I was seven."

"How honorable. A doctor always makes an excellent husband, too." She shot her daughter a sly smile. "I should put on some music."

Mrs. Sakagami turned back to Kiyo. "I bought a turntable and ten albums. Your mother always has jazz on. Some of the musicians are Americans."

"Don't put it on just for me. I must get home to study now." He rose. "Thank you for the refreshments."

"Do you have to go?" Sumiko's shoulders sagged.

"Please give your parents my highest regards," Mrs. Sakagami said.

Yuki clapped a hand over her mouth and backed away from the kitchen door. She wanted to laugh out loud. There were some things no amount of money could buy; Kiyo definitely being one of them.

THIRTY-EIGHT

What's a Treasure Worth?

After preparing dinner for the Sakagamis and cleaning up the kitchen, Yuki trudged to the bus stop; a telephone pole with the bus schedule tacked on it. Exhausted, she dropped onto a nearby bench, next to a man in a dark green jacket. Its pocket had a martial arts-school emblem. He picked at one callused palm, ignoring a pigeon pecking the ground near his shoes. They both got on the next bus heading south along the shoreline.

By the time the bus made two more stops before leaving the city, every seat was taken. Most passengers wore cheap, shapeless coats and sturdy but worn shoes. The attire of working folks who spent all day on their feet. Lines etched their weary faces. Dirt smudged the clothes of those working in fields, while cooks smelled of grease and spices.

A woman unwrapped a baby from a cloth carrier and bounced him on her lap. The infant reminded Yuki of her sister, and she felt a twinge of worry. The fourth week at her new job, the weather had been unseasonably warm. Her mother took care of Tomoko relatively well. Feeding her, even heating water on the brazier left stocked with kindling. Even so, seeing how late it was, Yuki tapped one shoe nervously. She worked longer hours for the Sakagamis and had to leave home earlier to walk to the city.

The bus lumbered along, the Bay to its right, and terraced fields – empty until spring – to the left. Fifteen minutes after she'd boarded, some familiar stucco houses along the road came into view. Soon the bus rolled to a stop on Tsukinoura Village's main street. Yuki was the only one who got off under the lone streetlight illuminating the town after dark.

She hurried down the side street toward home. No lights were on, but that was normal, to conserve electricity.

"*Tadaima!*" I'm home. She forced a cheery tone, untying her shoes in the entry, then flicking on the bare ceiling bulb dangling in the middle of the living room. It revealed a sight that stopped her cold: Kazuko slumped over the kotatsu table. Tomoko lying on the floor next to her, whimpering. The house was cold.

Her mother slowly raised her head. "*Okaeri.*" Welcome home, she said softly. "How was work?"

"Fine." Yuki smiled. "I'll heat up the kotatsu first, then make dinner." She dropped her satchel, went back out, and hauled in a bucket of charcoal. The kotatsu felt ice cold. She dragged the table and quilt off the pit, spread charcoal in the hearth below, and lit it. Then moved everything back and pulled the quilt up to her mother's waist.

Kneeling beside her sister, Yuki smiled. "Hi, Tomoko-chan, how're you doing? Need changing?" But she had already smelled the dirty diaper. "Let's get you cleaned up."

When Yuki untied the cloth, it was badly soiled and thoroughly soaked. How long the day must've felt to the little girl who lain in her own filth for hours. Yuki wiped her down, applied rash ointment, then wrapped her in a clean diaper. "There you go." Yuki picked her up and hugged her.

Tomoko gurgled back, the corners of her mouth twitching. Her version of a smile. "Why don't you sit with Mom?" Yuki sat her on Kazuko's lap and tied her upright with a length of cloth.

"Has she eaten today?" Tomoko, now two, ate regular food, but Kazuko still breast-fed her when she could.

"She nursed this morning, and also had lunch."

Yuki nodded. "I'll make something to eat."

After dinner, she told her mother she was going out to the toilet. Then she ran four houses down to Yamauchi Oshi's place. They'd been good friends when they were younger. Oshi still attended school, so Yuki rarely saw her now. But she was a responsible girl; one of the few in the neighborhood who didn't shun the Akaji family.

Yuki knocked on the nicely planed, solid-wood front door. Mr. Yamauchi was a carpenter and, while modest, his house was better built and much larger than Yuki's. Sturdy, well cared for. No one in their household had been afflicted with the Disease.

Oshi opened the door, eyes widening as she looked at her. "Yuki-chan! What's up?"

Like everyone in the Yamauchi family, her friend was tall and lanky, towering over Yuki. Her bangs were cut short, the rest of her long hair tied behind her. A thick, peach-colored sweater and long underwear – the kind everyone wore in winter under their clothes – added a bit of bulk.

"Can you talk for a minute?"

"Sure." Oshi stepped back and Yuki stepped inside the small entryway. "I have a favor to ask."

Mrs. Yamauchi padded over in slippers, wiping her wet hands on a clean white apron. "My goodness, we haven't seen you in a while. Come in!"

"Thank you." Yuki removed her shoes and stepped onto the smooth wooden floor. The house smelled of luscious steamed dumplings. She couldn't recall what they tasted like, it'd been so long.

Mr. Yamauchi who sat at a kotatsu reading a book, glasses perched on his nose, looked up at her. "Yuki-chan. Haven't you grown up! How's the family?"

Too ashamed to tell the truth, she said, "We get along all right." Kiyo was the only one she could confide in.

"I'm sorry about your uncle and father. They were good men."

"Thank you." The Yamauchis lived so close. Yet they didn't understand the devastation Minamata Disease had caused the victims and their families, either. Never offering food or money, not even stopping by to inquire if they could help.

He nodded and went back to his book.

"I'll make tea," Mrs. Yamauchi insisted.

"Please, don't bother. I won't be here long. I just need to talk to Oshi-chan for a minute."

"All right, but come sit under the kotatsu. It's cold." Mrs. Yamauchi went into the kitchen at the back of the house. The heat from the kitchen stove warmed the whole house, which had real interior walls, not just boards nailed on the outside.

Yuki sank onto the floor next to the entryway. Her old classmate sat across, looking down at her inquisitively. "You quit school."

"I'm a maid for a family in Minamata now," Yuki said.

Oshi dipped her chin and gaped, as if wondering what kind of mythical creature her old friend had turned into.

"I have to leave home a little after five," Yuki explained, "and I don't get back until seven-thirty."

She almost added that by the time she fed, cleaned and took care of her family she had no time left to paint. But her friend was practical; she liked math. She wouldn't understand.

"My sister can't keep going all day without her diaper being changed. The kotatsu needs to be re-stoked. Could you stop by after school and help?"

Oshi frowned. "Change diapers?" She made a face. "I haven't seen you in ages, and that's what you came over to ask about?"

"I'm sorry. But look – I'll pay you."

Ever since they were little, her neighbor had voiced a never-ending list of things she longed to buy, someday. Yuki hoped this hadn't changed.

Oshi rubbed her chin thoughtfully. "All right," she said at last, and held out a hand, palm up, for the money.

"I don't get paid until the end of the month. I'll bring it to you then."

It would hurt the household for her to give up even a fraction of the money. But she couldn't let her sister suffer all day, or her mother sit shivering in the cold.

"I'm supposed to work *every day* for a whole month before I get anything? How do I know you'll even pay me?"

"How can you say such a thing?" Yuki cried. Then she lowered her voice. "You've known me all your life. You know I'm honest."

"Hmm." Oshi's eyes took on a faraway look. "But changing stinky diapers . . . ."

"I really don't have any money yet." Despair clutched Yuki's heart, its nails digging in painfully. She couldn't think of anyone else to ask. No other neighbor would step into her yard, much less the house. If Oshi wouldn't help, her mother would huddle shivering under the kotatsu all day while Tomoko cried.

"Just think of all the things you'll be able to buy with the money," she urged.

"I've always loved your brooch," Oshi said, eyeing it.

Yuki polished the red- and blue-faceted glass gems every day. They must be sparkling under the bright lights in this house. She touched the brooch pinned to her sweater. "I love it, too."

"Remember when I tried to trade you my favorite red shoes for it? I loved them, but wanted the pin more. You wouldn't do it."

Most of her friends knew they'd always be poor. Their grandparents had been, and so were their parents. Logically, they too would remain so. That had always seemed preordained. But Oshi had fought that prospective future almost from birth, always wanting pretty, pricy things.

"You don't mean you still do?" Yuki asked. "That was four years ago."

"Want me to change your sister's diapers? Give me the brooch. Then I'll wait till the end of the month to get paid." A faint smile played on Oshi's face, as if she already assumed she'd won.

No, she hadn't changed at all.

"You want the pin *and* to get paid, too?"

She spread out her hands. "I'm entitled to a bonus for taking on the job. Unless you can get someone else."

Yuki's mouth went dry. She owned nothing else pretty, or of any value. The brooch was her sole prize. She'd found it when life was good, Uncle still alive, her parents healthy and energetic. When Minamata Bay had glistened clear and blue, full of sea life. The pin symbolized all the hope she'd ever had for her life.

Oshi huffed, "I guess you must not really care about your sister after all. I've got homework to do." She hopped up and went over to sit under the kotatsu. Turning away from Yuki, she pulled a textbook from a stack on the table.

Yuki felt sure she loved nothing more than she did her family and Kiyo. Yet . . . give up her birthday pin?

She just couldn't do it. She slunk home, ashamed.

The next morning, she piled double the amount of charcoal at the bottom of the kotatsu and lit it. She'd warned her mother the night before, "Be careful to keep your feet tucked to the outside wall of the pit." She laid two clean diapers on the floor within easy reach from where her mom would sit, then headed to work.

She scrubbed, cooked, and polished all day. Her body was busily working, but her mind was elsewhere. Would the embers keep the kotatsu warm until she got home? Could Mom's hands manage the diaper pins?

That evening, she jumped off the bus and ran all the way home. "*Tadaima*!" She sang out cheerfully.

"*Okaeri*," Kazuko responded. Tomoko, who lay partially under the kotatsu cover, looked up at Yuki, babbling her version of a greeting.

"Did it stay warm?" Yuki kicked off her shoes and rushed to the kotatsu. She lifted the cover. The pit was stone cold. The embers must've gone out hours earlier. "Oh, no."

As she piled on new charcoal, her mother said, "It stayed warm much longer this time. That was a good idea."

"How long?"

"Almost midafternoon."

Mom was lying. They'd clearly been cold for hours.

"Tomoko-chan." Yuki smiled at her sister. "Has she been changed today?"

"Yes, though I didn't clean her well enough."

"I'll do it now." When Yuki removed her sister's diaper, she sucked in her breath. Dried feces were caked on the girl's bottom. The diaper was heavy, sodden and cold. Yuki gave her a thorough washing.

Now she knew what she had to do.

Her dinner of tofu, miso soup and rice tasted like glue. Her throat was so tight it was painful to force the food down. She finally gave up and divided her meal between her mother and Tomoko. After washing dishes she again feigned a trip to the outhouse, then ran to the Yamauchis' place. The deep chill she felt on the way had nothing to do with the winter night; it was the despair of loss.

"You, again," Oshi said when she opened the door. She wore padded dark blue pants with a small white diamond design and the same thick sweater. She didn't invite Yuki in until her mother called from a room behind shoji doors. "Who is it?"

"Yuki-chan. Again," the daughter yelled back.

"How nice of her to stop by two nights in a row. I'll make some tea."

"She's in a rush. Only staying a minute." She moved over to allow Yuki into the entry, then closed the door.

Her father wasn't sitting in the front room tonight.

"Yes?" Oshi said. "I'm very busy."

"Will you still take care of my family if I give you the brooch?"

Oshi glanced away as if bored. "Sure, I guess."

Yuki stroked the beautiful glass gems for the last time, feeling an actual pain in her chest. She'd always polished it every day. Now the crystals glimmered up at her. The pin was beautiful. She thought she'd always own it. The brooch had become a reason to get up in the mornings, a reminder that not everything in life was ugly or full of pain and sorrow.

She slowly unpinned and then held it out. Her sweater felt strange without it; too light. Was this like the sensation soldiers who'd lost limbs reported feeling?

When Oshi's hand closed around it, Yuki thought her heart would crack. Without another word she turned away and flung herself out the door, already running.

The next day, she kept touching the spot where the brooch should be. Whenever she caught sight of herself in a mirror, her reflection looked strange. Wrong. As if she hadn't fully dressed.

She finished cleaning up after breakfast, did laundry and ironing, then tackled her first attempt at cleaning the imported chandelier, as Mrs. Sakagami had instructed her to do today. She moved aside the low table from between the sofas, set a stool under the light, and stood on it, carefully removing every delicate dangling crystal drop. She set them side by side on the soft sofa cushions.

In the kitchen, she made sure none of the crystal pieces touched the side of the sink, washing them under the faucet one by one. Then she got up on the stool again to wipe down the metal frame.

She was re‑hanging the last crystal when she saw herself reflected in it without her brooch, and its usual bright‑ly‑colored sparkle.

Do I look as strange from the side as from the front? she wondered, and turned her shoulders to study herself from another angle.

She swayed and lost her balance, arms windmilling to steady herself. No use; she was already falling. Instinctively, one hand grabbed the chandelier. The light swung wild‑ly and Yuki pitched forward, dragging it down too. She landed safely on the sofa, but heard glass shattering on the hard floor around it.

She lay still for a moment, eyes clenched shut, breath‑ing fast. At last she sat up and stretched her arms out. No blood there, nor on her legs.

Then she looked around and gasped, "Oh, no!" The chandelier's base had pulled free; the whole fixture sagged to the floor, its electrical cord dangling like a black snake from the wood‑paneled ceiling. The metal frame seemed crooked. Broken crystals littered the floor.

Stupid, stupid, stupid! She'd been preoccupied by the lost brooch when she should've been paying attention to her work.

Just then the front door banged open.

"*Tadaima!*" Sumiko yelled. And then she and her mother stepped into the living room.

Yuki sat frozen, mind gone blank with fear, staring back at them. Mrs. Sakagami gasped. Her eyes widened, traveling from the pieces of glass sparkling on the floor and then over to the light, a mere skeleton now, the bent metal arms holding only a few crystal pieces. Yuki and Sumiko only gaped at each other in horrified silence.

Mrs. Sakagami finally spoke, voice hard and low. "You *ruined* it."

Sumiko pointed at Yuki. "You wrecked the whole living room!"

Her mother's eyes welled with tears. She picked up a broken crystal and stroked it as one would a favorite pet. "My poor, precious chandelier."

"Oh, Mom, I'm so sorry." Sumiko murmured, patting her mother's back. She glared at Yuki. "Clean it up!"

"No." Her mother's expression was cold steel. "Don't let that idiot touch a thing. I've put up with bad cooking, but this is unacceptable. You're fired!"

Yuki bowed. "I'm sorry. I lost my balance on the stool. I'll pay for the damage."

The woman laughed. "As if you ever could! You're irre-sponsible. No respect for our belongings. People like you know nothing about values or ethics. Animals, groveling in dirt-floored hovels. I should never have hired a fisherman's whelp. Get out!"

Yuki recoiled as if struck. She calls *me* an animal without morals? A woman who spends her days drinking tea and playing games. *Yes, I made a mistake, but I took responsibility.* She opened her mouth to retort, *Fishers are poor only when it comes to money. We have principles. We're honest.*

But she bit her tongue, because she desperately needed this job. For her family.

She crumpled to the floor and hung her head. "I'm so very sorry! Take part of the repair cost from my pay each month. I'll work harder than ever, longer hours. Please, don't fire me."

"But I can't trust you not to break something else. Or even set fire to the house, next time. No. I don't want you here. Leave, now."

When Yuki lifted her head, both mother's and daughter's expressions implied they were looking down at a cockroach.

Yuki rose stiffly. "May I have my pay for the days worked, Sakagami-sama?" she asked, using the most honorific title possible.

"*Pay!*" Sumiko shrilled. She clenched the lone crystal and raised it as if to stab Yuki.

"I've worked three-and-a-half weeks of this month."

"Do you know how much that chandelier cost?" Sumiko pointed to the metal carcass hanging from its cord.

"Please," Yuki begged, "my family needs it for food."

"Get out!" Sumiko marched to the door and yanked it open.

"No. We won't stoop to her level." Mrs. Sakagami reached for her purse, dug out some coins, and handed Yuki her wages. "Now we're done. Go!"

Yuki shuffled out, limbs leaden weights. She'd been stupid, wasteful, taking the bus home every night. A costly extravagance. But she'd assumed her wages would continue, and they'd been more than enough to cover the fare.

Under a steely gray sky she dragged herself home, trying to think of other jobs to apply for. Homeowners wouldn't need her to garden plots until closer to summer, several months away.

One good thing, she thought as wind kicked up pebbles into her face: she could now get her brooch back. She wouldn't need Oshi's help with her family.

She arrived home just as Oshi was leaving. The wrongness of her beautiful brooch twinkling colorfully on her neighbor's sweater stabbed at her eyes. She blinked away tears. But now she could have it back.

Oshi raised her eyebrows. "You're home early. I just stoked the fire and changed your sister."

"I lost my job."

"Lost it. But why?" Oshi looked shocked.

"I accidentally broke a chandelier."

"Oh no!"

Yuki nodded. "Yeah."

"Still, that's pretty harsh. But you know rich people hate us. So . . . guess you don't need me coming over anymore."

"Thanks for helping out today. And, um, since you only came once, may I have my pin back?"

"You begged me to help. Now you want it back?"

"You know how much I love it. I never thought I'd lose my job. Please, Oshi-chan, I'll pay you for two days even though you came only once."

Oshi huffed. "You have a short memory. No one else would've helped. I only agreed to do this terrible job to get the brooch. It's mine. Not my fault you're so clumsy."

Yuki dropped to the ground and bowed. "Please, please, give me the brooch. I . . . need it."

"No."

Yuki sprang up and offered some coins from her worn change purse.

Oshi wheeled away, running home. She called back, "You don't have to pay for today. Consider it a favor from an old friend."

Yuki crouched in the dirt, weeping. A passing neighbor eyed her curiously, and she turned her face away. No one would understand. The pin had proved that somewhere there was always beauty in the world, even when life felt hopeless. She should've cherished it more, not simply assumed it would be waiting on the mat near her futon every morning.

Probably I've taken many things for granted, she thought. Believing my family or a prized possession would always be here. Maybe I should value even the bad things. Who knows, I might miss even those, too, once they've disappeared.

THIRTY-NINE

Father's Final Act

T he sun rose between two verdant hills, sending a beam through Kiyo's bedroom window. The light on his face woke him. In winter, light remained trapped behind the hill east of the city until well after breakfast time.

Spring's coming, he thought, sitting up and stretching. Meaning graduation from high school was also close – and the start of classes at Tokyo University. He looked forward to studying medicine there, but would miss Yuki. How often could he travel home to see her? She couldn't possibly leave Kazuko and Tomoko for as long as a trip to Tokyo would take.

He rose, thinking to bask by the window for a moment in the warm rays. But as it turned out, one thin slice of sunlight wasn't quite enough. Shivering, he quickly got dressed.

At the breakfast table, his mother was flipping through a women's magazine and sipping black coffee. Kiyo still preferred tea, but liked the coffee-bean aroma.

She glanced up and smiled. "Good morning."

"Has Dad left yet?" he asked.

"No, he's still in bed."

"Really?"

The new cook must've heard Kiyo talking in the dining room. The young woman came in wearing a black dress with white apron tied around her waist. Etsuko's new mandatory uniform for the help. She carried a tray for him loaded with toast, an omelet, strawberry jam, and a cup of green tea.

"Thanks," Kiyo told her. "Looks good." Then, to his mother, "Is Dad all right? He's usually up and gone long before I come down to eat."

"Probably just tired. He works too hard, but won't listen to me. You know how he is." She flipped a page in her *Vogue* magazine. "I'm planning a celebration for you end of March. Only three weeks away. Americans throw a party when someone graduates."

"Really? Thanks." Kiyo saw the pleasure on her face at the prospect of a party. Most of the guests would be his parents' friends and Dad's colleagues. He didn't care to spend time with a bunch of socialites and executives. But if it pleased his mother ... she was thinking of him, after all.

He bit into a thick slice of white toast. Crunchy crust, soft center, sweet strawberry jam. He washed it down with hot tea. As the warmth slid down, he imagined waves of peristalsis – muscle contractions – forcing his breakfast through the esophagus to his stomach. "The human body's a fascinating machine," he murmured.

"You've always been such a strange child," said Etsuko, shaking her head as she turned another page.

At school, Kiyo gazed out through the window of his literature class, his belly grumbling for a lunch that was still some minutes away. When he'd ridden to school earlier, the sky had been bright, a few wisps of white clouds streaking the blue. Now, thunderheads blocked any hint of sunshine, an opaque gray lid pressing down heavily on the Earth. How quickly the weather changes, he thought.

The classroom door suddenly opened, and the principal walked in, just as the teacher was writing a haiku on the blackboard. The short, bald man in a slightly rumpled suit whispered to him. A bored-looking girl who'd been fiddling with the ends of her hair dropped her hands to the desk-top, looking suddenly alert.

Kiyo saw why. Their teacher's mouth hung open, as if in shock. What was going on?

Just then the man took a deep breath and looked right at Kiyo. "Kuge-kun, please go with Ishida-san now."

Kiyo's mind whirled frantically and his mouth went dry. What'd he done to warrant a trip to the principal's of-fice?

The other students turned to stare. A boy across the aisle snorted. "What's your crime, egghead?"

All eyes watched as he slid from his seat and headed up the aisle. He remembered his anatomy book was still on the desk and lunged back to grab it. He always felt more relaxed with that in his hands. The principal appeared somber, so this was not going to be some merry meeting about a prize or a good test score. He might be glad to have his trusty book along.

He followed the man down the hall without a word ex-changed between them. Once inside his office, Ishida softly closed the door behind them.

"Kuge-kun, please sit down." His voice was kind; his eyes looked oddly moist.

Kiyo took a seat across from the small cedar desk, a sense of dread growing as the ashen-faced principal sank into his chair behind it.

"There's been, er, well, an unfortunate incident." Ishida swallowed audibly. "Involving your father."

Kiyo sat forward. "What sort of incident?"

"He, well . . . Kuge-san jumped in front of a train."

Kiyo sprang up, heart banging so hard his ribs ached. "What? Is he in the hospital?"

"I'm sorry, no. He was killed."

"What?" Kiyo shook his head. "No. Not possible. Dad works hard. Totally devoted to Chisso and to us. He'd never commit suicide."

The principal looked away. "The police are sure he did. Would you like some water?"

Dad is dead.

He hadn't shown up for breakfast, but Kiyo usually didn't see him then, anyhow. He'd come home last night well after Kiyo and his mother had finished dinner. As usual, Etsuko had sat with her husband as he ate, asking about his day, the normal routine. Kiyo had said good night and gone up to study in his room.

And yet . . . now he was dead. Gone, forever.

Why didn't I spend some time taking to him last night?

He'd thrown away his last chance for a conversation with his father, and instead read the everlasting anatomy book. So wrapped up in himself and his goals he'd never seriously considered the pressure his father had been under might prove fatal. Even though he'd clearly seen despair on Dad's face the last time he'd confronted him at the office. How hopeless and guilty he must've felt about not stopping toxins from polluting the Bay.

Kiyo jumped up from the chair. "I've got to go to my mother."

Ishida nodded. "Of course. The chauffeur's waiting for you outside."

Kiyo wanted to run like a small child to Fukuzawa. To beg him to hurry home. But his legs felt slow and heavy as he dragged himself out to the car.

The driver stood next to the black Nissan Cedric, shoulders slumped, eyes red. "Hello, Botchan."

Kiyo lost the last shreds of his composure as Fukuzawa's tenderly called him "young master."

"Fukuzawa-san!" He fell into the chauffeur's arms and bawled.

The chauffeur patted his back. "Cry all you like. He was a good man."

No one had embraced Kiyo in years; his parents had long told him he was too old for such displays. But now he must be strong. He took a few deep breaths, trying to dislodge the boulder obstructing his throat. Then he stepped away from the driver.

"I'm so sorry," Fukuzawa said.

"So it's true? Dad did kill himself?"

The chauffeur nodded sadly.

"But – why?" Then a new thought occurred. "Did you know he was going to do that? Tell me!"

Fukuzawa sighed. "Why don't you get in?" He opened the rear door. "It's chilly out here."

How could something this horrible happen on a morning that began so beautiful and sunny? The sky was solid gray now. A gust of icy wind slapped his face, startling him out of a fog. He nodded and got in the left-hand door.

Fukuzawa slid behind the wheel. After a moment, still facing the windshield, the driver began to talk. "Your father . . . he was always very loyal to the company."

"All employees are." Fukuzawa's jaw tightened, and Kiyo regretted interrupting him. "Sorry. Go on."

"He did his best to protect it despite its flaws."

Kiyo bit his tongue; he had to let the man speak.

"He knew organic mercury was in the wastewater."

"He told you that?" Kiyo gasped.

"The top people at Chisso have long known they were the cause of Minamata Disease."

Kiyo huffed, "Big surprise."

"Not right away, of course. But when hard evidence starting coming in from the researchers, they did their own tests. They've known for years."

Kiyo ground his teeth, but kept quiet.

"You see, your father didn't have many friends. Work was his identity. His life, aside from family. He couldn't tell anyone outside of work. He couldn't discuss the matter with anyone aside from the other executives there. Keeping the secret, pretending Chisso was not at fault . . . it was killing him. However cold he may have appeared to you, he felt deep remorse for what the company was doing to the victims. Yet he forced himself to keep the secret to himself for many years.

Too many, thought Kiyo.

"When people around the Shiranui Sea contracted the Disease – after the company changed the wastewater dumping site from the harbor to the Minamata River – he worried the pollution situation had become too obvious. That surely even the government couldn't continue siding with Chisso. He said nothing to me then, but around that time he appeared very troubled.

"Last year, I picked him up very late one night. It was the day you'd demanded he publicly announce the truth. And he wanted to, but still also felt bound to remain true to the company. Until recently he hadn't fully understood how much the victims suffered. When Dr. Hosokawa invited him to the hospital to visit the Disease ward . . . well, after that, the stress was overwhelming. He had to tell someone. He knew I was loyal, not only to Chisso, but to him. That I'd never reveal anything told in confidence. He broke down and cried. Told me the company had long known. And how he'd had to conjure up reasons Chisso was innocent."

"Wait. The company did install the Cyclator. Their wastewater's been clean for three years now."

"I said that, too. He told me the wastewater from plastics manufacturing wasn't hooked up to it. Only fertilizer and other products."

"So they kept dumping toxic waste into the sea." Kiyo slumped, all energy bleeding away. "Chisso is even more evil than I'd imagined."

"The guilt grew until he couldn't live with the shame anymore."

"Did he see the article about Chisso and the Disease that I wrote and tacked up on utility poles?"

"So you did write that. I thought so. Yes, but he didn't get angry. He even smiled a bit."

"I wonder if he knew. He never yelled at me about it." Kiyo raked his hair with his fingers. If only he could still talk to his father one last time. Had he guessed, about the flyers? He'd endure any punishment if only he could bring Dad back.

If only this, if only that, he thought angrily. My father is gone. We'll never speak again. It's too late. He leaned his head back on the seat. "And you knew he was going to kill himself?"

"No." Fukuzawa shook his head. "I knew he suffered tremendous guilt, and was feeling low. Quieter than usual last night while I drove him home. But I never imagined he could be planning . . . that. Maybe I should've realized and done something to help."

"It was my fault," Kiyo said. "Not yours. I kept pounding him about being wrong and heartless. Lately his face had a sickly pallor. I'd seen despair in his eyes. Yet, I still blamed him as if he alone had caused the Disease. Not knowing he'd actually wanted to help the victims, though his whole job was to manage discharges for the company. I never really listened to his true feelings, while he silently carried all that weight. I'm the reason he's dead."

Kiyo lunged for the door, wrenched it open, and vomited on the pavement.

Fukuzawa shot out of the car and came around to grip his shoulders. "Should I take you to the doctor?"

Kiyo wiped his mouth with a pocket handkerchief. "No. I'll be fine." He got back inside and closed the door.

Fukuzawa did as well, and started the engine. "Your father's death isn't your fault. Whatever choice he made would've been devastating to someone. I think this was his way of atoning."

In history class Kiyo had studied the samurai and their practice of dying with honor; killing themselves rather than falling into the hands of enemies. Also called Seppuku, disemboweling had also been a punishment for capital crimes . . . a self-inflicted one when a warrior had brought shame upon himself.

"Like committing hara-kiri. In his case, because of Chisso's refusal to clean up its wastewater."

Fukuzawa nodded. "And failure to apologize to the victims."

"But does dying absolve him of hiding the truth?"

"I hope so." The chauffeur sighed.

"Where did he die? Did you drive him there to do it?"

"No, no! He never called for me today. I waited and waited but . . . I finally called his office in the mid morning. That's when they told me." He hung his head. "If I'd driven him to work this morning as usual, maybe I could've stopped him."

He swiped a hand over his tear-streaked face. "He walked a quarter-mile past Chuo Station. Then threw himself in front of an approaching express train."

Kiyo felt as if he'd been plunged into a dark abyss. He'd felt sorrow when Yuki's uncle and father died, but now knew he'd never really understood how raw grief truly felt. How impossible to even speak of.

"He didn't come to breakfast," Kiyo said at last. "Mom said he was sleeping in. That never happens unless he's sick. I should've checked on him, I should've – "

"If you had, he would've told some story. There's no way to stop someone that determined. He could've done it anytime. If not today, then tomorrow. But you should know how proud he was of his family. He often told me you were very smart, and would become a doctor. You're still going to, aren't you?"

"Yes. Nothing can stop that." Kiyo caught the chauffeur's eye in the rear-view mirror and nodded.

"Now, I'm to take you to your mother at the undertaker's," said Fukuzawa.

The funeral home, the size of a modest clapboard bungalow, had a discreet sign mounted next to the front door: *Fukui Mortuary.* Fukuzawa had barely parked before Etsuko shuffled out of the mortuary, a lace handkerchief pressed to her face. Kiyo jumped out and ran to her.

"Oh, Kiyoshi-kun!" She slumped into his arms, sobbing. "You're the man of the house now," she gasped out.

Yes. Now he had to take care of his mother. To protect not only Yuki but her as well.

Not knowing what to say to a bereaved widow, he just held her. They hadn't hugged like this since he was a little boy. But now the top of her head only reached his shoulder. Her curled, stiffly-hair-sprayed bouffant scratched his chin; her gardenia perfume was too strong. That he should even think of such small complaints at such a moment made him feel like a monster.

A few drops of rain pattered down. "Should we go back inside?"

"No! Don't go in there," she moaned looking over her shoulder at the funeral home. "You don't want to see him. Let's go home."

Fukuzawa, still standing nearby, opened the rear door and bowed as Etsuko approached. *"Go-shūshō-sama desu."* My condolences.

Once they were both inside, she turned to Kiyo and grabbed his hands. "Why did Kichiro-san do such a thing? Was he that overworked? I never knew he was so unhappy. Did he say anything to you?"

Kiyo compressed his lips and glanced at the rearview mirror. Fukuzawa caught his eye and shook his head.

"No, Mom," Kiyo lied, patting her hand. "I don't have any idea why he'd do such a thing."

FORTY

Who Was Dad?

Kiyo sent his mother to lie down, then called his older brothers to break the news of Dad's death. Ichita and Tadahisa got on the train immediately. Since they'd had another baby, Ichita's wife stayed home; hauling three small children across the country would be too grueling a task.

As soon as they all arrived, the family gathered in the living room, sitting on cushions on the floor. Kiyo was relieved when Ichita announced that, as the oldest, he would take care of the funeral arrangements. Kiyo knew nothing about burials and memorials.

"Mother," Ichita asked. "Do you want to also have an *otsuya*?"

"A wake." She stared at her hands folded in her lap and replied in a weary tone. "I don't know how I'd get through that, along with a funeral and a reception."

Her eldest son nodded. "Yes, much too exhausting. How about just a funeral at the Minamata Buddhist Temple, followed by a reception?"

Etsuko nodded. "Thank you."

"Yes, good idea." Tadahisa gave her a small smile.

"And flowers in the usual tradition," she added.

"I'll order white and yellow chrysanthemums and lilies, then. Get them shipped from Okinawa. And only red meat for the reception?"

"Kichiro-san would've liked us to follow his prohibition against eating seafood," she said. "But perhaps we could have some shipped in from a different bay."

"Both, then." Ichita took notes.

"Please, do whatever you think is proper. I'm tired." She got up and shuffled away to her room, where she spent most of that day.

Two days later, on the eve of the funeral, all three brothers congregated under the kotatsu in the living room. Ichita, having called on the priest, caterer, flower shop and the hall, still wore his best suit.

"Ahhh," he sighed as he shed the jacket and loosened his tie.

Tadahisa and Kiyo wore cable-knit sweaters and khaki slacks. A bottle of their father's favorite, Suntory Whiskey, and three cut-crystal tumblers glittered under the light above the low table. Ichita poured generous helpings into each glass and they all raised these in a toast.

"To Dad," they chanted in unison. Kiyo's' older brothers knocked back half in one gulp. It took him two more to down his.

Ichita tapped the liquor bottle. "Dad always got the best."

"Tell us, Kiyo. What really happened?" Tadahisa said as he refilled their glasses.

Kiyo scooped peanuts from a ceramic bowl in the middle of the table, and tossed them into his mouth. "I don't know."

"No one just suddenly commits suicide." Tadahisa took another sip, staring at Kiyo suspiciously. "Did something happen at work? At home?"

"You're eighteen now. You must've noticed something was wrong," Ichita insisted. A frown line had etched itself between his eldest brother's eyebrows since the last time he'd seen him, three years ago.

Kiyo shook his head, swirling the amber liquid in his glass. The same cold hand that'd strangled his heart when the principal announced Dad was dead was back. Squeezing his lungs, making it hard to breathe. He didn't want to talk about it, but . . . everyone deserved the truth. "You know about Minamata Disease?"

"Sure. It's been on the news," Tadahisa said.

"Hosokawa Sensei, the doctor mentoring me, has been working on its cause. Seeking a cure, along with researchers from Kumamoto and Kagoshima."

"Okay." Tadahisa nodded. "And?"

He recited the studies performed: the cat experiment, the sludge research, diverting the wastewater to Minamata River then back to the harbor, the Cyclator not being hooked up, hair samples . . . everything. Then described the horrific symptoms, the pain. How some victims committed suicide.

Tadahisa poured more whiskey and took a large gulp. Ichita tapped his glass against the kotatsu table, frowning, sending an eerie clinking around the cold room.

Kiyo sipped one more mouthful to work up the courage to tell the rest. "He was at the office all the time, barely coming home to eat and sleep. We hardly ever saw him. And even then, he didn't seem to want to talk, so I quit trying. I should've made more efforts to find out what was going on." He cradled his head in his hands.

Tadahisa jabbed him with a fist. "Go on, tell the rest."

Kiyo mumbled into his glass, "He'd gotten so thin, even his hair. Mom kept hounding him to work less and eat more." He picked up the whiskey bottle, swirling the contents. "He must've just bought this."

"Hey!" Tadahisa elbowed Kiyo. "Talk!"

So he told them. What the chauffeur had said about Kichiro feeling guilty. "I argued with him so many times. It was my fault," he whispered.

Both brothers sat up straighter. Their eyes bored into him. "How so?" Tadahisa leaned so close Kiyo smelled the whiskey on his breath, heard him grinding his molars.

"I said he was heartless. That he only cared about business and profit. Didn't value human lives. That he was covering up Chisso's crime, making more victims. I didn't know he already felt terrible. I literally hounded him to death," he cried raggedly.

Tadahisa bolted from the room.

"It wasn't your fault," Ichita said, patting Kiyo's back. "He'd obviously been depressed for a while. Maybe the discovery of organic methylmercury was the last straw. There was no longer any way for Chisso to cover up their crimes. Dad may have been too ashamed to face the coming public outcry."

"You may not blame me, but Tadahisa-kun does." Kiyo sighed.

"I think mainly he just now realizes why Dad wouldn't let him join Chisso. Remember New Year's, three years ago?"

"Sure."

"Dad said he didn't want Tadahisa-kun to work there. After all this comes out, who knows if Chisso's going to survive? He was protecting him."

Kiyo slumped over the kotatsu table. Ichita was right. Dad had protected his second son just as he had the whole family, by forbidding them to eat seafood. He'd been loyal to everyone. And that loyalty had cost thousands of disease victims a normal life. In the end, he couldn't live with that.

"It's not your fault," Ichita repeated, gently thumping Kiyo's back. "He was caught in the middle. Whatever he did, he'd end up betraying somebody."

A large portrait of Dad, the photo the company had hung in their main office along with those of their other executives, stood in front of the Buddhist altar. Black ribbon draped the top corners of its frame. A large wreath of yellow and white chrysanthemums and vases of white lil-

ies adorned the platform below. Rows of folding chairs had
been set up for the mourners.

Etsuko wore her formal black kimono to the funeral.
The brothers, too, donned theirs. Ichita had visited a bar-
ber early morning for a haircut and a close shave. No occa-
sion had ever before necessitated Kiyo having a formal kimono, and suits were becoming more acceptable for most
events. Normally, his mother would've had their tailor
quickly make a new black suit, but she never mentioned
his attire, so Kiyo wore his navy one.

Kimonos were one size fits all, adjusted by folding any
extra material around the waist and tying the wide sash
over that, so he could have worn his father's. But Etsuko
had chosen to have her husband's body dressed in it. A kimono is always crossed in the front, left side over right.
But in death, Kichiro's would be crossed right over left.

Kiyo was given the task of accepting *koden*, the traditional condolence money. He sat at the entrance to the hall
at a small desk covered with a white silk tablecloth. A
large empty basket and a guestbook were the only items on
the desk.

Fukuzawa was the first to appear, carrying a white
envelope tied with a special black and white string.

When Kiyo saw the amount written on the front, he
protested, "This is far too much."

"No." Fukuzawa shook his head. "It's not nearly
enough. Call me whenever you need anything."

Kiyo's throat tightened. This man was the only person
who'd understood Dad's misery. He nodded. "Thanks."

The chauffeur signed the registry and dropped the envelope in the basket. Later, his mother would send thank-
you gifts worth at least half as much as the koden given.

All the Chisso executives, section chiefs, supervisors,
friends, city officials, and neighbors came. So did shop
owners who'd done business with the family. Kiyo was tak-
en aback, though, to see their former cook, who'd gotten

fired for something he had done. She wore a faded black dress and black shoes. Gray streaked her hair now.

"Yanagiya-san. You came," Kiyo gasped. "I didn't – "

"Botchan." She gave him a small smile.

The kind words made Kiyo again feel shame for allowing her to be fired. He, too, had made plenty of mistakes. Tears prickled his eyes. "I'm so sorry – "

"It's all right." She bowed. "I'm sorry for your loss. You're a good boy. You'll do fine." She handed him an envelope; the amount half of a cook's daily wages.

Could she afford it? But he only said, "Thank you."

Dr. Hosokawa stepped up next with a sympathetic nod and handed his koden to Kiyo. No one knew more than him about the father-son struggle over whether Chisso was to blame for the Minamata Disease. He patted Kiyo's shoulder and then, with a slight smile, took a seat in the back of the hall.

A dozen guests later, Yoshioka Kiichi of Chisso, walked into the hall. He headed directly for Kiyo. The president wore a cashmere coat and a gray-wool fedora. He had ordered the company's cover-up. He'd also shut down Dr. Hosokawa's cat experiment.

Kiyo's face grew hot. He glared at the man as he accepted the proffered envelope. Then abruptly stood and leaned close, whispering so only the president could hear.

"I know you ordered my father to cover up Chisso's crime, strutting around deciding whose lives are disposable. You put my father in an untenable position, until he felt he had no option but to kill himself. In deference to my mother, I won't announce it to everyone here, but the whole world will soon learn what a monster you are. Then it's your life that'll be disposable."

The president's lips parted. His eyes widened, and a hint of fear glinted there. "Condolences," he snapped and walked on into the hall.

Kiyo glanced at the koden before tossing it into the basket. The Demon of Chisso had given an amount equivalent to all the other executives' koden put together. Apparently he truly thought he could atone for his guilt this way.

Masa's family entered then, recited their condolences and presented their koden. The parents and daughter went on into the hall, but Masa lingered, shuffling his feet. "Sorry about your dad."

"Thanks."

"Let's go riding when it gets warmer."

Kiyo nodded. "Better yet, let's learn to drive."

Masa's face lit up. "Sure!" He quickly made his expression solemn again, and went inside to sit with his parents.

Kiyo was about to get up and join his family when Yuki entered. He stood to greet her. "Hi." Just seeing her already made him feel a bit calmer.

"I'm sorry, I can't stay." She wore an old jacket and pants. Grime rimmed her nails, as if she'd been gardening.

"It's all right." When he leaned over and thumbed a smudge of dirt off her cheek, she smelled loamy.

"Oh." She brushed at her face. "I'm moving rocks from one side of a garden to the other." She gave a little grin. "I have dirt all over me." Then she looked somber again. "You gave us generous koden when my uncle and father died. But this is all I have to offer you."

She held out a rolled-up paper. He smoothed it out to see a sketch of himself smiling as he stood before an older man; the latter's back was all that was visible of him.

Yuki pointed to the man. "That's supposed to be your father." But Kiyo knew. Her ability to capture people and evoke strong emotion was uncanny. Without even picturing his father's face, she'd depicted their love for each other.

He nodded. "I understand, and I . . . ." He couldn't go on. Why couldn't he and Dad have had this kind of relationship while he was alive? Why had he wasted so much energy being angry with his father? When he had children, he'd be sure to show them his love.

Finally he swallowed and said, "Thanks. This is how I want to remember him."

"I'm sure he was a good man, really."

Kiyo thought something looked different about her. Then he realized what it was. "Hey. You haven't been wearing your brooch."

"I traded it with someone, for . . . for my family." She smiled sadly. "I loved it while I had it, but it doesn't beautify my world anymore. You do. Art does. My family does. A piece of costume jewelry isn't important. I have the real thing. I'm the luckiest girl."

"I'm afraid I'll never be as mature as you." He was awed by her wisdom. With nothing but misery and obstacles thrown in front of them, by now most people would be bitter and angry. But she still saw hope and gratitude.

Yuki glanced into the hall and frowned. Kiyo followed her gaze; she was staring at the portrait of Kichiro propped up on the front table next to the incense bowl.

"Was that him?"

Kiyo nodded.

"But . . . he's the man who bought a peach for my family."

Kiyo started. "What?"

"We came into the city to get Tomoko-chan certified. A shop owner wouldn't take our money for a peach. She ordered us to leave. But your father bought it and gave it to me. I never knew who he was, before."

"Dad did that?" Kiyo gaped at his father's portrait, too.

"He was kind." She glanced behind her as if worried she was being followed. "I'd better get back to work."

Still shocked, Kiyo could only nod. As she rushed away, he called after her, "Thanks for stopping by."

His head was still spinning as he walked down the long aisle to join his family in the front row. How well had he truly known his father? Not very well at all, it seemed.

FORTY-ONE

Validation

Yuki and Kiyo strolled together to the All Kyushu Art Show. Cherry trees lining the street were in full bloom, creating a pink arch over the sidewalk. Yuki closed her eyes and breathed in the blossoms' sweet fragrance. April, her favorite time of year, a season of hope and new beginnings. And Kiyo, her love and most ardent supporter, was at her side. She hoped the artworks they'd view today would help lessen the sadness he still felt after his father's shocking death the month before.

The exhibit was being held at the same two-story brick Community Building as the annual Prefectural Art Show, where they'd first met Yuki's former mentor, Goto Sensei. As they approached the cube-shaped complex, she wondered if it would feel awkward, should they see her again, here. Whereas the end-of-the-year art show in Minamata was the most prestigious one in Kumamoto Prefecture, this competition today represented all seven prefectures on the island of Kyushu.

"How lucky the Show rotated to Minamata this year," she exclaimed.

"Very lucky." He smiled a bit, and she felt reassured that his grief was receding a bit. "And you look so pretty."

She smiled at the compliment. He'd borrowed an inexpensive kimono for her, from Fukuzawa's wife. This time Yuki wanted to portray herself as respectably as possible before its artist community. Even her best set of clothes would've been too casual for this gala.

To make sure they arrived within the first hour, Yuki had taken care of the needs of her mother and sister just before they left. As they entered the lobby she saw that the large rooms were already packed with art lovers gazing at paintings, etchings, and sculptures. Jazz music played softly.

"That's Hiraki Hideo on the drums." Kiyo pointed to a phonograph set up near the first room.

Yuki hadn't noticed the music until then, but she smiled and nodded. "I don't know who that is, but it's a great tune. You don't usually talk about music much."

"Mom loves jazz, so I've gotten to like it, too. I didn't think you were interested, though."

"We don't have a radio or a phonograph."

"I should've remembered that." His left hand was tapping out the beat on his thigh.

"See?" Yuki said. "Very catchy."

In the second room, he stopped in front of a small oil painting of an unspoiled-looking Minamata Bay and bent to read the signature. "Akaji?" He turned to Yuki. "This, it's yours?"

Her smile broadened. "Yes."

His laugh sounded joyful. "This is fantastic! Your best one yet. I didn't know you were going to enter."

"I didn't say anything because this show is juried, so I didn't known whether it would even be accepted."

"But it was! Having it hang here proves you're one of the best in the region. How many artists are accepted into this show every year, maybe forty?"

"Fifty in total. Thirty-five painters, fifteen sculptors, and ceramists."

"Hold on. Let's look around and compare."

He pulled her back to tour the other rooms hung with charcoal and pencil sketches, watercolor and oil paintings, gazing at each entry. At last he announced, "No question. Yours is better."

"Thanks, Kiyo-kun, but you may be biased." Still, she was so pleased at the compliment, she squeezed his arm.

"I'm not." He shook his head. "This is the best of show."

She wished she could feel so confident. Other artists chosen to show in the annual exhibit were mostly well known. Many made a living from their art. This was the first time her oils had been shown to anyone besides her family and Kiyo. She felt honored merely being part of the competition.

"This one's signed by Goto Hanako." Kiyo pointed to a study depicting a vase of colorful peonies which hung near Yuki's.

It was very good. She couldn't fault her former mentor's skills, no matter how unkind she'd been. "Yes. The colors are so rich and vibrant. It makes me feel cheerful."

"I guess. But not as good as yours," Kiyo said firmly.

"Oh," she gasped when she recognized a man across the room. His distinctive, wide dark moustache was familiar. He wore a stylish silver-gray suit, and was sauntering slowly around the gallery, pausing occasionally before one painting or another.

She nudged Kiyo and pointed discreetly. "That's Ando Makoto from Tokyo. The judge for this exhibit."

Kiyo glanced at him. "Is he famous?"

"Oh, very. Internationally renowned. One of the few from Japan. His realism is so true, you want to jump into the painting."

Ando Sensei paused as he studied each piece, sometimes stroking his pointed chin, or tapping one cheek with an index finger. As he approached her section of the exhibit, Yuki backed away. How would her tribute to the Bay make him feel?

He paused and gazed at the painting, standing close. After a few moments, he stepped back two paces, still studying it. His wide mouth twitched in a little smile that gradually widened. He nodded once, before moving on.

"He *liked* it," Kiyo whispered to Yuki, gripping her arm in excitement.

"I hope so." She couldn't let herself feel too much excitement yet. She was still a novice with almost no formal training. But her chest warmed at the thought that such a famous artist had found her painting somehow pleasing. That was enough, for now.

She and Kiyo were admiring an intricately-carved paulownia-wood turtle sculpture when Goto Hanako rushed past, carrying the scent of cherry blossoms on her gorgeous silk kimono, its deep indigo background patterned with white peonies. Yuki's pleasure in the perfume and the kimono evaporated quickly, though, as her former teacher looked their way and made a disgusted face.

"What are you doing here?" Goto demanded. "You're not welcome. We're a cultured group dedicated to creating beauty through art. Your indecency is a travesty."

Her eyes widened as she noticed Kiyo. "And you! The two of you still together, still behaving crudely in public. It's unacceptable."

Shocked into muteness, Yuki's first instant was to flee the gallery. She turned away to do just that, but then paused and chided herself, *You're an adult now. Stop acting like a frightened child.*

She pivoted back to face Goto. But just as she opened her mouth to defend herself, the two arts council greeters hurried over and bowed.

"What is the problem, Goto Sensei?" the male receptionist asked politely.

"I used to give art lessons to this . . . this *girl*." The artist flapped a hand toward Yuki.

"Ah yes. I remember. I introduced her to you a few years ago."

"Well, then I caught her and her, her . . . *him*." She inclined her head at Kiyo. "Together at my home while I'd been away, committing lewd acts."

"Lewd acts? In your home?" The female receptionist pressed a white-gloved hand to her mouth.

"We were not doing anything lewd," Yuki protested. Goto had no right to ruin her reputation in this society, a professional circle crucial to her future as an artist. "We had exchanged a single kiss when you walked in. That's all. There's nothing wrong with such a small gesture."

Goto sneered. "Oh, but if I hadn't walked in at that moment, you would've made love with him in my bed."

"Oh, no," whispered the female receptionist.

"That's a lie," Yuki said sternly. "Pulled solely from your imagination. I'm an honorable young woman. You're merely projecting your own prejudices on me."

"I want them thrown out immediately," Goto snapped at the receptionists, with a jerk of her head. It dislodged a hairpin, and her carefully coiffed updo began to uncoil. "Don't ever allow them in our group again."

The two art council members looked as if they wished to sink through the floor and disappear. As they hesitated, the woman wringing her hands, Ando Sensei approached. He held a large purple ribbon with the number one painted on it.

Everyone fell silent, staring at him.

"Ah. You've made your decision?" The male council-member's worried frown morphed into a bright smile.

"I have. And am delighted to have found such a brilliant painting executed right here in Kyushu."

"Oh! Thank you, Ando Sensei," Goto gushed. "Such an honor, especially coming from you. I've been to your gallery. I'm so happy to be included in your collection."

The judge smiled at her, then turned and bowed to Yuki. "Congratulations! I asked around; you are Akaji-san, are you not?"

"*Akaji?*" Goto looked stunned. Her face went scarlet.

Yuki froze; unable to move, barely able to think. Had Ando Sensei really said *her* name? Perhaps she'd heard wrong. Perhaps she was daydreaming? He stood between her landscape, and Goto's still life, still holding the ribbon.

Goto Hanako said, in a cajoling tone, "Oh, but Ando Sensei, surely you're awarding first place to *this* work, aren't you?" She gestured at her flower painting.

"I beg your pardon," the judge said. "I didn't mean to cause any confusion. I'm looking for *this* artist." And then he hung the first-place ribbon with a loop of red twine, on one corner of the framed painting of Minamata Bay.

I won? Yuki felt almost dizzy, as if she were levitating above the gallery's floor.

"You can't be serious. It's a dreadful mistake." Goto's scorn morphed to reverence. "You see, *I'm* Goto Hanako. *This one* is my entry." She moved aside as if to give him a better view of her painting.

Yuki shook herself back to reality. She should introduce herself. "How do you do, Ando Sensei? I'm Akaji Yuki." She bowed low for several seconds, showing respect for his fame and reputation.

"My goodness." The judge looked startled. "I didn't expect our first prize winner would be so young. And yet, the painting is deeply accomplished. It displays not just natural talent, but the kind of skill that normally takes many years to develop. How old are you, if I may ask, Akaji-san?"

Her face heated up. "I'm . . . well, eighteen."

"And who was your teacher?"

"Me." Goto suddenly yanked a pleasant mask down over her previous fury. "She's my student."

"Yes, Sensei, but for only three lessons," Yuki corrected. "And that was for watercolor. I taught myself how to paint with oils."

Ando Sensei shook his head slowly. "A gifted young woman, for sure. How many other works have you completed?"

"A dozen or so in oils, sir. Plus pencil drawings and many watercolors."

"I would like to see all of them. May I visit your studio?"

Yuki was seized with a moment of panic. "Umm. Well, I don't actually have a studio. I paint at home."

He smiled. "Splendid. Can we take a taxi there after the ceremony?"

Take a famous artist home with me? Her mouth dried up. "Well, I . . . . "

"It'll be all right," Kiyo whispered behind her. "Take the opportunity."

He was right. Being poor was not shameful. "This is my dear friend Kiyo-kun," she said. "And I would be honored, Sensei. But it's a humble place."

"I'm interested in your artworks, not your furniture." Turning to the receptionists, he asked, "Could we begin the post-awards reception now?"

The judge, plus all the artists, friends, and family moved to a separate room set up for the reception. Three young women in bright, flowered kimonos stood behind a long table covered with white lace. Three vases filled with light-pink plum blossoms and bright yellow rape-plant flowers adorned it. Bottles of sake, wine, and whiskey were lined up next to glasses and cups. The rest of the table was taken up by platters of delicious-looking hors oeuvres and stacks of small plates and napkins.

Ando Sensei asked for red wine. One of the serving ladies filled a glass for him.

"Look! There's *omanju, youkan, doumyouji* and *dango!*" Yuki pointed to the pink, green, and white sweet azuki bean desserts. How many times had she walked by confectionary stores and paused to stare in their windows at those sweet jelly, mochi, fruit, and azuki bean-paste crackers, wafers, and candies and longed to try even just one? Her mouth watered. Now she would sample all of them.

"Here, try this." Kiyo put a pink omanju on a dainty plate.

She eagerly took a bite and moaned softly, "Oh, delicious!" Next she tried the doumyouji: sweet pink mochi and red bean paste covered with a cherry blossom. "So that's what they taste like. Absolutely wonderful!"

Kiyo smiled. "It's a pleasure just watching you eat."

As soon as Ando Sensei downed his wine, he came over to them. "Should I request a taxi now?"

She'd hoped to also try the dango dumplings made from sweet rice flour, but said, "Oh, yes." If her work was selected for exhibit next year, she'd simply eat one then.

"Would you call a taxi for us, please?" the judge asked the receptionist.

"Right away." The man disappeared into a nearby office.

"How about my flower painting, Sensei?" Goto wheedled. "Akaji-san learned much from me, but I've been a painter for twenty-five years."

"Very nice." The judge said, barely glancing at her. "Akaji-san, let's go. I'm eager to see more of your work."

Yuki wrung her hands all through the taxi ride, as she gave the driver directions. Ando Sensei may have honored this entry, but what would he think about all the other paintings? And her family. Did he know anything about the Disease?

"Are all your paintings of seascapes?" he asked just then.

"No. I've spent a lot of my life on the water, so I like to do those. But I paint portraits as well."

"Oh? That is exciting. Collectors often want portraits of themselves. I look forward to seeing those."

"They're . . . a bit different from the usual portraits in shows." If the judge wasn't aware of what Minamata Disease could do to the human body, she feared he might be too shocked to appreciate them.

"Is that so? Well, I'm even more intrigued now."

Yuki bit her lip and sat back. The man had no idea about what he would soon be seeing.

When the taxi stopped in front of her house, Ando Sensei glanced around the street. "Where are we?"

Her heart sank at his wary look. With as much confidence as she could muster, she said, "This is Tsukinoura Village, a fishing village. My family have always been fishers. And this place is my home."

"Oh?" The artist shifted to gaze out at the small house.

She did too, to view it as he might be seeing it: hardly larger than a tool shed, crumpled newspapers stuffed between warped boards, front yard choked with dry, dead weeds. But his face expressed no distaste, only curiosity.

As they all got out of the taxi, Kiyo said, "The family doesn't have a telephone, so you may want the driver to wait to take you back to the city."

"Thanks for the tip." The judge spoke to the driver.

As they approached the house, Yuki prayed no broken roof tiles would slide off and injure the judge. Once they were safely gathered at the front entrance, she blurted out, "I'm sorry. We're poor."

Ando Sensei shook his head. "Talent is born in those of all cultures and classes."

"Before we go in," Kiyo said. "I'd like to prepare you. Have you heard of Minamata Disease?"

"It's been making the news in Tokyo lately. Ah, yes – it started here in Minamata Bay, no? A cruel, dreadful illness from what I've read."

"Well, fisher families on the Bay were the most likely to contract it. Yuki's uncle and father did. They've since passed away."

"How awful. I'm so sorry to hear that."

"My mother has it, too," Yuki added. "Though not as severely. And my little sister."

"Oh, no! They are home now?"

Yuki nodded. "Yes."

Even if Ando Sensei didn't like the rest of her paintings, she'd already been singled out for a great honor. And, she thought with an undeniable sense of satisfaction, the haughty Goto had not.

"Thanks for letting me know," Ando Sensei said.

"*Tadaima*." I'm home, Yuki announced, and opened the front door.

Her mother lifted her head from the kotatsu, where she'd been sleeping with Tomoko cradled in her lap. "*Okaeri!*" Welcome home.

The room smelled stale, but Yuki didn't want to open a window and make it colder than it already was. Tomoko gurgled a greeting, too.

"Oh, you brought guests?" her mother said, when Ando stepped inside. She smoothed back her short hair.

"Mom, this is Ando Makoto Sensei, a world-famous artist from Tokyo."

"Please, don't get up on my account," the judge said.

He seemed at ease, as if he didn't even notice the shoji doors covered in brittle, yellowed newsprint. Or the tatami floor so thin someone's foot might soon plunge through.

"I apologize for intruding with no warning, Akaji-san," he added. "This is my fault. I insisted on seeing your daughter's artworks, immediately."

Yuki was thankful, at least, that the whole family slept in the other room. A pile of clean diapers and the laundry were both in there.

"Please, come in. I'm Kazuko, Yuki's mother. This is my other daughter, Tomoko."

"Happy to make your acquaintance." The judge tugged a business card from his suit-coat pocket and politely held it out to Kazuko with both hands.

"I'm so honored." She accepted it just as respectfully, and spent several moments studying what was printed there. "Your name is Makoto, meaning 'sincerity' or 'truth.'

I believe one's name is important, and that a person grows into it. You have an honorable one."

"Thank you." The artist looked pleased.

"He judged the annual art exhibit, Mom. I won an award," Yuki said. She'd tell her all about it later.

"You did? Why that's wonderful." Kazuko beamed with pride. "Thank you, Sensei." She bowed from the kotatsu. "Yuki-chan, some tea for our guests."

"Right away." She hurried over to the kitchen to heat water.

"Please, sit here at the kotatsu," Mom offered. "Much warmer."

"I'll stoke it up." Kiyo added charcoal while the artist got settled under the futon.

Yuki was grateful she had enough tea leaves left for today. If only she had some cushions for the judge to sit on. Oh well, she thought, he'll have to take us as we are.

After everyone had taken a few sips of tea, Yuki rose and pulled away the old white sheet Kiyo had given her to cover the paintings leaning against the living room wall.

"Yes, yes. Please bring them out so I can see." The judge set down his tea.

Yuki first carried over seven other seascapes, three from the perspective of her dad's fishing boat.

"Lovely. You've even incorporated the bow and mast in some. They're just as beautiful as the one you exhibited. I would've given a first-place ribbon to several of these."

"Thank you." She felt so warm. One of the world's best artists thought her work was lovely. *Lovely.* She would cherish the word.

"The rest are portraits?"

"Yes, but perhaps not what you'd normally expect," she warned.

"Good! I'm tired of the same old serious faces floating above expensive suits and kimonos."

She set drawings of her uncle and father when they'd had the Disease in front of the artist. Also one of Tomoko, now almost two-and-a-half, being given a bath, her limp fingers splayed, a crooked smile lighting her face. Then the angry men at demonstrations. And the determination plain on Ishimure Michiko's face, to complete her mission and tell the world about the Disease. Even the smug police officers at the Chisso riot.

The last one was of Zumoto, the evil in his gaze marring not just his face, but his very soul, far more than any birthmark ever could.

The portraits showed all the ugliness, misery, and maliciousness she'd once endured, yet Yuki no longer felt unhappy, spiteful, or angry seeing them again. After the rape, she'd understood her mother and Kiyo would always love her. Almost killing Zumoto had made her realize that, though there were terrible people in the world, she would not become one of them. Recalling how close she'd come to drowning her own sister, she knew she'd never feel entitled to judge another person's value or second-guess their desire to survive. Instead, she'd keep showing the cruelty in the world by revealing the darkness within everyone. Only by acknowledging its existence could one keep that part of the self in check.

Ando Sensei was staring thoughtfully at the portraits, seeming mesmerized rather than repulsed, as she'd feared.

"Two of them depict your uncle and your father?"

"Yes. That's Uncle Higano, there, and this one is Dad." She still could not think of them in the past tense. They were with her, still. Then she explained who was portrayed in the rest of the portraits.

"You clearly show everyone's pain, both physical and emotional. I can see the frustration and anger in their eyes. The lack of caring in some of the others." The judge nodded. "Unique, and raw. Strong sensitivity. One would need great compassion and insight to paint with such perception. People will soon recognize your great talent, I predict. And I'd be honored to take all of these to sell in my Tokyo gallery."

"What?" Yuki and her mother exclaimed together.

"How much is the advance?" Kiyo blurted out. When the artist named his price, he howled and clapped heartily. "See? I knew you were great from the minute I saw you draw a cat five years ago."

"I can believe that," Ando Sensei said. "Such talent shows up early."

Yuki was speechless. The money offered would keep the family well fed for a year, with enough left over to fix the roof and floor. She exchanged amazed looks with Kiyo and her mother.

"Are you serious? I mean, about the gallery."

Winning the art exhibit prize said she was good. That alone had thrilled her. But she'd never considered selling her work. Never thought people would pay to hang her paintings on their walls. In Tokyo, no less!

"If you're willing, I could take them now." The artist pulled a wallet from his coat pocket and counted out cash on the kotatsu table.

"Oh, my!" Tears streaked Kazuko's cheeks. "If only Nobuyuki-kun was here to see this. Your father always believed in you."

Yuki picked up the bills. So much money and yet it felt so light. She'd only done what she'd felt driven to, not expecting to become famous or wealthy. Nonetheless, it all felt good. To be able to earn a living, and while doing what she loved.

"I was never sure before if they were any good," she murmured.

"Good?" Ando Sensei laughed. "I travel to exhibits and galleries all over Japan hoping, without much hope, to find a truly gifted artist with a unique style. Plenty of drivel out there; always the same thing. Your work is distinctive.

That's rare. Will you allow me to represent you? I'll pay you the same amount again, now, if you agree to sell to me exclusively."

"Exclusively?" Yuki asked, bewildered. "I'm not sure – " Not knowing any artists who sold work in galleries, she had no idea how the business of art should work.

"Fair enough. That *is* a lot to ask of someone who will soon take the art world by storm. I'll pay you double that advance to become your agent, plus fifty percent of the selling price."

"Fifty percent?"

"That's the normal rate. I'd be honored to introduce you to the world. Here." He dug in his wallet and pulled out every bit of the cash within. "That's all I have now, but I'll get the rest tomorrow."

Yuki hadn't meant he wasn't offering enough, merely blurting out her confusion. "Kiyo-kun, what do you think?"

Ando Sensei watched as Kiyo cocked his head. "I'm not versed in pricing art . . . but Ando Sensei is a famous artist, with a gallery well-known in Japan. That's why the council asked him to judge. They wouldn't invite an uninformed or unscrupulous person."

"And his name *is* Makoto," her mother said.

The sensei nodded earnestly. "I would not mislead you. I'll build your career as a painter with showings in my gallery, to which I'll invite prominent collectors." He scooted out of the kotatsu, and still on his knees, bowed his head to the floor. "It would be an honor to represent you, Akaji-san."

"Oh please, you don't need to do that." The only other time someone had ever bowed so reverently to her was when Kiyo had asked for forgiveness after she'd been raped. So the deep bow, though clearly well meant, made her uncomfortable. "I'd love to have you represent me. I still have a lot to learn."

The artist sighed, looking delighted. "Thank you."

The room grew quiet and serious for a moment until, suddenly, Tomoko laughed out loud. All tension fled as everyone else joined in.

"You're going to keep painting, aren't you?" Ando Sensei asked.

"Of course. I really couldn't do otherwise."

"As soon as you have five more, I'll come pick them up. I'll pay you as each piece is sold. Once your work becomes better known, prices will rise accordingly."

I've actually done it, she thought. Now I can officially call myself an artist. She'd never dared consider that something this good could actually happen. Yet she felt sadness, as well. She'd trade all of this to have her father and Uncle Higano back. To have Mom and Tomoko healthy again.

But that was not possible. Now the best they could do was to simply go forward: she with her art, Kiyo with medicine.

FORTY-TWO

Rise Above the Ashes

From the top step of their garden, Kiyo watched cherry blossom petals fluttering down. Some landed on his mother's black leather pumps and black dress. Six weeks after Kichiro had died, they were still not accustomed to a two-person household. The rooms seemed empty, suddenly too large. The smell of pipe tobacco clung faintly to the upholstery and tatami mats, as if Dad might still step out of one of the rooms and walk down the hall toward him.

How he wished that could happen.

Etsuko was making a valiant effort to keep the household going. Fukuzawa dropped in when he wasn't chauffeuring Dad's replacement, sometimes giving Etsuko a ride to the hairdresser's or a coffee shop to meet a friend. She made no more mention of a graduation party for Kiyo, though.

In the last two months, life had slapped him down, and then tried to grind him to dust. His father was dead, and he had not even suspected it could happen. Dr. Hosokawa, having determined the cause of Minamata Disease with the help of the university's researchers, had retired, saying his job was done.

Others had taken up his cause, though. Like Ishimure Michiko, the writer who'd accompanied Dr. Harada when he was studying infant victims of the Disease. The Mutual Aid Association of the Families of Minamata Disease Patients had petitioned the government to force Chisso to clean up its wastewater and the Bay. Other associations and committees were springing up to get assistance for the afflicted. The national media was now covering their plight, and international interest was also growing about the damage Chisso's heavy-metal pollution had done. Kiyo was about to leave for medical school, but the local groups seemed well equipped to move forward and resolve the cover-up. With all this momentum building, he felt certain Chisso would soon be held accountable.

It was time to accept change, and move forward. Today was the day he'd take the next step in his life.

When Kiyo arrived at Yuki's house, the doors were thrown open. She was sweeping dirt outside, though the broom kept snagging on splintered tatami mats. New ones were on order but they hadn't arrived yet.

Kazuko was staggering slowly around the garden, where snow peas already climbed high on tall sticks. She spotted Kiyo and raised a hand in greeting. Tomoko lay on a cloth in the grass.

Yuki stopped cleaning and met him as he parked his bicycle. "How are you? And your mother?"

He no longer had to bring food for them, of course, but after so many years it felt odd to arrive empty handed. Except for attending the art show, he'd been busy at home with family after the funeral, and with helping his mother settle Kichiro's estate. Whenever he wasn't at school, he stayed home and kept her company. She'd never seemed so fragile before.

"She's getting along all right, I suppose. I hope she starts listening to music again soon." The house was too quiet without her perpetual jazz records on the turntable.

"It must be so hard, though. Losing Dad and Uncle Higano was devastating."

"Yeah." He looked up and away.

Yuki must've climbed up and set large stones on the roof to keep more cracked tiles from sliding off. The house would have a new roof once summer arrived, a dream the family had held even before he'd met them five years ago.

"What's she going to do?" Yuki asked.

"She doesn't want to live here alone, after I go to university. So she's trying to decide where to live. Both my brothers have invited her to move in with them. She'd like to be with Ichita-kun because of the three grandkids. But Tadahisa-kun lives in Tokyo and she'd also really love to go back there. I said, why not switch every other year or something. She's thinking about it."

He knew his brothers would take good care of her. And he'd look after her whenever they both came back to Minamata.

Yuki nodded. "What's going to happen to your house?"

"It's been in the family for generations. So I'll live there when I come home on breaks from university, and after I graduate and practice medicine. She has a lot of friends here, too, and wants to come see them every now and then."

"That's nice. I'd hate to imagine strangers living in your lovely home."

"Yeah, me too." Bad enough to lose his father. Saying goodbye to the family home would strip away so many family ties and memories.

"Is everything else all right? When will you leave for school?"

The line of concern pressed between her eyebrows made her appear more mature. More adult. Of course, that was exactly what she was. She'd been forced to grow up even faster than he had. He'd at least had the luxury of being taken care of for most of his life. If supporting her family hadn't been enough of a burden, there'd been the traumatic events with Zumoto. Yet she was worried about him.

Her compassion seemed limitless. Could he ever hope to be as good a person?

"You know how everyone saves for – " He stopped abruptly. "Sorry. No, you wouldn't." Fishers were mostly forced to live from day to day, the lucky ones able to put away a little just for the next season. "My parents had already saved enough money for my education and their retirement, so we'll be fine."

"I'm glad."

"Also, I haven't had a chance to tell you all the news about Minamata Disease."

They sat side by side on a large rock next to the house. It had rained that morning; now frogs croaked from nearby puddles. Children chased each other along the road, laughing and screaming. Spring sunshine lit her smooth-scrubbed face.

In a few weeks, I'll have known her for five years, he thought.

Her eyes still shone like the faceted stones on the brooch she used to wear. The childish snub nose had gradually sculpted into an elegant, slender one. Her smiling lips were plump, rosy, perfectly shaped. Cropped shiny black hair swung across her cheeks. But what had always moved him most was the intensity of her gaze, the love behind her eyes.

He explained about Dr. Hosokawa's retirement, the continued work of Ishimure and the activism of the Mutual Aid Association of the Families of Minamata Disease Patients.

She shook her head, swiping away a tear with one finger. "So they finally allow us to know how it really happened. The evil that Chisso did to my family, to all those other people." She clenched a fist and shouted, "Damn them!" Then straightened and took a deep breath. "Ah, the sweet air of relief. Thank you, Kiyo-kun. During all those years, we would've died without your help." She lowered her head in a grateful bow.

"But my help wasn't enough, and anyhow I wasn't alone. When I had no bike Fukuzawa-san delivered everything, and contributed food, too. Yanagiya-san, our cook, actually sacrificed her job to help me do it. Masa-kun even bought us lunch, once, remember? And my mother gave food, too, though she didn't know it."

It was time now for the hard part . . . he hoped to make a good case, and convince her.

When he started to speak again, his mouth was dry as an old textbook. Could saliva really dry up instantly? He'd never seen such a thing in a medical book. But he'd wanted this for years. They were destined to be together.

Weren't they?

She'd surely say yes. She felt the same.

Didn't she?

Suddenly he wasn't sure of anything. His path, their future, had once been as clear to him as the waters of the old Minamata Bay. Kiyo and Yuki. That was what he wanted. Then why were his hands so clammy? Why was it getting hard to draw a breath?

She looked over at him with mild concern. "Are you unwell?"

The love in that gaze restored his courage. How many people could survive the horrors they had, together? Now the stars were no longer twisted in the sky. Maybe Yuki still lived in Tsukinoura – The Back of the Moon – but light would always shine on them, from now on.

He seized her hands. The skin was chapped and rough, the knuckles swollen from years of whacking them against hard walls while cleaning corners. Her fingernails were broken from countless hours of digging in other people's fields. They were the most beautiful hands he'd ever seen.

"Yuki-chan ... I love you."

Her frown dissolved, replaced by a broad smile. "I love you, too."

"Graduation is next week. And I'll miss you when I go to Tokyo University next month."

"I know. But you're going to be the best doctor ever seen in Japan."

He laughed a little. "I hope so. I'll come home on breaks. And you'll be busy drawing and painting."

She sat up straighter, as if she'd just gotten an idea. "When I've finished a few more paintings, I'll deliver them to Ando Sensei in Tokyo, myself. Then I can see you too. I'll pay someone to take care of my family for a few days."

"What a great idea!" He squeezed her hands gently.

"I'd love to visit his gallery. To see my paintings hanging there. Now that I don't have to work at another job, I'll have far more time to paint. Thank you for always believing in my art."

"Are you kidding? Anyone could see you're destined to be great." He hesitated, then blurted out, "Once I graduate and become a doctor, I want to marry you. Can you wait until then for me?"

"Yes. Yes! I'll be here." She wrapped her arms around him and squeezed hard, then leaned back to look into his eyes. "I'd feared the rape would tarnish me in everyone's eyes, yet you, and everyone else who matters, proved loyal over and over. But . . . . " she hesitated.

"What?" Oh no, he thought. She's changed her mind.

"Your mother ... Will she approve of a marriage to a fisher's daughter?"

He chewed on his bottom lip. He'd already considered this. His mother, like most parents of his friends, wanted their son to marry someone of a particular type. He knew the standards they professed: a young woman of the same or higher class, from a family of the same economic level. Preferably with a university-educated father. Also the family should have no record of criminal behavior or any members with serious diseases. But since the death of her husband, she seemed far less concerned about keeping up appearances. Longing only to be surrounded by her sons and grandchildren.

"I'll talk to her," he said. "She's changed in many ways since Dad's death. I think she'll accept that it's what we want."

He paused a moment, then rushed on. "As for Zumoto. There's no reason my mother need know of his despicable crimes. Let her see your wonderful art, your great talent. I'll take her to Ando Sensei's gallery when she comes to Tokyo."

Yuki smiled. "Now there's an idea."

"Yes. Mom admires all things Western. I think she'll be able to let go of the traditional notion of arranged marriage. Of choosing a spouse mainly for the good of the family." He nodded firmly. "Our generation will marry the person *we* choose, out of love. And she's going to be crazy about our future kids."

Yuki threw back her head and laughed. "Yeah, she will! I love you, Kiyo-kun."

They leaned into each other for a kiss, unrushed and lovingly. He never wanted it to stop. When at last they drew apart, her cheeks were flushed. From happiness, he hoped.

"What's going on?" her mother called from the garden.

"We're going to get married," Yuki exclaimed.

"Congratulations! Though truly, was there ever any doubt?" Kazuko laughed joyfully.

Yuki sprang up and went inside, bringing out her sketchbook and pencil. Kiyo tried to watch as she drew, but she grinned and angled the pad away, so he couldn't see. At last she turned the picture toward him. In it, they sat side by side on a sandy beach, in three-quarters profile, before a sparkling bay. His arm was around her waist, her head resting on his shoulder. Their expressions full of blissful contentment.

He pulled her close, breathing in dust caught in her hair, then sneezed. "That's our future. I've seen it too."

He kissed her again, and this time was sure her lips tasted as wonderful as a flower's nectar must seem to *mejiro*, the tiny green songbirds flitting about the garden behind them.

EPILOGUE

1976

The sun was setting behind the garden's trees and shrubs, casting long shadows. Yuki had already closed their living room windows to keep out the evening chill. Rice cracker wrappers and crumbs lay strewn across the table. The strong, rich aroma of coffee filled the room, mugs of that having replaced the earlier green tea. A fresh pot had been just the thing to warm Yuki, Kiyo, and Sawada Tanzan, who'd come from Tokyo to interview them for a magazine article.

The journalist flipped a note-filled page over, then continued scribbling furiously.

"Shinjirarenai." Unbelievable, he said at last, setting down the pencil, shaking his head. "I thought I understood hardship. Even believed myself to be worldly. But until I heard the story you both told me today, I didn't fully appreciate how . . . *Hidoi."* Horrible. "I hear the former president of Chisso and a supervisor of the factory face criminal charges for their role in causing death and serious bodily harm to the people of Minamata."

Kiyo applauded, erupting in satisfied laughter. "Magnificent! That prosecutor has guts, all right. I must have a chat with him. To force Chisso to pay eight million yen and medical expenses to all the victims, and additional compensation to fishermen groups, is a kind of reparation. But just paying money and issuing an apology isn't enough to atone for mass murder."

"What about the Diet passing the Pollution Laws that make damaging human health via pollution now a crime?"

Sawada asked, scratching another note. "We're the first country in the world to pass what they are calling an 'environmental law'."

"About time politicians quit kowtowing to big business and bring justice to our city," Yuki said. "Had they passed such laws twenty years ago, it would've saved tens of thousands of people from death and suffering."

The writer sighed. "Legislatures are never proactive. They merely react after bad things happen."

"I wonder if the forty-eight billion yen requirement for Chisso to remove the contaminated sediment in the Bay will actually be enough." Kiyo frowned.

"No telling, until the work's complete – and that may take ten years," Yuki said. "You know what else enrages me? *Our* prefecture must help Chisso pay for this fix. The damn company should pay for all of it."

"True. Yet that would also hurt the city. If the company went bankrupt, jobs would be lost. They'd quit paying altogether," Kiyo pointed out. "And, the prefecture did help with the cover-up."

Yuki nodded. "True."

"But will unpolluted sea life ever live in the Bay again? Dredging will stir up the mercury in the sediment again. I wonder, can we ever truly fix this mess? It's difficult to measure methylmercury in lower layers, so how will we know all the poison's been removed? Mercury levels in fish will still need to be monitored constantly."

"Easy to pollute. Hard to clean up." The writer shifted on his cushion to face Yuki. "W. Eugene Smith showed the world the horrors of industrial pollution through his camera lens. You, Kuge-san, have shown the suffering, pain, and the dignity of the victims through your art."

"You meant those paintings of my father and my uncle, made when I was younger. A show's opening next week in my Tokyo gallery titled 'Betrayed'. A collection of paintings and sketches I made of the victims and their families, before and after they contracted the Disease, showing the daily torment of those stolen lives. Also paintings of activists like Kawamoto Teruo, who organized sit-ins and tent encampments outside Chisso headquarters. He won an eight-year legal battle after being wrongly accused of assault. I painted Chisso executives and city people who'd scorned the afflicted too. And my cat Jiro. All the profits will go to help the victims."

"Oh, wonderful." Sawada nodded. "No doubt the work of one of the world's most famous living artists will have a huge impact. *Subarashii*," he added. Awesome.

"We've talked about the victims. Have you met any?" Yuki asked. "Would you like to meet my mother and sister?"

"Are they here now?" Sawada rose, glancing around.

"Yes, they live with us. We built an addition for my studio, and another wing for them and the nurse who cares for them during the day, while Kiyo and I are working."

"I'd love to meet them."

Yuki left for a few minutes, returned with her mother and sister. Kazuko, her gray hair cut short, walked in slowly but with great dignity. Her stylish tangerine blouse, loose silver skirt, and a thin white-gold choker lent her both a chic and distinguished air.

Yuki was behind her, pushing Tomoko's wheelchair as the skinny seventeen-year-old squealed in delight. Almost as tall as Yuki now. She was unable to stretch her mouth very wide, so her smile looked more like a gasp. Her dark hair fell in loose curls around her shoulders. A ruffled blouse and flared slacks helped fill out her bony arms and legs.

Kazuko settled in an upholstered armchair, facing the low table where Kiyo and Sawada still sat.

The journalist stood and bowed. "How do you do, Akaji-san and Tomoko-san? It's an honor to meet you." Then he asked Kazuko, "How are you getting along?"

"No worse, thank goodness. And, as always, Yuki-chan and Kiyo-kun take good care of us."

Sawada took his seat again. "I've heard your story. I remain in awe of such bravery."

"It was more like desperation. Nothing left to do but keep surviving," she said softly. "Tomoko-chan is really the brave one. Though always in pain, she manages to enjoy life. I'm glad you're seeing her on a good day."

"Still, I doubt I could've done half so well," the journalist confessed. "Tomoko-chan, I was not prepared to meet such a pretty young lady. And I like your perfume."

Yuki's sister covered her face with a splayed hand, as if to hide a blush.

Kazuko glanced at Tomoko tenderly. "She's only pretending to be embarrassed. She loves compliments, and meeting new people. But don't forget Yuki-chan, the bravest of us all. She got up in the dark, trekked for miles on an empty stomach, and endured abuse from cruel housewives and employers in order to take care of us." Her eyes glittered with tears; she smiled over at her daughter. "Yet, she let nothing destroy her passion for art. If you want to portray a hero in your magazine, write about her."

Yuki waved a hand dismissively. "Even when everything seemed hopeless, Kiyo-kun always reminded me to keep chasing that tiny sparkle in the darkness. Most men back then would've walked away after Zumoto's assault. Kiyo always stuck by me."

Her husband's face turned pink. "What fool would give up such a beautiful woman?" He downed the dregs of his coffee. "If we're done, Sawada-san, I must look in on a patient. Yanagiya-san, the family's cook when I was a boy."

"How fortunate she has such a distinguished doctor looking after her."

"She was very kind back then. Even forgave me for getting her fired. I can never repay her kindness and grace."

The writer slipped the notepad into his briefcase, and rose again. "Thank you for hosting me in your home," he said, as they walked him to the front door. "From what I've heard here, both of you were always champions to your families."

Yuki patted Kiyo's cheek, and they gazed affectionately into each other's eyes for a moment.

Then she said, "Perhaps. But the true heroes will always be the loved ones we lost, and the afflicted who still remain. They are with us still, like all the thousands of other victims of Minamata Disease."

THE END

Author's Note

This novel is based on the true story of Minamata Disease. Originally called the Strange Disease, it's caused by eating fish and sea life polluted with methylmercury. The Disease was first discovered in 1956, the point at which my novel begins. In the service of fiction, I've shortened the time period over which the historical events unfolded. The national government actually failed to acknowledge that Chisso Company was causing the Disease until 1968. The company, instead of taking responsibility, conspired with the prefectural and national governments to conceal its culpability for twelve long years, while more and more afflicted sickened, suffered, and died.

Methylmercury attacks the central nervous system, including the brain. Because there's no cure, thousands of people who did not die, including the congenital babies, still live with devastating disabilities.

Methylmercury, the most poisonous of all the mercury compounds, is organic mercury. In the 1950s, scientists did not know that inorganic mercury morphs into organic mercury when it's dissolved in freshwater or seawater. Since methylmercury is a heavy metal, it settled to the bottom of Minamata Bay and was finally found in the sludge there. Because Chisso discharged *inorganic* mercury, in the beginning there was confusion as to their culpability, since patients were found to have *organic* methylmercury in their system.

Victims and those who chose to stand up to Chisso were shunned, verbally abused, and pressured by neighbors and Chisso executives to keep quiet. Their homes and other assets, such as bicycles and boats, were vandalized. Some lost their jobs, and were refused other employment. Windows were slammed shut when they walked by. Marriage arrangements were canceled. The harassment described in the book happened, and was often many times worse.

The Disease victims finally managed to band together to sue Chisso. After a four-year trial, a verdict was rendered in March of 1973. The patients and the company agreed to a compensation agreement for consolation payments, covering costs the victims had incurred, and annuities, plus continued medical support. Once they were deceased, their relatives could not receive payments or reimbursements.

Even as he was dying of cancer, Dr. Hosokawa came to testify about his cat experiment and his opposition to moving the wastewater discharge from the Bay to the Minamata River. Other Chisso employees testified that the company's foremost goal was profit; that it'd disregarded employee safety and behaved with indifference to the results of the toxic chemicals it knowingly released. Even Chisso's president finally admitted the company knew World War II explosives in the Bay had nothing to do with the Disease.

The cost to Chisso of compensating Minamata patients, cleaning up the Bay, and reconstructing its factory procedures amounted to billions of dollars. In 2000, Chisso still employed 660 people; today it remains an important employer in Minamata. To make sure the company continues to pay its debt, the national and prefectural governments issued bonds of over two billion dollars to support Chisso financially. The company must repay 1.6 billion dollars of that aid, over time.

No one will ever know how many people were actually afflicted, but over 12,000 have been officially recognized by the government as victims. The same disease later broke out in other parts of Japan, as well as in China and Canada – also caused in those cases by mercury pollution from factories.

Kiyo, Yuki, and the other primary characters in this book are my invention. However, a number of the people who appear in the story were real.

Hosokawa Hajime was the director of Chisso Hospital; he did work hard to treat the victims of Minamata Disease and find the cause.

Ishimure Michiko championed the victims' cause. Despite terrible problems with her eyesight, she wrote tirelessly in newspapers, magazines, and also published a book meant to bring attention to the plight of the victims. Her "office" was a tiny, cramped room with poor light. She and her family were ostracized for speaking out. Her husband, a middle-grade teacher, was transferred to a remote rural school as punishment for his wife's activism.

Harada Masazumi was one of the dedicated doctors who worked in real life to help victims. He discovered babies assumed to have cerebral palsy actually had congenital Minamata Disease. He also worked out how that had occurred.

Yoshioka Kiichi was the president of Chisso Factory. He did have the Cyclator installed, but also knew from the start that wastewater from the plastics factory didn't pass through it.

Tsukinoura and other villages mentioned in the book were real, inhabited by poor families. Tsukinoura does, ironically, actually mean The Back of the Moon.

I also incorporated research done by scientists from the University of Kumamoto, and University of Kyushu in Kagoshima City, and have described their accounts as accurately as possible.

I relied greatly on Ishimure Michiko's book *Paradise in the Sea of Sorrow: Our Minamata Disease* as a resource to write this book. I also used *Bitter Sea: The Human Cost of Minamata Disease,* by Mishima Akio, as well as documentaries made by Tsuchimoto Noriaki, including *Minamata: The Victims and Their World.* Studying the devastation was heart-wrenching for one born and partially raised in Japan. Describing the horrible symptoms and plotting the story of how lives were ruined, or ended in suffering and death, was difficult. But I felt the truth needed to be told.

Environmental pollution continues throughout the world, sometimes unchecked, especially in less advanced countries. People (mainly the poor) living around polluted sites contract illnesses, suffer, and often die. Large, powerful corporations still deliberately hide toxic activities, even buying off government officials. They keep polluting for the sheer sake of profit. Globally speaking, more than nine million deaths a year are attributed to environmental pollution. There's only one way to stop this willful criminal practice. Concerned citizens must keep abreast of what's happening throughout the world, then speak up and demand change.

Northampton House Press

Established in 2011, Northampton House Press publishes selected fiction, nonfiction, and memoir. Check out our list at www.northampton-house.com, and Like us on Facebook – "Northampton House Press" – as we showcase more innovative works from brilliant new talents.

Printed in the USA
CPSIA information can be obtained
at www.ICGtesting.com
CBHW070528130324
5296CB00001B/2